D0559521

CAPTAIN NICHOLAS

Books by
Hugh Walpole

NOVELS

Jeremy at Crale Harmer John The Wooden Horse
The Gods and Mr. Perrin The Dark Forest
The Secret City Rogue Herries
Judith Paris The Fortress
Vanessa

THE LONDON NOVELS

Wintersmoon Fortitude The Duchess of Wrexe
The Green Mirror The Captives
The Young Enchanted
Hans Frost
Captain Nicholas

SCENES FROM PROVINCIAL LIFE

The Cathedral The Old Ladies

PHANTASIES

Maradick at Forty The Prelude to Adventure
Portrait of a Man with Red Hair
Above the Dark Tumult

BOOKS ABOUT CHILDREN

The Golden Scarecrow Jeremy
Jeremy and Hamlet

BELLES-LETTRES

Joseph Conrad: A Critical Study
The Crystal Box: Fragments of Autobiography
Some Notes on the Evolution
of the English Novel

SHORT STORIES

The Silver Thorn—A Book of Stories
All Souls' Night—A Book of Stories

WITH J. B. PRIESTLEY

Farthing Hall

CAPTAIN NICHOLAS

A Modern Comedy

BY

HUGH WALPOLE

GARDEN CITY, NEW YORK

Doubleday, Doran & Company, Inc.

MCMXXXIV

PRINTED AT THE *Country Life Press*, GARDEN CITY, N. Y., U. S. A.

FIRST EDITION

For

ROSE *and* OWEN

TURVILLE

Beware the Jabberwock, my son!
The jaws that bite, the claws that catch!
Beware the Jubjub bird, and shun
The frumious Bandersnatch!

LEWIS CARROLL

CONTENTS

PART I

THE SPRING EVENING

THE SPRING EVENING

"WHAT a beautiful evening!" Fanny Carlisle said to the little lady who was standing beside her.

It was one of her impetuous moments and, as was always the case, she instantly regretted her impetuosity. How odd the lady must think her, speaking to her thus in the middle of Bordon's, without any reason at all!

And yet she did not appear to mind.

"Yes, is it not?" she said, looking up and smiling. "So early in April, and so warm."

The room where the glass was had a beautifully remote air, and from the large window the late afternoon sun streamed in upon the glass, transmuting it, transforming the ruby and orange and blue into glittering, trembling flames of colour. The tall glasses, the round bowls, the tumblers twinkled, shone, and sparkled. They almost, if you were very romantic, appeared themselves to glory in the sun, which, perhaps, did not too often caress them. It was clever of Mr. Bordon to place the glass near the window and leave the rest of the room to the china. He had known that there would be these sunny days; he had even, Fanny Carlisle considered, arranged the large thin vases and the faint blue bowls on the highest points of vantage, for their hunger for light must be passionate. . . .

"It must be lovely for them—a sunny day," she said.

But the little lady could not follow her so far.

"It's too tiresome. My maid broke a blue bowl yesterday that my husband gave me five Christmases ago. I was greatly attached to it. My husband's away, you know, in Scotland, and I want to replace it before he returns. In fact I *must* replace it. He notices things. I felt *sure* that Bordon would have one like it. The man's gone to enquire, but I could see from his face——" She broke off to look again at the blue bowls. Poor things! They had been so happy in the sun and now they were worthless, valueless, might all be smashed into atoms and the little lady would not care.

"I was so *certain* that Bordon . . ." she murmured.

"What about this one?" Fanny asked, pointing to a pale blue bowl so thin and delicate that a breath would blow it like a bubble into the sky.

"Oh, no!" said the little lady, quite crossly. "That isn't in the least like it," and she looked at Fanny Carlisle as though it were most stupid of her not to have known.

"She's irritated by my height," Fanny thought. This often occurred to her when she was with strangers. She was tall and broad, felt herself to be clumsier than she really was, and this was because so often in her childhood she had heard the words: "Now, Fanny, *do* be careful! You'll knock that chair over!" or "Fanny—mind the table. Look where you are going!"

But the little lady was pleased with what she saw. She liked this tall straight woman with the dark hair and the kindly humorous face. She was not smart, but most certainly a lady—not one of these modern know-all women who gave themselves airs and thought they knew everything, although Heaven alone could tell whence they came

—for the little lady was something of a snob and as sensitive on occasion about her small stature as Fanny was of her height.

"He's a long time," she complained. "And I know it's all no use. It's so very irritating when they go off saying, 'I'll see what we can do, madam,' when you know that *they* know that there's nothing to be done at all."

"Well, I don't think that I can wait," Fanny said cheerfully. "I promised to be back by five, and it's half-past four now. My boy's at Westminster and he likes me to be there at tea time."

"Oh, you have a boy at Westminster, have you? My husband's brother went to Westminster. How small the world is!"

"Yes, we're a large family," Fanny said, smiling, impetuous again. "There are eight of us altogether!"

"Eight!" said the little lady. "Dear me! In these days! That does seem a lot!"

"Yes—there's my mother-in-law, my husband, my sister, my brother, and I have two boys and a girl."

"And you all live together, always?"

"Yes, we're a very attached family. At least I suppose we are. We all get along very well together."

"That's not at all the modern idea."

"No. I suppose it isn't. But I think we'd all be very sorry if the family was broken up. I always think it so odd in the newspapers and novels when they say that family life doesn't exist any more. But of course they have to write about *something*."

But the little lady shook her head. "Your case is very exceptional," she said. "All living together, I mean. Of course relations visit one another and so on, but staying in the same house . . . ! Don't you quarrel frightfully?"

Fanny laughed, shaking her head.

"No. Why should we? Of course we don't always agree, but that makes things more interesting."

"Well, I should be afraid if I were you. It's too good to last."

"Oh, I don't think so," said Fanny. "Nothing is."

This again she at once regretted, for it was platitudinous and, as her family often told her, the platitude was her danger. Only why, when a thing was true, was it silly to mention it? This would lead her too far, so she said:

"Those orange bowls are charming. With spring flowers they would be delightful."

"But it isn't an orange bowl that I want," said the little lady. "And I've been here half an hour. And I'm keeping you, too. What a shame! Really, in these big stores you'd think they——"

"Oh, it doesn't matter," said Fanny. "It wasn't important. Only some quite ordinary tumblers. I can get them anywhere."

At this moment the assistant, holding a blue bowl in each hand, appeared. He was a *very* thin man with a small pale yellow moustache, but his manner was so confident and superior that Fanny could not feel sorry for him.

"I think I've found the very thing, madam," he said triumphantly.

"Indeed, you have not!" said the little lady. "Neither of those is the least like it."

"I'm very sorry, madam," he remarked with polite indifference, as though he said: "I have excellent manners, but if you dropped dead at my feet this very moment I shouldn't much care." "Perhaps we can get you—if Madam isn't in a hurry——"

"Of course I'm in a hurry," the little lady, almost in

tears, replied. "And now I don't know what I shall do. It's too provoking. I thought Bordon's had everything. . . ."

"I'm extremely sorry, madam," said the assistant, pulling his primrose moustache. "Of course this blue bowl is very charming. We——"

But the little lady had gone, exactly as though the floor had swallowed her or the sun absorbed her into its splendour.

He turned to Fanny. "And what——?" he asked.

"Oh, it's only some tumblers," Fanny answered. "Quite ordinary ones. Half a dozen."

Very quickly she was supplied.

"Isn't it a lovely evening?" she said.

"Very fine indeed, madam. Has Madam an account or——"

"Oh, no, thank you. I'll pay now."

He went to wrap them up, still with his air of pleasant disdain which only his shoes, a little worn and wrinkled, belied. While he was gone Fanny looked again at the glass.

The sun now struck the room with its full power. The air sparkled and was shot with the trembling colour of the glass—pale as green sea water, rosy as evening cloud, frosty with the shimmer of ice on the windowpane, clear with the silver whiteness of crystal, these lovely things quietly surrendered to the evening. One tall vase of a blue as faint as a young hyacinth seemed to be part of the sun, to be withdrawn into outer air and lose itself in the evening sky.

"There's a smell of lilac," Fanny thought. "White lilac would look lovely in that vase."

2

Safely outside she climbed onto the upper part of an omnibus. Gazing through the window at her side, she marvelled that the world could be so beautiful. It was one of those hours when by a trick of light and sun London appears to be surely the queen of the world. She is not, of course, and we all know how, at the bidding of a tiny cloud, she can sink into primeval slime, but this afternoon she thought that she would let herself go. Through the window Fanny saw the spring evening at liberty. Carried through a rosy air, everything below her was unsubstantial, veiled in a mist that was primrose-coloured, and then deep in violet shadow—mists and shadows that seized messenger boys and ladies shopping and butchers at their reeking doors and antique shops with here a Persian rug and there a bowl of crimson, and newspaper placards, murderous and sporting—all these things were as whimsical as a play by a Scotsman or a children's poem by a member of the Athenæum. Somewhere around the chimneys the shadows failed, and above them the sky was as pale as the feathers of young canaries. Was it blue or white like a sea shell?

"If you wouldn't mind," said the lady in the seat with her. "You are sitting on my coat."

Fanny was never comfortable on the outside of one of those seats that are ironically designed for the sensitive egotism of ordinary-sized persons. Fanny was too large, and she could not see from the window as she would, so that it was delightful when the lady (who held herself stiffly as though Fanny had the plague or the chicken pox at least) departed and allowed her to command the scene. And command it she did! For now she could see all the humours of the street as though they were directed by her. She had only to move a finger and that lady with the parcels stayed where she was, imprisoned in the sunny haze, or the stout man trying to hail a taxi (he had a flower in his buttonhole) remained for ever hailing, an eternal figure in a master's landscape. And now they were in Piccadilly Circus where Eros, temporarily restored, caught the sunlight in his wings, and below the ground people dropped pennies into machines and slid down mechanical stairways. Here there was a hush. Everything moved softly, and the sky was exposed, a whole square piece of it, lit into infinity with one star quietly inquisitive. Then they went down the hill, saw people already on chairs outside His Majesty's Theatre, looked at the Trafalgar Square lions, considered the pictures separated from the spray of the fountains by that grimy wall of stone, down the hill again into a world of bells and legislators, of policemen and trees and hidden streets and small boys wearing top hats. . . .

Into Fanny's world, for she lived with her family in Smith Square.

"I'm sure I smell lilac somewhere," she said as she climbed down from her omnibus.

3

The face of the house where she, her sister, her two brothers, her three children had all been born always delighted her with every fresh vision of it. It was a tall thin house, the stone pearl-coloured, the windows high and rather narrow, the chimney pots a little twisted, four white steps to the door, and above the door a stone teapot that had been carved there when the house began its history somewhere about 1710. In a changing world—"and *what* a changing world!"—thought Fanny—the beautiful pale colours, the dignity and quietness of this house meant something. And then when you considered all the life that had flourished inside it—the brocades and patches, the sedan chairs that had waited outside the door, the teapot serenely watching them, and, later, the crinolines, the wickedly narrow waists, the young men with whiskers, the beards, the barrel organs, the screens covered with pictures from the Illustrateds, the births, the deaths, the quarrels and reconciliations—"and now!" thought Fanny. But at that she could wait no longer, but must, at once, let herself in with her key to see whether Edward was hungry for his tea, what Nell had done about the Frobishers, and whether Romney had sold the French picture to the rich American (now becoming in London so rare a bird!) as this morning he had hoped to do.

Then, inside the hall, these surmises were as though they had never been, for Janet was coming down the stairs and, at sight of her mistress, stopped dead and, in that husky would-be-indifferent whisper that was so especially hers, said: "Oh, what do you think? The Captain is here!"

Janet, who had been present when Fanny was brought into the world, whose whole life had been spent in one long determination never in any circumstances to allow a thought of emotion, pleasure, pain, or interest to colour her words, was on this occasion defeated. For her voice trembled as she spoke, and into her grey eyes there came that shadow of anxiety, of tenderness even, for her mistress, child, and friend.

"The Captain! . . . Nicholas!" and Fanny stayed where she was, almost dropping the parcel that held the tumblers.

"Yes. He's in the drawing room. And with his little girl. Them's his boxes."

She came down the stairs and stood beside Fanny, her tall gaunt figure drawn stiffly up as though she would defy the world.

They continued to whisper.

"But he never sent a line. He hasn't written for ten years."

"He's here, waiting for you, with his little girl!"

"He's come to stay?"

"It looks like it."

"Is no one there?"

"No, Mr. Matthew's out walking and Miss Grace is in her room and——"

But Fanny waited for no more. Thrusting the tumblers into Janet's hand she hurried upstairs, threw open the drawing-room door. There, in front of the fire, his legs extended, perfectly at home, waited her brother Captain Nicholas Coventry. Beside him a little girl in a rather shabby black frock was standing.

"Oh, Nicholas!" Fanny cried, and she rushed at him, almost knocking over a small table, threw her arms round him and kissed him as though she would never let him go.

"Well, Fanny!" he cried, when he was at last released. "This is fine! This is splendid!"

She was near to tears, her cheeks were flushed, her hair tumbled with the embrace.

"Nicholas! . . . And without a word! And after all this time! Oh, dear—but I was never so surprised in my life! Why didn't you write? Why didn't you telegraph? What does this mean? Have you come to stay?"

"Yes—Lizzie and I have come to stay if you will have us."

"Have you? Why, of course we will! And this is Lizzie! Why, she was scarcely born when I saw her last. You remember—that Christmas at Caroline's!" and she embraced the little girl, who was thin and pale and had large, round, dark eyes.

The Captain laughed, and his laugh was one of the jolliest in the world. He was a handsome man with as slight a figure now at forty-four as he had had at twenty, short, cropped grey hair, a little curly, a fresh rosy complexion, a short toothbrush moustache, and clothes that, if a little worn, fitted him quite perfectly. He was smart, he was neat, and he had small blue eyes. He patted her shoulder.

"Dear Fanny—this *is* a welcome. I didn't know how you'd take it. I said to Lizzie—'We'll leave our boxes in the hall, for they may not want us—it may not be convenient.' "

"Want you! Convenient!" cried Fanny. "Why, it's the most wonderful thing! But where have you been? Where have you come from? I haven't had a line for ten years, you know——"

"I know. I wonder I had the cheek to turn up at all. I said to Lizzie: 'If they do take us in, it will be the most marvellous charity, because nobody has behaved worse than I have. It's only,' I told Lizzie, 'because your Aunt Fanny is the best-natured, kindest creature in the world that I've any hope.' . . . We've come from Italy, from San Remo."

"From San Remo? Oh, but you must be famished!" She rushed across the room and rang a bell. She turned back towards them, her eyes shining, her hands outstretched.

"But it's wonderful to see you, Nick. And not a bit altered, just the same. A little greyer perhaps . . . !"

"And you're the same, too."

"Oh, no! I'm getting an old, old woman. Ten years!" She stood looking at them, smiling, tears in her eyes. It was too wonderful! Too . . . !

And then she was practical.

"But you'll want to wash. And they must take up your bags. Let me see! The Brown spare room. That'll be the thing. It gets the sun. I'll tell them to light a fire. And you'll like Lizzie near you. There's a small bedroom quite close that Edward used to have——"

Nicholas laughed. "It doesn't matter where you put us. We're regular gipsies, aren't we, Lizzie? Don't you bother about us, Fanny."

"Bother about you! Of course I'll bother about you." She then realized that Lizzie had not spoken a word, but continued to regard her with steady, unblinking eyes.

"You poor little thing!" She went up to her and kissed her. The child's cheek was very cold. "You must be worn out and *ravenous.*"

Rose the parlourmaid came in. Instructions were given. Fanny led the two travellers upstairs, into the Brown room (which wasn't brown at all, but had a wall paper with robins), and then Lizzie was shown the small room, and the boxes were brought in and the fires were lit.

After all this Fanny said:

"And now I'll leave you. Come straight down to the drawing room as soon as you've washed. The others will be all there in a moment. They'll be *so* excited!"

She went up to Nicholas and kissed him again. "Dear Nicholas! I hope you're going to stay for ever so long. You owe it us, you know, after the way you've behaved."

He patted her cheek.

"As long as you'll have us, Fanny dear."

As soon as she had left him she hurried up to the

schoolroom to see that Edward had his tea. Here, in this room with its picture-covered screens, its shelves with the old books, a worn rocking-horse without a tail, the children had lived, and now that Nell and Romney had grown up it remained with Edward as its only master. He regarded it now as entirely his, loved it with a passion, and resented intensely if anyone tried to alter even the smallest detail in it. Here he had his tea, his boiled egg, his toast and his jam. Here he pursued his own secret and mysterious life, and here he insisted that his mother should watch him cut the top off his egg.

He was waiting for her now, his school books piled on the table, his top hat thrown onto a chair, and his bright birdlike eyes watching the door. His features were plain, his complexion sallow, and his mouth large, but he was not unattractive, for he had energy, he had curiosity, and he was able to run his life (which seemed to him an extraordinary, adventurous, and most unusual life) by himself.

"I thought you weren't coming," he said to her gravely.

"I'm sorry, darling." She sat down beside him and poured out his tea. "But what *do* you think has happened? Your Uncle Nicholas has come with his little girl."

"Uncle Nicholas?" he said, with his eyes on the jam (he had expected for some reason that it would be apricot, and very disappointingly it was plum). "That's the wicked one, isn't it?"

"Wicked! No, darling. Wherever did you get such an idea from?"

"I heard Father call him a ne'er-do-well once, and I asked Mr. Foster what a ne'er-do-well was and he said someone who wasn't any good."

"Oh, that only means" (she watched him while he cut off the top of his egg, an operation that he performed with the most perfect dexterity) "someone who moves about. Ever since your uncle left the army he's been moving about. You see, after his wife died he felt lonely—and then he hasn't very much money. And he has a little girl to support."

"A little girl?" asked Edward. "What's her name?"

"Lizzie."

"Lizzie. Well, I don't think much of that for a name. Mother, all my algebra was right this morning. Paunchy seemed quite pleased for once, and, Mother, can Bond Minor come to tea on Saturday? He's not a bad sort if you know him, and he's been very decent about hockey. You see . . ."

And he entered into a long history. While he talked, her mind wandered. As a rule every detail of Edward's day (of Nell's and Romney's also) was absorbing to her. But now the consciousness that Nicholas was in the house, that he was, at this very moment, washing his hands on the floor below, that he had arrived and intended to remain—this great surprise drove for the moment even the family from her mind. She had always been a little shy of Nicholas, shy of him and adoring him both at the same time. He had been (and was still, no doubt) by far the cleverest of the family. It had seemed always that there was nothing he could not do if he cared to do it. That he had not cared had been astonishing to her. When, at the outbreak of war, he had at once joined up, that was part of his general courage and enterprise, but when, at the end of it, he had remained in the army she had been sorry. The army was not the place for his gifts. He read, he painted charming pictures, he was most modern in all his views. He has always been ahead of the others in his attitude to life—bold, audacious, Fanny often thought him. He had so much charm that people fell down before him like ninepins, and yet with all this, with his charm, his looks, his brains, he had not—as Fanny was compelled to admit—done very much with his life. What indeed he *had* done in the last ten years she did not know. He had married, towards the end of the war, Essie Lawrence, an odd, quiet, reserved little thing, and when Lizzie was a year old Essie had died of pneumonia in Paris. They had all written letters of sympathy, but not a word had been received in reply. The others had ceased to write: only Fanny had persisted, sending long family letters twice or thrice a year to the address of his bankers in Paris. He had never answered: she had expected never to hear again, and now here he was, as alive and charming and affectionate as he had ever been, here without a word, without even a telegram!

But the very sight of him had made her happy. Poor Nicholas—without a home, widowed so soon, with that sad, pale, silent little girl. She sighed.

". . . so I said, 'Well, keep it yourself—I don't want your silly old watch,' and he said . . ."

"Yes, darling. Is your egg all right?"

"Top hole."

"I must go down now and give Uncle Nicholas some tea."

Edward said nothing to that. When he was disappointed he said nothing. His mother always stayed with him for at least half an hour. He had lots more to tell her. So he said nothing and helped himself to jam.

She went down to the drawing room to find her mother-in-law and her husband and the tea all waiting.

Mrs. Carlisle was seventy-three years of age and a spare, fine old lady with white hair, a long nose, and a small determined mouth. When her son Charles had married Fanny Coventry she had lamented his fate as though he had lost an arm or leg. But that was quite natural, for so passionately did she love her son—her only child—that no woman on earth could ever be good enough for him. For twenty-three years she had maintained this attitude, and neither Charles's married happiness nor Fanny's good nature could modify it. Her commiseration, however, had been enlarged by her worship of Charles's children, who never, so perfect were they, could have a mother worthy of them. Apart from this, she liked Fanny. If Charles *had* to have a wife, and Romney, Nell, and Edward a mother, why, then Fanny was a good woman who did her best, and it was not *her* fault, poor dear, that she was placed in a situation altogether above her talents. That was old Mrs. Carlisle's domestic attitude. She paid an annual sum towards the upkeep of the house and, although what she paid was a great deal less than what she received, this gave her a right to interfere when she thought it proper—and she thought it proper quite frequently.

The other thing about her was that until the last two years she had "enjoyed" perfect health. Enjoyed was not perhaps the word because she had accepted this same health as her absolute right and had scorned her fellow human beings for their physical weakness. When, therefore, last year a little rheumatism had visited her legs, and her heart had begun once and again to trouble her, she had been greatly surprised and indignant, rather as though someone had been rude to her in the street or a man pinched her leg in an omnibus.

As to Charles, he was a square-shouldered, jolly-faced man with grey hair, a short sturdy body, and amused, tolerant eyes. He was, in fact, like five hundred and fifty thousand other men except to his mother and wife, who thought him extraordinary, and his children, who thought him an old dear.

He had been in the Stock Exchange all his life, like his father before him, and had retired three years ago. In these difficult times—it was the spring of 1932—his investments were not so flourishing, and he worried, sometimes, in the silence of the night about the future. At the top of the house he had a large room where he did wood-carving. Except for finance and one secret he had no troubles. He loved his wife and his children. His home was more to him than anything else in the world.

When Fanny came in she saw at once that they had not heard the news.

"Charles! Mother! Nicholas has arrived!"

She saw at once that neither of them was very glad. The old lady shut her mouth tightly and said not a word.

Charles said: "Nicholas! But why?"

"Why?" said Fanny, exasperated as in her impetuosity she so often was with Charles's slowness. "Why? Because he's come to stay—with his little girl."

"Come to stay?" said Charles. "For how long?"

"As long as he likes," said Fanny, wishing for a moment, as so many loving wives so often do, that she had married someone different.

"Where's he come from?"

"From San Remo."

"What's he been doing there?"

"Oh, I don't know. I've had no time to ask him anything. He's upstairs washing his hands——"

"Well, I'm damned!" Charles planted his hands on his stout knees. "What do you say to that, Mother?"

"What do *I* say?" The old lady tossed her head. "It's Fanny's house and it's Fanny's brother."

Just here, fortunately, Matthew came in. Matthew Coventry, who was forty-five, two years older than his sister Fanny and one year older than Nicholas, was a little man, oddly short beside his brother and two sisters, who were all tall. He was scrupulously neat in a dark suit and a blue bow tie with white spots. His round face was kindly and humorous and bore a striking resemblance to Fanny's, although his colour was pale beside Fanny's brilliance.

The trouble with Matthew was, as Mrs. Carlisle often pointed out to her son, that he *did nothing*. He had been once, years ago, a solicitor, but having some means of his own he had put some of it into the upkeep of the Smith Square house and taken up his abode there. He was perfectly happy. His most striking characteristic, at first sight, was his tranquillity. He brought with him, wherever he was, an air of rest and peace. Even Mrs. Carlisle admitted this: "I like Matthew about the house. He quiets you down, and that's the stranger, Charles, because he's undoubtedly mad."

"No, not mad," Charles would say, smiling. "Religious."

"Same thing," said old Mrs. Carlisle, who was, I'm sorry to admit, a complete pagan.

He came in very quietly now, and when Fanny said: "Matthew—Nicholas has come," he smiled and remarked:

"How nice! We haven't seen him for ages!"

He sat down, crossed his legs, and smiled at the old lady, of whom he was very fond. In her heart she liked him, too, but now, looking at him, she thought: "Really, it's terrible of Matthew—doing nothing with his life whatever and looking so contented. His religion ought to tell him that it isn't right." And she never reflected for a single moment that her beloved Charles also did nothing.

Matthew said: "Where's he come from?"

"From San Remo," said Fanny, pleased that someone had come in who would be glad about Nicholas. "And he's brought his little girl."

"Is he going to stay with us?"

"Of course."

"That's good."

At that moment Nicholas and his daughter Lizzie came in. Nicholas had looked spruce enough when he had arrived, but now he was as elegant, as slim, as straight-backed as an officer on parade. Lizzie was in her same little black dress. She held her father's hand and looked directly in front of her. Nicholas took her up to the old lady. "Old Lady," he said, "this is my beautiful daughter."

He had always in the old days called her "Old Lady," and for some reason she liked it, although in general she hated to be reminded of her age. She could not abide him, she despised him utterly, but nevertheless she liked him to call her "Old Lady."

She paid no attention to him but drew the little girl to her.

"So you're little Lizzie, are you?"

"Yes," said Lizzie.

"How old are you?"

"Twelve."

"Dear me, what a terrible age! You poor little thing, you look half starved. Nicholas, you haven't been looking after her."

He laughed, taking them all in with his merry eye. "Oh, *she* looks after *me!* Didn't you know? . . . How are you, Charles? Getting fat, aren't you? Hullo, Matthew! You haven't changed a bit! By Jove, it's grand to be here!" He sat down on the sofa, and Lizzie at once sat down beside him. "I don't suppose you any of you want me, but Lizzie and I couldn't help it. We just *had* to come.

Didn't we, Liz? And you can turn us out as soon as you like."

"*Had* to come!" snorted Mrs. Carlisle. "When for ten years you haven't been near us nor have you written to one of us."

He pulled up his trousers a little, gave his moustache a pinch; his bright blue eyes seemed to sparkle in the firelight.

"Oh, but I'm no good at all! You've always known that. I never write to anyone—I've got no conscience about anything. Besides, who cares to hear from me? What have I got to tell anyone that's of the slightest interest? But I've thought of you often—and talked about you. Haven't I, Lizzie?"

Fanny noticed that he was always appealing to his daughter but never apparently expected an answer from her. He planted his hands on his knees.

"Be nice to us for a day or two. We really need some kindness shown us. And then we'll move on again."

Fanny went up to him and kissed him on the forehead.

"Of course we'll be nice to you. We're terribly pleased that you've come."

He looked up at her, smiling, and touched her hand with his.

"We'll be nice to you," old Mrs. Carlisle said, smiling grimly. "If you'll be good."

"I can't be good," Nicholas answered. "It isn't in my nature. But I'll try to behave while I'm here." Then he went on, looking about him: "Oh, it *is* nice to be here! Just the same room—not altered a bit. How often in exile I've thought of the Bonington and Wilson—you could get a pretty sum for them now, you know—and the screen with the dragons, and the glass-topped table with the seals and garnets and gold boxes. Thanks, Matthew—I *will* have some of that cake—the plum one—and plenty of it."

The door opened again and Nell and Romney came in, so that all the family were now in the room save Edward, who was doing geography upstairs, and Aunt Grace.

Nell, who was twenty years of age, was very pretty, looking like so many of her age, half a boy with her short hair and slim figure. Her hair was fair and her face so youthful and so gentle in expression that the slight artificiality of the eyebrows and the carmined lips would have been masklike and unreal had they been at all exaggerated. She did not exaggerate, but painted and modelled just enough to be in line with her generation. She was wearing a little dark blue hat.

Romney, who was twenty-two, had a figure as slim as his sister's, but he was as dark as she was fair. He looked distinguished and superior to the run of young men, which was what he wanted to look, but in his heart he was afraid that he was not superior to anybody. He was often unhappy because he felt superior and inferior both at the same time. Life seemed to him increasingly difficult, and then there was the awful question as to whether there was any point in any of it. All his clever friends thought that there was no point. He longed for affection but assumed an attitude of cold heartless indifference—except to his mother, whom he frankly and openly loved although he thought her sometimes absurd and always behind the times. Once and again, in the secrecy of his chambers, he wondered whether to be altogether behind the times mustn't be rather comforting.

They were greatly surprised to see their Uncle Nicholas, whom they remembered scarcely at all. But they showed no surprise whatever and, after saying that they were glad to see him, devoted themselves to their tea.

Soon they were all talking together and Fanny could sit quietly by and watch them.

4

This was often the favourite hour of the day for her because, unlike so many families, they enjoyed meeting once a day and spending an hour in one another's company, removed from the rest of humanity if possible. Of course the outside world *did* come to tea at times, on occasion invited and on occasion because it had nothing better to do. Mrs. Frobisher, for example, was one of the latter kind. But, every week, there were days when no one came, and then they would sit, eat and drink, gossip, argue, and enjoy their hour. In this as in many other things they were an unusual family, and especially in the love that bound them all together. For though old Mrs. Carlisle might snort, Charles argue, Nell and Romney mock, and although they were not at all family-proud but regarded themselves as quite ordinary, nevertheless they cared for one another as they cared for no one outside.

Of course this couldn't last, Fanny often assured herself. Nell would fall in love, Romney marry, someone surely one day would attack their defenses. How strong was this family bond? Could they keep it? Yes. Fanny believed that they could. There was some underlying fidelity, trust, devotion here that was stronger than the world.

She had long ago been sure that this outside modern restless, reckless world must be accepted and propitiated. She herself neither understood it nor liked it. It was not *her* world, but it *was* the world of Romney, Nell, and Edward, so she tried to read their books, understand their pictures, and listened (often with alarm and a secret consciousness that all her tastes—religious, moral, æsthetic—were affronted) to their opinions on morality, marriage, art. She could not change these things. Nothing that she could say would alter anything, only because she loved them with all her heart she could show them that she was behind them in whatever happened to them and would love them whatever they did. Nevertheless Nell and Romney were *good*. She was sure of that and, whatever they might say, their ideas of honour and fidelity and courage were her own ideas. She could trust them anywhere.

And now Nicholas had joined the family. As she looked at him, laughing, joking, indulging to the full his famous charm, she smiled. What an extraordinary man! For there he was as though he had never been away, drawing them all in! He must be aware that old Mrs. Carlisle and Charles disliked him and didn't want him—but did that matter to him? Not in the least! He was confident, as he had always been, that he would succeed. And yet he had not succeeded—with more talents than any of them he was the failure. What, she suddenly wondered, was he living on? He had had years ago his share of their father's money, but she knew that also years ago he had spent it. He could not be earning anything now unless he was selling his pictures. Perhaps he was. . . . Perhaps over there in Italy he had become a famous painter.

So she suddenly said:

"Nick—what about the painting? Probably you're a famous painter now and we none of us know it."

He had been joking with Nell. (It was plain that he greatly admired her.) He turned, smiling, to Fanny.

"Oh, my dear, didn't you know? I've given it up long ago. I wasn't good enough. It's no use in these days being a second-rater. There are too many clever people about.

Then this modern painting, which is all I care about, is so easy to do badly that if you admire it you simply daren't try."

"I sold the Matisse today," Romney broke in. "I hooked the old boy at last. It was exactly like landing a salmon. But we got him. And at our price, too. All the same, he didn't do so badly. The price was stiff, but it was a *good* Matisse. A girl in a lovely red hat and a white feather."

"And what else?" asked Nell.

"Nothing at all except a silver garter. That was the trouble. He was frightened of what his wife would say. He brought her in finally, and the joke was that she admired it immensely."

"Well," began Nick, "I saw a Matisse the other day in Paris——"

But he was interrupted. Grace Coventry came in, flustered as usual. She was a large, stout, rosy woman, often smiling and generally bewildered. As she came forward she said:

"Isn't that dreadful? I went fast asleep. I was reading such an interesting book, too! And now tea's over. Well, never mind"—she smiled brightly on everyone—"I deserve it."

"Of course tea isn't over," Fanny said. "Grace, here's a surprise for you! Nicholas has come——"

"Nicholas!" Grace stood, confused, then she went rather timidly to him and kissed him. "Well, I never! I *never* did! How perfectly lovely!"

"How are you, Grace?" Nicholas said. "As blooming as ever, I see. This is Lizzie. This is your Aunt Grace, Lizzie, whom I've so often told you about. She'll take you into the kitchen and give you jam, and she'll bring you hot drinks at night, and if you ever have a cold she'll sit up all night with you."

Everyone laughed, and Grace tee-heed and laughed, too, and suddenly kissed Nicholas again and sat down on the sofa and took Lizzie's hand.

There had come in with her a large black cat. This cat was known as Becky Sharp for many reasons. One was that it had most brilliant and piercing green eyes, another that it was entirely callous about its almost incredibly recurring offspring, another that it was a cat always out for its own advantage and would attach itself ruthlessly to anyone who had anything to offer. Becky Sharp was one of Fanny's weaknesses. She knew all about its hard and grasping character, but she loved it, partly because she remembered the gay and enterprising kitten that it had once been. And the cat did *appear* to have an affection for Fanny. It followed her about the house, liked to settle on her lap, was distressed, apparently, when she was away.

It advanced now and stood beside her, looking up. Fanny poured its milk into a saucer.

"Yes, you know," Grace was saying, smiling round upon everyone and especially on Granny Carlisle, whom she always persisted in regarding as a weak, delicate old lady who needed looking after and protecting—"there I was. I went fast asleep, and it was at one of the most interesting chapters in Warwick Deeping's delightful book. I know you don't read novels, Nicholas. Let me put your cup down. No, I insist. . . . Yes, and oh, Fanny" (here she opened a large red bag which she always carried with her everywhere), "I forgot to tell you I bought the small hand towels and the other things this morning as I said I would, and they were two pounds two shillings exactly—you gave me three pounds, you remember. Here is the change."

"Oh, don't bother just now, dear."

"No, but I must. Or I shall certainly spend it myself."

She laid the little pile of silver on a small table, looked at it with satisfaction, then said:

"Shall I get your sewing, Granny?" (She always called Mrs. Carlisle "Granny" because the children did.) "Or would you like your book?"

"I don't want ANYTHING AT ALL, Grace, thank you. NOTHING WHATEVER. I'm going to my room very shortly."

Grace looked round to see what else she could do for anybody, and finding nothing she concentrated again upon Nicholas.

"But where have you *been* all this time, Nicholas? Where *have* you been? And never writing to one of us. Too bad. But there, I expect you've been so terribly busy. One's always so busy abroad. Thank you, dear." (For she had dropped her bag, which Nell picked up for her.) "And dear little Lizzie. We'll have to see what we can do to make her happy while she's here, won't we, Fanny? You shall come for walks with me, and there are lots of books in the schoolroom that I'm sure you haven't read. What do you like best to amuse yourself with, darling?"

Everyone waited for the answer, for until now the child had been quite silent. Only her father looked at her with ironical confidence.

"Thank you very much," said Lizzie. "I think I like watching people best."

"You see," Nicholas explained, "she's always with me, and I keep such *very* odd company that she has a good deal to watch altogether, don't you, Lizzie?"

"And where's she been to school?" asked Grace.

"She's never been to school."

"Never been to——! Never to school!" Grace raised her soft hands, which were small and beautiful. "Oh, but, Nicholas! What *have* you been about?"

"I don't believe in schools. I never learnt anything at mine. Lizzie can read, write, and speak Italian, German, and French, and she knows more about human nature than I do—so her education's all right."

Grace was about to exclaim again, but Charles interrupted in his slow way. (This was the family fashion, so long acquired that it was now like second nature, of checking Grace.)

"It has been one of the grandest days I've ever seen. I walked through the Park to Marble Arch. I never saw such colours!"

Fanny looked at him with a little anxiety. There had been something the matter with Charles during the last week. He was not happy about something. He was worried, she was sure. But she said nothing. Only her eyes met his, and they both smiled.

The little gold clock on the mantelpiece struck six, and there was a general movement. A family that is much together forms habits, and one of the habits here was that at six o'clock the family session was over and everyone went about his or her own business.

Charles got up, yawned, stretched himself. "Yes," he said. "One of the loveliest evenings I've ever seen. Spring. You could smell flowers everywhere. Now, Nick, make yourself at home. We dine at seven forty-five. Glad you've come." He put his hand for a moment on Nicholas's shoulder.

"Already," Fanny thought happily, "he doesn't dislike him as much as he did." She went off to see how Edward was getting on.

They all went their several ways. Soon the large room, with its pleasant glow from the lamps and fire, its silver-shining tea things, the large white bowl with early spring flowers, the old warmly coloured pictures, the bookcases and the deep-red lacquer screen, had only Nicholas and Lizzie for its occupants.

"Well, Liz," he remarked, "I don't think we shall do so badly here for a bit. What do *you* think?"

"I like the old lady best," she said. "I don't like the one with the red bag *at all.*" Her words had a slight touch of foreign accent.

She waited quietly for her father's next move.

She did not seem in the least astonished at it when it came. Nicholas looked, with a light glance, about the room, then with a little quick gesture swept the pile of silver that Grace had placed on the small table into his pocket.

Becky Sharp watched him with intent green eyes.

5

On the afternoon following Nicholas Coventry's arrival Charles Carlisle set out to say good-bye to a lady.

He was not accustomed to such farewells. He had tumbled into his father's business like a happy little duck into halcyon water. He was young enough when he fell in love with Fanny Coventry to be idealistic; he was still in love *and* idealistic. He adored his children and thought there were none like them anywhere. He considered the Smith Square house perfect, his club—the Atlas—the best in London, golf a wonderful game, and fooling about with a hammer and some nails and a piece of wood the most perfect of tranquil amusements. His health was excellent. But he was not such a fool as this sounds. His nature was cheerful and gay, but his heart was tender, and he had imagination. He also had common sense.

He had no very great opinion of himself, and it was

one of his weaknesses that he was easily convinced of the great merits of his friends, but he had courage, he could be obstinate and, if need be, almost fanatically loyal.

He knew quite well that the major part of his happiness came from his wife. He loved and admired her with a devotion that had in it patience, courtesy, honour, and humour—the four great qualities for any husband who wishes to pay marriage the compliment that it deserves. Like any other man he admired a pretty woman, and his thoughts were not always in his control, but, with the exception of his wife and daughter, he preferred like most normal men the day-by-day company of men.

He had known no worry that deserved that name, since Fanny's difficult delivery of Edward, until the last two years, when money suddenly began to behave eccentrically and the world, in general, turn towards madness.

But Romney was in a good business now, his family had no extravagant tastes; he could always, he was sure, find enough for them. Into this tranquillity, on January the Third of this present year, there had fallen the most astounding and troubling episode of his life. Its origin had been simple. On that evening Fanny was in bed with a cold, and he had gone alone to the theatre, a thing that he did sometimes, for he did not resent his own company and found that, when he was by himself, he noticed many interesting things that a friend's presence obscured. He had taken a seat in the dress circle and, at the first interval, thought that he would buy himself a drink. There was the usual impatient multitude fighting at the usual inadequate bar. He turned aside and saw a girl by herself, leaning against the wall in the corridor. At the first sight of her it was as though he were struck in the chest. She was neither especially beautiful nor especially young. Her hair was so fair that under the bright light of the theatre it looked almost white. She was alone and, he thought, in some distress. He was quite unable to prevent himself from speaking to her—it was as though he acted under some strong command. He asked her whether he could do anything for her. She thanked him and asked him to get her some brandy: she felt faint; she thought it was the heat. He fought his way to the bar and got the brandy for her, and they then talked. He discovered that she was an assistant in a flower shop in Knightsbridge. A week later she became his mistress.

6

He had thought that by this time he knew his character pretty well. He was not lascivious, he was not light-minded, he hated to do anything that could bring unhappiness to others. But this, although he went over it again and again in his mind, recalling the minutest details, sparing himself no accusations, examining it from every conceivable angle, he could not understand at all.

He had never been unfaithful to his wife before, he had never conceived it possible that in any circumstances he could be unfaithful to her. He was not a prude and was exceedingly tolerant to his fellow men. He did not believe himself to be of any exceptional moral strength of character, but, because he loved and admired his wife so truly, it seemed to him incredible that he could ever have relations with any other woman.

Christine Bell was in no way an exceptional woman. She was thirty-two years of age and had had, he knew, other lovers before himself. She had an easy, agreeable, friendly nature, but she was not intelligent or cultured. She had certainly at first been physically in love with him, but after some six weeks of their intimacy he fancied that she considered him as an older genial friend who was kind to her because he had a fancy for her. He was indeed kind to her. For some while he was like a man submerged in fiery and tempestuous waters. It was like that, as though he were living under water in some strange world where nature was changed, where houses were temples of coral, streets were paved with mother-of-pearl, and a dim green light shivered always in front of his eyes. And with this a fiery heat, so that his eyes burnt, his throat was parched, his hands were dry. A pitiful state for a man of his age! But he did not feel it to be pitiful. For some while he was in a condition of eager and excited exaltation. He considered no consequences, he wrote her passionate and foolish letters, he gave her extravagant presents, for which, to do her justice, she appeared to care very little.

Looking back, it was extraordinary to him that no one, during those weeks, noticed anything, but it happened that, at the end of January, Fanny, who had not been well, went with Nell on a cruise to the West Indies. It was, indeed, the consciousness, early in March, that she would soon be returning that woke him from his dream.

It was as though an enchantment had been placed on him and then as suddenly withdrawn. One evening, talking to Christine quietly in the little flat in Chelsea where she lived, he saw her as she was. He saw that she was a kind, ordinary, good-natured, commonplace woman and that he was in love with her no longer.

She, of course, saw it as quickly as he did and bore him no kind of resentment. She also was not in love with him. It seemed to her quite natural that these episodes should be bright, swift, and ephemeral. She had had a pleasant time, she had given him everything that he wanted, but he was not a sensual man and the permanent things that he wanted from a woman she could not possibly give him. She did not want to give them to him, for his passion, while it lasted, had seemed to her rather ridiculous. She thought of him as his children did—that he was a dear old thing, but—on the whole, for a continued affair, she preferred someone younger. This episode had not appeared to her in any way extraordinary as it did to him. They had both enjoyed their hours together, and she wished him all the luck in the world.

This afternoon he was going to see her for the last time.

As he walked along the King's Road—he had taken the underground from Westminster to Sloane Square—he was accompanied, it seemed, by a stranger, the man who had felt that crazy and fanatical obsession. He was on no terms any longer with that stranger, or on terms with him only enough to resent him.

This man whom he had once known was no companion of his any longer, but the effect of his company remained.

He turned down Manor Street by the Town Hall and, almost at the river end, arrived at a forbidding building with the appearance of a bishop whose countenance is noble but betrays private stomach trouble. There was grandeur everywhere, but it was a flaky, streaky grandeur; statues at intervals, but statues with peeling noses, wreaths of stone leaves and flowers soiled with bird droppings, and on the steps small fragments of newspaper that rustled and fluttered against the stone like live things.

He went inside, pushed the starting knob of the lift, and on the third floor found a door with a visiting card, a little grubby, inserted above the unpolished door handle. "Miss Christine Bell" it read.

She opened the door to him and, when the door was

closed, they kissed as they always did, but he did not put his arms round her nor did she wish him to do so.

In the sitting room, which had a yellow wall paper, a large bright green pouf in front of the gas fire, and two very silent canaries in a cage by the window, they sat one on either side of the pettish little fire which went, every once and again, "Put—Put—Put" in accents of irritable discontent. The rain began to beat against the windowpane, and suddenly one of the canaries uttered an excited, emotional little chirp as though it said, "Well, here's some life at last! Here's something to be thankful for!"

Christine did not pretend to be anything but weary. She had had an awful morning in the shop. This was her half-day, and didn't she need it! "The women were too frightful. All their nerves seemed to be on edge—especially that dreadful old Lady Hadden. She didn't know *what* she wanted. The narcissus was faded, although I told her it had come straight up from the country that same morning, and the white lilac was monstrously dear, which it *isn't,* and so on and so on. I could have smacked her old strawberry face, really I could, and there we have to stand, smiling and smiling. Oh, well, it's all in the day's work, I suppose." She lifted her eyes to his. She was wearing a grey frock and was almost, except for a little rouge on her lips, a shadow against the wall with her pale hair, her thin form, her long slender hands.

She *was,* perhaps, a shadow. These last months had been a dream; he had been in love with a ghost. And she looked at him, thinking more than ever that he was "a dear old thing." He was clumsy as a lover and absurd when he was passionate. She did not want him ever to touch her again, but she was very sorry that this was the last time that she would see his face, for he had one of the kindest, best-natured countenances in the world. It was his face really that she had fallen in love with, that she was even a little bit in love with still. She liked it when he was puzzled with something and wrinkled his eyebrows. She liked the good-natured crow's-feet that were marked near his eyes when he laughed. She liked his direct and honest gaze. Oh, he was a *good* man, and really this kind of thing wasn't his game at all. It was much better that it should end, especially as he loved his wife and his wife loved him. She wasn't one for breaking up married happiness. There wasn't so much of it about as all that.

She smiled at him and said:

"Here I am idling and you wanting your tea."

"Let me help," he said.

"Oh, no, you stay where you are."

When she came back with the tea he thought: "How well she does this! She ought to be married! It's a shame."

They talked of anything but the real thing. He told her of Nicholas's arrival.

"Not written to you for ten years!" she cried. "Looks as though he was making use of you, if you ask me."

"I don't know. He's not like other men. He lives from hand to mouth—he always has. I wasn't overpleased when I heard that he'd come, but now that he's there he's very charming, you know. He's got endless stories and is always in a good temper. My wife's delighted——" He stopped. He'd better come to the point, finish with it, and go.

"I'm terribly sorry this is the last visit," he said.

"Yes," she said. "So am I. I'm very fond of you—I didn't know how much until today."

She got up and kissed him on the forehead. Then she went to a shabby imitation Queen Anne writing desk and from a drawer produced a bundle of letters.

"Here they all are," she said, giving them to him.

"Every one of them. Every scrap. I'd like to keep them, of course—a sort of consolation in my old age." She laughed. "But it's wiser not. If you take my advice, Charlie, you'll burn the lot."

"I will." He didn't look at them.

She was an extremely honest woman. He knew that he could trust her.

"I haven't kept them all. There was one—oh, well, you know—after we had known one another about a week. I thought that really *was* risky. I burnt it."

"Thank you." He looked at her with gratitude and great liking. "There's only one thing makes me a little uneasy. There was one night—I was lonely, I missed you—I couldn't sleep and I got up and put on my dressing gown and wrote to you. It was the sort of letter you'd call silly—the sort you were always telling me not to write. I put it in an envelope and meant to post it in the morning. And then—do you remember?—when I saw you two days later you said you'd never had it—I've never known what I did with it. I should hate anyone to see it."

"Well, you *are* a silly! The way married men behave always beats me. Think of all the unhappiness there might be! And I hate people to be unhappy."

"Yes, I know. As a matter of fact I think I *must* have posted it and for once the post went wrong. It doesn't often, does it?"

He paused, hesitated, then went on:

"Look here, Christine. This is a bit difficult to say. But although we aren't going to meet again I'm awfully fond of you—I admire you so much. And then of course I'll never forget what's happened. And you've been so good ——" He stopped, stammering, while she watched him with amused, maternal eyes. As she said nothing, he went on:

"What I mean is—I wish you'd let me do something for you, something that will really help you. I want to——"

"I know," she broke in. "I understand. But it's all right. Don't you worry. I'm fine. If ever I'm in a hole I'll let you know. I promise I will. But I don't want to be dependent on anyone. You've been awfully good and generous to me. You're the kindest man I've ever known, the best-hearted. Really, you are. I don't want a thing, thanks very much. I'd rather not, really."

They had never been better friends than at this moment, never understood one another more completely.

She went on: "You know, Charlie, I've often wondered what you think of me—what you think I am, I mean. You're a simple soul in lots of ways, and I'll tell you one thing—you don't know much about women. You men who are devoted to your wives, you don't know anything about women at all. Really, you don't. Not even about your wife. When you're as devoted to a woman as all that, you don't see her as she is, not a bit. You think you do, of course. Now I know a lot about men. I *like* men, and you don't *really* like women. You sort of despise them, *really*. But I've known all sorts of men—bad, good, and indifferent. Oh, I've known some bad ones all right. I like being kind to men, poor things. They're so sentimental. What they want is to have the physical excitement *and* all the fine feelings—all going on together for evermore. And of course it doesn't, and when the physical excitement's over the fine feelings are over, too. And they're lost and bewildered, poor dears. Can't think what's happened. That's the nice ones, of course. As to the rotters—I know how to deal with them all right. But I've never taken a penny from a man and I never will. I've simply given a man a good time if he's wanted it and if I liked him.

And one day perhaps the *real* right man will come along —the sort a woman's always dreaming of. But by that time I'll be too old. Oh, well, there's always a dog or a cat you can look after. *I* don't worry."

She smiled.

"Of course I knew *this* wouldn't last. And a good thing it hasn't, too. Your wife must be a dear from what you say. I wouldn't hurt her for the world."

"It's the last flash of my youth," Charles said. "It will never happen again. I don't want it to. You were right there, Christine. I'm not the sort of man who can be happy leading two lives at once. If you hadn't been such a good sort I might have made a mess of it. And if I thought I'd done you any harm——"

She laughed at that.

"Done *me* any harm? Why, I've had all the fun. You've been sweet to me, Charlie. I'll never forget it. If you were single we'd go on being friends for ever and ever. But as it is it's better this way."

They stood together for a little, his arm round her waist, in front of the sputtering fire. They embraced, and she stroked his cheek with her hand. "You always shave so beautifully. You're so clean and you smell so nice, and your hair's strong and wiry. You're awfully strong really, aren't you? And I like your eyes best of anyone's."

She kissed him on the mouth. Then she pushed him to the door.

"There's your hat and coat. Funny! I know that coat so well and I'll never see it again. You'd better go or I'll make a fool of myself."

He went out.

In the King's Road he found that he was a little unsteady on his feet. A cold wind was blowing, driving the flares on the barrows into wild tongues of flame, and the bright cinema on the opposite side of the road, its poster of Wallace Beery and Marie Dressler splashing the dark wall with colour, seemed to him to be also a little unsteady, as though at any moment the twinkling lights might run down in flaming streams and flood the pavement with liquid fire.

It was so cold that he turned up the collar of his overcoat. And only yesterday there had been that wonderful spring evening! He had smelt flowers in the air.

London is suddenly dangerous. Every vehicle threatens you, and the houses shake their chimneys above your defenseless head. London can be dangerous, but only because some virtue has gone out of yourself. Virtue had gone now out of Charles. The episode was ended. He would never see Christine again. No harm had been done to anyone. No harm *could* come. . . . And yet for the first time since it began he was apprehensive. He had a strange fear that he would not get home to Fanny safely. For the first time he felt that he had done something shabby. But why? Christine was none the worse, *he* was none the worse, Fanny was none the worse. And yet there was some shabbiness somewhere, some concealed disgust.

His heart ached for Fanny. Like so many husbands returning to their good wives after an act of which they are ashamed, he wanted to do something for her, to give her things, to love her and make a fuss of her. . . .

Her goodness, kindness, generosity, simpleness of heart —he didn't deserve them, he took them for granted. He would remember in the future that he could not make enough of her. But the spring evening was gone. Buried in the underground, he could fancy the wind screaming overhead. The women and the men, tightly packed in despondent rows, looked wind-blown. At Westminster he got out of the train as though he expected someone to stab him in the back.

But no, it was only Frobisher, who got out at the same time. Frobisher was thin and bald and a little chilly in spirit, but that was because Mrs. Frobisher—who was warm and eager and never stopped talking—adored Frobisher so dearly that she had taken his soul into her keeping, so that Frobisher was a shell, a husk, poor man. But he didn't know it. He believed in his wife's estimate.

"Hullo, Carlisle!"

"Hullo, Frobisher!"

"Very cold wind."

"Yes, isn't it? After that glorious day yesterday. How's the painting?"

"Mustn't complain. Got to go up north tomorrow to paint a mayoress."

"Wife going with you?"

"Of course. We don't like to be separated, you know."

They parted.

Charles found his wife in her bedroom. He put his arms round her and held her close to him as though he hadn't seen her for months. Fanny was a girl, a child. He was her father and lover and husband and son.

They talked a little, sitting on the edge of the bed, her hand on his shoulder.

"Well, I must go down and see that Edward's all right," she said. She kissed him. "There's one thing. Grace gave me some change yesterday—for those towels. Do you remember? We were all together having tea, and she put it on one of the tables. I know I picked it up—it was some loose silver—but what I did with it I can't imagine."

"Never mind. I'll give you some more."

"Oh, it isn't that! But what can I have done with it?"

"How's Nicholas?"

"All right, I think. The house feels quite different. He's so jolly and friendly with everyone. But that's a funny little girl. She never speaks."

"She's shy yet," said Charles. "Edward will do her good." And then at the thought that he'd got Fanny safely, that they were together now, that he had no secret any longer, he caught her face in his hands, looked into her eyes and kissed them.

She was terribly pleased, and very readily those same eyes filled with tears.

"Why, Charles, whatever is the matter?"

"Nothing—only I love you."

"Well, that's no news," she said, laughing, and went to Edward.

7

That was *their* world. Captain Nicholas Coventry's is quite another.

> *"Families, when a child is born*
> *Want it to be intelligent.*
> *I, through intelligence,*
> *Having wrecked my whole life,*
> *Only hope the baby will prove*
> *Ignorant and stupid.*
> *Then he will crown a tranquil life*
> *By becoming a cabinet minister.*

"That, Eliza dear, is a poem written about a thousand years ago by the Chinese poet Su Tung-p'o. I have a remarkable memory for poetry, as you must often have noticed—and especially when it concerns myself. I, too, have been ruined by my intelligence."

He was standing, in shirt and trousers, arranging his black tie in front of the glass while his daughter, Lizzie, sat in a chair near his bed reading a book with a green paper back.

When he had tied his tie Nicholas turned round and looked at a small oil painting that rested against the arm of the sofa at the bed-foot. The sofa was of a faded rose colour, and the painting, which was by Sickert, was a study in dark red and yellow of a London street. It was in dull colours save for a bright green doorway in the foreground.

"*That,*" he said, "is a little masterpiece. I saw it in your cousin Romney's room and I asked him whether I might take it away for half an hour and look at it. He has four Sickerts that he bought when the going was good, before the prices went up. He may forget about this one. Sickert is the only living painter that England possesses. That is a masterpiece."

He went over to his bed to pick up his coat and waist-coat. He looked over her shoulder to see what it was that she was reading—the *César Birotteau* of Balzac.

"That's rather a stiff one. Such a lot of business in it."

"I like all the details," she said. "I like books that tell you *everything.*"

Then he laughed, for on the bed beside her there were three books. He picked them up. One was *The Head Girl of the School,* by Edith Thompson; another, *With Red-skin and Tomahawk,* by Henry Reeve; and the third, *Sea-Spray and Daffodils,* by Dorothy Merle.

"My God!" he said. "Did Aunt Grace give you these?"

"Yes," said Lizzie, looking up and smiling. "She says she has many more of the same kind."

"How do you like supper with Edward?" he asked.

"I like Edward. He's intelligent."

"Intelligent!" Nicholas cried. "I should have thought that the last thing he was."

"Oh, no!" She put her book down, that she might think more clearly. "Not intelligent, of course, about books and people and places. He's never been anywhere, and he's never read anything *at all*. But intelligent about his daily life. He can make me see it, the silly things they do. They wear high hats and they stick pins into one another. Also they think more about kicking a ball than anything else. I laughed when he told me, and then he laughed, too. I *like* Edward. He's very young for his age."

"And you're old for yours, don't forget," her father said. "Anyway, over here. We have to behave ourselves, Eliza. This will suit me for some time to come. If *only* I can stop my tricks . . ."

He stood looking at the Sickert, thinking his thoughts. His tricks were picking and stealing, making fun of those around him, interfering maliciously with their lives because they were so *stupid* and it was such fun to see what they would do! He wished no one in the world any harm, and when he encountered an intelligence as good as his own he greeted it instantly, as one robber baron, in the old days, greeted another. For it did not appear to him conceivable that in these days you could be, if intelligent, also moral. He could be kindly, generous, enthusiastic, but stupidity, old-fashionedness, roused his contempt, and his contempt could make him cruel. And as to the affections, he loved only Lizzie and himself. The world, he would say, had made him an outlaw—his hand was against every man's—but he liked it to be so! He had lived on his fellow humans, robbed and pillaged them his whole life long. He remembered how, when a child of five, he had stolen a small tortoiseshell box that belonged to his mother, and how greatly astonished he had been that no one discovered the theft. It had been so easy, and he had felt so pleasant to everyone after it! So all his life he had continued. He had been discovered once or twice, and the consequences of these discoveries were still with him—but *that* only made life the more exciting and amusing!

In general he had *not* been discovered. What happened as a rule was that someone invited Lizzie and himself to stay, found his company so charming that the visit was prolonged and prolonged. And then—oh, then the atmosphere changed. He wasn't so popular. Nothing could be exactly charged against him but some too venturesome love-making, some uncertainty about a check or a bibelot, or, more often, quarrels among the people with whom he was staying (who, until his visit, had been *most* harmonious!)—such trifles as these led to his departure. . . . Lizzie and himself, they moved on somewhere else!

He thought of all the places where he had been with great affection. He bore no one any malice. He might dislike them or despise them (the two were synonymous) at the time, but he soon forgot. And now he had flown, like a homing pigeon, back to his own nest. He had delayed this particular visit unduly simply because he had feared that his boredom would be so appalling! Fanny and Charles, Matthew and Grace, the Old Lady—how awful!

Necessity had driven him. These were hard times the world over. People were not so accommodating as they had been once. They hadn't the money. The world, in fact, was beginning to be alarmingly full of people like himself. Both Italy and Spain were at the moment uncomfortable for him. He disliked England with its dreadful climate and still more dreadful food. But there it was.

The Family might do for a brief while until Louise Brieux forgave him or the Pervises in Sicily saw what a mistake they had made in losing his delightful company!

And now!—well, really, he wasn't sure. He thought that the visit would not be so bad. They were *too* extraordinary, these people, after the company that he had been keeping—Fanny and Charles, Matthew and Grace—quite incredible! Their simplicity, their sentiment! Why, they still, in this year of grace 1932, believed in family life! They clung together like a brood of ducks on a stagnant pond! They loved one another! They looked up to one another! Even the young people thought their father and mother wonderful! He liked it, he admired it. It was something so novel and so refreshing that he positively admired it.

It was also something round which his sense of humour might play. Here was a game! He felt his creative power rising in him. He could make something of this, turn these good, simple relations of his into a new pattern.

And the girl was pretty, one of the prettiest he had seen for a long time.

That made him think of something. He said to Lizzie:

"Abel's turned up already. I'm going to see him to-night."

Lizzie did not look up from her book, only she said, as though into the very heart of the page: "He has been very quick this time, Papa."

"Yes, hasn't he? I don't know how the devil he finds out. But he won't get anything out of me. He can do his damnedest."

Propped against the leg of the looking-glass was Arthur Waley's *170 Chinese Poems*, and Nicholas was learning one of these by heart. This was one of his tricks, a trick of which he was peacock-proud, for he had a quite extraordinary memory which might, had he wished it, have been put to real uses. As it was, he was Macaulay-like in his genius for quotation. He could spout anything, poetry or prose, suiting his words to his company, bawdy with the bawdy (*and* he could be bawdy!), pious with the pious (satirical then, but they never detected it), and when with those who shared his own enthusiasms—an odd magpie heap, Christopher Marlowe, Proust, Donne, Calverley, Peacock, Joyce's *Ulysses,* Webster and Tourneur, Spengler and Amanda M'Kittrick Ros—he could, for a moment, drop his conceit, his malice, his monkey acquisitiveness. Of modern and living English writers he admired only two—the author of *His Monkey Wife* and the author of *The Orators.*

But he cared for books as he cared for music and pictures, acquisitively, to snatch these things and make them his and then, like the emperor of all the lovely things in the world, to deal them out, to flash them before the eyes of his subjects. It really seemed to him sometimes that Marlowe and Donne and Webster had written only for himself. That was why he made a pose of despising Shakespeare, because he knew that he was too great for his capture.

He turned round to Lizzie and threw her the book.

"Hear me this," he said. "Page thirty-two—'Meeting in the Road.' "

Like a child, with his hands clasped in front of him, he repeated:

"In a narrow road where there was not room to pass
My carriage met the carriage of a young man.
And while his axle was touching my axle
In the narrow road I asked him where he lived.

'The place where I live is easy enough to find,
Easy to find and difficult to forget.
The gates of my house——' "

He paused.

" 'The gates of my house——' Damn! What's next?"

" '—are built of yellow gold,' " said Lizzie.

"Oh, yes:

" '—are built of yellow gold,
The hall of my house is paved with white jade,
On the hall table flagons of wine are set,
I have summoned to serve me dancers of Han-tan.
In the midst of the courtyard grows a cassia-tree—
And candles on its branches flaring away in the night.' "

He chuckled with satisfaction.

"There! That's pretty good. I only read it through twice. And now I'll never forget it again. You've got a clever father, my girl."

He bent down and kissed her.

"Here, you go to bed soon. Don't sit up all night reading. I've got to go out after dinner and see Abel."

She nodded, and he went out humming.

8

On the way downstairs he met the servant Janet coming up. He paused to let her pass.

"Mustn't pass on the stairs, Janet," he said cheerfully. "It's unlucky."

But she didn't answer; only, her tall figure drawn to its full height, quietly went by.

"She detests me, that woman," he thought, and for a moment considered someway in which he might vex her, for, like all egotists, he hated, like a child, to be disliked.

They all went down to dinner. Nicholas sat between Nell and Grace, and he made himself charming to both of them. Family meals had become something quite different since Nicholas's arrival. Before, they had been a little dull—homely, comfortable, but a little dull. Nell and Romney were often out, and the older people asked one another questions about the day and concentrated on their own personal well-being. Grace always had plenty to say, but nobody listened. Old Mrs. Carlisle came down sometimes, but lately had had, very often, her dinner in bed. It was noticed that now that Nicholas was here she came down every night. Fanny was quiet, seeing that everyone had what they wanted.

The food, Nicholas thought, was good for English food. He was pleased about that, and Charles had some good wine in his cellar. Before Nicholas came it had been only on special occasions that it appeared, for neither Charles nor Matthew cared much about it. But now Nicholas said: "Jolly good claret, old man," and Charles was pleased.

Romney and Nell had agreed in the past that family meals were pretty awful, but now everything was different. Everyone drank more, and Nicholas's stories were wonderful.

"The amount he knows," Romney said to Nell. "The places he's been and the things he's read."

"Yes," said Nell, who had not surrendered yet. "When you spend your life living on other people you have plenty of time to notice things."

Nevertheless she herself admitted that he was wonderful company. But she didn't like him. Why, she was not sure. It was the way that he looked at her, almost as though they shared some secret together. And she had told him nothing. He couldn't know about Hector Collins, for instance. . . . Not that there was anything to know, of course.

The only one of them all who did not like these gay meals as much as the old ones was Fanny. She had enjoyed the quiet comfortable coziness, and both Charles and Romney, she thought, drank too much. And Grace was silly sometimes. Nicholas seemed to *want* her to be silly.

And then, after a thought or two like this, she blamed herself. How ungracious when Nicholas was so kind and jolly, when he had made himself so quickly at home with them all! They had never had so gay a time . . . no, they had all needed waking up and here was Nicholas doing it for them. Dear Nicholas, the same clever, generous, irresponsible, warm-hearted boy that he had always been. As she listened to him she felt a wonderful pride in him. He was her brother, and she was sure that he was cleverer than anyone else in London. So clever was he that she found herself now a little shy of speaking in the rash careless way that had always been her habit. He was never unkind or rude, but sometimes now when she said something it *did* seem foolish, and she fancied that the others thought so, too. Only her sensitiveness, and it did not really suit her to be careful. Her considered remark was sometimes as silly as her spontaneous one, she was afraid. She wished that she had had a better education, but she and Grace really learnt *nothing* at that school in Wiltshire. Young people today knew so much about everything. She wondered, in fact, that Grace had so little fear of exposing herself. She never seemed to see that the others were laughing at her, or if she saw she did not care.

So she watched to see that everyone was happy, and said as little as possible. And then after a while she was afraid lest they should think her *too* quiet. So she joined in.

"The fact is," said Nicholas, laughing, "that Einstein doesn't care whether his theory is right or not. What *he* wants to do is to learn the violin."

"Well," said Fanny, "I know that Romney thinks he's wonderful, but there was a picture in one of the papers the other day of his 'Genesis' and I'm *sure* no one could——"

Of course they all laughed at that, and even Grace cried triumphantly: "You mean Epstein, darling—the man who put that thing in the Park. They said it was meant for the birds to drink out of, but I'm told the birds won't go near it—frightened of it, and I'm sure I don't wonder. . . ."

"We're two silly old women, Grace and I," Fanny thought, and wished that Charles at least had not laughed. He did not know much about Epstein himself, come to that.

But it was Nicholas who said:

"It's all very well your laughing at your mother, Nell. The next generation will be laughing at *you* very soon."

And that did not really make it better because, until he said that, Fanny had not thought that Nell *was* laughing at her.

They talked about what they would do after dinner. Now that Nicholas was there they played bridge—Nicholas, Nell, Romney, and Charles. They did not talk and read books round the fire any more. Matthew went to his room, and Grace and Fanny read, but they felt self-conscious. And Nicholas was so good at bridge. Charles and Romney lost money every night.

However, this evening it was not to be.

"No. I've got to go out and see a friend," Nicholas said.

They were all sorry.

"Yes, an old friend. I knew him in Italy."

"Ask him to a meal," said Charles.

"Oh, thanks very much, but I don't think you'd like him. He's one of my *bad* friends."

Everyone laughed. Nicholas and his bad friends! It sounded most romantic.

Abel Mandez was lodging at a hotel called "The Prince Regent," off Victoria Street.

"Like his cheek," Nicholas thought when he read his badly written, badly spelt note, "to get as near as he can." But indeed Abel had been quick this time! How the devil had he known? Nicholas himself had decided to throw himself on the family only a day or two before his actual arrival. At the shabby little hotel in Paris where he and Lizzie had been staying, Abel had made no appearance.

"He knew that I hadn't a bean," Nicholas reflected. "He thinks now that I've come into cash again. But I haven't yet. The day that we turned up in London I positively hadn't a sou. And all next day only that scrap of change I picked off the table." But last night Charles had lent him fifty pounds—and that was only a beginning. Young Romney and his pictures, Matthew and his kind heart, Grace and her sentimentality. Oh! there was lots to be done here!

"And so Abel jolly well knows. I shouldn't wonder if he's got the whole family at his finger ends already. Marvellous fellow!"

As he walked from the house down the little silent street, past the school, under the archway into the lights and bustle of Victoria Street, he felt, with a warm almost animal pleasure, his other life streaming in upon him—the life of risks and adventures, rascals and scoundrels, the life without law or principle that was really his. Once upon a time this had been a world rather thinly peopled and exceptional enough to be almost melodramatic. The high lights in it—the flight from Jamaica, the death of his wife in Paris, Bawtrey's suicide in Monte Carlo, the thieving in Rapallo, Saunders's death in Venice, these might once have been called melodrama. Novelists threw bright colours on just such incidents as these, drab and unromantic though they always were in reality, comprised of discarded tram tickets, the week's washing, wine splashed on a marble-topped table, a barber's impertinence, a fit of indigestion, a woman's cold. . . . Yes, once exceptional enough to be lurid, but now the whole world was composed, it seemed to Nicholas, of just such figures, just such incidents. He moved surrounded by a constant company of men, out of a job, ready to do anything for money, by suicide, murder, and robbery with violence. One figure led to another. Touch Abel and you found Marston, have a meal with Marston and he introduced you to Likiadopulos, drink with Likiadopulos and he asked you to meet Mme. Balzac. . . . Always a little lower. . . .

Certainly, during those last months in Italy, he had kept some queer company, and on the whole it was as well that he had pulled himself out of it when he did. But the thing that he loved was the contrast of these two worlds. To pass, as he was now doing, from the English domesticity of the house in Westminster, the quiet old-fashionedness of those people who all felt so safe, who lived, even in these days, with the habits and morals and blind security of old Victorian England, to appear to be one of them, to mimic their tones (but was it mimicking? he was by birth and breeding one of their very selves), to compel their trust, to make them fond of him and proud of him—and then, with one step, to pass into this other real world where society was disintegrating into chaos, where there were no laws, no rules except that the cleverest collared the booty—yes, *this* was a sensation that stirred his blood!

It would be fun tonight, sitting in the shabby little room with the aspidistra and the smell of drains and stale tobacco (he knew the room before he had seen it), to tell Abel in his own humorous fashion that this time he should not have a penny from him, that he could hang on as long as he liked and starve for all Nicholas cared, and then to see Abel, as so often before he had seen him, smile and roll one of his poisonous cigarettes and say that *he* didn't care, that he was in London for his own pleasure, that he had written to Nicholas only to send him a friendly greeting, and so on and so on. . . .

But then (for now he was nearing the street) Nicholas for a moment paused. He really, this time, did not *want* Abel's company. He liked this place—it was new and refreshing, this simple and childlike atmosphere. It was good for Lizzie. He felt an affection for all of them, the Old Lady, Fanny, Grace, Charles, Matthew, the children. For a time at least he would try and behave. It would be amusing for a while to play at being one of themselves. Although everything in which they believed was nonsense, that very fact made them, for the present at least, rather touching to him. It was so long since he had seen people like this, living, breathing people who believed in God and the family and wedded bliss. Fanny was as strange to him, after all these years, as some queer bird in a zoo. Over and over again in these last days, listening to her innocent prattle, he had had to pinch his mental self to persuade it that this was actual.

That they believed in him and trusted him touched him very little, for, in these days, that anyone should believe in anyone implied an imbecility that deserved almost any punishment!

But he was, in truth, grateful to them for giving him a new sensation, and *while* it was new he did not intend to spoil it. So—let Abel keep off! He would jolly well see to it that he did!

So, murmuring to himself:

"The gates of my house are built of yellow gold,
The hall of my house is paved with white jade,"

he entered the portals of the Prince Regent.

9

Opening the door, he found himself in a little stuffy hall, with a large palm, a soiled settee, two shabby chairs, and an aperture on the left; behind this last a stout woman with untidy yellow hair was seated.

"Good-evening," he said, smiling his charming smile.

The lady looked up, scowling, then seeing so elegant a gentleman, patted her hair and looked at him expectantly.

"Is a gentleman, Mr. Mandez, staying here?"

She turned over the pages of a book.

"What name?"

"Mandez."

"No, I don't think—oh, yes——"

"He's expecting me."

She leaned forward and cried: "Henry, see if the gentleman in Number Ten is in."

A long, thin youth appeared apparently from the middle of the palm.

"What name?" she asked.

"Oh, never mind—say the gentleman he's expecting."

Henry disappeared.

"Nice weather we're having," she remarked.

"Yes, aren't we?" said Nicholas, very friendly. "It will soon be proper spring."

"Yes—I like the spring. What I mean is, you know the winter's over."

"Business good?" Nicholas asked.

"Oh, mustn't complain—not what it was, of course, but then nothing is, what with the slump an' all."

He could see that she was stirred with a great curiosity. It wasn't often that a gentleman like this visited the hotel. She couldn't take her eyes off him.

Henry appeared.

"Gentleman's in his room," he remarked. He, too, stared at Nicholas as though he had never seen anything like him.

"Take the gentleman up."

She leaned out, looking after him. Another lady appeared from nowhere. They began an eager conversation.

The stairs were dark and smelt—as Nicholas had expected—of drains, sour beer, and tobacco. The passage was so dark that the doors were invisible, but there was a knock and Mandez stood there, his lighted room illuminating him. Nicholas went in, closing the door after him.

So here was little Abel again, just as he had been in so many other places, the room with its frowsty smell, untidy litter, so like all the other rooms of his that he might be a snail who carried his house on his back.

Nicholas sniffed.

"I say—open the window a minute."

As Nicholas looked at the man it seemed to him, as it always did after an absence, that he was greeting part of himself. Abel Mandez was short and sturdy, with a round childlike, plump, brown face. He had great breadth of shoulder, width of chest, strong arms, but his legs were small and meagre. He had small hands and feet. His hair was of a jet-gleaming blackness, and his brown face clean-shaven, almost bare of eyebrows, naked. He had black eyes, very white teeth which he often showed because he smiled continually. He was a Jamaican half-caste. He was dressed very quietly in a dark brown suit, and he was wearing brown bedroom slippers. The backs of his brown hands were covered with thick black hairs. His little eyes, his mouth, his whole body were smiling, for he loved Nicholas more than any man, woman, or child in the world. He loved him and blackmailed him, robbed him, stole from him.

"Well, Abel," Nicholas said after he had watched him open the window. "How are you? What a filthy room this is!"

It *was* filthy with its stained wall paper, a bed unmade, a basin with dirty water in it.

"Yes," said Abel. "I've been sleeping all afternoon."

They sat down near to one another.

"How are you, Captain?" said Abel. "It's damned good seeing you again." Indeed, he could not take his eyes from Nicholas. He looked at him, grinning, as though he had never seen him before, as though he had never known that there was anyone so splendid in the world.

"Have a drink?" said Abel.

"No, thanks. How did you know where I was?"

"Why, Captain, sure. I know everything you do, every

place you go. Sure I do. You know that. I'm your friend."

Nicholas looked at him and thought that yes, that was probably true. Abel was perhaps the only friend he had in the world. Yet he would rob him without mercy, murder him perhaps if there was enough reward offered. But he would be sorry afterwards—he would be sorry and lonely and unhappy for the rest of his life.

"Yes—well—all right," said Nicholas. "I've only come in for a moment—just to say that it's no good your hanging around this time. There's nothing to get, and after tonight I don't see you again. Understand?"

Abel crossed his little legs while his fingers were busy rolling a cigarette.

"Certainly, Captain, I understand. How's Lizzie?"

"Never mind about Lizzie. I've only come back here to say the one thing. You'd better get back to where you came from."

"Sure. How long are you going to stay where you are?"

"Never mind how long. I'm with my own people, and that's just where you don't come in. If you show your face anywhere near me while I'm in London, I'll have you gaoled."

"Why, yes, I understand." Abel drew his chair a little closer. "But don't go for a minute. It's good to see you again. I miss you something terrible—honest I do."

And Nicholas felt it also. This man had been mixed up with so much of his life, with all the rottenest part of it. To be with him was so easy, familiar. He could be himself. There was nothing to conceal. Abel was bad all through, there was nothing he would stop at if his passions of lust, fear, greed, jealousy were driving him. And Nicholas liked that. He liked a man who would stop at nothing and about whom there was nothing concealed, no nonsense, no hypocrisy, no fine sentiment. Yes—but this time Abel must keep off.

He got up. "No, I mean it. Every word of it. I've come here only to say that. Don't let me see your dirty little face or handle one of your mean little letters while I'm here. I've said this before, and you haven't believed it. But now you've got to believe it or you'll be sorry."

"O.K., Captain."

Abel also rose. They stood close together, Nicholas by far the taller, magnificent, superior; the little man like a dog, watching, at his feet.

"I haven't a sou in the world, Captain," Abel said.

Nicholas took the loose change from his pocket and put it on the table.

"There! That's all I have on me."

"That'll do for the present."

"It's got to do, now and ever. I'm sick to death of your following me. I'm going to lead a respectable, English, God-fearing life—the sort of life you haven't the least notion of."

"O.K., Captain." Abel swept the silver into his pocket. Then they both laughed. Nicholas couldn't help himself, for it was like being at home again to see that round plump face, the small sparkling eyes, the restless brown hands.

Nicholas moved to the door.

"Well, that's enough. I've told you and you've heard. You don't need telling again. If you come near me or interfere in any way whatever, I'll break your neck."

Abel put his hand on Nicholas's arm. For a moment they stood close together.

"Good-night," Nicholas said sharply and went.

10

About a fortnight after Nicholas's arrival Fanny woke one morning burdened with a sense of distress. As always when one wakes to an immediate awareness of misfortune, time must pass before the actual cause is realized. And now she lay, looking at the soft morning light that moved like water on the ceiling, and wondered wherein her unhappiness lay.

But was it unhappiness? Rather it was discomfort, vague, nebulous, hovering about her heart as the dim shadowed early sunlight hovered on the ceiling. Something was not quite right. She thought first, as on waking she always did, of Charles and the children. So far as she knew, all was well with them. Charles, the sheet drawn up to his ear, slept warmly beside her. They were such old-fashioned people that they still slept in the same bed as they had done throughout their married life. She listened to his soft, sibilant breathing, looked at his ruffled hair and one hand clenched on the outside of the bed. Yes, there was nothing the matter with Charles.

Everyone in the house was well—well and, as far as she knew, happy. The house itself was happy. As she often did she went imaginatively through it, visiting the rooms, caressing with her mind the dearly loved furniture. It stood about her—warm, comfortable, loving. In the hall the painting of her father, stout, rubicund, sitting in his room, Cæsar, the dog that he loved best of all his dogs, at his feet. The dining room now would just be catching the first light, the silver on the sideboard faintly gleaming, the antlers over the fireplace, the large white marble clock that had ticked so ferociously all night keeping guard over the room while everyone slept; the drawing room with the lacquer screen and the Bonington and the Persian rug with the dark purple flowers, the great set of ivory chessmen, the Castles on horseback, the Knights with their lances, the Bishops in their mitres—the famous set which had been passed down through the family generation after generation. . . .

And then the bedrooms. Romney sleeping, she was sure, with the bedclothes flung off him; Nell snuggled up like a bird in a nest; Edward with his head crooked in his arm—yes, all was well with the house and everyone in it. Well, then, what was wrong? She sighed and instinctively, without knowing it, put out her hand and felt Charles's stout arm beneath the bedclothes as though for protection. She was well herself. She had slept the night through without dreams. She was ready for all the tasks and pleasures of the day. Well, then, what?

Was it the general state of the world which she had, like so many others, for so long disregarded? Was it now forcing itself upon her, all these poor men unemployed through no fault of their own? America not understanding England. England not understanding America. Germany and France still hating one another, that terrible Russia, greedy Japan, and, only yesterday, Janet telling her about her cousin in Newcastle who had been out of work for a year, with three beautiful little children—"and him ready to work at anything if he could only find it." Yes, it was partly that, perhaps, although what could Fanny do about it, knowing so little about politics and having to believe what the newspapers told her, although they were most unreliable as everyone knew? She felt in her heart an ache of sympathy for all the world. It seemed wrong that they—her family—should all be so happy and comfortable and safe when there were so many in such distress. Safe? Were they safe? It was then that sharp actual fear attacked her. Somewhere there was danger—danger to herself, to those whom she so passionately loved. Danger? But where was there danger? Not here, not in this house. The light broadened through the room. The clock on the mantelpiece struck seven. Great shafts of light stroked the carpet, and beyond the window she could hear the sparrows chirping.

Charles turned. He muttered. He stretched his arms. He raised his head and yawned.

"Hullo, old lady, what time is it?"

He took her in his arms and kissed her. She lay against his chest, her heart beating on his. She pinched his cheek, brushed back his hair from his forehead.

"It's just struck seven and it's a lovely morning."

"Oh, Lord! Good—another hour's sleep."

He lay back, one arm stretched over his head, breathing deeply, happily, his pyjama jacket open. But he did not turn over and sleep again. Her hand had found his, and he knew from her pressure that something distressed her.

"What is it? Anything the matter?"

He put out his arm, and she rested her head inside it, lying close against him. He rubbed his eyes with his free hand and yawned again.

"What are you awake for?" he asked. "Been having dreams?"

"No—I've slept beautifully."

"Well, then, what about a little more?"

"Yes, of course. You turn over and go to sleep."

But he was so sensitive to her, knew so well her moods and joys and fears that he could not mistake her apprehension.

"No, there's something the matter. What is it?"

"Nothing. Only—I've been awake and thinking."

"Thinking? That's a bad thing at this hour of the morning."

She murmured:

"Everything's all right, isn't it?"

"Of course everything's all right. What shouldn't be?"

She kissed him again. Her hand rested against his cheek.

"I wish Romney hadn't told that story last night," she suddenly broke out.

"What story?" Charles asked sleepily.

"That one about the hotel and the old lady."

"Oh, *that* one!" He sat up, yawning ferociously, stretching his arms. "There was nothing in that."

"No, I know." She hesitated. "Only he wouldn't have told it a year ago—not among all of us, I mean."

He lay down again, drawing her close to him.

"We're old-fashioned, you and I. The things we wouldn't have done when we were young—well, what I mean is, times are changed."

"Yes, I know."

But that wasn't what she meant. She lay against him, thinking. She suddenly realized *how* glad she was that she had got Charles. In these strange, shifting days it meant everything to have someone with you on whom you could entirely rely, someone who would never deceive you, who belonged to the whole world of trust and fidelity and honour.

So many husbands in these days deceived their wives, and although she was determined to be broad-minded and generous, to condemn no one, to move, as well as she was able, with the times, yet if she had not Charles, how difficult, how lonely sometimes, life would be!

She turned and kissed him.

"Charles, don't think me silly, but you don't *know* what it is to me sometimes to feel so sure of you. Everything else is changing. The children are growing up, and sometimes I think I'm losing them, but you—I can trust you in everything—you never fail me——"

Rather surprisingly he moved away a little.

"You mustn't trust anybody, Fanny," he said.

"Not trust——?" She sat up. "What *do* you mean?"

"Oh, nothing. Only we all have our queer times."

"*You* don't. You never change. It wouldn't be *you* if you did." She went on: "I suppose Nicholas will get a job soon."

"A job? What sort of a job?"

"That's what he's here for, isn't it? He's so clever. He could do *anything*."

"Yes, well, it isn't so easy to get a job these days—not for a man of his age."

"Oh, but he *must*. He can't stay here for ever doing nothing. Of course, it's lovely his being here. He brightens everything up. But he'll have to get something. What will he live on?"

"Yes; as a matter of fact I lent him fifty pounds the other day."

She turned towards him, startled.

"Oh, did you? That was good of you. That was just like you. But you shouldn't. That wasn't right of Nicholas."

"Oh, he'll pay it back in a week or two—when his money comes from Paris. He's got a lot there, he tells me. But it's tied up in some way."

He took her hand in his.

"Don't you worry, old lady. I won't let Nicholas rob me."

"No, of course not. Nicholas is all right. It's only that

he takes everything lightly. He's so irresponsible. He was always the same, even when he was a little boy." She added: "You didn't like him when he came. You like him better now, don't you?"

"Yes, I must say I do. He's not a bad chap. He makes you laugh."

She lay there and thought about it. She must take care not to be a killjoy, not to seem old to them all. She did not seem to herself to be old, but she supposed that she could never be rid altogether of her upbringing.

But then, in the silence that followed, Charles lying on his back, quietly dropping off to sleep again, the light pouring into the room like water, she was attacked by one of those moments of acute loneliness that come to all of us and to no one of us more than to him or her who is dearly loved. It is as though a voice, certain and timeless, whispered to us: "You *shall* not live by bread alone," and at once we are aware of a consciousness far truer, far severer than the material one. Our daily values are seen suddenly to be false. We are helpless without our own naked courage, our most intimate relationships with others are shadows, and the long journey ahead of us has no familiar landmark, no companionships, and is inevitable in its ruthlessness. At such a moment of perception we can either deny the reality of our experience or accept the conditions. All our later history may depend on the choice we make, although afterward we find other excuses for the consequences. . . .

But Fanny's loneliness seemed to her now a new loneliness. Suppose that everything were taken from her—Charles, the children, the house. Suppose that it were true, the thing the little woman had said in Bordon's that lovely spring evening—"It's too good to last? The world is disintegrating. No one can hold together any more;

nothing is stable, and the family love and devotion that they had had for so long, was that to shiver into pieces with the rest? How did she know any longer what Romney and Nell and even Edward were thinking and doing? Perhaps now they *pretended* to love her because it was their duty, because they did not wish to hurt her. She had told Charles that she could trust him, but could she? How did she know what he was like when he was away in that strange man-world of his? She saw them all meeting, these men, and they became at once strange animals with horns and hoofs, their heads close together mocking at women, wanting them only for certain needs, and then, as soon as their needs were satisfied, trotting off, moving herdlike across the open plain, their heads up, sniffing the free air, happy at their release. . . .

She had been so deeply absorbed by the family that she had made no women friends. You could not call Mrs. Frobisher a *friend,* nor Millie Westcott (kind and good-hearted though she was), nor Rose Lane. And if Charles went and the children . . . She was beginning to tremble. She was in an absurd state. What had caused this? Who had caused it? It was as though she knew that on the other side of the bedroom door a dark figure was standing, his head forward, listening. . . . The long mirror on the dressing table, slanting forward, caught the chairs, the carpet in a silver glaze. All was unreal in that world. And behind the mirror there was another world, and behind that another. Who was safe?

"At least I have Edward," she thought. "He is there." But no. He, too, was moving into a world away from her, talking with his companions of things that she did not understand, listening to stories that he would not wish her to hear. Edward whom, so little a time ago, she had suckled at her breast, his tiny hands moving up to her cheeks, and his eyes, wondering, absorbed, altogether trustful, searching her face. Now he, too, was going.

Charles woke up again.

"Time to get up," he said.

II

In fact and in truth Edward was just now keeping something from his mother. He had had a very strange week.

Like all boys he had his own secret world; in this world he moved as an Indian moves in the jungle judging by a broken twig here, an imprint in the dust, the sound of underground water. This world was completely satisfactory to him, and even those for whom he cared were allowed only glimpses into its fascinating mystery.

And this world did not include girls. He despised them profoundly, and, as it seemed to him, for excellent reasons. They could do nothing. When they threw a ball or ran they were absurd. They could not talk about anything that was of the least importance. When they asked questions they were ridiculous.

And now, out of the blue, without warning, this girl had been thrown into his life. When he came home, his mind busied with all the important things that had to be considered, she sat at table with him. The event of the day that he preferred to all others (although he would confess this to no one)—the tea hour that he shared alone with his mother—was now entirely spoilt by the presence of this girl. The room that had been recognized by all the world as his own private kingdom was now invaded by this girl.

It was not that she asked to share anything with him.

She was not like other girls. She did not run or throw balls. In fact, she played no games; she despised them utterly. She seldom spoke unless spoken to, but would sit there, reading a book or writing on a piece of paper, or simply sitting, with her hands folded, staring in front of her. She never laughed, she never smiled—only, if Aunt Grace had taken her for a walk, she would, on her return, have a look on her face that was *almost* a smile.

He was not by nature a cruel little boy, but he tried, at first, to entice her to do things that would make her look foolish. He turned a somersault (he was clever at somersaults) and dared her to do the same, but she looked at him with such an air of cold surprise that he was suddenly less proud of his somersaults than he had been.

Then, one evening, she helped him with his sums. She was *marvellous* at sums. She did them in no time at all, and he boasted about this at school. "We've got a girl at home," he said, "who can do sums as good as anyone. And she reads French books like English."

She had travelled, he discovered, almost over the whole world. It appeared that in Rome she had seen the Pope, and in some other place a sailor in a blue shirt had stuck another sailor with a knife while she stood looking on. Most astonishing of all, she had seen a woman produce a baby. He knew about babies—they talked about everything at school. He had a clean, independent mind, and all the things that did not belong to his world he disregarded. Babies most certainly did not belong. Nevertheless her account was interesting. He kept it to himself, even from his closer friends, who would have been greatly excited at his recital. He saw that Lizzie took everything with the greatest calm, and he learnt from her to show no excitement. Only one side of her experiences he loathed and, after the first anecdote or two, gave her clearly to understand that he would hear no more. All of this concerned the ill treatment of animals, for he understood that in Italy and Spain and other countries where she had been they stuck sharp pins into donkeys, beat horses until they had sore places, and knocked dogs against the wall. At one of her more horrible stories (which she related in a perfectly calm and unperturbed voice) he went suddenly very white and was sick, there and then, on the floor. The next time she attempted such a narrative he rushed at her, pulled her hair and kicked her black-stockinged legs. She did not cry. She made, at the moment, no attempt at retaliation, but half an hour later she came up behind him, pulled his head back, dug her sharp little fingers into his neck and nearly throttled him. That was their only physical contest, and she told him no more stories about animals.

Once she gave him an account of the magic that people practised in Sicily. You made a little doll of wax, stuck pins into it, melted it on the fire. Then the person of whom you were thinking died in great agony.

"Gosh! I don't care," said Edward. "You can't do anything to me!"

Then she took out of her pocket a dirty little lump of wax with two black pins for eyes.

"You wait and see," she said, and, sure enough, next day he had toothache. It was true that it was an old tooth that had often given him trouble before. Nevertheless, there it was.

On the whole, however, they maintained a rather friendly neutrality.

One thing disturbed him. He had always thought that his mother knew everything. Now, very plainly, she did not. Lizzie knew many things that his mother did not. One day he asked his mother where Palermo was. She said it was in Corsica. He did not correct her mistake but reflected on it.

He was very cross with Lizzie that evening and teased her about cricket, of which she knew nothing at all. He said to her with scorn: "Why, you don't even know what a wicket-keeper is!" and that night, when his mother came to say good-night, he hugged and kissed her with more than his ordinary ardour.

But, after this, he was puzzled. Coming home from school was not quite as it had been—it was not so good and it was better. When he was *at* school he surrendered altogether to the school atmosphere. Life was very busy there; there was something going on every minute of the time.

Until the last fortnight, however, he always, as he approached his home, felt all the pleasures of the Westminster house close him in. He was extremely happy at home. People left him alone, he liked them all, was interested in a hundred things that went on in the house, and, above all else, treasured his independence in his own room, ruling his own kingdom.

He always knew every day what the house would be like, the smell of the pot-pourri at the top of the first staircase, the stutter and clangour of the old brass Georgian clock with the face of a grinning sun, the view from the window on the second floor—a square of small quiet street, a tree, a corner of the church tower—all these things were his and he was theirs. This was home as no other place ever would be all his life long.

But now they would be home no longer, for Uncle Nicholas and Lizzie had changed all that. You never knew what Uncle Nicholas would be at. He would stand in front of you making faces and reciting a funny poem about two drunken sailors in a boat at sea, or he would do a trick and take a ribbon out of your ear, or he would say: "Now—as man to man! What tricks have you been up to today?" and would add: "You can tell *me,* you know. I'm so wicked myself that nothing that anyone else can do can shock me."

He made in some mysterious fashion the whole house different. Even when you knew that he was out somewhere, you expected to see him turning up in a doorway or from behind a curtain, smiling, cheerful, and saying: "Now then, out with it! Tell me your secrets!"

He and Lizzie were so *different* from anyone else Edward had ever known. They did not think the same things good and the same things bad as other people did.

Of one or two acts Edward was deeply ashamed, although he would not *say* that he was—as for instance when they had teased Blake Minor because he had a sister called Lucy. They called Blake Minor "Lucy," and Edward had made him cry because he wrote "Lucy" all over the front page of a calendar Blake had.

Edward had strutted about after doing this and had pretended to be very proud, but he had not been proud really. After all, if anyone laughed at Nell he'd give them one, and Blake was a silly ass to cry. Nevertheless, Edward had been ashamed.

When, however, he told Uncle Nicholas this one day, Uncle Nicholas had laughed, had said that there was nothing to be ashamed of and that it did Blake Minor good. Then Uncle Nicholas was wonderful at imitating people. He could imitate anyone and especially Aunt Grace. Edward had always rather liked Aunt Grace. Of course she *was* silly sometimes, especially when she had one of those letters from the man in Winchester who was supposed to be in love with her (fancy being in love with Aunt Grace!), but although she was silly she was nice, would give you anything she had, and was never out of temper.

But Uncle Nicholas imitated her. Gosh! he imitated her until you *had* to laugh. He told Edward it was a secret between themselves and, right before your eyes, he would seem to swell, be all fat in front, and his eyes would stare just as Aunt Grace's did, and he would say in that breathless foolish way that Aunt Grace had: "Yes, I've got a letter from John and he says the weather in Winchester has been quite fine these last days, only there was a thunderstorm last Thursday and I've found *such* a pretty book for dear little Lizzie. I'm sure she'll love it—I know I did when I was a girl . . ." all muddled up and catching his breath with his hand on his heart. You could *swear* that it was Aunt Grace! Edward must laugh, but at the same time he felt uncomfortable, and when he was with Aunt Grace could not look her in the face.

But this was the principal difference that Uncle Nicholas and Lizzie had made—that they had brought into the house with them the sights, sounds, smells of another world. Edward's imagination was fed with all these things: hot, blazing streets, little dark rooms where you ate strange dishes, long high staircases lit with the cold radiance of the moon, hills that looked like spotted animals, and beaches that stretched for miles above a sea as purple as grapes and as green as a parrot. It must be fine to see these countries, not to know where your next meal was coming from, to carry a revolver in your pocket, to hear music and dancing in the room above the street. Edward must travel. It was absurd that Lizzie, who was not as old as he, should have seen all these things while he himself had seen nothing at all.

The Westminster house was not so wonderful. It was filled with old things that had been there for ever and ever. Perhaps, one day, Edward would run off and join Uncle Nicholas somewhere. He kept these things in his heart. He no longer told his mother everything that was in his mind.

12

Romney, also, like his young brother, was finding his home not what it had been three weeks earlier. He had been for a long time finding life very queer and very difficult, but, unlike the majority of his own generation, he kept his troubles to himself—absolutely to himself—and it was not until a day early in May that he talked to anyone about himself. Of all people the confessor that he chose was his Uncle Matthew. The way of it was this.

He had suffered a severe disappointment on that afternoon. While he was sitting at his desk in the little room at the Churchill Galleries someone told him that he was wanted on the telephone. He knew who it must be—Harry Rait.

"Hullo."

"Hullo, Romney, old man."

"Is that you, Harry?" (He felt his heart hammering.)

"Yes, of course." A little pause. Then Harry's voice again. "I say, I'm most awfully sorry, old man, I can't come tonight."

(Romney had known it. He had known it all the time.)

Sick with annoyance, hurt pride, and a devastating sense of loneliness, he said sharply:

"Why not?"

(He knew so well the way in which Harry, who was not imaginative, paused while he summoned up excuses.)

"Why, you see, old man, it's like this. I'd forgotten all

about the Bromleys. Clean forgotten. I promised them weeks ago. It's bridge, and you know what it is—if one doesn't go, one ruins their whole evening and so——"

"Oh, all right," Romney answered savagely and put down the receiver. He hadn't intended to be savage. He hated to lose his temper with Harry, simply because Harry didn't mind in the least if he did, and he, Romney, hated to realize that Harry didn't mind. Harry wouldn't mind now. Harry wouldn't care if he never saw Romney again, and returning into the exhibition room, facing the celebrated sculptures of M. Kaminski which everyone admired and no one would buy, Romney swore, for the one hundred and second time, that *he* didn't care if he never saw Harry again, either, and for the one hundred and second time knew that it was a lie.

The sculptures of M. Kaminski were very fine indeed. There were six—"Torso," "Woman Running," "Solar Plexus," "Bird in Flight," "Rabbit," and the vast accumulation "Mother Earth" in the middle of the room.

Romney looked at these and hated them, although but an hour ago he had thought them magnificent. Behind them, on the walls, were the flower paintings of that promising young Frenchman, M. Paul Fléhot.

Two young women were standing there lost in admiration.

"These are the sculptures of Kaminski?" the more elderly of the young women enquired.

"Yes, madam. And the flower paintings are by Fléhot."

(Idiot! She was holding a catalogue. Why enquire?)

"Very fine! Magnificent! Don't you think so, Doris? They are for sale, I suppose?"

"Of course, madam."

She gave the "Torso" a prod.

"What is the name of this one?"

"Simply 'Torso.' "

" 'Torso.' How fine! Isn't it fine, Doris?"

"Absolutely divine, darling."

"You should look," Romney went on, "at Fléhot's paintings. Many people think him the finest young painter in France. This one"—he pointed—"is especially magnificent. His sense of colour is really superb. Those reds, those greens . . ."

"Yes," he was thinking, "I'm damned if I'll bother with Harry any more. He's always doing this kind of thing. And I'd ordered the dinner." He broke off. The woman was speaking.

"They are for sale, I suppose?"

"Oh, yes, they are for sale."

She turned to her friend.

"Doris, aren't they divine?"

"Simply divine, darling."

He thought: "It's only because I give in to him about everything. If I stood up to him a bit . . ." But it wouldn't be any use. If Romney stood up to Harry, Harry would simply fade away. He wouldn't care. How to make him care? How to hurt him? How to——?

"What's the name of that one?" the woman asked. "I like that one."

"It's called 'Chrysanthemums.' "

"Oh, those are chrysanthemums, Doris, those are chrysanthemums. Aren't they lovely?"

"Simply lovely. And I like that blue one over there. Don't you like that blue one, darling?"

"Yes. Lovely. What's that blue one called?"

"Oh, that's called 'Pansies.' "

"Pansies! How darling!"

". . . If only I could give him up," he thought. "If only, on my way home tonight, I could say: 'Well, that's the last time I bother with him. After all, he doesn't care for me. Not a bit.' "

"Well, we must be going now," the woman said. "They're simply *too* lovely."

Marston came towards them and stopped them. Marston was so very clever; he could make people buy the most unlikely things, things that they didn't want and would for the rest of their lives detest. Marston had all the qualities that Romney hadn't. He was charming to everyone alike, he was never cross or put-out. He had in fact no private life at all, but existed only for the Churchill Galleries. His broad handsome figure, his smart, alert walk (a *little* automatic, as though a screw were turned in the back), his pleasant, easy, very English voice (so English that you must especially believe that he was speaking the truth when he praised foreign pictures)—all these things charmed visitors, reassured them and made them in the end proud of themselves (for he would say: "Well, it's funny you should pick that one out. Martigue himself thinks that's his best, but you're the first one here to see how good it is"). He had all the gifts that Romney lacked, but Romney had the taste. Marston had no taste at all. He simply did not know one picture from another; when a discerning visitor appeared it was Romney who dealt with him. For Romney had a true flair. What is taste? Is there such a thing? Only Time and Mr. Clive Bell can decide. But Romney knew in his bones—somewhere in the middle of his spine—when pictures and sculptures were alive and when they were not. Alive for him, for him alone? Surely that says nothing? But his opinion was shared by the Tasters. The happy men whose lives are occupied in tasting different blends of tea know when tea is good. So the Tasters of Art. Romney was a Taster by instinct.

Today, however, he could taste nothing. Life was sour on the tongue. He was going home.

"I'm off," he said to Marston.

"Oh, I say—are you? It's early. Cardiff said he might be in and buy one of the Fléhots."

"Well, if he comes tell him Numbers Three, Nine and Fourteen are the best. He doesn't know. But Number Nine is a beauty really. Tell him it will be double its price one day. That will fetch him."

As he went out he put in his pocket a small wood-carving of a young negress. It was tiny, but beautifully alive and made of a lovely bronze-coloured wood (that gold bronze that is also amber). It was carved by a young sculptress who, living in Kingston, Jamaica, occasionally sent work to their Galleries—work always original, brilliant, and strong. She had sent two or three large pieces and one or two of these small figures.

She was not known yet in Europe, but she would be. He had bought this for himself after it had been on show some six weeks. He loved it. The wood glowed like metal, and the face of the young negress, carved though it was in only a few lines, had in its gaze something ardent, wondering, poignant.

As he passed into Leicester Square he felt that his personal history had reached a crisis. Something must be done and done immediately about a number of things, and especially about his friendship with Rait. He had known Harry rather more than a year now. He had met him first when a friend, Dick Armour, had invited him to luncheon at the Junior Army and Navy. Unexpectedly Rait had been there. Romney had at first resented it, for he had wished to talk to Armour alone, but during the meal he had fallen a victim to Harry's charm. What *was* his charm? Wherein did it lie? For Romney it was at first perhaps that Harry was so ordinary—Romney spent so much of his life with the eccentrics. Harry was square, solid, monosyllabic, a proficient at games, a stockbroker and a contemner of all the Arts. He was as simple-minded as the bulldog that he kept in his rooms. He was altogether a perfect hero for one of the more moving poems of J. C. Squire. He was Georgian Poetry personified, splashing through the mud of a country lane, cheering his side at a Rugby match, smoking his pipe contentedly in a tempest of rain on an English hillside and saying with kindly but patronizing assurance: "What you want to spend all your time mucking about with those bloody pictures for, old boy, *I* can't imagine. But thank God all this art means nothing to me."

Very irritating, you might imagine. But not to Romney, for Harry was free entirely from all those complicated obsessions, that dim edgeless pessimism, that half-insane inanition, that beset and befogged almost all of Romney's set. Harry asked no questions of fate. Once assured that his digestion was working properly, that he made money enough for his simple needs, that his golf did not deteriorate, he was at peace with the world. He was kindly, generous, and never out of temper. He had bright blue eyes, a ruddy complexion, and when he laughed he was a joy to see. He was as yet a bachelor, but awaited the right girl with a serene assurance. And when he married he would have three children, would have a cottage near Sunningdale and as many dogs as the cottage would hold.

That is the kind of man he was, and Romney loved him. Romney was greatly disturbed about his own sexual nature. He had had as yet no physical relationship with any women; he did not know what it was to be in love with a woman. He knew, however, very well, that he was not sexually abnormal. Everyone everywhere nowadays spoke quite openly of these things. In his own set especially you were considered to be intellectually superior if you had somewhere a sexual twist. A number of men like Forrester, Bancroft, Hudson, made no attempt to conceal their abnormality. But Romney disliked the company of abnormal men and women. He judged no one; he accepted the modern view that these were matters of psychological and not moral decision. It was simply that the sexually abnormal dwelt in a world that could not be his. Their passions, their preoccupations, seemed to himself the passions and preoccupations of maimed and defective people, as though they lacked a limb or were deaf or blind. He would have been truly sorry for them had they in any way needed his pity, which it was evident that they did not. They were, on the whole, he perceived, happy and contented with their lot and would not change it if they could. He was as foreign to their world as though they had been Chinese, having their own tongue, manners, customs, and traditions.

At the same time there was ever increasing in him a horror of casual physical love. He felt this to be priggish and prudish. He hid it from everyone, but he knew that his friends perceived it, speculated about it. The loneliness that sprang from it was often very bitter indeed. He had a romantic and obviously quite foolish view of the possibilities of human relations. He could see that very often people ruined their relationships with one another by being greedy and possessive; also that views changed when the novelty of physical passion died. Yet once and again he saw magnificent human relationships, relationships that burnt steadily with an inner flame. This glorious thing existed—then why not for him?

He was not in love physically with Harry Rait, and yet it gave him physical satisfaction to be with him, to see him move, smile, speak. This came, he fancied, from a kind of deep hero worship, hero worship not so much of Harry in person as of the things for which Harry stood—his courage, imperturbability, kindliness, common sense. The more he saw of him the happier he was to be with him and the more thoroughly he realized that for Harry this was an ordinary casual friendship, that Harry could not conceive that men should have emotional feelings for one another, and that he would be dumb with disgust did anyone suggest it. And yet at this time Romney's love for and admiration of Rait was the mainspring of all his finer feeling, it was mixed in with his passion for art, his love of his family and even, dimly, his apprehension of God.

For here were the other two emotions that separated Romney from the set in which he lived. The three things that Romney's friends most thoroughly despised were family relationships, religious beliefs, and patriotism. They had good reasons for their scorn of all these things and were quite fair and temperate in their attitude. Almost without exception they regarded their parents as poor, stupid old muddlers who had made a mess of life not only for themselves but also for everyone else.

Only the other evening at a cocktail party at Ben Johnson's, Peggy Furnival had declared: "Well, would you believe it?—Mother actually tried to insist on my staying in. She said I'd promised. Of course I'd done nothing of the kind, and as I explained to her I never could have promised to be in at one of the family dinners. They are simply too awful for words! She got quite excited and talked of all that I owed to her and Father. 'Well, really, Mother,' I said, 'did I ask to be brought into the world? I'm here simply because you and Father were in love with one another. You've brought me into a world that's a complete mess, and a mess that your generation have made.' I didn't want to be unkind. They really *are* pets, both of them, but this idea that we owe them something—it's really too fantastic!"

Romney knew well enough that everyone did not feel like this—there *were* exceptions—but, looking around him, it was difficult to find anywhere a family that *was* a family. Often enough it was the fault of the parents. Women like Mrs. Montague, who was fifty if she was a day, dressing to look younger than her daughters, and old men like Clay Robinson, a grandfather if you please, chasing young girls about London quite notoriously.

But nowhere did Romney see any family devoted in the way that his family was devoted. He did not know whether in their case it *was* family feeling, for he was sure that if anywhere he had met them—his mother, his father, a girl like Nell, a boy like Edward—he must have thought them delightful. His mother of course belonged to her own time and generation. She said silly things sometimes, she was impulsive, but where in the whole of London would you discover anyone so warm-hearted, so touchingly honest, so generous-natured? They were all bound together by a deep emotion of trust and confidence. They liked to be together. They looked forward to the evening when they would, all of them, warm and cozy inside the Westminster house, share their experiences. Why should this be so unusual a phenomenon? Even Uncle Nicholas plainly thought it very odd and, because he thought it odd, Romney began himself to question it—for Uncle Nicholas was a jolly, fair-minded man of the world who had seen more of life than they had.

Finally there was Romney's apprehension of God. This was the most doubtful of all his emotions, for, in truth, he could be sure of none of it. Among his friends there were two Roman Catholics—Wilfred de Cordova and Larry Whyte. These two believed in and practised their religion.

But for the rest—and outside his own family—he had not a friend in London who had not, entirely and completely, discarded the old absurd notion of a God, a First Cause, or whatever you pleased to call it. One or two of them quite frankly regretted that it was no longer possible for a sane human being to believe in anything at all.

"It must have been jolly in the old days when you thought that someone was looking after you and that, if you were good enough—even at the very last moment—you were in for a splendid Eternity."

They did not give themselves airs because they were wiser than their grandfathers, but Romney noticed that their stern and fatalistic conclusions were, as a rule, founded on very little. The vastness of the planetary system, the waste and ruin of the late war, some catch phrases and a sort of very genuine personal humility—as though each one said: "Well, I'm not very much myself—an unimportant arrangement of chemical matter. It would be really too arrogant of me to presuppose an immortality for myself. And if there *is* a God, well, then, He must be pretty ashamed of Himself by this time."

Romney did not know why it was that he had this persistent sense of religion. It certainly did not come from any family influence. He loved his mother, but her childish beliefs seemed to him too simple for words. Uncle Matthew was the religious member of the family, but Romney had never had with him an intimate talk about anything. Uncle Matthew led a life quite apart from the rest of them. He was a dear old boy, never out of temper, generous to a fault, but he had his own life absolutely, visited by his own friends (and queer enough some of them looked!), and subject, it was said, to dreams and visions that, although they did no harm to anyone, certainly marked him out as not quite right in his head.

No, Romney was not a visionary. He was quite practical; he did not believe in visions. It was simply that there was something within himself that would not let him alone. "Indigestion, old boy," Harry Rait would say. "What you want is a pill."

13

As he walked out into Leicester Square he felt, with every step more strongly, that he had arrived at a crisis and that something must be done about it. Something must be done about his loneliness; he could not go on as he was any longer. Then, stopping to light a cigarette, he wondered, with a sharp stroke of perception that was almost like a revelation, whether it were not his Uncle Nicholas who had roused him to this sense of urgency. He had not as yet had much talk with Uncle Nicholas, but he had listened to him, he had watched him and, quite beyond question, he had been influenced by him. Uncle Nicholas seemed to have an answer to everything—yes, and a sensible answer, too. It was not that he was dogmatic. He spoke always with a laugh and an airy wave of the hand, as much as to say: "This is only the conclusion I've come to. There may be nothing in it. Don't think I'm judging anybody."

This was, to Romney, what was so exciting about Uncle Nicholas—that with all his knowledge of the world (he had travelled everywhere), with all his wide interests (there was almost nothing in which he was not interested), he never dogmatized. He offered an opinion, drew a picture, related an anecdote, and left you to draw your own conclusions.

He deferred to you in your own subject (absurd really the humble fashion in which he listened to Romney about pictures, or to the Old Lady when she was anecdotal about her youth), was surely the least conceited man in the world. Nevertheless, already Romney was aware that many things were absurd to Uncle Nicholas, most things perhaps. He did not believe, Romney was sure, in Family Life, in God, in Patriotism. And yet he was wise and kind. He would not laugh in your face whatever your opinions were. Somehow, since his arrival, the house was changed. Something was happening. Romney, very sensitive to atmosphere, was pulled in two opposite directions:

"I don't want any change. We were very happy as we were."

And then:

"Something is coming. Events are preparing. Life will never be the same again as it was before he came."

Looking up, startled by his sudden apprehension of some hidden drama, he was aware of how lovely a face London was wearing at that moment. The space of brick and mortar between Leicester Square and Piccadilly Circus is a very mysterious one: it is hard to believe that it was not always so. Only yesterday—if, taking Time as we should, we greet the Neanderthal Man as our brother—when the swamp oozed and sputtered under the thick dank boskage of the overgrowth—it was at this spot that the light was dim, that the coils and intercoils of tangled fibre hung lowest over the sullen stinking slime. Neanderthal Brother, brutish of jaw, sly of winking gaze, paused here, apprehending his enemy, before he paddled forward to find his kill. And now, leaving the Shakespeare statue and the click of billiard balls and the new garish Palace of

Pleasure to guard the Square, you slip, for a brief moment, into a no-man's-land where all peoples of the world may meet, regardless of caste, of financial status, of home or country. Beyond you gleams the Circus, and beyond that are the dusky sheep of the Green Park; here are the ghosts of a Society for ever vanished and the lonely sheet of sky that like a wall, of steel, of woolly fleece, of bird's-feather blue, of a raging fiery sunset, is independent of social change, does not care that there are shops now where once there was Elegance, that will guard this little space with the same beauty, the same immortality long, long after the little stir of humanity has died into silence.

So, pausing for a moment outside the Prince of Wales's Theatre, Romney beheld London transmuted. Above the Lyons' Corner House the sky splashed its blue with waves of rose, recklessly splendid, while beneath it hither and thither figures hurried and paused, the traffic murmured like a beaten drum, and in the air there was a confused gentle breath of petrol, of tobacco, of flowers and, at the last, simply the London breath—London quietly resolving to be London although they might turn her ancient courts into shrill parlours of coconut-shy and Peeping Tom cabinets, and plaster flaring portraits of nude abandoned houris on the bosom of her theatres.

Everything was transmuted. Gold dust was in the air. May had come with carnations and starry evening skies and the first beat among the vegetable stalks of the Prelude to *Die Meistersinger*.

It would be a lovely evening—not so lovely as that spring evening weeks ago when he had walked from the Galleries as though he were stepping into a new world—the very evening, he remembered, of Uncle Nicholas's arrival—*that* evening he would never forget—but lovely as the first May evenings in London are always lovely, promising, reassuring, consoling the doubting human heart.

He took off his hat and looked up. "What we want," he thought, "is to believe in ourselves more. We have despised one another for long enough. There's a new time of confidence coming."

Three men and a perfect lady almost knocked him down. He apologized. "Star-gazing," said the lady.

It was at that moment, as he approached the Circus, with the Pavilion's cinematographic entertainment bidding him enter, that he determined that he would speak to Uncle Matthew. At once. He would find out what Uncle Matthew thought of all this. He had walked a little out of his way. He turned down the Haymarket, his face set towards Westminster.

Letting himself in, proceeding quietly upstairs, he passed an old man with a white beard. He had seen this old man before. He was one of Uncle Matthew's friends. A very quiet old man, whose step made no sound, with very bright blue eyes and clean but shabby garments. The old man bowed, murmured "Good-evening," and passed down into the hall where the maid was waiting to let him out. Romney went into his room, took the little negress from his pocket and placed her reverently on his table, then turned and went up to Uncle Matthew's room.

Outside his own door he almost stepped on Becky Sharp, the cat. She seemed, he had noticed, to have the power, like certain birds and lizards and snakes, to change into the colour of the background against which she stood. Not that she was not always black, and black with a shining intensity, but with the blackness she was also at times invisible, invisible except for the intense watchfulness of her green eyes.

Now he almost fell over her, but she bore him no

malice, only walked quietly beside him, along the passage to Uncle Matthew's door. There, when he paused, she paused too and looked at him curiously and, he could have sworn, scornfully—as much as to say: "You surely are not going in *there,* are you?" When she saw that it really was so she walked, with quiet purpose, away.

He knocked on the door. "How very odd!" he thought. "In all these years I've never entered this room except to ask a question or deliver a message—never with any intention of staying there." It was strange how, in this house, they all had their own quarters to which on the whole they obstinately kept. Was it Uncle Nicholas now who was drawing them together?

He heard Uncle Matthew's voice bidding him enter.

He knew the look of the room, of course. It was wide and high, and books ran to the ceiling on all sides of it. There was only one picture—a large copy in colour of Leonardo's "Virgin of the Rocks" that hung between the two windows. Romney disapproved, of course, of all copies in colour, but of this which Uncle Matthew had bought in Dresden he had to admit that the dim green shadows, the pale, lovely face of the Virgin, had in themselves a real beauty which the whole room reflected.

In the centre of the room was a table covered with a deep blue cloth. On the cloth was a plain white bowl. On the mantelpiece was a fat round tobacco jar. Uncle Matthew was sitting in an armchair reading.

When he saw who his visitor was he smiled.

"Why, Romney!" he said. "What can I do for you?"

Romney was shy. They were all, when it came to it, shy of Matthew because he lived quite definitely in another world than theirs. He had never bothered any of them with the slightest hint as to what that world might be like; he had never shown the slightest wish to lead any of them into it. But they were all well aware that his life was full, active, and exceedingly interesting. He had the look, in spite of his quiet ways and his indifference to speech, the calm of a man who is always happily occupied. He could say a sharp thing sometimes, too. He might be a saint, but he was not meek. He might love all mankind, but that was not to say that he suffered fools gladly.

"I don't want anything," Romney said, smiling. "Or rather—I do. I want to talk."

"That's splendid. Sit down there. That's a very comfortable chair. Fill your pipe."

Romney sat down and filled his pipe. He did not know how to begin.

Matthew helped him.

"Do you know?—this is the first time in all these years that you've come in for a talk. I've often wanted you to. I even knew that you would one day, but I wasn't going to press you. We're all free in this house."

"I didn't think," said Romney, "that you'd want to be bored with me."

"That's very modest."

"No, I don't mean it modestly." Romney hesitated. "I don't mean that I'm not worth talking to. No one thinks that of themselves really, do they?"

"Oh, yes—some people do," Matthew said.

"Well—not *my* friends anyway. What I meant was that you've always seemed so settled in your life—as though you'd made up your mind about everything; and I've made up my mind about nothing."

"About nothing?" said Matthew.

"No, nothing at all. I'm influenced by everything that comes along. Six months ago I read Lawrence's *Plumed Serpent,* and it seemed to me the most marvellous thing ever. Then I read someone's book about him and he was awful—so self-centred, always squealing, false to his friends—and I didn't want ever to read anything about him or by him again. So it always is. I can't find anything to hang onto."

"And so you thought you'd come and see if I had anything?"

"Yes, in a way. It was like this. I was coming from the office. The sky was lovely. I'd just bought a little wood-carving. I was excited and dissatisfied. I'd just had a great disappointment. I thought I'd come and ask you some questions."

Matthew looked at him with great affection.

"Fire away then."

Romney smiled. "I like this. I like this room and everything. Why haven't I been in here before? The first thing is about myself. My disappointment this afternoon was because a friend of mine wouldn't go out with me this evening after he had said that he would. That isn't very serious, is it? But in a way it is, because it showed me how awfully fond of him I am. Almost as though he were a woman. And that's what worried me. Because I've never been in love with a woman, and I care for this man so much. I was wondering whether I were homosexual. But I know I'm not because I'm uncomfortable with men who are. I would hate to be—not because I think they can help it, but because—oh! I don't know—because I want to be sane, square in the middle of life. It's a handicap to be abnormal. Everything is twisted. Why don't I fall in love? Why do I mind so much when this man chucks me?"

Matthew struck a match and relit a pipe. Bending over it he said:

"I shouldn't worry. You've got plenty of time. People talk and write too much about these things. You're normal all right, but we're all a mixture, and different people rouse different emotions in us. I expect you're a bit idealistic."

"That sounds priggish," Romney said. "But I think a lot of my generation are like me. Girls aren't as romantic as they were. They are too close. They don't hide anything. We want love to be something rare, a little out of our reach. Friendship seems rarer than sexual love sometimes."

"What's this friend of yours like?"

"Oh, he's absolutely ordinary. He cares for none of the things I care for. I'm fond of him, because he's so steady and safe. I like to be with him, to be near him. I don't think there's anything physical in that, and yet I was sick with disappointment this afternoon. He doesn't care a bit for me as I do for him. I know that. And yet I cheat myself, I want him to need me. But he doesn't. If I died tonight he wouldn't care."

"I had a friend once," Matthew said, "for whom I felt like that. And yet I'm normal enough. I think we divide love up too much. Love whom you will, but keep the quality fine. There are lots of different ways of doing that. But you can't mistake it. If the fineness is there, you'll know it. If it isn't there, drop it. Be your own judge." He crossed his legs. "Don't expect too much of anyone else. Expect a lot of yourself, though. And don't be too solemn about yourself—which I expect you're inclined to be. We're all very comic—very comic indeed."

"Yes. I know we are. But if you think yourself *very* comic you don't have much confidence about the things you try to do. You know—sometimes I go to a restaurant with friends and I suddenly see myself in a glass and I think I'm too awful for anything. Eyebrows and a nose and a slit of a mouth. I'm so tired of it. I've seen it so often. Then I sell a picture to someone and I think I'm grand."

Matthew was so clean and fresh, Romney thought. "It's as though I'm seeing him for the first time. And this room for the first time." Matthew was wearing a bow tie of light grey with white spots. The sharp ends of his collar gleamed with an intense whiteness. He was so quiet and friendly and restful. They looked across at one another smiling.

"Well, what's the next thing?" asked Matthew.

"The next thing is connected with the last thing. Except for this man there's been nobody who mattered to me except all of us—the family, I mean. We've grown up taking it for granted, our loving one another, being so happy together. I've never thought it odd that I should love Mother and Father and Nell and Edward. Or," he went on, smiling, "that we should have uncles and aunts in the house and like them to be there. Well, suddenly, in these last few weeks I've realized that what we have hardly anyone else has got any more. Or at any rate all the intelligent people now think the family's a mistake and a danger like nationalism. All in a moment I've realized that I might lose this—that it might be broken up, that something would come and tell us we're all silly to believe in one another, to care for one another. You see, if I were to lose my friend *and* the family—if I suddenly thought Mother silly and Father lazy and our evenings together a bore—why, then I'd have nothing left at all."

"Why should you?" said Matthew. "After all, your mother *isn't* silly and we do all care for one another. It's something *real* that holds our family together. If it's real it can't be unreal."

"No—but what's real or unreal? Isn't it the way we

look at it? There are so many ways of looking at things. Your way, for instance, and Uncle Nicholas's."

"Ah, yes—Nicholas."

"It's since he came that I've felt so unsettled. Some of the things I've thought fine I'm not so sure of when he's there. It's almost as though there'd been a little earthquake in the house and all the things that you had believed to be steady had rocked for a moment."

Romney looked at his uncle.

"You don't like Uncle Nicholas, do you?"

"Why should you think that?"

"Oh, one can feel it. And Uncle Nicholas feels it, too. He's never quite at his ease when you're there. You're the only one of us who doesn't."

"It isn't dislike," Matthew said. "It's only that we don't believe in the same things."

"You know," Romney went on, "in the drawing room the other night after dinner it was almost a battle between you. You didn't say anything, but the room was full of it. The house isn't quiet any more. Events happen underground. The other night at dinner Mother said something that I thought silly, and I snapped at her. I wouldn't have dreamt of doing that two months ago. I saw that she was hurt. I was awfully ashamed of it."

Matthew said not a word.

"Perhaps it's because everything's changing just now," Romney went on. "It's like going downhill in a car when the brakes won't act. Somebody whispers in your ear: 'You're rushing into chaos whether you like it or no.' But we ought to have more power, oughtn't we, Uncle Matthew? Not only over events but over ourselves. Chaos itself oughtn't to matter if we're sure of ourselves. And I'd like to fight to keep us together. Whatever happens, nothing can separate *us*. That's what I'd like to say. But I'm so weak. I don't respect myself. I don't find anything I can believe in except beautiful things like pictures and music, and even they are changing their values all the time.

"But tonight when I felt my friend had chucked me and that we were all different at home, it was as though I had no ground for my feet. Between Leicester Square and Piccadilly it was as though I were standing on a swamp. I hope you don't think I'm talking awful nonsense, Uncle Matthew."

"No, of course not."

"And so I thought I'd come and ask you—why, when everyone else is so uncertain, you're so sure, and so happy. . . . It's your religion, I suppose?" he added more timidly.

There was a pause. Then Matthew said:

"Do you think I'm happy? I suppose I am. If I am it's because I don't think about myself much any more. Oh, well . . . think! If I had the toothache I'd think all right. But I don't think how I *am,* whether I'm happy or not."

"Why don't you? It must be wonderful not to bother."

"Oh, because there are other things more important. That's a priggish answer, isn't it? Very noble and all that. It isn't noble. It's simply what's happened to me—that for a long time now I've lived in another world where the values are different."

"You mean religion—God?"

"Not religion certainly—but God, yes." He broke off. "Look here, Romney," he said at last. "Do you really want to talk about these things? There's nothing more interesting if you *are* interested, nothing more boring if you aren't."

"Of course I want to talk about them. That's what I came here for."

"Yes, but I hate to preach. I don't particularly want to make you better, you know. Or make anyone better. What's good for one isn't good for another. Propaganda's awful—or props of any kind. All that anyone's got to do is to find out what's true for himself. Your own truth. That's your job. I'll tell you what I've found out to be true for myself if you like, but that doesn't mean that it's true for anyone else."

"Oh, no," Romney said eagerly. "That's just what I want to hear—how you've discovered something to be true and what that something is."

"How quiet this room is," he thought, "and how beautiful! The ground's steady. It's been rocking under my feet for weeks."

"Look here," Matthew said. "It will be time to dress soon. We'll talk another evening for as long as you like."

Romney saw that he was shy, that he had suddenly closed in upon himself as the petals of a flower close. But he was determined to get some kind of answer before he left the room. He felt as though, if he went away now, he would never return and an irreparable chance be lost.

"No," he said. "I want just to hear from you what you've discovered. Then we'll talk another time if you'll let me."

"I haven't discovered anything," Matthew said. "Or at least only one thing. I discovered some years ago that for me it was wiser always to be ready—waiting to receive—rather than to go out and try to take what I thought I ought to have. To let it come to me rather than that I should go to it."

"To let *what* come to you?"

"God if you like. The other life. The life inside. The immortal life."

"Then you believe that you are immortal?" Romney asked.

"I believe," Matthew said, "that there is something immortal inside me."

"And it's that that makes you happy?"

"Why do you harp on this happiness?" Matthew said, smiling. "That isn't the point. The point is that you should let the tree have plenty of light and air and good soil."

"What tree?"

"Confucius called it the Tree of Heaven. That's as good as another. Look here! I knew that we should get like this—loose and symbolic. I'll give you a fact or two. Nietzsche says somewhere that life's either wrestling or dancing. That's partly true. But there's a third way—waiting to receive what comes to you and then cherishing it. Twenty years ago, in 1912, I was in love, passionately, desperately in love with a married woman. It's a commonplace little story. She also was in love with me. I wanted her to leave her husband, and she, quite rightly, would not. We parted. Life seemed altogether over for me—empty, useless. Then one evening I came into my room—I wasn't living here then—and it seemed to me as though I had a visitor. Oh, I didn't *see* anyone—but I felt as though someone were talking to me. After that it was as though a seed had been planted inside me. A new life began, timidly, shyly, to grow. I didn't want it. I was as cynical about it as Nicholas could ever be. I tried to disregard it, but it wouldn't be disregarded. Things that had been important seemed important no longer. I began to see things that I had never seen before. It was as though I had been shown the existence of a whole continent—yes, a world inside this other one—inside or outside, around it, intermingling with it. And the things of this world, its laws, its scale of values, its beauties have become increasingly real to me as I've grown older. This tree, this world, this life—I don't want to be pretentious about it. I wouldn't argue from my experience of it that there's life after death or that it is what men mean by religion. I only know that it's real to me, now, at this moment. It's so real that the material world is often unreal—unreal in its detail, I mean. I suppose it would be simpler to say that I have an inner life and that it is more active than the outer one." He laughed. "My dear boy, don't think that all the material things aren't real, too. I love my food and my friends and some work I do (although you didn't know it, did you?) and theatres and the country and all of us in this house. The two lives intermingle. They are one and the same life. One enriches the other."

Romney said: "You're awfully lucky. To have that, I mean. If one hasn't got it one can't pretend."

"No, of course not. All you can do is to wait and see what happens. Not to demand anything, but also not to miss a chance, not to close yourself up. Not to say that anything is nonsense."

But Romney secretly was disappointed. He had thought that there would be more than this—it was all so vague and formless.

"Then you wouldn't call it a religion?" he asked.

"Oh, no, not a religion, simply an experience. As though I'd walked down a country lane and met someone who took me to a beautiful place and invited me to stay there."

"And it's changed your life?"

"Well, of course. Everything and everyone I come into contact with changes my life. So of course this has done. Many things and people are valuable now. I wouldn't even have seen them once. Many things are unimportant now that once would have worried me. This other world is created in love. That doesn't mean, you know," he went on, laughing, "that I love everyone, never lose my temper, never have indigestion any more or am not peevish if I do have it. Indeed no, I'm a very imperfect citizen of that world, but I know the qualities that make it. It's like learning Chinese. Slowly, I'm picking up the characters."

"Do you know other people who have had your experience?" Romney asked.

"Oh, yes. Gradually we meet one another. One here, another there."

"Then it has no dogmas, no sect, no name?"

"All dogmas are right if they feed the Tree. Every man must find his own—the one that suits him."

Romney moved restlessly in his chair.

"Uncle Matthew—don't think me rude—but most people today—most people of my generation, anyway—would think it most awful nonsense. All imagined by yourself, I mean."

"Of course they would," Matthew said. "If they haven't experienced it. And it's right they should if that's what they honestly think. The only thing they can't do is to take it away. I'll give it any name that pleases you. I'll say that I believe in God as a beneficent power—I'll say that Christ was the one perfect citizen of this world that the other, the outside world, has ever known. I'll say that once you are aware of this life in you, you can't deny it, you can't do anything but live it. But I'll say, most of all, that you must keep yourself open, let it flow into you, let it work on you as it will. And I'll say that it's a definite practical experience, that once you've known it, you can't deny it any more than you can deny a voyage to South Africa if you've been there."

"Are there any rules," said Romney, "that you have to

obey? Do you say prayers? Do you go to any kind of church?"

"Rules? Not rules so much as values. Some things are better than others. Charity is better than meanness, love than hatred, self-forgetfulness than egotism, cheerfulness than grumbling, attention than chatter, humour than pomposity—and always to lose yourself in something larger than yourself. Prayer? No, conversation rather. You have a constant friend. You talk together. Churches? All and every church. All and every place. There are no exclusions——"

He shook his head.

"There you are! You asked me. There's no miracle, no revelation. I'm no priest or prophet."

They were silent. The last lights of the May evening thinned the leaves of the trees beyond the window so that they were fragments of shadowed gold against a sky white with radiance. The room was dark. Romney sighed.

"I can only repeat," he said, "that you're lucky. Perhaps I'll be lucky too one day."

14

Now it so happened that, at the very moment when Romney and Matthew mentioned his name, Nicholas was standing in the passage outside Matthew's room. He was standing, a smile on his lips, a wine-coloured carnation in his hand, and he was humming a song from *The Cat and the Fiddle*.

He smiled because he felt happy, the wine-coloured carnation he had stolen from a vase in the drawing room, and he was humming for the same reason that he smiled.

He was standing in the passage outside Matthew's

room because he was not sure what his next move would be. As a matter of fact, his next move was to be a very important one, trivial though at the time it seemed. But he did not know that.

He sometimes halted thus in the middle of the house, listening to its beating heart—the stirring of the clocks, the breeze behind a curtain, a step muffled by walls, someone singing. And when he halted thus he pleased himself with the fancy that he had only to move this or this to set all the patterns changing. There they were, behind their different doors, waiting for him to move the game on a stage further—as a chess master's hand may hover over the board.

He believed immensely in his powers. He was, in fact, a most amiable self-satisfied man—amiable because self-satisfied.

And he was especially amiable and therefore especially ready for good-natured mischief this afternoon, because he had won at the Young Bachelors ten pounds after some excellent games of contract. The Young Bachelors was an obscure little club in Rupert Street that existed only for gambling purposes. It was exactly what Nicholas required, for it was obscure, on the whole honest, and all of its members, save one or two, played games less well than Nicholas played them. He was glad that, on the whole, it was honest, for he preferred to win by natural talent. If, on the other hand, unnatural talents were called for, well, he could do his share. But he saw himself making a very pretty little income at the Young Bachelors for a long time to come.

Now he was not sure what he would do. Should he have a serious conversation with Lizzie, or be kind and teasing to Fanny, or read some chapters of the Maurice novel in his room, or write a letter to Speranza Portugales, to whom he had now written half a dozen and received no answer from her? (But soon she would succumb and receive him back again. After all she had really *given* him the bracelet. She had said carelessly, "You can have it if you want to," or, if those had not been *exactly* her words, they were so near as not to matter. And then once she had given it to him it was surely his to sell if he wanted to?)

What should he do during this hour before dressing time? He realized then that he was standing outside his brother Matthew's room. Should be go in and tease *him* for a bit? But he was not *quite* sure about teasing Matthew. Matthew was the one member of the family whom he had never liked. He was the only member of the family he didn't like now!

He recalled how, when they were children, he and a big boy from over the way had stripped Matthew of his clothes and shut him up in the coal shed. He had escaped later and, besmeared with coal, had walked, quite naked, through the house up to his room. He had not been shy, ashamed, or irritated. He had been seen by some female guest walking up the stairs. That had not disturbed him, either. Very aggravating. "I don't believe I'd be what I am if it weren't for Matthew," Nicholas thought. That was perhaps unfair, for they had gone to different schools. Their lives had been always separate. But Matthew was the one and only human being whom Nicholas could not charm. No, he could not!

"Dear old Matthew," Nicholas thought. "What a ghastly prig! He's in there now talking religion to someone, I wouldn't mind betting." He little knew how accurate he was!

So, jingling his money in his trouser pocket, he moved away. He would chatter to Lizzie (from whom he wished to learn a number of things), read his novel, dress slowly. He understood that there was a dinner party tonight, a little dinner party with some bridge afterwards. He would, almost certainly, win a few more shillings before the end of the evening.

Then he paused, because he nearly fell over the cat. He had not seen it. He cursed it pleasantly, but Becky Sharp liked him and, purring, rubbed against his trouser. She had a purr like the beating of a baby drum in a baby jungle—muffled and important. So, pausing, he saw that the door on his right was ajar. Inquisitive as ever, he peeped in. It was Grace's room and there she was, sitting at a table in the window busily writing.

He liked Grace best of all the family, for Grace adored him, and he loved to be adored. She had always worshipped him, had slaved for him when they were children, had never looked for any rewards, and now, on his return after so many years, had at once surrendered to him again, wanting to run messages for him, to serve him in any way, protesting indignantly if he were criticized, laughing at his jokes whether she understood them or no.

Poor old Grace! He would do anything for her in reason. He recited wicked poems to her (and she had no idea that they were wicked), entertained her with incredible stories about the West Indies and Italy, kissed her and teased her and made her life, as she confided to Fanny, one long, bright holiday.

Peering through the door, he wondered what it was that she could be doing. She was completely absorbed, huddled up in her chair, leaning forward, her stout, shapeless figure hugging itself. She was writing furiously.

He walked in, softly crossed her room, stood behind her, then, with a laugh, put out his hands and covered her eyes.

She screamed. Then, with an excited giggle, said: "I know. It's Nicholas. I can feel it's your ring."

He took his hands away. "Yes, Nicholas it is. It's cheek, my coming into your room like this, isn't it?"

"Oh, no—*you* can."

His curiosity had realized that at once she had covered, with her hand, the paper on which she was writing. There were other sheets, and these too she drew in to the shelter of her purple blotting book. She was writing a letter. But to whom? There was a mystery here.

"You shouldn't leave your door open if you don't want your inquisitive brother to come in, Grace dear."

"Oh, was it open? I'm sure I didn't know, but I'm always doing things like that, and I've been shopping with Fanny. It's such a lovely afternoon, and I've got something for Lizzie that I'm sure she'll simply love."

He sat down on the edge of the bed and looked at her with his quizzical good-humoured patronage.

"What on earth are you doing writing so intensely like that all by yourself, you funny old thing? One would think that you were writing a love letter."

He saw at once that his random shot was correct. She *had* been writing a love letter!

She blushed, laughed nervously, and closed her fat hand even more firmly on the mysterious sheet of paper. Nicholas had heard, of course, that Grace cherished an attendant gentleman somewhere in the country. Grace herself quite often made allusions to him. None of the family had ever seen him. Grace had met him several years ago when on a holiday in Bonchurch. The splendid letters that he wrote to her were her great joy. Nicholas of course wished to see one of these letters. He was interested in everything human, and the thought that dear Grace, middle-aged, stout, and foolish, had a lover was queer indeed and also, although he would not admit to tenderness, rather touching. As he looked at her now he had a memory of Grace, a little girl with a flushed face and tousled hair, pushing into the hand of a small ungracious boy who had come to tea a ring with a ruby (the fruits of a cracker) and murmuring huskily: "I want *you* to have it!" Fanny and Grace! Foolish sentimental girls, foolish sentimental women. . . .

"Writing a love letter!" Grace murmured. "Nicholas, how absurd! You should know me better than that. Whom would I write a love letter to?"

"Your enigmatic courtier in the provinces."

"You're teasing me, but of course it does mean a lot to have someone care for you at my age, and I must say that I'm properly grateful, and sometimes on a lovely afternoon like this when everyone is looking so bright in spite of the bad times—for they really are awful, aren't they, and it looks as though there'd be Mussolinis everywhere presently, and perhaps it would be the best thing in this country after all—what I mean is, Nicholas, that an old woman like me does want a friend to prevent her from being lonely."

"Nonsense, Grace—you're not old and you're not lonely."

Nicholas leaned, lightly, on the back of her chair.

"Now this letter, for instance—what kind of things do you write to him about?"

"Oh, little things—what I do and what people are talking about and how everyone is—oh, dear! I don't know—you *are* a tease, Nicholas!"

He noticed that one of the sheets had slipped from the purple blotting book. He pinched her ear, slowly, playfully drawing her kind, flushed, excited face towards his.

She was always excited, poor Grace. Everything moved

her to extravagant emotion. She was excited now, greatly pleased that he should be there, thinking it worth his while to spend his time with her. Wonderful that he should be interested in her little doings, the dazzling, brilliant, teasing Nicholas!

He looked over her shoulder, talking nonsense, smiling into her eyes, and read these sentences:

"And so, darling, beloved Grace, you can understand that when I took my customary walk after supper I was thinking so much of you and wishing that you could be with me and help me to solve some of my difficult problems . . ."

Darling, beloved Grace? But the letter was in Grace's handwriting. It was this that she herself had written during the last half-hour!

He stood back a little, still with his eyes on hers. Her cheeks flushed a deeper crimson.

"Grace . . . you've been writing this love letter to yourself!"

"Oh, Nicholas!"

With a long-drawn sigh, her body trembling, she drew back from him, never taking her eyes from his face. His smile, kindly, teasing, affectionate, cynical, was steady, dominating. He had her in his hands to do with as he would.

"Oh, Nicholas!" she whispered again.

Once more he tweaked her ear.

"You wicked old thing! Who'd have thought it? Deceiving us all—well, I'm damned!"

"It isn't wicked, is it? It doesn't do anyone any harm?"

"Wicked? No, of course not."

"And you won't tell anyone, none of the others? I'd die of shame if they knew."

"Tell them? Why, of course not. What sort of brother do you think I am?"

He moved away and sat down on a small chair near the bed. He leaned forward, nursing a knee with his elegant hands, looking at her in the kindest, friendliest fashion. He had never, in all his experiences, known anything so funny! Poor old Grace, sitting in her bedroom writing love letters to herself, imagining a lover, deceiving the family. . . .

He said:

"But, my dear, whatever do you do it for? What fun do you get out of it?"

"It isn't fun." Her voice was timid, almost beseeching. "No one has ever been in love with me, not really, I mean, although there was a Captain Barnett used to come here and he took me to the theatre. He kissed me in the taxi. . . . Oh, that was years ago, of course! And now, of course, no one ever will be in love with me, and it seems so unfair. What I mean is, Nicholas, I shall die without ever being made love to, and I didn't mean this to go on when I began it. I just wrote one letter one evening when I was feeling lonely, to keep myself company as it were, and then it went on, and then——"

She broke off. She stared at him, her eyes now brimming with tears. She was becoming, now, with every moment, more excited. How often she had longed to tell someone of this—how impossible that she ever should! And now Nicholas knew—what a fool he must think her, and yet he looked at her with a kindly smile, he *seemed* to understand! And, oh, if he only did! How wonderful for her to have a friend to whom she could sometimes talk, someone sympathetic, comprehending . . . Words began to pour from her.

"You see, Nicholas—no man could ever understand—

but every woman wants to be loved and to have children, doesn't she? Of course I was never very good-looking, and the people I cared for never seemed to care much for me. And then there was God."

"God?" asked Nicholas.

"Yes—always hanging over one—watching everything one did. Oh, I know children don't believe that any more these days. They don't believe anything, not Santa Claus nor fairy tales nor a single word you tell them. Look at your Lizzie! But they all did when we were children. I couldn't tell even the whitest of lies—and I used to tell lies sometimes because I was frightened of Papa, although he was ever so kind, but when he was angry he was so *very* angry. In any case—what was I saying?—oh, yes. God's Eye seemed to be everywhere, in the garden, down in the tool shed—do you remember at Moreton, Nicholas, when I caught you there one day kissing Minnie Simmers and stood guard for you ever so long outside and caught a cold which lasted for weeks? Anyway, I was silly, I suppose, but there were both God and Papa watching everything. Fanny was more venturesome. I've always thought Fanny had a bit of the pagan in her, and you remember that time when she went on with Lionel Holford, although Papa didn't like it at all, and she didn't care a bit. I never would have dared. I was always a fearful coward. But what I mean is that if I hadn't been so afraid of God I might have had more chances. Because men want you to go part of the way, don't they? But I never dared. So here I am, an old maid writing letters to herself. It's dreadfully silly, isn't it?"

She ended with a nervous, almost hysterical laugh, for she had realized, quite suddenly, that she had put herself entirely in Nicholas's power. If any of the others were ever to know—Romney or Nell or Charles—oh! she would die of shame! She would throw herself into the Thames! She put out a hand and timidly touched Nicholas's sleeve.

"You won't breathe a word, Nicholas, will you? Please, please. I should never be able to face any one of them again—and I'm so fond of them. I know how silly it is, and I should never have told them that I had a friend. I've always known it was wrong, but he's become quite real to me now. I know just what he's like and how he lives. And there are times when I think that if I went to Winchester there he'd be at the station——"

She broke off.

"Of course, dear Grace. I won't breathe a whisper. It shall be *our* secret. No one in the world shall know. But can't you find a *real* man to write to? I'm sure there are lots of men who are as lonely as anything and would be only too glad to get letters, such charming letters——"

She shook her head.

"I don't know. You'll think me very queer, Nicholas, but if it was real there'd be sure to be something wrong. He'd want to meet me perhaps, and then he'd be disappointed when he saw me, and there might be something about him I didn't like—he'd have purple veins in his nose or an irritating cough. You never can tell about people, can you? Whereas now he's what I want him to be and he's always the same, so very kind, with perfect manners. . . . Oh, dear! you'll be thinking me more foolish every minute!"

But what he *was* thinking was: "This is what comes of all that pre-war humbug—all that nonsense about God, and women never being allowed to look a man straight in the eye."

He had an instant of revolt, of disgust. For a moment he positively hated this family—Matthew and his religion, Charles and his wood-carving, Fanny and her domesticity, and this old maid clutching her silly, sentimental letters. It was then, at that instant, as he looked at Grace, at the pictures on the wall—a view of Edinburgh Castle, "Christ with His Parents in the Temple," a seascape of sand and waves under a yellow sun, the innumerable photographs, the pincushions and toilet articles, a pair of red faded bedroom slippers with dubious fur at the edges—it was then that he had his first impulse of real malevolence. He *had* a right to rob and plunder and disturb these people, if he wished! Individually they were good, kind, sentimental souls, but they stood for a life that he detested—a sham, romantic, soppy, stupid Mumbo-Jumbo world! It would be good for them all to learn how unreal and false they were! He kissed Grace lightly on the cheek.

"I must go and dress. It's ever so late. Your secret's safe with me, my dear!"

15

Fanny had one thing in common with her daughter Nell—that she never could prevent happiness from breaking in. This was as it should be with a pretty young girl like Nell, but it must, she sometimes in these days reflected, irritate other people in a middle-aged woman like herself. Middle-aged women, even in these modern times, were always silly when they behaved like children.

On this particular afternoon, however, she and Nell had so greatly enjoyed their shopping, and the sun, and the bright faces, the colours of bronze and rose and bright pale green, the sunlight as it caught the silver of the motors and the glass of the windows and the great patches of carnations and roses in the baskets of the flower sellers, that it was difficult *not* to be happy.

And yet, as soon as they entered the Westminster house, some of Fanny's happiness left her. It was late, but they would have a cup of tea, and indeed the drawing room, soaked in the May sun, was empty.

Fanny sank into a chair.

"Where is everyone?" She pushed a bell. "We'll have a cup of tea even if it *is* late. Just as we are! How quiet the house is! Where *is* everyone?"

(Yes, Matthew and Romney were together, and Grace and Nicholas were together, and Charles was at his wood-carving, and the Old Lady was asleep, Edward was cutting a picture of footballers out of a paper, Lizzie was writing a letter.)

"And there's the dinner tonight. The Pontifexes and Claribel. Granny isn't coming down, so there'll be ten of us. Claribel's brother couldn't come."

"I'm glad of that anyway," said Nell. "I hate Claribel's brother."

"Hate! Darling, how violent you are!"

"Well, he's *so* conceited—just because he can do sums in his head. And he has an eye like that damp blue bone that fish have in railway-train meals."

"Very sweet she looks," Fanny thought, "in that mouse-grey with the dark red carnations. Such a child still and yet so very modern." They were like sisters, and then like mother and daughter, and then sometimes like complete strangers who found one another's habits very odd.

"I must stop wanting to take my children in my arms and love them," Fanny thought. "That stage is over."

She and Nell had been at one all that afternoon and now they were separated. She looked across at her daughter almost with timidity. She had talked, as she did when she was happy, eagerly and carelessly, unafraid that Nell would not understand. But now, quite suddenly, she was afraid of everything. This dinner tonight . . . Mrs. Pontifex was so very commanding. She always knew what was right for everyone. And Claribel Birch who was so beautiful and so discontented. She would make eyes at Nicholas, at Romney—age meant nothing to her.

When Fanny was hostess in her own house she talked too much. She knew that she did. She wanted, so badly, that everything should go well. Those dreadful pauses that came, arising like ugly monsters from under the dinner table, pointing their fingers at you! She ran in always to slaughter them, and then she could see what Mrs. Pontifex was thinking. Often she did not care. She had her family all about her. She was too happy to mind what strangers thought. But tonight she *would* care.

She took off her hat and stroked her dark hair. She turned to Nell, who was pouring out tea, and said:

"I talk too much, darling."

"Talk too much?" said Nell.

"Yes, dear—oh, not with you and the others, of course—but I shall tonight. I feel it in my bones, and Nicholas will think it a pity and the Pontifexes will discuss it going home. Oh dear! I've been so self-conscious these last weeks. I never used to be."

Nell's attention was not yet fixed. She was thinking, "I nearly told Mother about Hector this afternoon: would she have understood? Would she have minded? Mother is such a darling. She is always so determined that she will understand everything. Sometimes we are just like sisters, and then she's a whole generation away. I want to look after her, to protect her, to shield her from everyone, and then she makes me feel shy. She *will* wear such bright colours. She gets so enthusiastic. . . .

"No, darling," Nell said. "You don't talk too much. You talk too *fast* sometimes."

"Do I? Yes, I think I do. I must go up and see Edward."

"Oh, don't bother for once. You look tired. Let me arrange those cushions. Lie back." Nell came over and arranged the cushions, then bent down and kissed her. As she did so she thought of Mamie Pontifex who was always looking after her mother, although you would think that Mrs. Pontifex never needed to be looked after by anyone. Mamie, indeed, made a business of it. It was as though she said: "Everyone accuses my generation of being unfilial. Well, they're wrong. Look at me!"

Fanny caught Nell's hand.

"Stay here a moment. I feel tonight as though I were losing you—you and Romney and Edward."

"Losing us!" said Nell, kneeling down and looking up into her mother's face.

"Yes. Oh, well, of course I am in a way. I mustn't grumble. You've all been sweet to me. Women have a hard time anyway. If they have lovers they lose, and if they are domestic they lose."

"I suppose," said Nell, sententiously, "we all lose one way or another."

"What a thing to say at your age! Sometimes you're fifteen and sometimes you're fifty."

She stroked Nell's hair, which was very fair and curly. Nell now had the face of a child. And yet she already knew so much that Fanny would never know.

"Is it better, Nell, do you think, that all your generation know so much so soon?"

"What—about men?"

"For one thing."

"Yes, we can look after ourselves better than your generation could."

"But doesn't it make you hard sometimes and cynical?"

"No, I'm not cynical," Nell said. "The generation older than mine was. They had the war to look back upon. We're looking forward, and although the world is in the most awful mess—still, there's all the more for us to put right."

"And are you confident that you will?"

"Oh, no, of course not. It will be right in some places and wrong in others as it always has been. But there are things we can do."

"As for instance?"

"Not be furtive about sex as you all were. Not be frightened by things. Clear the slums away—oh, I don't know—lots of things!"

"Are you happier, do you think," asked Fanny, "than we were as girls?"

"No, I don't think so. But happiness isn't everything."

"Yet you want other people to be happy."

"Yes, I do." Nell jumped up. "Yes—I want everyone to be happy one day and just and kind. But of course they won't be. Still, one can try."

She looked beautiful just then. Often she did not. Her face was immensely expressive—as honest a face, Fanny thought lovingly, as any in the world.

Fanny said: "Kiss me again, Nell, darling. Once more before I go up to dress. Oh, I do wish we weren't having a party this evening!"

16

And in fact, at the very start there was a catastrophe—for the soup was cold.

Fanny could not understand it. During all the years that Mrs. Baldwin had been their cook the soup had never been once cold. Mrs. Baldwin was famous for a number of things—for her temper, her game leg, her green-tailed parrot (her husband had been, in his life, a sailor, had brought her a parrot from Africa; she said that death should not part her from it), her long-legged, dishevelled son who, with a perpetual cold in the head, visited her at certain times to demand money of her, her hatred of Becky Sharp, whom she could not abide (Napoleon, the parrot, also detested her). For all these things and many more she was celebrated in the family, for she was a "character," as you could see at once when you looked at her grey eyes, her moustache, her mountainous bosom, and listened to her game leg tapping out its temper on the kitchen floor—but most of all was she celebrated for her cooking. Fanny was afraid of her, even Janet was shy of her. No one in this world was familiar with her. She was a friendless woman and proud of it!

Nevertheless she could cook—she had the touch, the flair, the *je ne sais quoi,* the artist's certainty, the epicure's arrogance, the Maskelyne magic. She could cook. For the first time in her career the soup was cold.

But uneasiness had begun before that. Fanny, receiving the Pontifexes and Claribel in the drawing room, wondered, quite suddenly, as though someone had whispered in her ear, whether her bosom were not too bare and her dress too highly coloured. This was the first time of wearing. How she had loved it when she had seen it at Miss Fatima's! Watching the girl sway from side to side, it had seemed that the crimson velvet had a life of its own.

"Exactly the thing," Miss Fatima had said. "With Madam's height and Madam's lovely dark hair."

It had seemed "exactly the thing" upstairs, "exactly the thing" when she had gone in to kiss Edward good-night and he had said: "I say—that's *grand!*", "exactly the thing" when, entering the drawing room, she had found Matthew and Grace there and witnessed their approval (although Grace had no taste at all, poor dear), "exactly the thing" until Nicholas had come in and then Claribel. Claribel was in black and had that tragic, dishevelled appearance that so wonderfully became her. She looked on these occasions like one of the women in the *Rape of the Sabines.*

Fanny saw in an instant that Claribel though the crimson dress absurd, and then a moment later Nicholas confirmed it. Why? How? By what movement or gesture? With Nicholas one never could tell. He was very grand himself, sparkling and dashing and all-conquering. One of the Romans perhaps, and with one glance at him you could see that Claribel was sure of it.

And then Mary Pontifex was in black, too, entering the room like a general leading his army to certain victory—so that it was disappointing to find that the army, when it arrived, was only Bertie Pontifex, fat, placid, and, in some indefinable way, superior to his dominating wife.

But *why* were they all in black tonight? Just to make Fanny feel flamboyant, you might suppose.

"Stunning dress you're wearing," Bertie Pontifex said as they went down to dinner, but that meant nothing, for Bertie always paid compliments to women—just to show his independence of his wife.

Fanny knew at once that the soup was cold, for she saw Mary Pontifex raise a spoonful to her mouth, taste it, start, then with determined politeness pursue the hard necessity. But, until she tasted it herself, Fanny could not credit it. Mrs. Baldwin and cold soup! But there it was—not to be denied. The soup had that discouraging, shivering, vanished warmth about it that only bad cooks know.

Fanny looked around her. No one else appeared to be suffering. And then she caught a glance from Charles. He, too, was aware.

The salmon was all right, and she breathed again. The strange sense of impending calamity that had been hanging over her ever since she had entered the house that afternoon lifted a little. On one side of her was Bertie Pontifex, on the other Nicholas. Next to Nicholas was Claribel. On either side of Mary Pontifex were Romney and Matthew.

"It isn't a party," she had said to Mary Pontifex. "Almost entirely family. But we thought you and Bertie would like a little bridge."

"My dear, I *loathe* parties," said Mary Pontifex, lying with that brazen confidence common to all successful generals.

And yet, somehow, in a curious indefinable way it *was* a party. It was, Fanny thought, as though all her family were guests—even Charles, with whom for so many, many years she had shared the same bed.

They were there to criticize, she felt. If anything went wrong they would let her know it.

It was presently made clear to everyone that Mary Pontifex had been seeing a play called *Wings Over Europe* and reading a posthumous work by D. H. Lawrence called *Apocalypse*. She had a voice incisively clear, brilliantly penetrating. It was said that when she whispered secrets to a friend at a table in the Carlton Grill, gentlemen in the Old Kent Road started in astonishment. It was not that her voice was loud—but rather that it cut the opposing ether as with a knife.

She talked about the younger generation.

"I believe in knowing what the young people are doing. I admire the young. Lawrence was undoubtedly a genius.

The young man who wrote *Wings Over Europe* seemed to me exceedingly clever. Why don't *you* do something, Romney?" she threw across the table. "I don't know what it is you *are* doing—pictures or something, isn't it?"

Romney murmured.

"Well, come and have tea with me one day and I'll give you some advice. Do you know Stephen Morrison?"

No, Romney did not. He was blushing. His hatred of Mrs. Pontifex was fanatical.

"No? But where *have* you been? He edits the *Friday Review.* Quite the most brilliant of the weeklies, and he told me only the other day that he wanted more young men——"

"I can't write," Romney murmured.

"What nonsense! Of course you can. Don't tell me. You haven't tried."

Charles came in here.

"He's doing very well where he is," Charles said. "He knows more about pictures than any other young man in London. And as to writing it seems to me that there are far too many writers as things are. All stepping on one another's toes."

But Mary Pontifex, as it happened, was more militant than usual, because Bertie that same afternoon had refused to tell her where he had been between four and five. She was irritated. She had not wished to come to the silly dinner. What had induced her to promise on the telephone? She was in her most dangerous mood because it seemed that nobody loved her, nobody followed her advice, nobody thought her clever. She was never more certain of her own brilliance than when others denied it.

"The matter with you, Charles," she said, "is that you are not aware of what is going on." She smiled at him. "Don't think me rude, but I do feel it's most important that we shall all keep up with the times—terribly interesting as they are. Look at France! *And* America! Who would have believed it?"

Everyone looked at France and America. Then Nicholas said:

"Have you ever been in the West Indies, Mrs. Pontifex?"

She looked across the table, smiling brightly.

"No. Why?"

"Oh, you should go one day. You should study the habits of the Parasol Ant. You should watch it as it goes along brandishing a piece of leaf very much larger than itself. When it arrives at its nest it chews up what it is carrying and adds this to its nest. The nest becomes a kind of mushroom garden, and on this the ants plant a fungus which grows and produces multitudes of pearl-like bodies. These the ants eat and feed their larvæ with them."

"How interesting!" Mrs. Pontifex said. "But I don't quite see——"

"It's only," said Nicholas, "that France and America don't seem quite so important after you've watched the Parasol Ant for a bit."

Everyone laughed. Mrs. Pontifex laughed, too, but uneasily. Was this dangerous-looking man (you could see that he was an adventurer) mocking her? Were they all mocking her? She was suddenly lonely and longed for her daughter, Mamie, who, if she had been here, would at once have rushed to her defense. And when she felt lonely she felt angry. Fanny had laughed with enthusiasm, not at all because she understood the point of Nicholas's remark, but because there was danger in the air and laughter was safest. Mary Pontifex, who in any case considered Fanny a fool, thought: "She's laughing at me.

Fanny Carlisle of all people—and in that absurd dress she's wearing!"

But the introduction of the Parasol Ant into the conversation had general consequences. Nothing that evening quite recovered from it. Life in these days is dangerous. We none of us know, from minute to minute, where we may be. It was as though Nicholas, with his smiling charm, had threatened everyone at the table: "If you don't look out I will tell you about something worse than ants."

The immediate result was that everyone began to talk at once: Bertie Pontifex about the Stock Exchange, Grace to Matthew about the Buchman movement, Romney to Claribel about Ernest Milton's Shylock, Nell to Mrs. Pontifex about a cocktail party where Mamie Pontifex had been.

Of these Nell was the bravest, for she disliked Mrs. Pontifex as deeply as Romney did, but something told her that her mother needed assistance, that the party was going badly even as her mother had said that it would, that Mrs. Pontifex must be placated because she was angry.

But, as she talked, smiling, a little hurried and breathless, she thought how odd it was that Uncle Nicholas, with one word, could bring a country that she had never seen so vividly before her. Her picture, of course, could be nothing like reality. It seemed to her now a brown island (Nicholas had told her once that it resembled a crumpled piece of brown paper) filled with naked brown people, and over its surface ants, chewing large leaves, crawled in intolerable numbers.

Others also were thinking of Nicholas.

"Oh, but, Matthew," Grace was saying, "I wonder you are not more interested because you've always said that religion is the most absorbing thing in the world, and there really hasn't been a movement in our lifetime—what I mean is that although Dr. Buchman himself is an American, he does seem to have a kind of universal understanding, and I've been to one of their gatherings—house parties, they call them—where they all tell openly about their faults and failings——"

"I shouldn't care about that at all," said Matthew.

"Oh, well, you mightn't because you've got on so far—what I mean is that you're so religious already—but for young men who think about nothing but sport and going up to London for the night it's really splendid——"

"It would only make me lose my temper," said Matthew.

Grace dropped her voice.

"I'm not enjoying this much, Matthew, are you? I think it's silly of us all to have dinner together so often. I know Nicholas thinks it is."

"Why—has he said so?" asked Matthew.

"No, but you can see that he does."

Thinking once more of the Parasol Ant, Grace, in spite of herself, shivered. How horrible! Ants in thousands upon those sands, crawling over the earth, chewing as they went! She looked at Matthew for reassurance, as in fact she had done ever since she was a baby. For Matthew with his bright friendly eyes, round face, round body, his cleanliness and tranquillity, his understanding and inevitable loyalty, was, perhaps, the person whom Grace loved best in the world—Matthew and Fanny.

As she looked at him she thought:

"How dreadful if he and Fanny knew what Nicholas knows! If Nicholas were to hint . . ." Even now it seemed to her that across the table he might, with a wink, with a gesture, fill her soul with terror.

"Oh, why did I ever tell him? *What* induced me? But

he could get anything out of me. He always could when we were children. He always will. . . ."

But it was not a glance from Nicholas (busily laughing with Claribel) that she caught, but rather a sudden interchange of smile and glance between Matthew and Romney. They had smiled at one another across the table, and in that smile Grace caught something of Matthew's shyness and Matthew's tenderness.

"He is shy of all of us," she thought, "and yet he would do anything for any of us. Nicholas—he doesn't know what shyness means, but he only pleases himself. And yet anywhere, if they went out together, it would be Nicholas who would be noticed, Nicholas who would be popular."

She liked to think of people, to study them. In the letters that she wrote to herself she described people until they were as intimate to her as her own family.

"Oh, yes, dear," a letter would recount, *"I forgot to tell you Miss Spink looked in last night. She was just as scandalous as ever. I really had to stop her because she was saying* such *things about Dr. Bennett."* Or: *"I think you'd like the Hartleys, darling. She had a dreadful operation last year—something internal, and they say it was quite a miracle that she recovered, but now she is going about again, although her hair has gone quite grey. . . ."*

Oh, yes, she knew Miss Spink and the Hartleys and Dr. Redmond and old Mrs. Cass as well as well. They were her world, they kept her alive, they and John—John who cared for her and longed for her and . . .

She pulled herself together. Really they would think her strange, staring in front of her and not speaking to anyone. And Nicholas had said that it was all nonsense. Well, it *was* all nonsense, come to that. A little crazy perhaps. But she wouldn't give it up. She would just die without it. And they mustn't know. She must speak to Nicholas again and make him promise once more . . .

Then she saw that it was her favourite sweet—the best thing that Mrs. Baldwin made. This was an ice pudding with dates and cherries and nuts, flavoured with maraschino. A wonderful pudding that was Mrs. Baldwin's secret.

Grace was frankly greedy. Why not? At her age and with her figure she had ceased to worry about diet. What if she *were* stout? John in Winchester did not care. . . . He had said to her, again and again, in his letters: *"I don't like thin women. Now Miss Spink is painfully thin. . . ."*

When her turn came she helped herself liberally. Her eyes beamed as she tasted. But what was wrong? She tried again. Why, how horrible! Mrs. Baldwin had used salt instead of sugar. At the same moment she heard Fanny cry out:

"Why, she's put salt in by mistake!" and then: "Mary, don't touch it! Bertie!—she's put salt instead of sugar!"

Bertie said: "Oh, it's all right. I don't notice anything." But he did.

Mary Pontifex in a voice that would have cleared the Albert Hall: "Well—really—it's not so bad. Ice cream always tastes salty. What you should do, Fanny, is to get a cook from Mrs. Marchant in Sloane Street. Remind me and I'll give you a note to her."

"Oh, but," Fanny cried in an agony, "it's too absurd, because Mrs. Baldwin has been with us for years—hasn't she, Charles?—and she's the most perfect cook. Everyone knows. Why, you yourself, Mary, have said often . . . No, no, Rose. Take it all away. Nicholas, don't think of eating it. But I can't imagine what has happened. The soup was cold, and now this——"

"I could have told you long ago," Mary Pontifex began, but again Charles came to the rescue.

"It's all right, Fanny, don't upset yourself. Accidents *will* happen and here's the savoury. . . ."

But in Fanny's heart there was a dreadful foreboding. For weeks past she had been waiting for something to happen. She had known that all was not right in the kitchen; Janet had been strange, moving about the house like a prophetess, and when Fanny had asked her whether she were unwell, simply shaking her head and in her own maddening way merely replying:

"I'm perfectly well—perfectly."

Yes, Janet. But Mrs. Baldwin? This was unheard of. She was as proud of her dinners as Julius Cæsar of Britain, or Leonardo of his newts and lizards, or Einstein of his violin. Not that Fanny was thinking of these analogies. She was thinking that she must keep a very tight hand on herself.

She knew from long and often-repeated experience how, from afar, the lack of self-control approached her. At first no more than a cloud the size of a button; a button of a cloud, a fist of a cloud, a balloon of a cloud, and then the whole sky is dark, there is a whirling wind, and she is saying things that she will ever, her life after, regret. Now it seemed to her that everyone was sitting round the table waiting for her outburst.

The strange thing was that there would be other dinners when the cold soup, the salt in the pudding would not matter the slightest. Everyone would laugh. The little accidents would but increase the friendliness.

Tonight it was different. Every movement, every word, was dangerous. She must not lose control.

Nevertheless when the ladies went up to the drawing room, with a smiling word of apology to her guests she left them for a moment and visited Edward's room.

He still, big boy though he was, insisted on the night light of his babyhood. By its dim shaded colour she saw that he was fast asleep, lying on his back with his mouth open. He was not a beautiful child. There was nothing lovely about him now.

But for her there were all his irreconcilable characteristics: his obstinacy and sudden melting submission, his secrecy and moments of unexpected revelation, his hatred of sentiment and touching dependent affection, his growing manliness and clinging babyhood, his courage and cowardice, his separateness and his close intimacy as though he were yet in her womb.

He was still hers.

She bent down and kissed him, then turned him on his side. He didn't wake. She stood there in the half-dark, terribly near to tears.

What was this sense that everything was slipping from her? Why did she feel tonight that her own family was hostile?

"I'm a fool. I've always minded everything too much. I've never laughed at myself enough. What does it matter if the soup *was* cold and there was salt in the pudding? The world won't stop because of it. But I do *hate* Mary Pontifex tonight. Why should I care *what* she thinks?"

So she stood there for a little while summoning control. She kissed Edward again and went down.

In the drawing room Claribel was explaining to Grace how rude men were:

"Of course I know they can't help it, poor things. If they see a woman about it's like a moth and a candle. All the same when it comes to pinching you in a bus——"

"No one ever pinches me," Nell said, laughing.

"Oh, well, when you're my age! But all the way from Hyde Park Corner to Bond Street. And you know what the traffic is along Piccadilly now. We were five minutes without moving."

"Why didn't you get out of the bus?" said Mrs. Pontifex.

"Well, how could I? I was positively wedged in. If looks could kill! But he was one of those men who are quite shameless!"

How disgusting, Fanny thought—and after all Nell was only twenty. And could it be true that men today were like this? And Nell so pretty. Why, it was only the other day that she had been a schoolgirl with plaits down her back. Men! She saw them like Nicholas's ants crawling about the earth, chewing leaf and flower. . . .

"I'm afraid you'll think me rude, Claribel," Mary Pontifex said, "but the women who get pinched are the women who want to get pinched."

Claribel was furious.

"Are you trying to tell me——"

"I'm not telling you anything, Claribel, my dear. But if anyone knows anything about men I——"

The men came in.

But Claribel paid no attention to the men. She was swung into her Cassandra mood, a mood enjoyed by her so greatly that she surrendered even her anger with Mary Pontifex.

"Oh, you may say what you like, Mary! I don't care who hears me. The fact is—and we all know it but some of us haven't the courage to face it—that we are at the end of our civilization. Everything is going to pieces—

everything! Our money, our homes, our governments—soon we won't have any security, any safety. It will be worse than the Middle Ages. Talk of pinching!" She gave one of her famous Cassandra laughs. "It's the plain and elderly ones that will be lucky! There'll be wolves again in Hyde Park, we'll live in huts and wear skins, gnaw bones in our fingers, and the men will hunt with packs of dogs through the jungles of Piccadilly."

Fanny burst out then with the first of her three absurdities of the occasion.

"Whatever you say, Claribel, there'll always be spring evenings."

Everyone looked at her. What on earth did she mean? She seemed, they all thought, to be far more excited than the occasion warranted. They did not know that she saw Edward flying for his life across Trafalgar Square, pursued by wolves, and Nell hiding in the Burlington Arcade from fierce men, clad only in skins. . . .

"Spring evenings?" said Mary Pontifex.

"Oh, yes. How silly you must think me, but really, Claribel, you're talking such nonsense. I only meant I've never forgotten one evening last April. I was coming back from shopping. I've never *known* such an evening—so beautiful. I only meant that however bad things get there'll always be those evenings. . . . Oh, do forgive me! I'm forgetting my duties. Now what about bridge? How shall we play?"

While they were arranging the tables Nicholas was thinking: "It's true what that silly woman says. We are going back to lawlessness again. And a good thing, too. There'll be pickings for everybody. What a dull old age I would have had thirty years ago, but now——"

He thought of Abel, with whom he had spent last evening. Behind Abel there was that old life. Riding down to Montego Bay—deserted then. . . . That strange old negro with the scar on his leg, and the witchcraft, the scent of the thick smoke of the fire, the saucer with the blood, the chicken screaming in the yard, and beyond the open door, the white sands bordering that lazy, warm, pellucid sea . . . Abel and that woman living with him in the dirty Chelsea hotel, her old blind father . . . Abel ready for anything . . .

Here the drawing room with the solid furniture gleaming in the firelight, the high bowl with the wine-streaked carnations, the two bridge tables, everyone smiling, quietly talking. . . .

In a moment, staring in front of him, the room seemed to him to be thick with trees—the giant cotton tree, the calabash, the annatto with its rosy-coloured flower, the star-apple tree with the golden-bronze of the leaves, the yellow of the Jerusalem thorn. . . .

"Now that's right," said Fanny. "You and I, Claribel, with Romney and Charles."

In the end it worked out differently, for Claribel was at the other table with Romney and Nell and Bertie. How had this occurred? Another of the misadventures of the evening. Fanny had determined that she would not play with Mary and Nicholas. She was not a bad bridge player when she was quite at her ease. With friendly people who were not aghast at some small blunder she could keep her head. So long as auction was the fashion she had known where she was, but contract, unless the atmosphere was friendly, was terrifying. The risks of the bidding, the sense that one careless word might lose your partner thousands of points, bewildered her before she started.

She had realized the danger. She had planned that she should be at a table with Charles and Romney and Claribel, for Claribel thought too much about herself, the way that she was playing, a possible flirtation with some gentleman, to be a good player.

Now, at the last moment, Charles had arranged it. Dear Charles! He always maintained that Fanny was an excellent player in the making, but that she would never improve except in the best company. He would not, of course, realize that she was terrified of Mary Pontifex and Nicholas. He could not know how dangerous this evening was for her! He led her like a lamb to the slaughter.

And slaughter it was. She forgot everything that she had ever learnt. She was supposed to belong to the Culbertson school, and she had a card on which were written all the proper declarations. But Fanny had never been good at mathematics. She played contract well when her head was clear, when the atmosphere round her was friendly, when nobody minded losing a shilling or two.

But tonight she was opposed to Mary Pontifex. Fanny did not know that Mary had considered that at dinner she had been mocked; that she was determined now on revenge. But Fanny *did* know that the atmosphere was grim, the air thick with animosity.

So she made every possible mistake. After the first rubber she tried to leave the table and persuade Grace to take her place. But Grace was an *awful* player, the more awful in that she thought that she was rather good and looked on bridge as a kind of Halma or Snakes and Ladders. Neither Charles nor Charles would hear of Fanny's retirement. Nicholas foresaw a nice little addition to his week's earnings.

So Fanny played and made blunder after blunder. The only time that she won was when playing with Nicholas, and these games she hated most of all, for Nicholas was tender to her, careful of her as though she were an egg in a basket. Even then she made one ridiculous bid and he looked at her. She flushed. She felt quite isolated from the other three. She might have been behind prison bars and Nicholas and Mary had kindly come to pay her a visit!

"Poor Fanny," they would say in their freedom and irresponsibility. "But it's really her own fault that she's come to this. Her foolishness has brought her here."

But it was Mary Pontifex's play that maddened her. Nicholas of course was a real player, in a higher class than the rest of them, but Mary, Fanny was convinced, was, in cold reality, no better a player than herself. Mary had a commanding way with her. She would make a mistake and dare the whole world to tell her that it was one. No one, however good a player, conducted successful post-mortems with Mary. But she was a coward. You would not suspect it of her, but so it was. And you cannot play contract well if you are a coward.

Fanny knew this, and when at last the end came and she and Charles had lost five pounds a piece (which in these days they could ill afford), Mary Pontifex's self-satisfaction was a dreadful thing to witness.

"Never mind, Fanny," she said as they moved away towards the fire. "Come and have a quiet game with me some time. What you want——"

"I don't need you to tell me what I want, Mary dear," Fanny said in a trembling voice.

These words were enough. They unlocked the gates.

Afterwards looking back (as she often did, for this was the crisis in the succession that led to the later catastrophe), she wondered whether even then, tired though she was, she might not have held on to the end had it not been for Nicholas's glance at her. He had not intended her to catch it, but, sensitive as she was just then, it was almost more than she could bear.

It said as though in words: "I've a terrible fool for a sister. I wonder if anyone else suspects it. I'll protect her as long as I can."

She cared for Nicholas so much, admired him so, had found him so splendid all these weeks in the house, that his glance at her stung her more fiercely than any of Mary's superiorities.

Something snapped in her brain. A long way off a voice whispered: "Now you're going to be foolish. You're going to burst out with a lot of things that you will always regret."

But her head was a hot whirling ball, the dinner had been a ghastly failure, civilization was tumbling to pieces, Charles through her had lost far more than he could afford. . . .

So she said: "I don't need *you* to tell me what I want, Mary dear." Had her voice not trembled, all might even then have been well, but the agitation behind the words caused everyone to look at her.

And then Mary laughed.

"Certainly, Fanny. I never offer help where it's not wanted."

Fanny made a last effort to save herself. It was as though she were on the edge of a high cliff. One push and she would be in the tumbling, stormy waters. She smiled.

"Don't think me rude, Mary. Only I played bridge so frightfully. I don't think I'll *ever* play again. What will you drink, Mary? Charles, find out what everyone wants."

Then Mary gave Fanny the final push over.

"Yes, a little lemonade, Charles, please. Yes, Fanny, I

agree. I don't think you've got the *card* sense. It's something quite special, like playing the piano. And of course now bridge is so scientific . . ."

So over Fanny went.

"Really, Mary dear, you'll be giving bridge lessons soon. I believe they're very paying. I'll come and learn if you're not too expensive."

As she spoke she knew that everyone in the room was wondering what had come over her, that the children were uncomfortable, Matthew and Charles sorry, Nicholas amused, Claribel delighted.

("Oh, you fool, you silly fool," the voice whispered. "You *will* regret this!")

"Now you're rude, Fanny," Mary said, looking at her with great dignity.

"I don't care if I am," said Fanny, wishing that she could steady her voice. "Sometimes, Mary, you're quite insufferable. Oh, I know that this is my own house, but I don't care. It's time, Mary, that someone told you. You'd think we were all school children—always telling us where to go, what to do."

Mary looked as though she could not believe the evidence of her ears, as though she were a commander receiving the news of one of his most important officers' disobedience, as though she were Queen Victoria defied by Mr. Gladstone.

"Fanny!" she cried.

"Yes, I know." ("Oh, you'll regret this, you silly woman!" But it was *not* herself. It was some devil, some demon who, for the moment, possessed her.) "I don't care if I *am* rude, Mary. All the evening you've been telling me what I should do, and what my children should do. Where I should get a good cook, and that I mustn't play bridge any more. And you're *always* doing it, as though you knew all about everything and were superior to everybody."

Mary Pontifex turned to the door.

"Come along, Bertie. It's time we went home. I won't *forget,* Fanny. . . ."

But Charles sprang forward.

"I say—don't mind Fanny—she's tired."

And Bertie said:

"Hold on, Mary, old girl."

But Mary Pontifex was not accustomed to "holding on."

"No, thank you, Charles. It's evidently time we went home. We've outstayed our welcome, I fear. Come, Bertie."

She went. And Bertie followed her.

When the door closed (Charles hastening after his guests) before the eyes of the astonished family, Fanny sat down on the sofa and burst into tears.

17

From Matthew's Journal

. . . It's the quiet that I love, that I'm too fond of altogether, I don't doubt. For me it has been an exciting day, first Danny coming in with the news about his son's job, then Romney's unexpected visit, and lastly poor Fanny's outburst this evening. I suppose, as I told Danny, the truth is that I'm a moral coward. I was no help to Romney at all, and yet how often I've longed for him to come in just as he did! How often I've thought of the talks we would have! Why did I fail? It's the old trouble of being unable to convince someone of experiences that they can't dream of having! Never surely before has there been so wide a division between the two worlds! Reading Aquinas the other day, and then shortly after a life of Newton, I realized afresh that in the things of the *soul* we have not advanced one whit—nay, gone back. Who can write or feel or think today like this?

"You are a distinct portion of the essence of God; and contain a certain part of him in yourself. Why then are you ignorant of your noble birth? Why do you not consider whence you came? Why do you not remember, when you are eating, who you are who eat, and whom you feed? Do you not know that it is the Divine you feed, the Divine you exercise? You carry a God about with you, poor wretch, and know nothing of it. Do you suppose I mean some God without you of gold or silver? It is within yourself that you carry him. . . .

"Being, then, the work of such an artist, will you dishonour him—especially when he hath not only formed you, but given your guardianship to yourself? . . .

"I answer that I have not yet so much dignity as the case demands. For I do not yet trust to what I have learned and accepted. I still fear my own weakness. Let me take courage a little, and then you shall see such a look, and such an appearance, as I ought to have. . . .

"Such will I show myself to you . . . noble, tranquil!

"What, and immortal too, and exempt from age and sickness? No. But sickening and dying as becomes the Divine within me. This is in my power; this I can do."

As I copy these words I know them to be true—as true today as when Epictetus wrote them, true long long before he was born, true long, long after I am gone. But in the world for which Newton cared they go for nothing, and it is his world and his alone that has made the modern spirit. Why have not both worlds gone hand in hand to make this modern one? If it had been so, what a grand life we would all now be leading! How proud we would be, not for ourselves but because we know that we carry God within us!

And yet I, who know this for as sure a fact as that I am sitting here, at two in the morning, with the window open in front of me and the warm air streaming in upon me—am I proud or confident? Yes, I was confident enough when Danny was sitting beside me, believing the things that I believe. But when Romney, wanting help and new confidence, came and appealed to me my cursed shyness seized me. I hung my head and muttered some words and he went away disappointed.

They talk so much, I notice, in the papers of reconciling religion and science, but of what value would that be to us when we all deny ourselves, are so contemptuous of ourselves and the world in which we are living? It should have been an easy thing for me to have said to Romney—"I know that God is alive in me and in you and, because of that, we should be proud men, happy and confident, caring nothing if our bodies are blown to pieces, eaten by a cancer—I *know* the difference between what is ephemeral and what eternal, and yet am I not like anyone else, bewildered by the selfishness, the greed, the cruelty—these things in myself as well as in the outside world?" How can I persuade Romney that we must be proud men, carrying our heads high, when I am myself so weak and cowardly?

And yet the secret life goes on, and I know it to be true. I should go out and fight more than I do, for there *is* a battle. But it seems that as the inner life grows in a man it draws him away from the outer, making him selfish, greedy for his own quietness, wanting to be only with those who feel as he does. . . .

And dear Fanny! I felt with her tonight all her fear and apprehension. And I could do nothing. During dinner I was longing to say to her—"This is nothing. Laugh at it. There is no enemy in the house. It is just as it was three months ago." And to put my arm round her as I used to do. At Fenchurch, for instance, when the pony ran away coming back from Bewling and she was so brave while Grace and that silly girl friend of hers (I've forgotten her name) were screaming. Then when it was all over and we were alone in the schoolroom she cried. . . . And when she was rude to the old Miss O'Malley and Father was so angry, I understood *why* the words poured out from her and how the thought that that old flea-bitten dog had been ill treated made her see poor Miss O'Malley as a kind of Borgia and that she didn't *mean* what she said. For so long now she has been tranquil and happy, loving us all, the house, her life. But she must *be* loved, be needed. If she isn't, her old moods of despair come back to her so easily. And I, knowing all this, could do nothing for her tonight. My cowardice again. Afraid of a scene.

But if I am "not ignorant of my noble birth," how is it that I can be so inactive? I spend my life now with those who believe as I do and with those who *want* to believe. And meanwhile, outside us and disregarding us, untouched by us or by the things that we know to be true, there is the whole mass of mankind.

O God, make me less of a coward. Make me more responsible for Your power within me. Grant that this rich happiness of my own experience may be the experience also of increasing numbers of men! Above all help me that I may "stand still from the thinking of self, the willing of self."

Also that I may never lose my wonder at this experience of life.

Nec requies, quin aut pomis exuberet annus,
Aut fetu pecorum, aut Cerealis mergite culmi,
Proventuque oneret sulcos, atque horrea vincat;
Venit hiems, teritur Sicyonia bacca trapetis,
Glande sues laeti redeunt, dant arbuta silvae;
Et varios ponit fetus autumnus, et alte
Mitis in apricis coquitur vindemia saxis.

For Thine is the Kingdom, the Power and the Glory,
For Ever and Ever,
Amen.

END OF PART I

PART II

FANNY'S HOUSE

FANNY'S HOUSE

On a cold and windy afternoon early in September, Fanny was shopping in Bond Street and Edward was her cavalier.

To say that she was shopping is possibly an exaggeration. She had been lunching with the Frobishers and had brought Edward by request because the Frobisher boy, Cyprian, was on holiday and needed company. Cyprian —what a name to give the poor child! Fanny was sorry for him before she knew him. She had not seen him for a number of years. Last time he had been only six years old and ill in bed with stomach ache. He still, it seemed, had stomach ache. Nothing you gave that child agreed with him. He was now on a new diet—bananas and goat's milk—but even that wasn't satisfactory. What had really happened to him was that Mrs. Frobisher had absorbed him just as she had absorbed Mr. Frobisher, and the child *liked* to be absorbed! He adored his mother. It was, in fact, a splendid mutual-admiration nucleus, a grand manifestation of *one* way of making family life a success! As Mrs. Frobisher tossed and preened her neat little head and moved her neat little body inside her neat little costume, proclaiming how wonderful a success everything Frobisher was and how happy they all were, Fanny doubted more and more as to the real happiness of her own home circle. The awful thing about Mrs. Frobisher was that in her company you became mean and revengeful. You longed to call out: "Oh, but look at your little boy! He has to live on bananas and goat's milk!" or "Yes, Mr. Frobisher's pictures may be popular, but you know that he has no personality at all. He is never reckoned among the interesting painters. He has been producing for years these excellent versions of English country life, but there's nobody inside them. Nobody at all."

And Edward looked at Cyprian with dismay. He simply wondered how a boy could be like that. He was polite for his mother's sake but hugely relieved when they made their departure.

"He must get sick of bananas," he said to his mother. "He eats twelve a day."

"Well, it won't be for long," said Fanny cheerfully. (Her spirits began to rise again immediately.) "They'll be trying another diet soon. Mrs. Frobisher is thinking of quite a new doctor, and they are sending him to a school especially for delicate boys."

"Gosh! That must be an awful kind of place!" said Edward.

They went to Bond Street because Fanny loved it so.

"We can't really buy anything," Fanny confided, "because I haven't any money, but we can pretend we're going to."

"Are we very poor now?" asked Edward.

"Well, you see, since Father retired he's only got his investments, and investments are bad at present. They go down and down."

"Shan't we be able to live in Westminster soon?" Edward asked.

"Oh, yes. It isn't as bad as that. We own the house,

and Granny and Uncle Matthew help. But we've got to be careful. Just like everyone else."

"People don't look as though they were being careful," Edward said, gazing on the splendours of Bond Street.

Fanny almost pressed her nose against the shop-window panes. She could never tell which shop she preferred. They had taken a bus up Regent Street, walked along Oxford Street and started down Bond Street from the Oxford Street end. Here, on the left, one glory succeeded another. At Walpole's the linen was enchanting. Then there was the picture shop with the queer, modern pictures which Romney would appreciate. They were altogether beyond Fanny. Today there were two pictures—one of a naked lady whose skin was as scarlet (she was holding, for no especial reason, an orange in her left hand), and another was of a fishing village running violently down a steep place into the sea.

"Why's she holding an orange?" Edward asked.

"I don't know, darling," said Fanny. "Perhaps she's on a diet like Cyprian."

Then they came to the bookshop whose window was filled with books from "the late Mr. Arnold Bennett's library." Among these was a copy of Malory, priced only five shillings, and when Fanny saw it she determined to buy it for Edward. She purchased it and, when they came out again, gave it to her son.

"You must take care of it, Edward, darling. It's very exciting to read. All about King Arthur's Round Table."

"Have you read it?" Edward asked.

"No, as a matter of fact I haven't, but then I'm terribly uneducated. I don't want you to be like me. But you must keep it always because it belonged to Arnold Bennett."

"Who was he?" Edward asked.

"A very great writer, darling."

Then they came to the dog shop, about whose delights there clustered a small group of amused people. On the upper shelf in the window sat a proud Pekinese who was pretending that he knew nothing at all about a fox-terrier puppy in the lower shelf, wildly barking, frantically excited.

Edward was hard to draw away from this window.

"I'd like that puppy," he said wistfully. "If I saved my money, Mother, and you sold this book, don't you think——?"

"We'll see," said Fanny impulsively. "I'd love to have it. I daresay we could manage——" Then she pulled herself up. Charles would never allow a puppy. She threw the dog a longing glance and lured Edward away. . . .

They passed the dignified portals of Colnaghi, the shop with the leather bags, the shop with old silver (always in its window were silver knives, tied together in bunches, silver knives with bright green handles) and then a window—well, Fanny simply stayed, rooted to the ground, gazing. One dress only was displayed, alone in its glory, a dress of silver gauze. What was there about it? Why was it so lovely? And did she not know that she would be absurd in it, far too old, far too tall? It was a dress for a young girl, for Nell perhaps. And at that thought she longed—longed so passionately that it hurt her heart in her breast—that she might buy it for Nell. Absurd, of course—it would cost pounds and pounds—pounds and pounds. . . . Only last night Charles had warned her against extravagance, and she had said: "Isn't it about time Nicholas got a job?" and he had said: "Why, Fanny, you don't grudge Nicholas . . ." Yes, she was beginning to grudge Nicholas, and she wanted that dress for Nell so terribly that she could understand exactly why a hungry man broke the glass of a baker's window and the magistrate said: "What are things coming to when a man deliberately . . ."

"Don't you think," said Edward's voice in her ear, "that if I asked Father to give me my next birthday present *now*—after all, it's in six weeks anyway—and he mightn't mind a dog if I looked after it myself . . ."

Nell had been so sweet lately. She hadn't had a new dress for ages. And Fanny *did* grudge Nicholas. There he had been in the house ever since April, staying at home even in August when Charles and Fanny and the children had gone to Cornwall, and it had been very strange, coming back last week, to be received by Nicholas exactly as though he owned the house. Of course she loved him and he was her brother, but the house wasn't as it had been before he came. Nothing was the same. And who was that strange, foreign brown man she had seen coming down the stairs yesterday, humming to himself? One of Nicholas's friends, but he didn't look at all trustworthy . . . and after all, was Nicholas himself quite trustworthy, for he had never repaid Charles's fifty pounds and had taken that old picture of the fishing fleet from the drawing room and hung it near his bed? She sighed. No, she must not buy the dress. She turned away.

"Come along, dear, it's time we went home. Tea time."

And then, as she turned, she was happy again. The skies were grey, the afternoon was darkening, but the more because of that Bond Street shone with splendour. In spite of the traffic it was very quiet. And yet it should be quieter. It should be the one street where there *was* no traffic and, in the lighted splendour of the evening or on a hot morning of a summer day, you would hear nothing but the footsteps of men and women, passing, loitering, smiling, bowing to friends. Behind walls of glass were presented the treasury of the earth, gorgeous books in morocco, pictures, crimson and blue and green, Tang horses of rose, Chinese plates of crystal, cases of rich leather, silver knives with green handles, ropes of pearls and collars of diamonds, carnation and rose and lily, and queen of them all, the dress of silver gauze waiting for Nell who, alas, would have to wear that same white silk with the rosebuds, of which, as Fanny knew, she was most patiently weary.

"What would you buy, Edward," Fanny said as they walked away, "if someone told you to make your choice?"

"I'd buy a puppy," said Edward.

"And after that?"

"Well, I do want a box of tools," said Edward, who saw that this was an opportunity. "Father said he would give me some of his old ones, but he likes them all too much."

"I'm sure I don't know who *does* buy all these things," Fanny said. "Everyone says they haven't a penny any more."

They stopped again to look in at Asprey's window and gazed at Noel Coward in a silver frame.

"There must be *some* rich people left," Fanny said.

Then, to give Edward a treat, she engaged a taxi to take them home. This was an extravagance, but Edward's pleasure was a delight. She sat with her arm around him and thought of all the things she would do when Charles's investments went up again. She had had a very happy afternoon.

"Gosh!" Edward said, "I would like to have that puppy!"

Then she received the worst shock of her life—yes,

really the worst. Nothing so bad as this since she was born. . . .

She had rung the bell for tea and was standing there wondering where the others could be when Janet appeared.

"Why, Janet——!" Fanny said. She knew at once that something was wrong and she knew, at the same time, that after Charles and the children she loved this tall bony woman in the grey print dress more than anyone else in the world.

"What's the matter, Janet?"

"May I speak to you a moment alone, mum?"

"Why, of course. Come up to my bedroom. I want to take my hat off."

As she led the way she wondered *what* the matter could be. Things had not been right downstairs for a long time. Ever since the night of the dinner when Fanny had been rude to Mary Pontifex, Mrs. Baldwin had been reserved, "brooding," as Fanny put it. She hadn't liked it when Fanny spoke to her. But then what was Fanny to do—the soup cold and salt instead of sugar in the pudding? But all that Mrs. Baldwin, with a shrug of her huge shoulders and a twist of her moustached upper lip, had found to say was:

"Things in the house aren't what they was."

No, they were not, and as Fanny pushed back her bedroom door, looked round smiling and saying, "Come in, Janet," she sighed. Even Cornwall had not been as easy as usual.

She went to her dressing table, took off her hat and turned around. "Now, Janet, what's the trouble?"

Janet stood, her hands folded in front of her, as rigid as a lamppost.

"Sit down. We can talk more easily."

"No, mum, I'd rather stand. It's this——" She swallowed in her throat. "I'm thinking of retiring."

"You're—what?"

"Of retiring. I've got a little house in Hampstead—in the Garden Suburb. My brother—the one that had the jeweller's in Camberwell and was a bachelor—he left it me when he died. It's been let all this time, but I've got my savings, and there's my sister Angela's girl would be willing and glad to come and live with me."

She stopped. She could not say another word. The two women stared at one another.

"But, Janet," Fanny said at last, "you're the greatest friend I have in the world."

"And I'm sure you're mine." All pretense of official relationship was dropped. "I never thought that we would be parted, not until death came and separated us. But there it is—I think it would be best for me to be going."

Fanny pressed her hand on the dressing table that she might steady herself. She thought—"Now don't lose your head over this. Janet doesn't mean it. She's only got a complaint of some kind. I must find out what the complaint is." So she said, looking straight into Janet's eyes—eyes of perfect loyalty and faithfulness:

"Now, Janet, don't talk nonsense. You know we couldn't bear to be separated, either of us. Now what's the matter? What's been troubling you?"

Janet closed her lips—and when she closed her lips, as Fanny well knew, she closed them. She became as obstinate as Balaam's ass and, in her own view, for excellent divine reasons.

"Nothing's been troubling me—at least nothing I would trouble anyone with."

"Ah, then something has. Is Mrs. Baldwin upset about something?"

"She's often grumbling. She's made that way. I pay no attention to her grumbling. Never have."

"Then, Janet, what *is* it?"

"Nothing that you can cure. I'm not so young as I was, and a home of my own would be a change, like."

"Nonsense, Janet. You'd be bored in a week."

"Maybe I would. Maybe I wouldn't."

Fanny wanted to shake her. And she wanted to kiss her.

"Janet—you owe me something. And I owe you almost everything. Let's be honest. We love one another. We have seen one another through trouble. Life isn't going to be easier as we get older. The children will be grown up soon and I shall need you more than ever. Are you going to desert me?"

"No, I'm not." Janet's slim face puckered almost as though she were going to cry. Her upper lip trembled.

"Tell me what it is."

"No, I can't."

Fanny put out her hand and took Janet's.

"Let me tell you this. I haven't been happy either this summer. I need you beside me more than ever before——"

"Well, then, don't you see——" Janet broke out. Then stopped.

She pulled herself together, smoothing her dress with a hand that trembled.

"I'll stop for the present," she said.

She gave Fanny's hand a pressure and walked from the room.

2

Nell was in love with a married poet. His name was Hector Collins. She was not sure that she was in love until she looked back upon him from the crowded bathing beaches (once silent and mysterious moon-shadowed coves) of Cornwall. Then she knew that she loved him and wanted always to be with him that she might cook his food better than Lottie, his wife, cooked it, that she might earn money for him, that she might give him peace that he might write his epic, "The Wilderness."

Hector was ten years older than Nell, but he looked younger. He was thirty years of age, and you would suppose that he was in his first year at some university. When he and Nell were together they appeared to be brother and sister, for they were both very fair, very, very youthful, innocent, and helpless in appearance. Lottie Collins, Hector's wife, stood over them like a beautiful protecting goddess, for Lottie was both the loveliest and the stupidest woman Nell had ever known or was ever likely to know.

On the occasion when Nell had first met Hector (it was at a grapefruit party—at that time a *new* idea for a party, now a *very* old one), Nell had said, "Who is that lovely woman?" and Hector had answered, "That's my wife, and she's not a woman, she's an imbecile."

Nell had asked him whether he should talk about his wife like that and had said that no woman *so* lovely could be an imbecile.

"Oh, but that's nonsense," said Hector. "Don't you remember the girl in Trollope's novel who marries Planty Pal? Don't you read Trollope? Well, I assure you Lottie couldn't be stupider. She's stupid enough to tell everyone she *is* stupid—as though they don't at once find it out for themselves. But you'll soon see."

Nell soon did. It was quite true. Lottie was incredible. But how lovely she was! She was of the type that wins those International Beauty Prizes—"Miss England,

19— '—and then a little later writes articles saying how simple it is and that one lather with warm brown mud ("and be sure not to remove it until the morning") before retiring at night . . . Lottie was just like that: dark brown hair in wonderful waves and then a cluster of curls above the nape ("only five minutes at night. Each curl must be separately treated of course . . ."), a marvellous figure with bust and hips of precisely the right measurement, lovely hands and feet. . . . Oh, yes, and it was true that she did almost nothing to have it just so. She ate what she liked and slept when she wanted to and, beyond plucking her eyebrows, took no especial steps. . . . She was too stupid to be proud of her beauty. She didn't care whether she were beautiful or no. She didn't want to attract men. What she liked was marshmallows, plenty of sleep, and the pictures. She *adored* the pictures! She could go, she declared, every afternoon and evening of the year and never tire. But the odd thing was that even at the pictures she slept as often as not, slept with her fingers arrested in the search for a "hard" chocolate in the chocolate box, slept with the smile of an infant on her beautiful features.

Unfortunately she and Hector were dreadfully poor. He had married her, quite frankly, because her beauty had knocked him silly, but why *she* had married him . . . She was really too stupid to know why.

So they lived in a very stuffy and melancholy little flat in a sort of fortress off Sloane Square. A woman came in, two or three times a week, and "did" for them. They went out for their meals. The flat was always in a state of disorder that made Nell's heart ache. The first reason for loving him was that she wanted to make things tidy.

A queer thing about Lottie was that, half asleep as

she always appeared, she resented quite sharply any interference. Her big beautiful brown slumbering eyes suddenly flashed. Oh, yes, and she would say:

"Leave it where it is, Nell darling. We'll see to it later. . . ."

For she adored Nell. She stood over her (she was quite statuesque) and patted her golden head and stroked her cheek and said, in her husky, slumbering voice: "Nell, *darling* . . . how sweet to see you."

Hector did his best to earn. Just now he was a super in a *surréaliste* play at the Rose Theatre. *Surréaliste* plays were almost out of fashion—this was the last there would be—but he manfully did his best as an automaton clerk, one of six sailors in a brothel in Marseilles, an algebraical formula, a sign of the wrath of God, and a saxophonist in a jazz orchestra representing the Seven Deadly Sins. The play would not run long, he told Nell on her return from Cornwall, and then he did not know what he would do.

But he was a real poet. He belonged to the new school, poets like Auden and Day Lewis and Spender, poets no longer hopeless like the generation before them but confident of the future.

A small volume of his poems called *We Climb the Mountain* was published by the Hogarth Press.

His epic, "The Wilderness," however, was the thing. He was not boastful of this—nor unduly proud. He was certainly glad that it would resemble in no way Georgian poetry, but otherwise made no claims for it.

Its theme was that of a London ruined and deserted, a very old theme indeed. No specimen of the human race remained any longer on the planet. He wrote of the creeping invasion of the Wilderness. The wild cats invaded the foyer of the Rose where now he was performing. They clustered about the stall, their fiery eyes blazing at the painted backcloth, tattered and torn, of a bathing beach on the Lido with gay parasols and a purple sea. In the middle of Piccadilly there was a cavity where the road menders had been at work, and here the rain had made a pool; in this pool the moon and stars were reflected, and a dog, furious with hunger, gazed angrily at his own impotent longings. High tall grasses sprang up about Eros, and wild yellow flowers hung above his naked thighs.

Then the Wilderness begins to feel its power. In Streatham and Surbiton and Croydon the jungle grows. Through the windows of the little red houses tendrils creep and seize with tingling appetite the cheap mirrors green with mould, climb about the beds, and choke the fireplaces. From the floors there sprout strange pale fungi, and through the doors and down the passages roots push their way, and young trees grow from the heart of the dining-room table.

His epic was to begin thus. But the true (and, as he felt, utterly individual) theme was then to develop. For to the Wilderness God again returns and, bending down to the jungle, with eyes bright with a new hope, surveys the scene.

"I will make another attempt," He says, and once again creates. But this time not Man. That has been too tiresome a failure.

This time He will make a new creation, part man, part bird, of the essence of light, light changing into light, form into form, for it is because of his Individuality that Man has failed. Now there will only be agents of the Divine Will making a small fragment of Heaven out of the Wilderness. . . .

"I *must* go to the Regal tonight," Lottie would say. "It's Clark Gable in *Love in Peril*—too divine."

And again, later, across seas and continents, would come the husky, slumbering voice: "It's Clark Gable, darling!"

Hector was, in spite of his apparent sophistication, still a child, as were most of his companions. He was a child because he was bewildered by the things that life did to him. He had not reached the maturity of realizing that there was something in life more important than his personal fate.

He could not, for instance, understand why he had married Lottie, or why, intelligent as he was, he failed to make more money, or why men like Temple and Forsyte succeeded as writers and he did not. He was a better artist than they, but they, in spite of the condemnation of them by all his circle, were not so truly bad that he could comfortably despise them. His father was a clergyman in Northumberland and lived there with Hector's mother in a happiness and tranquillity that seemed to Hector quite incredible. "Don't they *know* what's happening to the world?" he would say. He realized, however, that they possessed something that he had not. It could not be *only* their religion. It could not be *only* their love for one another.

It was on the afternoon following Nell's return from Cornwall that they spoke to one another honestly for the first time, in the untidy little room, Nell sitting on the sofa, Hector standing by the window.

"Lottie will be in any minute."

"I mustn't stay," Nell said. "I only looked in to see how you were. Why didn't you write?"

"I don't write letters," he said, "unless it's *absolutely* necessary."

She leaned over the arm of the sofa, looking at him. She herself recognized that they might be brother and sister. She wondered whether it were a vain narcissism in her that she should love him. But she could not tell because she had never loved anyone before.

"That isn't true," she said. "You've written me lovely letters."

"Glad you liked them," he answered, smiling. "Do you know, Nell, how alike we are? I never realized until I saw you what a lively pale gold my eyebrows are, what a fine white forehead I have, and my figure—it's superb!"

"I was thinking the same thing about myself," she said, laughing.

"Well, I'll tell you why I didn't write." He spoke slowly, staring at her. "Because I love you."

"And I love you," Nell said. "I didn't know until I was in Cornwall this time."

They didn't move, but stayed where they were, looking at one another.

"Perhaps it was because I didn't write. It made me seem more valuable."

"No. I was bathing one morning with Edward and I suddenly knew."

"What are we going to do about it?" he asked.

"I don't know. What do people do?"

"They sleep together and get tired of one another. Or they run away and quarrel, or they never see one another again."

"That seems a silly thing to do," said Nell.

"Perhaps they feel that that's the only way to keep their fine emotions."

"I've never been in love before, so I don't know," Nell said.

He came over to the sofa, sat on the edge of it, and put his arms around her. They kissed. This moment was so very much more glorious than any that Nell had ever known that it was as though she died—soon to be born again into another existence.

After a while Hector said:

"We won't make a mess of this, will we—like everyone else?"

He walked about the room, laughing.

"Oh, I'm so happy! . . . I'm so happy!"

Then Lottie came in.

"Hullo, you two!" She came up to Nell and kissed her. "You sweet pet! I'm so glad you're back. Where have you been? Oh, yes, I know, Cornwall. I'm simply dead. Isn't this room in the hell of a mess?" She threw her hat onto the floor and lay down, full length, on the sofa.

"I must be going," Nell said. "I only came in for a minute."

"Oh, don't go," Lottie said. "We'll go out and have tea somewhere."

"No, I must go. Mother's expecting me."

When she was in the Westminster house again she could not believe that everything could be so different. the whole affair—and by "affair" the heavens and the planets and the wind in the deep gullies of Mont Blanc are intended, as well as the cellar where Charles's wine is kept—had rings on its fingers and bells on its toes. She burst into the drawing room expecting to find the dear family (for she loved them all now) and instead saw the room in a kind of rosy smoke as though sunset clouds had descended, and in the middle of this Uncle Nicholas waiting for his tea.

He saw at once how happy she was. "By Jove, she's lovely!" he thought, for Nell was like a vase that changes its colour with the flowers it carries. Her happiness was opaque, shining, and the clearest, truest silver against Nicholas's polished steel. But he had from the day of his arrival liked her best of the family. He liked her youth, her courage, her audacity, and he liked her because *she* didn't altogether like him. "But she will. I'll make her." She and that old cross-grained servant and Matthew were the three now in the house whom he did not control.

When he felt (quite honestly) generous and affectionate, as he did now, he was charming. He was excited, too, because in two hours' time he was off to see Mrs. Agar and Abel. It was happening here as it always happened with him wherever he was. He had only got to *be* there for situations to develop on every side of him. Up they piled, the atmosphere becoming ever more charged—and then one day—bang! What an explosion!

This was what he loved—to be such a failure and yet so powerful. What an ordinary handsome conventional English gentleman and officer he appeared! And yet—*how* he could stir people up!

And this girl had something of the same quality. The only one in the family. He would make something of her, show her a thing or two. She should surrender to him more completely than any of the others. She seemed to surrender to him now because, although she did not like him, she was so happy that she must come close to anyone and everyone.

"Where are they all?" she asked.

"I don't know. I rang for tea. Your mother and

father are out, so there's only the Old Lady and Grace. The Old Lady's got rheumatics in her left leg."

Even through her happiness she realized how completely now he owned the room and everything in it. He stood there, his legs spread, his handsome body perfectly balanced, like a triumphant rooster proclaiming his mastery to the sun.

"Well, *you* look as if you'd had good news," he said, lightly holding out his hand to her, which she for a moment lightly took. Then she moved away and sat down.

"One must be happy sometimes," she answered, "at my age. Why shouldn't I be happy?"

"Oh, you *should* be! Even I'm happy sometimes, a penniless old failure like me."

"Do you really think you're a failure?" she asked. "Or is that a pose?"

"Oh, I never pose. I am the only completely honest man alive in the world today." Looking at her his eyes, little sharp points of light, dancing over her, he proclaimed:

"It makes no difference abroad,
The seasons fit the same,
The mornings blossom into noons,
And split their pods of flame.
Wildflowers kindle in the woods,
The brooks brag all the day;
No blackbird bates his jargoning
For passing Calvary.

"Auto-da-fé and judgement
Are nothing to the bee;
His separation from his rose
To him seems misery.

Today, Nell," he said, "your bee and your rose are one. Keep them together as long as you can."

She knew his habit of quoting poetry and thought it an intolerable affectation, showing off. But now she was not so sure. This was perhaps a step in his purpose like so many other things with him. She was sharp enough to know that he was always, morning, noon, and night, intent on his own purposes.

"Who's that poem by?" she said, looking at him ironically.

"It doesn't matter who it's *by,*" he said. "Poets sting and die. Or should do. *She* did."

The maid came in with the tea. He waited until she had gone, then he said:

"Some young man has told you that he loves you."

"Shall I pour out?" she asked. "Or wait for Aunt Grace?"

"Who ever waited for Aunt Grace?" he said, smiling maliciously. "Save the gentleman in Winchester. She is, I don't doubt, writing a letter to him at this moment." He raised his head and listened almost as though he could hear her writing. "The longer you stay in this house," he said, "the less walls count. In another six months they'll all be made of paper. Now, Nell—who's the young man?"

"Why should there be a young man?"

"Of course there is. I hope he's nice. He's probably married already."

"Yes, he is," she said, to her own complete surprise. She had not dreamed of telling him. But he had invaded her happiness, pushing his way in, gaily, lightly. It was as though he had been there from the beginning. Now that she had told him she was rather glad. There was no other member of the family to whom she could speak, and Uncle Nicholas knew more of the world than anyone else. He could advise her. Leaning forward, her eyes shining, her cheeks flushed, she told him everything.

He was deeply interested and was at once so kind, so wise, so friendly that for the first time she liked and trusted him.

"It mustn't be spoilt," she said. "Don't you see, Uncle Nicholas? It's the finest thing that has ever happened to me or ever will happen. And he can be a *great* poet. He can really. It will make all the difference to his work if I don't let him down."

"Let him down? Of course you won't let him down!"

"Of course I may." She shook her head impatiently. "Don't you see, Uncle Nicholas, what a chance this is? Everyone says how disappointing life is, that marriage is always a failure, that no two people love one another long—and if *we* can make it last they are wrong—everyone's wrong."

"And what of the young man's wife?" Nicholas asked, nibbling a biscuit, looking at it with appreciation, and nibbling again.

"We shall have to tell her, of course."

"Will she like that?"

"Oh, no—I suppose not—I don't know. She's so funny. She doesn't seem to mind about anything, and then quite suddenly if you touch anything of hers she wakes up and is angry."

"Then I shouldn't tell her."

Nell leaned forward, clasping her knees. Nicholas thought that he had never seen anything so lovely, for the flame glow of the fire very delicately caressed her throat and cheeks as though it were sharing her happiness, and her shadowed hair was light gold against light.

"Not tell her?" Nell considered it. "No, no. That would be horrid. Anything secret . . ."

"Are you then going to explain everything to the family?" He sat down, took a small plate of black-and-white china, and helped himself to strawberry jam.

"No—not now at least. It's only just happened. I don't know what we shall do. We mustn't hurt anybody—that's the chief thing. The moment anybody's hurt it's spoilt."

"Very difficult," he said, licking a finger, "when your friend's married——"

"Yes, it will be difficult," she agreed. "But love always is, isn't it?"

"Always."

"Well, then—we are no worse off than anyone else." She smiled. She was radiant. "We are better off. No one can stop us loving one another."

"Aren't you going to eat anything?" he asked.

"No." She looked up at him. "Uncle Nicholas, you won't tell anybody, will you? None of the others? Not just yet?"

As she asked him she was aware that this was the first real secret of her life. She had hoped never to have any. Already, within an hour, honesty was difficult.

"I, my dear? Tell anybody! I'm the most perfect keeper of secrets. I——"

The door opened and Grace came in. He looked up at her, laughing. "I keep secrets wonderfully, don't I, Grace?"

She flushed, looked about her to see who was in the room, then gave him an almost piteous look.

"Why, yes, Nicholas, of course. How should *I* know? Oh, Nell, darling, there you are. No one else in. I meant to have gone out and got that book from the Library, the one about Esquimaux that Charles wanted. I promised him that I would, but I believe I had forty winks and it's not nice out, is it? The sun has gone in and the clouds have been racing along—yes, dear, not too strong. And what have *you* been doing with yourself, darling?"

"Why," Nell wondered, "did she look at Nicholas in that uncomfortable way? I have noticed it before. She seems to be afraid of him." As she helped her aunt she wished that she had not been so impulsive. Half an hour ago there had been a secret between herself and Hector. Now it was shared. She went up to her room to be alone with her happiness.

3

But she would have been surprised had she known how greatly Nicholas had been touched. This emotion was now, at this moment, looking at Grace with cynical kindliness across the teacups, quite real. The world that he intended that very evening to inhabit had little about it to correspond with Nell's freshness and inexperience and youth—"but, by Jove," he thought, "they talk and write so much about the sophistication of the young these days. It's superficial. There's no change a skin down. Nor, perhaps, in any of us."

Before going up to wash he went out for a five minutes' stroll. He wanted to think about things, to see where he was. Mrs. Agar, Abel, old Mme. Litvinoff—he would be with them all very shortly and must take a line. Abel wanted more money. By God, he himself wanted more money! Things were moving—in this house and out of it.

He strolled down the street and stood looking up at

the great black pile of the Abbey above him. In the semi-dark it stood there like a mountain breasting the tide. Hanging, as it seemed, to the corner of one of the towers was a brilliant star, fiery and angry, as though it were indignantly battling for its place against the shreds and patches of ebon cloud that swept about it. A wind was up. The little street where he stood was quiet enough, but he indulged the fancy that the whole town was heaving about him. Standing on a beach at night, the breakers advance and then, under a dark sky with a line of white foam, hang suspended. So now the Abbey seemed to breast an advancing sea, and the murmur of traffic, two streets away, full of rhythm and also with that hesitating break that the waves have, confirmed the illusion. What was he doing to these people with whom for the moment he was living? Why not leave them alone? But, looking up at the star, he shook his head. This was a cracking, crumbling world. Law and order were gone or going. That Abbey there stood for nothing any more save a few sentimental, broken, discredited traditions. He must occupy himself, amuse himself, feel his cleverness. Only that child. He would not hurt her. He would give her some good advice. And then he thought of his own Lizzie. How different human beings were! How unique everyone! Nell and Lizzie! Himself and Matthew! Fanny and Mrs. Agar!

Was there perhaps, after all, something like a soul, something personal and separate? But again he shook his head at the star—and strolled home.

He changed into a dark suit and went to give Abel something to eat at the "Crab-tree" restaurant in Soho. This evening was important. He must come to some decision both about Abel and about Mrs. Agar. He did not like coming to decisions. Again and again in the past he had wandered into some position, and all he asked was to be allowed to stay there quietly. But, because he could not keep his finger out of any pie but must always maliciously stir and probe, positions refused to remain static. And sometimes the new positions were so opposed to one another and so intricate that he had not time to prepare for the crisis. It came, and all that happened was that himself and Lizzie slipped away by the next train, leaving the most horrible mess behind them. The complication in the present position was that he was really happy where he was, and on the whole Lizzie was happy too, although he could never quite tell what Lizzie was feeling. Well, leave it alone then. He had his comfortable room (into which he had now been able to insert from other rooms a few decent pictures, a small Persian rug, a pair of George III silver candlesticks, one or two odds and ends), comfortable meals and the company of his *own* people. (For, after all, was not blood thicker than water? But were they his own people? It seemed incredible.) He was comfortable and safe and living practically for nothing. Well, leave it alone then! Ah! there was the trouble, he could not. He hadn't *asked* to interfere, but how could he help it? How could he sit down quietly and watch their silly sentimental lives and *not* interfere? The things they believed in, the affection they pretended to have for one another! Charles, Grace, Fanny, Matthew! And those two children! They could not, no, they *could* not, step out into the world with only those obsolete old people to advise them!

He was never aware so sharply of the dying, vanishing world that still pervaded that Westminster house as when he moved into the world of the outlaws, his *own* world. For he *was* an outlaw, had been one for many years, and the only difference today from the past was that once he had been the exception and now he was the rule. In this new chaos everyone cheated, robbed, and plundered if it were reasonably possible. Anyone would do *anything* for money. He did not pretend that Abel and Mrs. Agar and John Flagstaffe (how the circle spread once you touched it!) were normal and average people. There were millions of law-abiding normal citizens still doing their best to exist honestly in this present topsy-turvy world. But they were finding it with every day more difficult, and with every day the Agars and Abels and Flagstaffes were penetrating further, growing bolder and more daring, showing law and order—the *old* law and the *old* order—to be ever more helpless, more completely unworkable.

Sitting opposite to Abel at a little corner in the Crabtree, he thought to himself: "Thirty, twenty years ago even, they would have put this little rascal into gaol and kept him there." He didn't wish even now to be seen in any very public place with Abel. The little man was wearing a dark blue suit and a dark blue tie. His sleek shiny black hair was neatly brushed and his brown cheeks as smooth as the back of a hairbrush, but he looked the pirate he was. Cheerful, humorous, delighted to be with Nicholas, but a pirate, and a dangerous one.

The Crab-tree was a dark stuffy little pothouse, but most convenient for dinners such as this. On the walls were pictures of pugilists. The food was good and the proprietor, a Greek called Cavafy (a slur on a noble Greek poet), was a tall bony skeleton with a broken nose.

"Well, how are things?" asked Abel, grinning. He couldn't take his eyes off Nicholas. He was always so deeply delighted to be in his company.

"Oh, all right. Look here, Abel, you're not to come into the house again. My sister saw you the other day and thought you looked very queer."

"Very good." Abel leaned his arms on the table. "But tell me—how is it about money? It looks a very wealthy house."

"Well, it isn't. I've told you before. My brother-in-law has only his investments, and they are down like everyone else's."

"Mine are down, too," Abel said. "I haven't a bean."

"That's just," said Nicholas, "what I want to talk about. I told you at the beginning, months ago, that you are only wasting your time here. I shan't have any more money to give you. I'm only just subsisting myself."

"Ah, now, Captain," Abel said, smiling. "You are always telling me those stories. You've been telling me them for years."

"This time they're true," Nicholas answered sharply. "You remember—months ago—when I came here first I told you the same thing."

"We haven't done so badly," Abel said reflectively. "And I like London. So do you. And I've done something for you. I've found Mrs. Agar."

Then into Nicholas's eyes there came a look which Abel knew well. Nicholas ceased to be a gentleman.

"You'd better take care," he said. "You've followed me and blackmailed me and annoyed me ever since I left Jamaica. I'm lazy. I let things run on. But now I'm with my own people. Having none yourself, you don't know what that means. What it means is that things are different from the past."

He paused, drank his wine, wiped his lips, then went on:

"What it means is that you shall have a hundred

pounds in the next three days, you will leave England—go to hell if you like—and never speak or write to me again. If you bother me, I put the police on your track. They'll be glad to hear of you in Paris or in Marseilles or Genoa. Almost anywhere. Even here in London perhaps."

Abel drank his wine, smacked his lips appreciatively.

"That's good wine," he said. He filled his glass and raised it. "I drink your health, Captain." He drank his wine again. "Now why all this unkindness? I've treated you well this summer. I've had very little money from you. I've looked after your interests. Sure, I'm glad you're happy to be home. But it won't last for ever. You know it won't, Captain. You'll be moving on and then you'll need me again. I'm your friend. I worship the ground you tread on. I admire you to death, and that's a compliment because I know everything about you, and admire you all the more. Why should we part? And as to this police business, you know that's nonsense. Think I'd give away your secrets, Captain? Why, no—not to save my own skin. But in a police court, under pressure, things come out by accident. They're devils for catching you. We're too old friends to part, and that's the truth."

Nicholas's gaze softened.

"You play your game cleverly, don't you, Abel? I admire you for it. You're one of those men with only one purpose in life—not like my dear relations, clogged up with sentiment—never knowing what they want. All the same it's true—this time. I've settled down. I don't want you round any more. You can try all your tricks, blackmail me as you like, but you get no more out of me. I'm settling down. You don't belong in this world where I am now."

Their meal was finished. Abel peeled a dry wizened

little apple, set his teeth into it, and waved his hand in the air.

"We'll leave it, Captain," he said. "I quite understand what you're feeling. I shan't be in your way. Just a pound or two to keep me alive, and in return you haven't a friend like me—not one anywhere who'd do for you what I'd do for you."

"No, I believe you. You'd cut my throat for twopence." His lazy indifference, so strangely mixed in him with his passion for interference, crept about him. "I mean it, though. You'll soon see that I do. Our ways are parting."

"Yes. Very good," said Abel, smiling. "But not to-night. We go and see Mrs. Agar—yes?"

Mrs. Agar lived with the old Russian, Mme. Litvinoff, in an apartment in Clarges Street, next door to a restaurant.

Her rooms were very charming, quiet and in the best of taste. Over the mantelpiece was a very warm ruddy flowerpiece by Matthew Smith. There was a piano (for she played admirably), two or three excellent pieces of old furniture, and a fine Persian rug of dark purple with a border of small orange flowers.

She herself was as quiet a woman as you ever would find, a tall figure, dark brown hair, a pale, kindly, and rather gentle face. She had blackmailed a number of people in her time, including a famous cabinet minister, an admiral, and a very rich Lancashire manufacturer. She was responsible for at least three suicides and had broken up a number of very happy homes. She had never herself been in any trouble, enjoyed life to the full, felt affection for all the world, and never said unkind things about anyone.

When Nicholas and Abel came in there were also present Mme. Litvinoff and a fat, cheery, jolly-looking man called John Flagstaffe. Mme. Litvinoff looked like an old, wizened, wrinkled monkey. She was beautifully dressed and wore a necklace of small fine pearls round her skinny throat. She smoked cigarettes incessantly from a long amber holder. She had a sharp cracked voice and spoke with a foreign accent. Flagstaffe, who was as good a confidence trickster, blackmailer, card-sharper, and pimp as there was in London, beamed good nature. He had once "done time," but it was a long while ago, and he had, with the greatest friendliness in the world, forgiven everyone concerned in the affair.

Nicholas detested him. He didn't like old Litvinoff, either. In fact this company was altogether too low for him and he despised himself for being there. Mrs. Agar, however, attracted him more powerfully than any other woman he had met since Dora Lenning two years ago in Rome. Women were, of course, his great weakness. He knew it well and was quite philosophical about it. It annoyed him, however, that at his age and with all his experience he should once again feel this temptation to submission. What he hoped was that a little intimacy with Mrs. Agar would cure him.

There had been no sign as yet that Mrs. Agar (whose Christian name was Beatrice) wished to be his friend. And he felt instinctively that she despised him for his companionship with a rat like Abel.

Tonight, however, everyone was very friendly. Flagstaffe had a passion for music and especially for Mozart. He was talking about him now. He lay back in his chair, his fat round thighs stretched against the blue stuff of his trousers, his cheery face lost in a tender happy smile.

"Oh, yes, there's nothing like the G minor Quintet. That's the best of the whole lot. The loveliest piece of music in the whole world. You know—with the two violas. Tum-te-tum-te-tum-te-tum." He beat on nis stomach with his fingers. "The fourth movement—the Adagio—my God! that's the most tragic thing that ever was. And then the Allegro at the end—sheer happiness. And he was only thirty-one when he composed it! Marvellous! To know so much about life. Or the songs—the 'Abendempfindung.' Go on, Beatrice. . . . Just play the theme—you know—tum-te-tum-te-tum . . ."

Mrs. Agar smiled. "What a bully you are, Johnny! All right. But only for a minute."

She sat down at the piano and played the "Abendempfindung," humming softly, and the "An Chloë," then slipping into the last movement of the G minor Quintet. . . . Then she rose abruptly, shutting gently the lid of the piano.

"That's enough," she said. "Now take Tatiana away, Johnny. It's quite time you went."

"I'm pair-fectly ready," Mme. Litvinoff said, rising.

Flagstaffe dragged himself out of his chair and stood, his big bulk slightly swaying, humming to himself the "Chloë."

"What are you off to?" Nicholas asked, looking up at him, thinking what an ox of a creature he was, seeing him bend forward very slightly and take the throat of a man kneeling on the carpet in front of him and slowly, slowly squeeze it. What man? Oh, any man.

"Never mind," Flagstaffe said, laughing. "We're off to amuse ourselves. We leave you to do the same."

When they were gone and the three who remained had talked a little while longer, Nicholas said to Abel:

"Don't forget, my friend, you have also *your* engagement. It's quarter to ten. You'll be late."

Abel had no engagement, except to be near his admired Nicholas. For a moment Nicholas thought that he would disobey. His forehead was quite suddenly covered with little wrinkles as a pool is fretted by a breeze. Nicholas had often seen this before, and it was impossible to explain to himself why it was so obscenely unpleasant. It meant that Abel's temper was disturbed. He did indeed hesitate—but then, without another word, with only a nod of good-night, departed.

So they were alone, sitting in front of the fire. Mrs. Agar produced a work basket and a round frame upon which she was working a gaily coloured tapestry of birds and flowers.

"I envy you that," Nicholas said. "How silly that it should be thought effeminate for men to do needlework."

"Is it?" she asked. "Quite a lot of men do."

"Oh, yes, I suppose so. I had forgotten that the sexes are changing."

"Are they?" She looked at him with her large, quiet, beautiful eyes. "Captain Coventry—why do you have that awful little man around with you?"

He crossed his legs. "Abel? Is he so awful? Ah, he's mixed up with my past."

"Yes, but one gets rid of one's past when it's as unpleasant as that."

"He's difficult to get rid of," Nicholas said quietly. Then, his hand lying over the edge of the chair until it almost touched her knee, he said: "You know—I think Flagstaffe is quite as nasty as Abel—nastier. Abel would cut your throat for a shilling, but until he did so he would be loyal. He's seen me through a good many nasty places. But Flagstaffe is, I should imagine, loyal to nobody."

"Oh, John!" She bit off a piece of bright blue thread. "I know how to manage *John*. His faults, habits, weaknesses—whatever you like to call them—are so simple.

Once you know them you know *him*. But *your* friend—you could never be sure of him. He's another species. He's one of the very few men I've ever been afraid of." Then she laughed. "But don't let's waste this pleasant hour. Do you know, you interest me very much, Captain Coventry?"

"I'm honoured," he said, making a little mock bow. His fingers touched the stuff of her dress.

"No, I mean it. May I be frank?"

"Please."

"Well, then—you look so conventionally English. You are living, you told me the other day, with your sister and her family, who are, you say, most conventional. You like living there. And yet—there is Abel and, I should imagine, a most unconventional past."

"*Is* there anything strange about it? I can tell you at once. It's the contrast that I enjoy. The two worlds, one threatening the other. I like to see what is going on in both—to see one being invaded by the other. Just as Flagstaffe enjoys Mozart and has gone off this evening to—what has he gone to do?"

"I don't know," she said. "I never ask questions. Yes, I see. That's interesting. And your sister and her family—do they realize what is happening?"

"Who knows *what* they realize! It's their complacency, I suppose, that stirs me up. I like to disturb it."

She moved away from him a little, bending over her tapestry.

"In what way are they complacent?" she asked.

"No. That's the wrong word. They're not complacent, they're blind. They can't see that all the things they believe in are no longer there."

"What, for instance?" she asked.

"Oh, patriotism, the family, religion."

"I wonder whether they *are* gone. The Russians, the Italians, the Germans—they're patriotic enough. Sometimes it seems to me that just now it's only the English who are not. The family? Yes, people are more restless, certainly. And religion? Many people are still very religious."

He moved his legs. "Oh, I don't know. Let's say they still believe in goodness, that there's a God who watches over them, that the best man wins——"

"Well, doesn't he?" She turned round. "You know, Captain Coventry, I sometimes wonder——" She broke off. The door opened. A maidservant stood there. "Well, Annie, what is it?"

Nicholas turned and saw that the maid, a young pale-faced girl, was frightened. His consciousness of that fright, the sharp hardness in Mrs. Agar's voice, had changed the atmosphere of the room.

The girl murmured something. He could not catch the words, but Mrs. Agar got up.

"Excuse me a moment," she said.

After she had gone he caught himself listening for a cry. In that brief "Well, what is it?" he had realized another Mrs. Agar. He was suddenly sorry for the famous cabinet minister.

He stood in front of the fire waiting for her return almost as though he were on his guard—for, certainly, these people were dangerous.

4

It happened that on this same afternoon Charles Carlisle had returned home about six. He went up to see his mother, who was kept to her room by her rheumatism. The old lady was in no very good temper. Her left leg jagged her with pain as though it had a personal grievance against her. It had quite suddenly occurred to her that afternoon that she might, sooner or later, have to die. So fine had her physical health always been, and so easily had she obtained her wishes and satisfied her needs, that she had never actively considered herself as mortal. Of course one day she *would* go—everyone did—but not until she was ready and had informed Death that, tired of the present set of circumstances, he might now, with her gracious permission, carry her off to another.

Then, reading the memoirs of Madame Roland and revelling in the Abbaye and the tumbrils, quite without warning, a voice seemed to shout from somewhere: "Off with her head!" The pain in her leg leapt at her and gave her a terrible twisting. The book dropped to the floor, and she found that she was very near to tears. Death! It was absurd! To be *nothing!*—the seasons proceeding with their indifferent punctuality, motorcars crowding the streets, people shopping, feeding, drinking, sleeping, herself forgotten, the very furniture of this house outlasting her!

She was a strong-minded old lady, and it did not take her long to summon her resources and put Death where he belonged—but, after this moment, her security was gone. . . .

She had always regarded herself as important. It mattered to the world in general that she should be there. Now she saw clearly that it did not matter in the least; it did not even matter to her immediate family. They would go on perfectly without her. She badly wanted company and so was very glad indeed when she saw her son come in.

"How are you, Mother?" he asked her, sitting down beside her.

"Very well indeed, thank you, Charles."

"Is your leg troubling you?"

"Not in the least." (Aren't I? said her leg, and shot her a severe twist.) Her face trembled in spite of herself, and Charles saw it, but of course gave no sign.

"What have *you* been doing?" she asked.

"I've been having a talk with Bentley." Bentley was a stockbroker. "Things are bad and don't look like getting any better. If only the Americans would hurry on with their beastly election——"

"Oh, the Americans!" She spoke as though they were a savage tribe in Central Africa. She had no use at all for the Americans, knowing—like most of her compatriots—nothing at all about America. "I've no patience with the Americans," she said.

"Whether we've got any patience with them or not, we're all in the same boat. We depend on them and they depend on us."

"I don't know what's coming to the world," she said restlessly. "Or this house either."

"Why, what's the matter with the house?" he asked, laughing.

"That's the worst of you, Charles. You go about with your eyes shut. Why don't you say something to Fanny?"

"Why—what's the matter with Fanny?"

"I'm sure her temper's very queer. She was very short with me yesterday. Very short indeed. She takes advantage of my leg being bad."

"I'm sure she doesn't," Charles said indignantly. "Fanny's all right."

"*Is* she?" The old lady tossed her head. "Everyone's

been noticing how queer her temper is. Why, you yourself said after that evening when she was so rude to Mary Pontifex——"

"Oh, that's ages ago. And Mary deserved what she got."

She laid her hand on his arm.

"I know what I'm talking about. I'm not a fool. Nicholas came in to see me last evening——"

"Oh, yes, and what's Nicholas been saying?" he asked sharply.

She grinned, tapping her dress with her old dry fingers.

"I like Nicholas. He amuses me. He's got no conscience, no conscience at all, and his little Lizzie knows the most dreadful things. I wonder Fanny trusts Edward with her——"

"Yes, but what's Nicholas been saying to you?" Charles asked, frowning.

Old Mrs. Carlisle adored her son, worshipped him, thought he could do no wrong. But if she had a *little* criticism of him it was that he was too cheerful and complacent. He just went along with his wood-carving and his walks and his worship of Fanny as though everything were eternally for the best. So she was pleased now when she saw that she had disturbed him.

"How can I remember what Nicholas said? He's always making a joke about something."

"No, but about Fanny? What did he say about Fanny?"

"Oh, nothing particular. But his two sisters seem very quaint to him, I'm sure. Remember, he's known them longer than we have, Charles. I've always said that Fanny and Grace and Matthew have got a lot in common —a family similarity. As though when they were children they did nothing but read the Bible and learn Collects.

Now don't be angry, Charles. You know that I'm very fond of Fanny, although I don't think she's good enough for you. I never did."

"She's too good for me," said Charles. "The longer I live with her the more I marvel at her goodness, her kindness——"

"Oh, yes, we know all about that," his mother interrupted sharply. "You're something of a simpleton too, Charles, not to have discovered after all these years that no woman likes another woman to be praised to her face, not even an old woman like me. However, what I wanted to say is that Nicholas knows something about Grace that amuses him very much. I tried to get it out of him, but he said it was a secret. He knows something about Nell, too."

"Nell?" Charles cried. "What can he possibly know about Nell?"

"I've no idea, but you can take my word that Nicholas and that Lizzie know things about all of us. Fanny didn't realize what she was doing when she brought *him* into the house."

"Fanny didn't bring him in," Charles retorted. "He brought himself in."

"Oh, well, however it was," the old lady said, smoothing her dress.

"Anyway, if he's saying things about Fanny he'd better go."

"*I* never said he was saying anything about Fanny."

"Oh, yes, you did, Mother. If anyone bothers Fanny, out they go."

"Dear Fanny!" murmured Mrs. Carlisle.

"She hasn't been quite so well lately," Charles went on, almost to himself. "I don't know why. She wants to economize, and it isn't easy in a house like this."

Then she saw that he was really disturbed, her dear Charles, her adored Charles. She loved his thinning hair and his eyes wrinkled with kindness and his broad straight back and his rosy cheeks. Everything about him she loved as though she were bathing him in a small round bath in front of the fire, a thing that she had done, it seemed to her, only yesterday.

So she kissed him and held his strong firm hand in her own hot thin one, forgetting her leg and the thought of imminent death.

After leaving her, in the lower hall Charles met Romney. He saw that he had his hat and coat.

"Hullo, going out?"

"Yes, Father, I'm dining with a man."

They stood there smiling. They were very fond of one another. Charles thought his son a good-looking young man with a wonderful knowledge of pictures and a warm heart. Romney loved his father very much more deeply than he knew.

"Sold anything today?" Charles asked him.

"No. Things are getting difficult. No one's got any money for expensive pictures. We're going to have a show soon of young painters and everything's going to be very cheap."

Charles saw that he was impatient to be gone.

"Well, enjoy yourself. Going to the theatre?"

"Oh, no. Just having dinner."

"Good-night, then."

"Good-night, Father."

Harry Rait, with whom Romney was dining, had rooms in St. James's Street, very nice rooms above Rumpelmayer's. This engagement had been fixed a week ago, and ever since it had been made Romney had been expecting to hear Rait's voice on the telephone, saying:

"Most awfully sorry, old man, but I quite forgot that I had promised . . ."

But this time it had not occurred. Romney had himself rung Rait up that morning to remind him, and Rait had answered: "Why, of course, old man. Everything's prepared—sumptuous meats, gorgeous wines——"

Romney cut him short with:

"We won't go out anywhere, will we? I want to talk."

"Right-oh," Rait had answered.

But Romney had fancied that there had been an echo of disappointment in the air. Harry liked to go to a musical show or a boxing match.

"I'm not great at talking," he said. And it was true.

However, tonight there Harry Rait was fixed into his own room, no escape possible. Romney *wanted* to talk to him. He wanted to explain, if he could without making a fool of himself, why it was that Harry meant so much to him. He wanted to explain it to himself and so rid himself of some of the uncertainties and fears and perplexities that had worried him so deeply during these last months.

Over and over again he had thought to himself of what he would say to Rait, of the way in which he would overcome his own shyness so that he could break down the barrier that existed between them. For there *was* a barrier. It came partly from Rait's own dislike to speak of his feelings and partly from Romney's sensitiveness. For Romney was so easily repulsed. In his heart he felt that no one could really like him and that his loneliness was a just thing, only what he truly deserved. And yet if someone *did* care for him, how much that affection would do for him! It would destroy his self-distrust. With Harry behind him, believing in him, he could, he thought, do almost anything! If he showed Harry that it might be that Harry, reticent though he was, would give some sign of his own affection for him. A very little sign would be enough.

But he must be careful. Harry hated scenes or any emotional display. Romney had no intention of being emotional. Very calm and matter-of-fact he intended to be. Crossing the Park, he saw the clouds flying along like yachts in a race. Or, rather, like herons, he thought, and one cloud had so long and eager a neck that it must surely soon break. And it did so. Just as it broke, the pale evening sky of the colour of watered milk seemed to quiver above the Park trees as though it hoped that it would blaze with a miraculous sunset. There was no blaze, and the wind-darkening expanse swept the grass, the little chairs, the stubborn trees, the loiterers, into a world where life must now, for many an hour, be secret.

As Romney passed St. James's Palace he decided to change his life. He must become somebody. Why live otherwise? He raised his head. St. James's Street ran uphill in front of him as though it would lure him into the delights of Piccadilly—"We are sober here. Tobacco, boots and shoes, clubs. Dull things for a young man in these times." The lamps threw into relief the silver-grey of the Palace walls, shabby a little perhaps, smelling of spiritual smoke, echoing (but very faintly now) the thunder of history.

"I'll change my life," Romney thought. "If Harry believes in me and cares what happens to me," someone added.

It was plain enough that Harry saw no reason, in earth or in heaven, for contemplating, in *his* personal instance, any change. Everything in his rooms, even to the round brown shining jar of tobacco, was rooted to the soil. There were no mental microbes here, but an exceedingly healthy mind, and Romney knew at once that this was what he needed, these solid leather armchairs, this row of pipes, each pipe in its little hole, these coloured prints on a brown-papered wall of riders leaping hedges, rosy-faced men in ditches, and hounds streaming across a field, this fireplace with white and brown tiles, this piano that quite obviously was never opened unless songs from the Harrow songbook were to be played on it!

Harry himself! Yes, this was what Romney wanted for friendship; here was someone whom Romney could admire, a man made out of the bulwarks of England, square and set, ruddy with country walks and golf played as the priests once served the Oracle—no doubts, no awful moments, no mystical sloppiness, no Freudian dreams, no denial of man but no affirmation of him either—here was the friend that Romney needed. All through dinner, which was plain and good (but the wine was rather ordinary although Romney drank a good deal of it), Harry was as kind as kind could be.

There was always, when he was with Romney, a slight suggestion of humouring the convalescent, as though Romney had but recently come out of hospital, was well on the road to recovery; sea air (if he could only be persuaded to take it) would put him right. This was a quite genuine kindness in Rait. He regarded artists of every kind as a physical culturist regards invalids. When he met an author (and this wasn't often) he would say, in the friendliest fashion, "Writing anything?" and when they replied (as they always did) that they were, he would cry, "Good. That's the stuff to give them!"

So now, in this same manner, he asked Romney over the mutton and roast potatoes how the pictures were getting on, and when Romney said not so awfully well because no one had any money just now, he frowned with kind concern and added: "Of course, old man, they do ask the most dreadful prices for things I wouldn't go into the next room to see. And they do these reproductions damned well nowadays. This modern colour photography has fairly got pictures whacked in my opinion."

Romney loved to hear him. Harry was so honest, so true—no humbug or pose or affectation. Romney had every day so much of the other thing. He watched Harry while he cut the bread. It was like Siegfried forging the sword.

"I hope," he said, "you don't mind our staying in to-night."

"Not a bit, old man. Not a bit. There is some of that all-in wrestling at the Ring that I thought we might have gone to, but they have it every Thursday. No, as a matter of fact, I'm a bit weary if the truth be known. I was at Sunningdale all the afternoon—went round with the Pro. Jolly useful man. How are your people?"

"All right, thanks."

"That's good. Don't you get a bit sick of living at home, though?

"No, I don't think so."

"Well, I should. Not that I'm not fond of my people, you know. I often go down to see them. But it isn't quite like being on your own. Shall we move into the other room?"

Seated in the leather armchair, Romney looked at his friend with apprehension. He had read somewhere that when people come and talk to you about their aspirations you had better, before they leave you, count your silver spoons. He felt that already Harry was counting his spoons.

"Well, now tell me all about yourself," Rait said, sitting down, filling his pipe from the enormous tobacco jar.

"Oh, there's nothing much to say about myself. I'm getting along all right."

"Is that uncle of yours still with you?"

"Oh, yes."

"Bit of a cynic, isn't he?—from what you told me."

"Not a cynic exactly—but he's travelled a lot, and of course we must seem rather old-fashioned in some ways."

"I don't like those cynical chaps," Rait said. "Always downing everything. There was a chap this afternoon—Thatcher he's called—thin hungry-looking sort of bloke. Wanted me to go round with him, but I knew better. He's a holy terror. Thinks Russia grand and all that sort of thing. I said to him the other day, 'They wouldn't let you play golf like this in Moscow.' And he said, 'Their climate's different.' The man's an imbecile."

There was a pause.

Rait said: "All right, old man? Got everything you want? Have a whisky?"

"Not just yet, thanks," Romney said. Then he plunged. "Look here, Harry. I'm glad we haven't gone out to-night. There's something I've been wanting to say for a long time. You don't mind my talking a bit, do you?"

"Of course not." Rait looked at him with the benevolence that was most genuinely part of his nature. He liked to help his friends, and he liked to know that he helped them.

"Anything I can do?" he said. "You're not in a mess with a woman, are you?"

"Lord, no!" Romney laughed. "There's nothing the matter. It's about us—you and me—that I wanted to say something."

He paused. He plunged on.

"You see, we're so very different. I sometimes think that it must be a bore for you having me for a friend."

"Not a bit, old man—of course not," said Rait generously.

"We're so different. All our tastes are different. I think that's why I like you so much."

"That's all right, old chap," said Rait. "We're damned good friends, and I'm glad we are."

"Are you?" said Romney eagerly. "That's what I wanted to know—if you are *really* fond of me. It will make a tremendous difference to me if you are."

Rait bent down and relit his pipe.

"Why, of course I'm fond of you," he said. "We're pals—that's what we are. And when men are pals there's nothing more to be said, is there? What I mean is that if a man's your pal he can be away for years and you never see him or write or anything, and then when you meet again you pick it up just where you left off."

"Yes, that's just what I mean," Romney said quickly. "That doesn't seem to me friendship. Friendship's something that has to live, has to be fed all the time. You've got to know one another better and better, find out one another's faults and like one all the better for them. If you never see your friend or write to him, I don't see that that's friendship."

"Do have a whisky, old man," Rait said. "Help yourself."

"Yes, I think I will," Romney said.

He got up and knew that his legs were trembling. His impulse was to say good-night and go. He was making a terrible mess of this. He would write a letter instead. But he helped himself to a strong whisky, drank it while he was standing there. Then he poured himself out another. Now he felt better. He knew what he wanted to say. He pulled his chair nearer to Rait's and sat down.

"I've been wanting to say this for ages, Harry. You've no idea what you mean to me. Of course I love my father and mother and sister, but outside them you're the only person in the world I care for. I know that it's bad form for Englishmen to show their feelings. I'm shy as anything myself. But sometimes one *has* to speak out when it's so terribly important. Well, you are terribly important to me. I'm pretty lonely really. I don't make friends easily. I pretend to have lots of confidence, but that isn't real. If you believe in me and are fond of me I could do almost anything—or that's what I feel. You're strong in all the ways I'm not. You could help me a most awful lot. Don't be angry with me for talking like this. I think of you so much when you're not there. There's nothing in the world I wouldn't do for you if you'd let me. I promise not to bother you with this sort of talk again, but I had to know how you feel. I couldn't go on without knowing."

There was a silence. Then Rait said:

"What you want, old boy, is a woman. You'd be less lonely then."

"No, no!" Romney cried eagerly. "Don't you see that this isn't sexual? That's why it's so hard to put into words what I mean." He stopped for a moment to make his words simple and direct. "Have you ever heard of a writer called Lawrence?" he asked.

"He chivied the Arabs or something, didn't he?" Rait said.

"No. That's another Lawrence. This one was a novelist and a poet. He died a couple of years ago."

"I don't read novels," Rait said. "I don't seem to have the time."

"Yes—well—that doesn't matter. I only read one,

called *The Plumed Serpent,* and thought it grand. Then I read a life of him by someone and hated him. Then the other day Uncle Nicholas—the one I've told you about—advised me to read *Women in Love.* Well, that's got superb things in it. Of course there's a lot of mad sex stuff in it, but there's one bit about a man riding a horse that's frightened by a passing train. . . . You'd think that first class. I know you would."

"I must read it," Rait said politely. "What do you say it's called?"

. . "*Women in Love.*"

"*Women in Love.* I'll get it from the library. I belong to Harrod's, but I haven't taken a book out for ages."

"In *Women in Love,*" Romney went on eagerly, "there's an extraordinary scene. There are two men in the book who are in love with two women, or rather the women are with them. One of these men, who's really Lawrence himself, is very fond of the other man and he wants to find some relationship with him that goes beyond physical things. He's sure that somewhere there *can* be a relationship between human beings that's perfect, but sex gets in the way of it and spoils it. One evening these men are in a library alone and they strip and wrestle. They wrestle until their bodies are all in. They get *beyond* their bodies. And for a moment they do touch this further relationship."

"My God!" said Rait. "Do you mean they take their clothes off and wrestle in a library?"

"Yes," said Romney. "You see——"

"But why a library? Damned odd place to wrestle in. They must have been batty."

"Oh, never mind the library!" Romney said. "Anywhere would have been the same."

"It wouldn't have been if the police had been around," said Rait.

"Yes, but what I want to say is this—I feel for you the best, the finest things any man can feel for another. I'm sure that we could have a friendship that would reach that state that Lawrence means. I think that all men will reach it one day and that it's the only hope of the world. If we all think nobly of one another——" He stopped. He got up. "Oh, I don't know. Of course you think I'm talking rot."

"Not a bit, old man. Not a bit," Rait said.

Romney came and sat on the broad, shiny shoulder of Rait's chair. He put his arm round his friend.

"I'd die for you if you wanted me to," he said huskily.

Now there was a very long silence indeed. Rait did not move. The clock struck a quarter to ten. The silence grew ever more appalling. Then Romney moved from the chair. He stood looking into the fire.

At last Rait said: "That's all right, old chap. Of course I'm not a sentimental man. I keep that for women." He knocked his pipe against his shoe. After a while he said: "Why don't you join Sunningdale?"

"I'm afraid I hate golf."

"Oh, you shouldn't. It's the grandest game out. When you're bringing your handicap down it gives you something to think about, I can tell you."

There was another long silence. Then Rait said:

"I went to *Casanova* again the other night. That's the third time. Have you been yet?"

"No, I haven't," said Romney.

"Oh, you ought to. The dancing is damned good." Rait mentioned one or two other plays. Then at last Romney, coming away from the fireplace, said:

"Well, it's time I was off." He smiled brightly.

Rait got up and, very slowly, knocked his pipe out against the tiles of the fireplace.

"You haven't minded my talking like this?" asked Romney.

"Why, no, of course not, old man. Say anything you like. He must be a queer writer, that chap. What did you say the book was called?"

"Women in Love."

"Women in Love. Pretty thick some of it, I expect. I must read it."

After another pause Romney moved towards the passage.

"Have another whisky, old man."

"No, thanks," Romney said. He put on his coat. "Thanks for a ripping evening," he said.

"That's all right, old chap. I'll ring up one of these days."

"Right you are. Good-night."

"Good-night. You know your way down?"

"Yes, thanks."

5

I have always felt a very real sympathy with those authors who feel it their duty to say something about the weather. When I say "author" I mean "novelist," for it is a sign of these stupid and exasperating times that every lady over thirty reads six novels rather than one short poem, and this has the odd result that poets today must call their beautiful poems novels in order to have them read at all.

So that it is novelists, or poets disguised as novelists, for whom I feel sympathy when they are compelled to write about the weather. For they will be abused whatever they do, they will be told that they have arranged the weather as a suitable garment for the emotions of their characters—Egdon Heath itself has been reminded that it is too subservient to the emotions of the reddleman.

For myself, I believe that the creator of human beings is also compelled at one and the same time to create the weather. In *Lear,* who made the storm? Would there have been a story worth telling had there been that night an anti-cyclone stretching from the Azores to the Duke of Gloucester's castle? The gods, whom Lear so constantly evokes, doubtless in a fit of idle peevishness, provided the storm, and the leader of these gods was Shakespeare himself, bringing with him his own very special and splendid lightning and thunder.

No one can deny how deeply, into the very farthest nooks and crannies of our souls, we are influenced by weather—that is, all the sensitive ones among us; and what novelist but deals principally in sensitive souls?

For all this, let the novelist darken his skies and his heroes' spirits at one and the same time and he will be told that he has done it for effect. He has done it, all you nincompoops, because it was so. It is high time that someone spoke out on this business, for we have had years now of this pretense that a man (and a woman also) is arranging and manipulating a series of events and consequences in order to obtain praise, money, the envy of relations, the chance of pillorying a dear friend, the filling in of some intolerably boring hours.

On the contrary, the creator is led by the hand and shown a marvellous congregation of persons, facts, themes, ideas, crimson sunsets, intolerable critics, meals of champagne and oysters, grubbing in the ash bin, the moon obstinately rising, indigestions and cancers, stealing money from a blind man and leaving five thousand pounds to the local hospital, God in His glory and the rabbit quivering in his trap—all this and more, far, far, more he is shown. He may select what he will, and according to the kind of creature that he is, so he will make his selection. Yes, indeed, he will select wrongly, stupidly, blindly, arrogantly, because none of us is perfect, and even Shakespeare could write of Gloucester's eyes with savagery worse than Goneril's.

But the matter is from God—storms and icicles and the cowardly fears in man's heart and his reckless, daring audacity. Let's have done with this pretense, my dear friends and ignorant babblers, that man is the creator. God is the creator and man the blundering, blind selector of the material that God offers to him. Nor, friends, need we blush when we speak of God now that, in our stories, we make so free with water closets. We are brave enough these days to venture anything.

And so it is with the weather. If my friend, my dear brother, my novelist companion, brings, after all the adroit dealing possible to his talent, his hero and heroine into a lasting embrace, do not chide him because the moon, like a blossom from a Japanese plum tree, is rising above the milk-white line of hill, or, when the villain of the piece (who is blameless, because it is Freud who has made him) brings the widow and the orphans with sorrow to the grave, the country lanes should be ankle-deep in mud and a thin rain hiss upon the iron roof of the Methodist chapel. These things are so, and true love can make any moon cherry-coloured, and a thunderstorm provokes malignity in the most generous of breasts.

So (for I will not deny that these plain truths have been provoked out of self-defense) it was with all the human beings gathered together in the Westminster house

—with Mrs. Baldwin and Janet and Rose the parlour-maid, with Charles and Fanny and Grace, with Edward and Lizzie, with Romney and Nell, with Matthew and Becky Sharp, with old Mrs. Carlisle and Captain Nicholas Coventry.

For it happened that on a certain afternoon and evening towards the end of September of this year 1932 a terrible storm broke over London—terrible because it had thunder at its heart, and the sky, busy with its own private quarrel, dropped lower and lower above the town, lying with the weight of all its malignant power upon the brains and eyes and hearts and entrails of millions of men, women, and children who touched suddenly the hand of the Devil himself, without knowing their dark neighbour.

It is but seldom that citizens look up at the sky in London—they have so many other things to do. For one thing, they carry their life in their hands. For another, there are many bag snatchers. When, however, the heavens are black, the houses shine with a white unwholesome radiance as though struck with leprosy. Then you look up and say that a storm is coming.

London is brave enough, but more than most cities it cowers beneath a threatened storm. The trees in the Park shiver, the dusky sheep huddle together, the traffic rises to a stream, and the cinema houses are suddenly crowded.

This especial storm struck the town about three of the afternoon. The thunder rumbled, at first nonchalantly, as though behind the walls of the Ritz, the lodging houses in Bloomsbury, the tenements in the Old Kent Road, every one had been inspired to move the furniture.

Then there is a clap—Jehovah ordering the curtain to rise. Then the thin, delighted patter of the rain and the scurry of hastening feet. Somewhere a young lady in a shop plucking the eyebrows of another young lady says: "Here comes the rain, madam. It will be cooler now."

Above St. James's Park the sky is as black as ink, and birds, flying, have wings of silver; the water of the lake is flurried with little dark lines. Lower and lower comes the leaden sky. Hurrying to a doorway you bend your head as though the expected blow will be averted by that submission. Then the thunder breaks and the rain falls in sheeted steely splendour.

This was the second day after Romney's evening with Rait. There was, it seemed, little eagerness, that afternoon, on the part of the millionaires to buy pictures, and so he made an excuse and went home early. This was because he thought that there might be a letter from Harry waiting for him.

All yesterday, all today, he had thought of nothing but this. At every ring of the telephone he had started from his chair. This was foolish, for Harry was dilatory. He would not write; he would not telephone unless it were to say that he was otherwise engaged. He never did. But Romney, allowing his imagination to spring up like the glorious Phœnix, had now created from the ashes of that barren evening something of the fairest beauty. It was true that the evening had, on the surface, been a failure, but, he told himself, he knew Harry so well. His friend was undemonstrative (and Romney would not have him otherwise). The things that Romney had said would be very new to him, and at the first contact he would shrink. But afterwards, going over them in his mind, considering their true meaning, he would begin to realize that here was something offered to him that he had never known—a loyalty, an intimacy so rare amongst men that it would never come to him again. Romney did not pretend that he himself was anyone extraordinary to have for a friend.

Far from it. But the thing that he offered was extraordinary—a friendship without self-seeking, pure, honest, unselfish, without anything base. . . . Here (for he was hastening home to escape the storm) he laughed. What a silly, priggish colour he was giving to it! Let him content himself with his intentions and leave the rest to develop as it might. Nevertheless, passing under the archway and entering the quiet, reserved patience of the Abbey precincts, he could not prevent a little glow of happiness. It had seemed at the time a failure, but now he was glad that he had spoken as he did. Next time it would be easier. Harry himself would have more courage and would show him where especially he could help. And he, on his side, would forget his shyness and would be free, as he had never been with anyone, to formulate his ideals, to prophesy how man might be noble again, might . . . Here the thunder clapped, as it seemed, right above his head, and the little street appeared to rock under the sudden onslaught of the rain. He ran, pulled his key from his pocket and, his cheek cool and fresh with the raindrops, let himself into the house.

The hall was so dark that he switched on the light, then saw that there was a letter addressed in Harry's hand waiting on the table. He snatched it, tore off the envelope, and read:

"DEAR ROMNEY—*This is not an easy letter to write, but I have been thinking things over for twenty-four hours and have come to the conclusion that we had better not meet again. I have for a long time felt that we were not well suited as friends because our tastes and interests are so very different. I am a plain ordinary sort of chap as you must have long recognized.*

"*After the other evening I realize very clearly that our*

lives are going different ways. I hope, Romney, that you won't think too badly of me if I give you a word of advice. Some of the things you said the other evening would be misunderstood by most men although of course it's all right with me. You find a nice girl, Romney, and you'll be all right.

"Wishing you the best of luck always—Yours,

"H. R."

He heard a step and, looking up, saw that his mother was coming down the stairs.

"Why, Romney!" she cried. "Home so early?"

And he, rushing up the stairs, passed her without a word.

7

It had long ago occurred to Fanny that especial excuses, attentions, ceremonials, observances, seemed to attend, in this world, everyone but herself. For example, Mary Pontifex might be outrageously rude and people would say: "Oh, well, there's something in what she said. Mrs. Baxter asked for it." But did she, Fanny, for five minutes lose her temper in her own house, the effects of it continued to reverberate down the ages. She had always been one of those to whom her friends, her husband, her children spoke frankly. That again caused her to wonder. What *was* it about her that invited this frankness (so swiftly converted into personal rudeness!) when with others friends and relations walked as though on egg-shells? It was not that she had not, when she liked, a very pretty temper that could not snap back at the best of them. But there seemed to be two different ways of losing your temper—either you shattered the universe and caused those in your company to swear that never, oh, never again would they risk such a terrifying experience —or simply you made your friends a little shy, uncomfortable, and sorry for you. Fanny's temper was of the second kind. So it happened that it was her common experience that someone should say to her: "You know, Fanny, you *must not* be so sensitive! Why, the other day at the Moults', when that awful young man with the rabbit teeth who writes told you you knew nothing about modern poetry, you blushed like a schoolgirl! But *of course* you knew nothing about modern poetry. You never read . . ." "Why," thought Fanny, "does she say all this to me? She wouldn't dare say it to the Frobisher woman, nor to anyone else I know. What *is* it about me . . . ?"

Whatever it was, it was clear enough that even her own children now treated her rudely, brushed past her on the stairs, did not answer. . . . But Romney was upset, and not by herself, but by some letter that he had been reading. Romney was in trouble.

Once more, as so often, so often in the past, she must check, beat down that impulse, the strongest of all things in her, to hurry after him and help him, comfort him, tell him that she would stand by him, against the world, against the Devil himself. . . . But they did not want that, these modern children. They could, and did, stand up for themselves. What advice could their mothers give them, the mothers who had grown up in a world where they were hooded and deceived and sentimentalized, an old preposterous dead-as-a-cinder world?

Fanny knew that Nell and Romney loved her. She must be content with what she had. But she could not bear to think of that white, suffering face of Romney's! What *was* it that the letter had done to him? Had some girl rejected him or tantalized him and laughed at him? Romney had much of her own sensitiveness in him. He always hated to hurt her (although of late he had not been quite so careful perhaps!).

She stood there at the bottom of the stairs, beating down her longing to go to him. Then she heard the rain lash the window by the hall door. What a storm! How dark it was beyond the window! The storm attacked the house as though it had some personal spite against it. She remembered that Edward would be returning from school and although he had so little a way to go he would be soaked to the skin. She looked about the hall, undecided as to her next step. She was thinking of Romney, longing to go to him. . . . How queer a colour the storm stirred beyond the window and how unnatural the white glare of the electricity! She switched it off, and at the same moment the lightning struck the hall with its wicked brilliance as a hand slaps a face.

The hall door opened, a flurry of wind and rain blew in, then she heard a voice saying:

"Oh, please—I cannot shut it. The wind is *too* strong!"

It was Lizzie in a small black hat and a waterproof that dripped. Fanny switched on the light again and stared for a moment almost as though she had seen a ghost, so unexpected was this thin child with the pale face, the long black legs, one wet lock of black hair falling almost into her sharp burning eyes from under her hat. It was her eyes that gave her life—but there was something too in her attitude as she stood now by the door, lonely, isolated, unhappy. Fanny's heart warmed to the child whom in all these months she had never in the least understood, of whom she had been even afraid. Now was her chance perhaps.

"Darling, how wet you are! Come up to the schoolroom, dear," Fanny said, "when you've taken off your wet things. Edward will be back soon."

The child nodded and ran up the stairs in front of her. Fanny, on her way up to the schoolroom, paused at the landing window on the second floor. The sky, breaking in between the roofs, chimneys, and the high grey face of the church, was black, with spaces of white that moved like stirring pools between cliffs of cloud. The rain came down in a glittering wall against the arrogant black sky. As she looked, a burst of thunder was so loud that it seemed to shake the floor on which she was standing. It was like an attack on the city. In the schoolroom she stood wishing that Edward would come and thinking about Lizzie. It was very unusual for her spontaneous nature to be for so long in company with another human being and achieve so slight a contact. But she was shy of other people's reticences, although she gave herself at once, completely and sometimes rashly, to anyone who seemed to need her. It had been quite clear through these months that Lizzie didn't need her, but she felt that behind that strange silence and self-dependence there was a deep and unhappy loneliness. This might be, she was fully aware, only another example of her own sentimental explanations. She was always, like many affectionate characters, thinking that others were herself and then finding that they were not.

But in any case she was sure that for Edward's sake she must try to discover some contact with Lizzie. For Edward and Lizzie were friends.

The door opened and Lizzie came in.

"Father's having a bath," she said.

"Is he?" Fanny answered, coming to her. "What a funny time to have a bath, in the middle of the afternoon!"

"Yes. He told me through the bathroom door that the weather was so dirty that he had to do something about it."

Fanny sat down in the old shabby schoolroom chair, put out her hand, caught Lizzie's and drew her close to her.

"Do you mind storms?" How thin the child was, how cold her hand, how pale her face! But the child did not shrink from the contact—only, as she always did, she held herself upright and was independent of everyone, everything, herself. . . .

"Lizzie, dear—have you been happy here with us? I've often wanted to ask you. I *want* you to be happy."

"Yes, Aunt Fanny," Lizzie said.

"You haven't *seemed* happy always. I've wondered sometimes, but didn't want to interfere."

Lizzie's black hair was cut in a straight line across the marble pallor of her forehead. Under this forehead her black eyes looked out like sentinels flashing steel and so sharply on guard that you shared their fear of surprise.

As a rule you saw her eyes first and wondered that they could be so alive and bright, as though she had been crying. But she never cried. Your second question about her, Mrs. Frobisher, who was always gaily talking about people with the abandon of a gramophone record gone wrong, said, was—How *could* a child be so old for her years? A foolish question, because years as years have so little to do with age. And the third question was—Why won't she make friends? She certainly wouldn't make friends with Mrs. Frobisher, who had all the virtues except sincerity—an important one in Lizzie's eyes.

But quite suddenly now she made friends with her Aunt Fanny. It was as though something menacing in the storm, or some private knowledge she had, stirred her ironic pity and so her affection.

How could she not be ironic? At any rate now she said, allowing Fanny's hand to hold hers:

"Yes, of course Father and I are *more* happy in Sicily, which is the place where we've been most happy of all. Do you not think, Aunt Fanny, that people in London are not grown up yet?"

Fanny certainly had not thought it. But there were *some* people, of course, who would never grow up. Grace for example.

"In what way, dear?"

"You see—in Italy and Spain and France no one thinks that people are not wicked. In England everyone *pretends* that people ought to be good. They cannot understand why they are not. But of course everyone is wicked."

This was terrible to Fanny. A child so young. And what of her influence on Edward? And what kind of a man must Nicholas be to bring up his child thus?

She put her arm round Lizzie's thin, bony little waist and drew her closer.

"Oh, but people aren't wicked!" she cried. "I'm so much older than you, dear, and although your father has taken you everywhere, still you must see that people are weak but not wicked——"

"What do you think wickedness is, Aunt Fanny?"

"To be wicked," Fanny answered, staring at the window where the storm now, with a face as black as ink, pressed against the pane as though it would break it, "is to do wicked things without being sorry for them. To *want* to do wicked things."

"Yes," said Lizzie. "But what *are* wicked things?"

"Why—my dear—everyone knows."

"No. Everyone does not, Aunt Fanny. In Syracuse when we lived there a woman killed another woman because she was jealous, and everyone thought it fine. In this house if you say 'bloody hell' everyone thinks it wicked. Nobody does in Paris."

Fanny answered: "*I* think that *is* wicked, whatever they say in Paris."

She felt then the child's body tremble under her hand.

"I know what you think *I* am, Aunt Fanny—what you all think—all except Edward. Father says it would be better for me if I had been with other children more, but I don't mind. I am by myself. Other children are stupid because they believe things that aren't true. When I grow up I shall believe *only* what I see for myself, not what anyone says. I like Edward because he is honest. I listen in this house to what everyone says, but I like best to be by myself. When it thundered just now I walked in the street by myself. That's what I like. . . ."

Fanny kissed her.

"It's terrible to be so alone, darling. Will you talk to me sometimes as you are doing now? I will never tell you what you ought to do. Only—don't believe that people are wicked. They *mean* to be good——"

The lightning flashed through the room. Everything for an instant shone with a cold splendour.

"Yes," Lizzie said. "I don't mind talking to *you,* Aunt Fanny."

The door opened and Edward came in. His top hat, his overcoat, were soaked. He threw them on the floor.

"Oh, gosh!" he cried. "Did you see the lightning, Mother?" He was delighted. The water shone on his nose.

"Pick up your things, Edward."

He picked them up. He was grinning with pleasure.

"Take them down to Janet. She'll dry them."

He danced about, holding the hat and coat. "It's never going to stop! I hope it goes on for ever and then the river will flood. Perhaps it will come into the kitchen."

Fanny kissed him. She felt his clothes.

"No, you're not wet. That's a good coat we got. Only change your socks. Now run along and take those things down."

He made a laughing defiant face at Lizzie. "You don't have storms like this in other countries."

"Of course you do," Lizzie said. "Much worse."

"No, you don't," said Edward. Then he went.

The pressure of the sky on the house was terrible. Fanny's head ached as though it were a new head which the storm had supplied.

"Lizzie, dear," she said, "there's one thing. Remember that Edward is very young for his age and you are old for yours. Don't tell him things that will make him old too quickly. When you have children you will want to keep them as long as you can."

"I think," Lizzie said, "that it will be a good thing when Father and I move somewhere else."

"Oh, no—don't say that."

"It's always a good thing when we move. People never like us after a little."

"I shall always like you," Fanny said quickly. "You can always come back to me—whatever happens."

Lizzie, looking at her with an old penetrating stare, said:

"Yes, Aunt Fanny."

So, carrying her headache with her like a heavy black parcel with a bomb inside it, Fanny went to her room to brush her hair. When her head ached it helped to brush her hair, to wash her face and hands, and to think of something very pleasant. She was aware, as she sat at her dressing table, that it was taking her all her time now to remember pleasant things, and this, she discovered, was because everyone in the house was developing personalities. Until six months ago she had loved them all and known them so well that she took them for granted. Now she was not sure what any of them might say next.

And she was right, for there was a tap on the door. She said, "Come in," and there was Janet.

She knew at once that Janet was leaving her. She put down the brushes and said, with a kind of cry of despair: "No, Janet, I can't stand it! This storm is dreadful. I have the most awful headache."

"I'll come another time, mum."

"No. I know what you're going to say."

"Yes, mum. I must leave at the end of the month."

"Then," Fanny said, "perhaps you won't mind telling me what the reason is."

"I'm very sorry, mum. I'm behaving badly, I'm sure, but I've stood it as long as I can."

"Stood *what?*" The thunder was rumbling as though they were moving furniture in distant rooms.

"Well, I'd have told you last time. . . . It's the Captain."

"Captain Nicholas? What has he been doing?"

Janet's look of dull determined obstinacy was, as usual, infuriating.

"Never mind, mum, what he's done. Since he came into the house last April I've not been wanted. It isn't for him to know, of course, how I've worked my fingers to the bone, willingly so long as I was wanted. But he's hated me from the first. I've done my best for your sake. There's nothing I wouldn't do for you. But maybe if I go now you'll understand what's happening."

"Happening? What's happening?"

"It's not for me to say. I'm only a servant."

"You know you're not only a servant, Janet."

"That's as may be. Perhaps when I'm out of the house you'll see you haven't a better friend anywhere."

Then Fanny, driven by her headache, lost her temper.

"Come, Janet. Tell me what Captain Nicholas has *done*."

"Best leave that, mum. It's sufficient, I'm sure, that he hates the sight of me, to say nothing of the fact that an hour ago he called me a tiresome old bitch."

"Janet!"

"Yes, mum. I wouldn't repeat such words, but you asked me."

"He can't have. . . . You must have misunderstood."

"Not at all, mum. On the way to his bath at three in the afternoon, wearing one of the master's dressing gowns——"

"But what had *you* done? You must have done something."

"All *I'd* done was when he ordered me to go down and bring him a whisky, I suggested one of the maids——"

They looked at one another.

Fanny nodded.

"Very well then, Janet. Perhaps it *is* better. . . ."

7

The cat, Becky Sharp, felt the storm tingle within her body. It was part of her and she part of the storm. She moved about the house in delicate silence, having first watched the rain from her place at the pantry window, then passing with majesty and pride into the passage, up the stairs, then, as she always did, pausing to look at the pair of gold birds on either side of the clock in the hall (for these would one day be hers; she would tear them feather from feather), then up the wide staircase, into the drawing room, out again, up onto the higher landing that now was dark, close with the storm, like a box, and smelling faintly of mice.

Here she stretched out against the wall and licked her black glistening fur. All her movements were assured, contemptuous, arrogant. Contemptuous she was, for she despised everyone in this house. Long ago she had realized that no one in this place had her own reserve and control. They made noises, rushed hither and thither, demanded her friendship, were ridiculously pleased when she purred or rubbed her soft strong body against their persons, were excited when she drank milk for them, were distressed when (often from mere boredom) she showed her displeasure. They delighted in none of the things that were of value, did not lie in a streak of sun, did not hunt at night, must ever, in their restlessness, move from a place where it was good to be, could not concentrate on what was best for themselves and, having found it, hold to it.

She despised them so deeply that she never thought of them at all unless they denied her something that was her right or forgot her necessities. She used them to her advantage but never considered them.

Her life was immemorial, eternal. Her world was infinity, an infinity starred with fragments of light, heat, smell, food, rhythm. Least of all were they aware of her wildness, of the times when she was primeval, howling in love or battle or lust or hunger, or drawn tight into a centre of pause before the spring, concentrated on her kill. Immortal and primeval she perceived the immortal and primeval instincts. Such instincts now inhabited this house. Something stirred now in the light and dark, between the sound and the silence, that had not always been there. With her consciousness of it grew her pleased participation in it.

All through the house now there was the jungle air. As she stole softly from wall to wall, her eyes intent, she smelt the promise of delightful danger and, best of all, the night, dark to all but her, was now alive when for so long inside the house it had been so empty. She waited, her eyes shining like green stars. . . .

Now, unexpectedly, a door opened. Someone came out and almost stepped on her, but as he passed she caught the smell of a garment that she knew, a long thick soft garment that was scented with soap and tobacco, sometimes very dry and warm, sometimes damp and clammy to her fur. She followed it.

At the end of the passage, just as a roll of thunder drummed through the walls, the wearer of the garment stayed. Purring, she rubbed her soft warm body against a naked leg. She looked up, slanting her eyes, and saw that he was so deeply absorbed, looking at something, that he did not feel her gentle rhythmic pressure. Then she was aware that he was possessed of some warm powerful sensation. His leg trembled against her body. The jungle-consciousness passed from him to her. They shared a wild, feverish excitement. It was as satisfying to her as a saucer of milk. He passed into a room, closing the door, unaware of her, shutting her out.

8

Nicholas had intended that afternoon to go out. Subconscious, although he would not recognize it, was the determination to call on Mrs. Agar. It would be better that he should not do so; nevertheless . . . But he did not go out. He saw the storm piling up behind the pale and crooked chimneys, and something in the heavy foreboding air decided him to remain in the house until the storm should be over. Then, sitting in his bedroom, engaged with one of Ezra Pound's *Cantos,* he decided that he would have a bath. His natural gaiety had for the moment forsaken him. Something told him that his situation (the only situation that could conceivably matter to him) was developing too swiftly for his comfort and he must think about it. The best place to think about it was in a hot bath. Moreover he loved to be clean. He could not be too clean, and soap, bath salts, fresh underclothing, these things would be very good on a day as sultry and difficult.

He wandered into the passage, thinking that he would order a drink; he passed Charles's dressing room, the door of which was open, and, lazily entering, saw Charles's purple dressing gown lying across the end of the bed. He liked purple; it was his favourite colour—wine-coloured carnations, Homer's wine-stained sea, a still-life of purple wineglasses painted by William Nicholson, owned by Mrs. Appia in Rome, all good things. He put on Charles's purple gown and, humming (for now, like a child, he was happy again), he wandered back to his room. He undressed, looked at himself naked in front of the long pier glass, wondered appreciatively that he should still have so fine a figure, speculated on what Mrs. Agar would think of it, collected his sponge, nailbrush, bath towel, Ezra Pound's *Cantos,* put on Charles's dressing gown and sauntered off again.

Nearing the bathroom door he encountered Janet. He hated the woman. He hoped that he would embarrass her by appearing before her thus, early in the afternoon, almost naked. A crash of thunder broke above the house.

"Well, Janet," he said, "I am about to have a bath."

"Yes, sir," she said.

The passage was narrow. She had drawn herself up stiffly against the wall. What a pinched dry face the old woman had! How pleased she was with her neatness, plainness, primness! Yes, he hated her. But he smiled his most charming smile.

"What a storm!" he said. "That's why I am going to have a bath."

"Yes, sir," she answered.

He stood full-square; if she passed him she must brush against him: that would amuse him.

"And I tell you what I want, Janet," he continued. "A nice whisky and soda."

Janet looked at him but said nothing. He was irritated.

"See that there's one in my bedroom, will you?"

"I will tell Rose, sir."

"Too grand to do it yourself?" he asked, smiling. "Why *are* you so grand, Janet? It would interest me to know. You think that you're simply magnificent, don't you, and that no one in this house can hold a candle to you. I expect you're right. All the same I suppose you're paid for your job like other people. Not that I ever see you doing any work. I don't blame you for that. *I* don't do any work, either. But then no one pays me anything."

She did not move. At last she said:

"Would you mind letting me pass, sir?"

"No, but wait a minute. I want to know, as we *are* talking man to man, why you've always hated me so?"

She looked him then straight in the face.

"It's not my place," she said, "to have feelings. I do my duty."

"Well," he answered, "that's just what I question. Not

that I've a right to question anything, of course. Still I *am* one of the family."

"It's for my mistress," she said, "to know whether I do my duty."

"Yes, I suppose it is. But my sister has a warm heart. She would put up with anything."

Then, really irritated, he snapped out: "Do you know what you are, Janet? Just between man and man. You're a tiresome old bitch."

Then he went on into the bathroom.

When he had the water exactly to the right temperature and was lying down in it, he reflected that it was most foolish of him to lose his temper. *That* surely was the unforgivable folly in anyone. It showed that his nerves were on edge and that it was indeed high time for him to consider in all its aspects his situation.

The great question was: Would he stay or would he go? If he went, where would he go to? Nowhere. At the present moment there was no house in the world ready to receive him. And in addition to that he had, at this moment, exactly two pounds three and sixpence halfpenny. Moreover he liked it where he was. Not, he thought as he curled his toes in the delicious water, that he liked anyone in the house very much, save possibly, the girl; and his brother, Matthew, he disliked extremely.

Here he was conscious of a real grudge against life. He was the most amiable of human beings—given a little, a very, very little, just enough to live upon, a room or two, a picture, a book, a small luxury, those things plus security and he wished everyone well, would be charming and kind and generous within his means. But it was exactly this security that was always denied him! There wasn't a more charming, sweeter-natured fellow in the world. But how could he continue to be charming and good when he had to fight, every minute of the day, for his very existence?

Nor was he growing younger. In spite of the fitness of his firm and well-tended body his hair was thinning, there were slight rolls of flesh about his middle, he was weary when three years ago he wouldn't have been, he lost his temper with a silly old servant. He was not so confident of his wisdom and control as he had been. He had not the power over Abel that he had once had. Abel was a danger. And, most menacing of all, there was Mrs. Agar and her world. He knew that that world was a lower one than any that he had ever inhabited. He was not yet its inhabitant, but he was slipping into it. It was a *lost* world, a world where one false step meant ruin and disaster. Some of its inhabitants had already experienced that ruin. Once you were down there, *really* there, you never climbed up again. You were done for.

The storm had made the room very dark, and he had switched on the electric light. He had propped Ezra Pound's *Cantos* between the soapdish and the wall. Turning on his side he read in that cold unreal illumination:

We also made ghostly visits, and the stair
That knew us, found us again on the turn of it,
Knocking at empty rooms, seeking for buried beauty;
And the sun-tanned gracious and well-formed fingers
Lift no latch of bent bronze, no Empire handle
Twists for the knocker's fall; no voice to answer.
A strange concierge, in place of the gouty-footed.
Sceptic against all this one seeks the living,
Stubborn against the fact. The wilted flowers
Brushed out a seven years since of no effect.
Damn the partition! Paper, dark brown and stretched,
Flimsy and damned partition.

He shivered. His bare flank, out of the warm water, was chill. "Flimsy and damned partition" and the thunder rolling menacing, aloof, beyond the window. He had come to a parting of the ways. His personal case was more desperate than it had ever been, and that sense of desperation would drive him, were he not careful, into company that would, he knew clearly, damn him for ever. To avoid it he must stay where he was, and to stay where he was he must have money. He must have money from Charles or Fanny or Grace—from all three of them perhaps.

Then (and here he sat up and turned on the hot water again) there was Lizzie.

Yes, there was Lizzie, the only person for whom, besides himself, he cared. She had seemed for a long while to be part of himself and so the easier to care for. She had, since she was a tiny child, responded to persons and things exactly as he himself might, coolly, ironically, always keeping her head, never afraid and never enthusiastic. And so, from this, he gathered that she was fond of him. But was she? Upon his soul he could not be sure. And now, since their stay in this house, he had become less sure. Were they affecting her, these people? She was, it seemed, attached to the small boy Edward, surely a most unattractive child. She did not dislike, as one would have supposed she must, her walks with Grace. She found Fanny kind.

She was changing—but then she was growing. But if he lost her——! At that a slight shiver (bath water, like tea, was never as hot at the second brew) struck his body. The thunder rumbled and the little room was close with a thick packed heat. He buried his body deep, allowing only his face to emerge, while the hair on his chest, like a sinister water plant on a pond's fringe, wavered on the surface. If he lost her he would be alone, and the thought of that loneliness was suddenly appalling to him although, his whole life long, he had defied loneliness, laughed at people who needed props, mocked the lusts of the lustful and the sentiment of the sentimental.

But of course he would not lose Lizzie: they had done too much, seen too much together. She had taken life as he had shown it to her and had shared his values. But suppose that she no longer did so? Curse these aunts and uncles and sticky family ties! He would remove her from them before it was too late. But could he? Leave the family, and on the further side of the ditch were Abel and Mrs. Agar! He was growing old. He was losing his power of decision. He was becoming altogether too serious and solemn. Meanwhile he needed money, *must* have it. About that one could not be too serious. He sat up and began to sponge himself and, as he did so, had the sense that something or someone was waiting for him outside the bathroom door. Someone was crouching there. He felt, in his nudity, oddly unprotected and alone. This damned thunderstorm gave you all kinds of ideas!

He got out, dried himself, and, with a malignant splash, Pound's *Cantos* fell into the bath, which was gurgling with malicious satisfaction. This added to his ill temper, for it was a rare book. He had procured it from Paris, Pound being altogether too clever and erudite for the English. He picked out the book, which seemed, through its dampness, to have lost suddenly both its cleverness and erudition.

Then he remembered. Charles had said, some months ago, that he could have the purple dressing gown if he liked. It had been hanging in Charles's cupboard, and Charles had said that he was too old now for purple and that he scarcely ever wore it. Now that he had got it he would keep it! This cheered him, and, whistling, he stepped out into the passage. Here, in its obscurity, he nearly fell over the cat. Then, as he reached the broader light above the stairs, his hand in the pocket of his gown touched a paper. He drew out a letter. This was in an envelope, unfastened, and in Charles's hand. He took it from its envelope and began to read. The first part of the letter was as follows. There was no date and no address:

"DARLING—*I am writing this late at night or rather early in the morning. I haven't been able to sleep. I did go off for a moment and then I woke, then lay here as though I never would sleep again as long as I lived. How I have longed for you to be here! Just that you should be sitting in the chair near the bed and talking to me so that I should hear your voice and sometimes touch your hand. Is this love nothing but madness? You take it so calmly. I often wonder whether you care for me at all. And why should you, an old dull man like myself, so unused to these things, so blundering and clumsy and stupid? How patient you are with me! And meanwhile I am in a fever. I think of you all day and often, as now, all night as well. I thought I was so happy and contented before you came, with my wife and children and home, and indeed, God knows, I love them still. But they are no longer enough and never will be again. The worst of it is that I am not ashamed but only proud that you should care for me. You do, don't you? I would die, I think, if you did not. Anyway it is already morning and today I shall see you and have you close to me. . . .*"

"My God!" said Nicholas. Then he added: "The silly old fool!" But Charles! Charles! He never would have conceived such a possibility! Charles to be unfaithful!

Charles to write such turgid nonsense, to leave such a letter in his dressing gown! And the woman—who was she? And Fanny—what would she say if she knew? Charles of all people in this world!

He thought that something was rubbing against his bare leg. He looked down, but there was nothing there. Yes, he would keep the purple dressing gown—a valuable garment.

9

At that same time Matthew was entertaining two of his friends in his room. His friends were called Danny Oldfield and Bob Orange.

Danny was over sixty and looked more, for his hair was snow-white and he had a small wrinkled anxious face, very charming when lit up with a smile or a question. His shoulders were bowed, for he had been a bank clerk until two years ago when an aunt had left him a little money. He was a widower, lived alone in two small rooms near Victoria Station. His blue suit was well worn, but he was as clean and fresh as an apple tree. Bob Orange was a sturdy young man with nothing very special about him. He did not resemble an apple tree or a nice friendly dog or a strong wave of the sea or any of the other things that poetic writers think of. He was just a sturdy young man. Danny was the first of this now large body of friends. He was, in fact, the beginning of it all. One fine day Matthew had sat beside him on a seat on the Chelsea Embankment and they had begun to talk. They talked about God and found that they thought very much alike in that they were both conscious of some contact, enduring, persistent, and powerful. Danny came to see Matthew, and they soon found that they were friends.

Then Danny brought with him a man who lived on the same floor as himself, a thin cadaverous widower, swallowed up in spectacles, called McTavish. McTavish brought his daughter Mary. Mary brought an elderly spinster, Miss Murdoch.

After a while they thought they would have some definition. They were not a society and were determined never to be one, but they needed some very simple expression for their conduct of life. So they pledged themselves (very gently and without any kind of sharp term) to contemplation, work, and love. That is, they said that they would try to be quietly alone during some part of every week, they would not be idle, and they would endeavour to be generous, warm-hearted, and tolerant. This last did not mean that they would love, indiscriminately, their fellows. Miss Murdoch, for instance, could not abide Mr. Sellars, the second-in-command at the office where she was. Nor had she any intention of abiding him—he was a nasty, mean, lecherous old man. Nor did Mr. McTavish care for Mrs. Graham, his sister-in-law.

"None of your saints on purpose for me," he said fiercely, glaring at Matthew through his glasses. "I wasn't born a saint and I shan't die one." But they had this in common: they believed in a spiritual world and wished that their consciousness of it should grow, should pervade their daily lives, should transmute the material world as sunlight soaks into a landscape. Because they all, different though they were, shared this common experience, their friendship developed very naturally. They made allowances for one another, were so grateful that they were no longer lonely that they felt generous toward one another. They talked freely and unselfconsciously about God and, while keeping their private independence, shared, when they wished, their experience. But no one demanded a confidence of another nor did anyone judge another's private life. The habit of securing, an hour or two every week, silence, and quiet grew with practice. It did not make their actual daily life less real; it was as though they passed into another room, closing the door behind them.

After a year or two they numbered some fifty or sixty persons, and they hired a room in the building where Danny was. Here they met, had supper together, talked and engaged often in violent discussions. There were no rules, no obligations. People joined them and fell away again. Some wanted a more definite creed, others were shocked at the indifference, as it seemed to them, to the backslidings of sinners, others demanded ritual. Some, who were religious, had yet no consciousness of a spiritual world. Some were too quarrelsome and argumentative to be endured. Some were fond of scandal and gossip to the exclusion of everything else. Some joined them because they wanted material help and were always after borrowing money.

It might indeed have had no continuous life had it not been that half a dozen of them shared so deeply their common experience that no disappointments, quarrels, differences of opinion, could separate them. These six were Matthew, Danny, Mary McTavish, young Bob Orange, a friend of his, Sam Somerset, and a jolly middle-aged woman who kept an antique shop, Milly Crowder.

Orange and Somerset were fond of roaming. Orange was a commercial traveller—he dealt in hosiery—Somerset was a motor mechanic, and the two of them moved over much country. So, through them, the body of friends grew. In one place or another people sprang up. But there was still no organization in any official sense, and it was better, Matthew said, that there should not be one. Now on this dark sombre afternoon with the sullen storm pressing about the house, Matthew realized how deep and true this thing was. Danny might have been his friend in any case, for he was a delightful man, gentle, kind, humorous, modest, intelligent, and it was amazing to Matthew to think that Danny had been sitting for years in that bank and had never been discovered by anyone to be remarkable. How many thousands upon thousands there were in London whose personalities had the strength and the sweetness of fruit and flower, who nevertheless, by the monotony of their work and the grind of money necessity, developed through the years a kind of hard, grey skin, obscuring them even to themselves!

Danny he might have loved in any circumstances had he had the luck to find him, but with Orange he would have normally nothing in common. He was a good enough young fellow, but his tastes, his way of seeing things were all alien to Matthew. Their bond was their mutual experience. Orange lived as though he had visited some marvellous country whose people and cities and plains were for ever filling his vision. He was no saint. He was greedy, vulgar, lustful, cheap, sometimes mean, sometimes drunk, often a coward. He never spoke of his spiritual life to anyone unless they wished it. He had his virtues. He was self denying as well as greedy, tactful as well as vulgar, chaste as well as lustful, rare-spirited as well as cheap, generous, most times sober, often brave. But through all these twenty selves there ran this *one* self —the self who had made a journey. And slowly the twenty selves were being changed, and from them all one personality was rising. He looked a red-faced, large-limbed, football-loving young commercial traveller. He looked as though he would bluster, bully, be beaten into angry shamed silence, have furtive, fuddled love affairs, drink and gamble his money away. And he looked, if you studied him, like a child in happy possession of a secret.

There was nothing, however, in the least mystical or precious or beautiful about him. He sat now in Matthew's armchair, his legs spread in front of him, his head back, entirely at his ease, telling them of his adventures in Salisbury. He had done some good business there by a bit of luck, although times *were* so shocking, and then he and a fellow called Mason had spent a night and a day on Salisbury Plain. The funny thing had been that an old man called Barbury had insisted on accompanying them. They hadn't wanted him. They had warned him that as likely as not they would be the whole day out there without exchanging a word, that they were going to read the New Testament. At this old Barbury had roared with laughter.

"What! You two young bastards! Reading the Bible!"

He had thought that they were going to some farmhouse, pick up two girls perhaps, anyway drink at a pub somewhere.

But, after all their warnings, he insisted on coming. They slept at some farm. In the middle of the night old Barbury, who had been drinking, was ill, but after that, was resigned and quiet as though he had suddenly thought of something. What he had thought of was clear in the morning when he explained to them at some length a new way he had discovered of cheating his customers. (He was a grocer.) All the same they took him out with them on the Plain and walked him off his feet. But it wasn't the walking he hated so much as the silence.

Orange and Mason never exchanged a word until they were back in Salisbury that evening, and the effect on Barbury was that he was frightened of them and frightened of the Plain and frightened of himself. Next morning, before Orange returned to London, Barbury sought him out and talked about giving up his grocery business. What he wanted to do instead he didn't know. He thought he might travel and see the world a bit.

"But of course he won't sell his business. I bet he's putting sand in his sugar already. But it was funny. He'd lived all those years in Salisbury and never seen Stonehenge. He was so tired in the afternoon that he saw things. He saw the Plain was like the sea. It got on his nerves, our not talking. The last bit he followed us like a little old dog. He wasn't a bad chap."

Orange had met friends in Glastonbury and Warminster and Longbridge Deveril and a number of other places.

He must say they were all very happy. "It gives you a different sense of values. I don't mean that I'm not dead nuts on selling my stuff, more than ever I was. And I need to be, too, because it gets harder every day. But if you don't—well, there are other things to think about. And there's another thing. If you get in the habit of thinking about Christ, He's always nearly turning up. What I mean is, everyone you meet seems to have a bit of Him—without their knowing it, of course. I knew a man once who felt that way about Shakespeare. He'd read the plays such a lot that he saw him everywhere. He'd describe him—you know, long thin fellow with a beard and breeches, humming to himself or drinking; very friendly chap, he said he was. . . . Well, I must be getting. Taking a girl out to a show. What a storm! Listen to that rain!"

He got up, smiled at them both, said: "See you next Friday," and went. On the stairs he met a small boy, soaking wet, and grinned at him. "Posh house," he thought. "I'd find it a bit cold myself."

After he was gone Matthew got up and switched on the electric light. He looked out of the window at his favourite tree, whose leaves now were furred with a silver whiteness against the black sky. Great drops of rain like gay plums broke on the pane. He went back to his chair.

"That's a nice boy," he said.

"Yes," said Danny.

"You know, Danny, I've been happier during these last weeks than ever before in my life, I think. Going with you to Glastonbury, then helping with that hospital at Portsmouth, those two days with you and Mary on Exmoor—especially that evening when the sky turned inside out and that moor pond was full of stars. And the man standing with his sheep on the edge of space. Do you remember? We'd been silent for hours, and the woman stopped us, asking you if you had a match. They wanted to light a fire. And we both saw a child with the woman. We *both* saw it, mind you. And then there was no child there. We'd been overdoing the silence *that* day, Danny. The fact is our three points are getting too damned easy. Contemplation can slip into mere laziness, work into busybodiness, and as to love—well, if you only spend your time with people you like, who think as you do, loving them isn't difficult."

"You're a queer one, Matthew. You've been struggling your life long, so you tell me, to get some kind of peace, and now that you've got it you want to break out of it again."

"No, Danny, you're wrong. But there's a mystery here. This life that we have now—this inner life—it's like

Alice in Wonderland's well. The deeper you are the deeper you get. It pulls one in further and further. You look up from its safe darkness and see men as trees walking. And you don't care whether they're trees or no. I'm more selfish, Danny, now when I'm working at all sorts of things with you and the others than I was when I was lazy here by myself. We're in danger of becoming a kind of enclosed band, away by ourselves. And self-satisfied too! Orange is a nice boy, but didn't you notice when he talked about that old grocer who went walking with them on the Plain that there was a kind of self-satisfaction? Pharisaical a bit."

"Yes—now you mention it——" said Danny.

"It's extraordinary," Matthew said vehemently, "how difficult it is to be real. We now—you and I—we *know* that God is real, but to be genuine and modest and kind ourselves although there's Christ to guide us . . . ! It's as though we forgot some essential central point. Like poor Beaverbrook, for example, who is always shouting to us to keep out of European wars—forgetting that the moment the Germans were to take the Channel ports we'd be for it whether we liked it or no. There's something as simple as that we're missing—or I, at least, am."

"Yes," said Danny. "But the closer we get to Christ the closer to the solution."

"Yes—and that's the miracle. The Gospels are simply collections of sayings, anecdotes, stories, pieces of gossip, brought together from where you like. And yet together they make that central unique loveliness—nothing the least like it in the world's history before or since—all made up of incongruities that merge naturally into harmony. So with one's own life—one's got to merge the incongruities!"

Danny said quietly: "Don't you worry, Matthew—everything's all right."

"Well, it isn't as a matter of fact," Matthew said. "I've been neglecting my own people. Things are wrong here in this house."

"What's the matter?"

"Well, you know, I've told you, how we all live independent lives here. We can because we're all so fond of one another. Up to the spring of this year we were all as happy as anything. But since then everything's been going wrong. My sister Fanny, for instance—there wasn't a happier woman in the world. She's one of these simple-minded women, you know—just lives for her husband and children. Lately she's been very unhappy. Only last night, she said something about a lovely evening last spring when she was coming home and London was like fairyland. 'It will never look like that again,' she said. 'Or I shan't see it if it does.' And the boy's gone broody, and my other sister is worrying. I've seen all this for weeks and I haven't done a thing. I'm a coward, Danny. I hate to meddle in other people's affairs. But I've got to. I've got to stand up and do something about it."

"Do you know what's made the change?" asked Danny.

"Yes," Matthew said slowly. "I do. It's my brother."

"The one you told me about?"

"Yes. He's a queer man. He likes to upset people. We never got on, even when we were small. Everything I believe in he laughs at. He likes to disturb people. It flatters him. He wants to show us all that our affection for one another is nonsense. He positively *hates* our belief in one another. He'd like to show us all up."

"He may be right from his point of view," said Danny.

"Yes, he may be. All the same I can't see Fanny and Grace and the children lose their happiness and do nothing about it. He's got to stop it or go——"

They heard the thunder roll beyond the window, and they got up and stood side by side, looking at the rain.

"I must be off," Danny said.

"Won't you wait until this is over?"

"Oh, no, thanks." He found his bowler hat and umbrella. "See you Friday," he said.

After Danny had gone Matthew took out his Journal:

I have suddenly realized that I've been too happy these last weeks—a kind of self-satisfaction. How incredibly hard it is to live decently—except perhaps for those unselfconscious people who move in the right direction by instinct. Although if one knew all about *them* one might discover that they have their difficulties. . . .

Our Father which art in Heaven—lead us not into temptation . . . but He *does* lead us as He Himself was led. There's been a storm raging all the afternoon, and while Danny and Orange were here I kept feeling that He also was in the room with us—taking shelter from the storm as though He too needed protection just as we do. Or would want us perhaps to *feel* that He needed protection so that we might love Him the more actively. But it's with myself that I'm dissatisfied. As the thunder was rolling and the rain lashing the panes it seemed to say: "You're all very happy, you and your friends, inside there, but it's cowardly evasion—that's what your religion is coming to."

Perhaps it is—at least I *know* that I'm a coward. And I'm especially afraid of Nicholas, of his sort of irony. I don't know how to deal with it. I never did. As a small boy I would lose my temper, which was just what he wanted. Or I would be silent, which amused him. And now how I hate to go out and confront him!

Did Christ sometimes shiver with nerves before He met the Pharisees! I hope so. Yes, I think so. He was never sure that the power would be given to Him. He must have known that the moment *had* to come of "My God, my God, why hast Thou forsaken me?" But my cowardice is appalling. That, I suppose, is why I snatched at this life here, surrounded by people who loved me, safe, undisturbed.

And so I have gone on from security to security. The first time that I wondered whether it was right was when Romney came to see me and I failed so badly. And now I *know* that I'm shirking what I should do. If it were only anyone but Nicholas! Our childhood has made me subconsciously dread him and be awkward with him. He is clever when I am not. He can laugh at me so easily. But I know that we will none of us be happy again until he has gone. I'm afraid of him, for the others as well as myself. Why do I feel such scorn of myself tonight? This self-contempt is a miserable thing. We must all think nobly of ourselves and then we will act nobly. I *won't* be afraid of Nicholas. Let him mock. "Too late I loved thee, O Thou Beauty of ancient days, yet ever new! Too late loved I thee! And behold, Thou wert within, and I abroad, and there I searched for Thee! Thou wert with me, but I was not with Thee! Things held me far from Thee which, unless they were in Thee, were not at all. Thou calledst, and shoutedst and burstest my deafness. Thou flashedst, shonest, and scatteredst my blindness, Thou breathedst odours, and I drew in breath and pant for Thee. I tasted, and hunger and thirst. Thou touchedst me, and I burned for Thy peace."

10

The storm, like smoke driven by the wind, scattered away. All the rooftops and chimneys glittered after the rain. A slight breeze ruffled the river which, under pale gleams of the evening sun, caught ripples of light like feathers scattered by a multitude of birds. A freshness, as though the busy streets were evening meadows, touched wall and pavement and the hurrying wheels of the traffic. The sun blew out across the clean-washed sky like a trumpet.

11

About a week after the storm Romney came to a decision, and it was his Uncle Nicholas that brought him to it.

The effect upon him of the reading of Harry Rait's letter had been overwhelming. He was in some ways, at this time, like many boys of his period—cynical and worldly-wise in expression but very romantic and even idealistic at heart. He mocked with others at the very ideals that secretly he cherished. While loudly proclaiming that every human being must, in this new age, have absolute freedom of conduct, he kept on himself a severe and almost ritualistic guard. He did in reality believe that somewhere, for someone's finding, there was a Holy Grail.

It was quite true that his love of Harry had been religious in its idealistic creation of an image. It was partly because of this that Rait (who never analyzed anything) had felt so uncomfortably ill at ease in his company. It may seem incredible that anyone as ordinary as Rait could become to another a sort of mystic figure; such things happen every day. Now one sentence in Rait's letter had destroyed completely all Romney's worship of him. This sentence echoed and reëchoed in Romney's brain. It might almost be said to keep him company from now for ever, as some sentences, some scenes, some accidents do. One must, in fact, be careful about letter-writing. The sentence was:

"Some of the things you said the other evening would be misunderstood by most men although of course it's all right with me."

It was the complacent self-satisfaction behind the sentence that killed Rait for ever in Romney's eyes. But it not only killed Rait; it killed, once and for all, his young belief that you could trust the understanding of others. He saw now what a fool he had, for so long, been. He had, it was true, been himself uneasy about his own unsophistication, which was why, some months before, he had talked to Uncle Matthew. But he saw that, all through life, one must be on one's guard. Even with one's closest intimate one cannot tell the truth. (He was in after years to find out, most happily, that this was not so.) The great harm that this letter did to him was to make him for a long time to come less honest, less frank. The child in him was slain.

But he did not blame Harry. He blamed himself. He looked back on the past two years and saw nothing but folly, ignorance, blindness. He had created Rait in his own image. He had made that most fatal of blunders—assumed that some other human being would be as he wished simply because he wished it.

He was thrown back now into a passion of cynicism, irony, and distrust. One thing he must do—put himself right about women. He would have a mistress, several perhaps. He would show the world that he was virile, scornful of ideals, just like all the other men in this cynical age.

Only—he did not know quite how to set about it. Uncle Nicholas, perhaps, would show him.

But, before he had his talk with Uncle Nicholas, he encountered his mother. His love of Harry being gone, he discovered, to his extreme annoyance, that he ached for affection from someone. Not that Harry had ever given him very much; imagination had lent its assistance. This need for affection disgusted him. After all he was to be a man now, and his love of his father and mother had too much of the child about it.

Nevertheless it obstinately remained. He only hoped that the life he was now about to lead would chasten it.

His love for his mother was extremely powerful; it was built up of a thousand memories, tendernesses, jokes, troubles, intimacies. Even now, fresh-grown cynic as he was, he had to confess that his mother was a darling. He knew, beyond argument, that she was worth a dozen Romneys, which was a pity just now when he wanted to feel very self-confident, wise, and superior.

So he was very cross indeed when she came into his room; he just back from his work and busy rehanging a picture.

"Oh, I didn't know you were there!" she cried. She was flushed with the number of things that she was doing, her hair was a little disordered; he disapproved very strongly of her occasional untidiness.

"What do you want, Mother? I do wish you'd knock before you come in."

"I know!" She stopped and looked at him like a guilty child. "I always mean to and I forget."

"You've come to tidy up. I do wish, Mother, you'd leave my room alone. You can't say that I don't keep everything tidy myself."

She sat down on the edge of the bed. Romney was standing on a chair, holding a hammer in one hand and in the other a Sickert interpretation of houses in Bath, bright and shining although menaced by a purple rain cloud.

Without a word she got up and held the picture for him while he knocked the nail in the wall. This, whether he liked it or no, established a relation between them. He got off the chair and stood back, admiring it.

"Yes, it looks exactly right there. It gets just the proper proportion."

She sat down on the bed again.

"Now that's a picture, Romney, I *can* understand. I do think your room's nice, dear. It's wonderful what you've done to it!"

She looked round appreciatively. Like most of the women of her generation she had never had much æsthetic education, but she loved beautiful things and had a natural inborn taste.

"I like that head of a girl so much. Who's that by?"

"Duncan Grant."

"And that snow picture with the green stream. That's always one of my favourites."

"Yes. That's by John Nash. I tell you that every time you come into this room."

"Well, I think it doesn't much matter who does things if they're good. All the fuss as to whether Shakespeare wrote his plays! In my opinion they were written by at least ten people. They're all so different. And oh, Romney, *that's* lovely! What a darling! May I look at it? I've not noticed it in here before."

She went to the little wood-carving by the Jamaican artist. She picked it up and handled it.

"Oh, dear, I *do* like that!"

He smiled. He was delighted. Try as he might to be modern he must love his mother, who liked the right things so naturally.

"Yes, that's by a woman. She lives in the West Indies."

"Oh, it's exquisite! One shoulder's higher than the other, but I suppose she means it to be! *What* a quiet, kind face she has! And it's been made by a woman. Well, I *am* proud."

Then, still holding the little figure, she turned round to him with a face rather like that of a piteous child and said:

"Romney—what do you think? Janet's going!"

That, indeed, was news for him. He stopped where he was and suddenly, a child as he was, exclaimed:

"Janet!—Going!"

She nodded her head.

"I've known it for some time. I've said nothing to anyone except Nicholas—not even your father—because I hoped all the time she would change her mind. She spoke to me first a long time ago. Now it's settled. She's leaving us next week."

"Janet leaving us! Oh, but it's impossible. But why? What's the matter? And Uncle Nicholas—what's he got to do with it?"

"He's got everything to do with it. It's because he's been rude to her that she's going."

"Rude? Why, what did he do?"

"He lost his temper one day and said something shocking."

"I can't believe it. He never loses his temper. She must be imagining it."

Fanny shook her head.

"Oh, no. He admits it."

"Well, then, he must apologize."

"He has. I went to him and told him. He said at once: 'Oh! I'll apologize,' and he did, quite charmingly. He said that I must be there when he did it, and I must say no one could have been nicer."

"Well, then—there it is."

"Oh, no, it isn't. You know how obstinate and provoking Janet is. She stood there as stiff as a tree and listened to him. When he'd finished, all she said was: 'I bear no malice, I'm sure.' It's plain that she can't endure him. Afterwards she said to me that she was very sorry but she was an old woman and tired out and so on."

"What nonsense," Romney cried. "Why, she's as energetic as ever she was."

"Of course she is. But nothing would persuade her. I—I——"

Fanny sat down on the bed. He saw that her eyes were filled with tears.

"She's been with me always. She's the best friend I have in the world. She's always been so loyal and so wonderful if anyone's ill, and so good with the other servants——"

She stopped, giving a little gasp. Romney was as soft-hearted as she. He had imagination, too. He knew what this meant to her. He sat down on the bed beside her, putting his arm around her.

"Never mind, Mother. She'll come back. She's sure to. She'll find she can't get on without you."

She sat closer to him, getting immense comfort from her contact with him.

"I hope so, I'm sure, but I don't think she will—not while Nicholas is here."

Romney took her hand.

"But Uncle Nicholas is all right. I must say if he did lose his temper, it's about the only time he ever has! He's charming to everybody."

She sighed. "Yes, I know he is. Nobody has charm like Nicholas. But he *has* upset the house a little. Ever since we've been back from Cornwall things haven't been the same."

"Oh, haven't they?" said Romney. "I haven't noticed."

"Well, I don't know whether I ought to say anything—but I'm afraid he's borrowing money from your father. And then Grandmother being ill has made things difficult."

"*That's* not Uncle Nicholas's fault, anyway——"

"No, of course not. But Grace is unhappy about something. And—*you*'ve been worrying, haven't you?"

"Oh, never mind about *me!* That's not Uncle Nicholas's fault, either."

"No—but——" She straightened herself up. He could feel her hand tighten on his. "I've been full of fancies myself. Perfect nonsense—as though someone were trying to take you all away from me."

"Take us all away!" Romney laughed. "As though anyone could!"

She smiled. "Of course they couldn't—not really. But I've always known that it couldn't go on for ever. Our all being so fond of one another, so close, being together. You and Nell will marry, Edward will grow up. That's all quite right, of course. But I mean something deeper than that." Her voice sank. She looked down at her lap. "I mean that you should grow to think differently of me, despise me a little, think me stupid, not want to see me any more. I expect that every mother of my age has that kind of fear. And that's where Janet was so important.

I mean that I was sure that she would always be with me. While she's in the house I feel safe."

"Safe!" he said. "Why, Mother, what are you afraid of?"

"I don't know," she answered. "I never used to be."

Then he cheered her up, petted and consoled her.

She ended with: "And now, dear, I must go. Don't think of what I've said. All silly nonsense. But it's such a relief to talk to someone."

After she was gone he sat down and tried to think of things clearly. But he could not. Everything was disordinate. He had been brought up, like every intellectual young man of his time, on Proust, and now he had been reading the four volumes of M. Jules Romains' endless novel. The fourth volume in its cheap French paper was lying beside his bed now. That was exactly what his life seemed to him at the moment. Bits and pieces. He had never supposed that he could write, but now it occurred to him that he could write a very good novel indeed about himself in his present manner. Very easy. No wonder so many of his friends were writing novels! Not of course that he could be as clever as M. Romains, but he need not worry about arrangement or form. There he was in his room and the Sickerts were on his wall and Mr. Sickert himself was probably taking a photograph of a lady whose portrait he was painting. Outside Sickert's room the tram was rumbling by and an old man with a dirty moustache was selling the evening paper while his wife at home, in a filthy room crawling with bugs, was reading in the *Daily Sketch* of the Hon. Mrs. Langbridge, who, at that moment, was drinking her fifth cocktail in a room all glass, shining steel, and white marble. The Prime Minister, Mr. Ramsay Macdonald, was no doubt drinking his tea at his desk in a room all emptiness and windows, while Norman the Butcher was reclining in a chair, snoozing before his wrestling bout at the Ring. In the hospitals people were sinking into space under anæsthetics, while Mrs. Patrick of The Hollies, Brixton, was scolding the small maid for breaking the handle off the best teapot, and rows of people at the Regal Cinema were watching adultery in New York. At Geneva they were wondering what America was going to do, and in Russia the machinery was dropping to pieces, while Harry had just made a splendid drive onto the ninth green, confident now of doing the hole in three. . . .

And here was he in the centre of this with no centre at all. That is, he was empty, miserable, lonely, and death (so long as it was painless) would be preferable.

Later, when he had dressed and found himself alone in the drawing room, he had a moment of something more than negation. He was, for one brief instant, actively frightened.

He was standing in front of the round mirror with the carved border of gilt flowers, arranging his tie. The mirror embraced half a picture of still-life—flowers, fruit, and a needlecase—a corner of the Japanese screen, amber and crimson, and a square table with some books and a silver tray. All these things reposed in the mirror with what Romney, in his present mood, could not help but think a complacent self-satisfaction. He had that sudden instinct, common at moments to all æsthetic fanatics, of general destruction. He would not care if he destroyed everything in the room. It was crowded, clotted, stifling. And then, without a moment's warning, Uncle Nicholas was standing in the mirror! There he was, foreshortened a little, but smart, erect, beautifully dressed, and motionless. He was stiller than the still-life itself! How softly he had come into the room, and what was he watching Romney for?

Romney swung round.

"Hullo, Uncle!"

"Well, Romney—admiring yourself in the glass?"

"Oh, no—only seeing whether my tie was straight."

Romney looked at him. "I say—Mother's most awfully distressed about Janet going."

Nicholas lit a cigarette.

"Yes, I know. It's a damned shame. It was all my fault, too. I lost my temper one day and cursed her. I was no end sorry afterwards because I know what she means to your mother. I did all I could. I apologized handsomely. No good."

"Could you speak to her again, do you think?" Romney asked.

"Of course I will if you think it'll be any use."

"It might. You're awfully good at getting round people, Uncle."

"Thanks for the compliment, if it *is* a compliment. But no, I'm afraid Janet's one of the people I never *will* get round. She detests me."

"Oh, no, I'm sure she doesn't!"

"I'm sure she does . . . However, I don't mind trying." Nicholas smiled at Romney. "The truth is, old boy, I'm a bit of a nuisance in the house, I'm afraid. I'll be off soon. There's a job I've heard of in Spain—Barcelona."

"Oh, no," said Romney. "We'd miss you like anything. The house is quite different since you've been here."

"Is it? Perhaps it's not a change for the better."

"Of course it is," Romney said. "You've woken us all up."

"I don't think your mother thinks so—or your Uncle Matthew. He was saying something this morning—quite friendly, but suggesting that I've been here a long time."

"Oh, Uncle Matthew! He's always dreaming. He doesn't see things as they are."

"No, I don't think he does—or not as *I* see them."

Romney hesitated. Then he said:

"Uncle Nicholas—will you do something for me?"

"Of course I will—anything in the world but lend you money."

"Will you let me take you out one evening? We'll dine somewhere and go to a show."

"Of course. I'll be delighted."

"I want," Romney went on, "to talk to you. You know the world. You can advise me." He hesitated. "About women, for instance. I'm most awfully ignorant—I——" He stopped.

"Why, of course," Nicholas said. "But what about your father? Why don't you talk to him?"

"Oh, Father! He doesn't know anything about women."

"How do you know?" Nicholas asked.

"Why, of course he doesn't. He's never looked at a woman except Mother."

"I wouldn't be too sure," Nicholas said. "You never can be sure about anyone."

Romney took this in. "No, I suppose you can't. All the same I *am* sure about Father. Besides, anyway, it's difficult talking to one's father. He knows too much about one. He can't see the wood for the trees!"

"And I can?" Nicholas laughed. "All right. We'll have a night out. But don't blame me afterwards."

"No, of course not," Romney said eagerly.

"Well, I don't know," Nicholas said slowly. "People *do* blame me afterwards. I've often noticed it."

He put his hand for a moment on Romney's shoulder.

12

But it was not, as it happened, with Romney that Nicholas's next step was taken.

There came a day—Wednesday, October 19th—which was to prove one of the half-dozen most important days of his life. In Jamaica watching the road to Constant Spring for a brown man with a basket, once in his pyjamas on a cold night in Rome bowing to a lady at the door of her bedroom, once in Sicily turning over the body of a man lying face downwards on the kitchen floor, once nursing Lizzie through a fever in Paris, once climbing naked onto the roof of a villa near Cannes in the early hours of the morning (he hadn't a stitch: he walked down the country road afterwards stark naked), once in a bedroom in a filthy little hotel in Camberwell writing out a check for Abel—these were old historic occasions. Now Wednesday, October 19th, 1932, was another. That day, by a combination of incidents, brought him to a decision which affected the lives of a number of very different people, from Janet's niece in a little house in Hampstead to Mrs. Arthur Paradine, all that day in bed with a cold, in her charming house in Regent's Park, and entirely unaware that Captain Nicholas Coventry existed.

How strange! Because Captain Nicholas lunched with his niece, had tea with Mrs. Agar, an argument with his brother Matthew, and a quarrel with his sister Fanny all on the same day, Wednesday, October 19th, *therefore* some years later Janet's sister Angela married a butcher in Glasgow, Mrs. Paradine's brother, Major Watson-Harvey, committed suicide in a flat in Half Moon Street, and Edward, Fanny's youngest, won a prize for a historical essay on "The Revolution of 1688." To say nothing at all about Fanny Carlisle's life, which was altered entirely by the events of this particular day.

The events, taken separately, did not seem so very unusual, and later, on looking back, Nicholas saw the luncheon as an especially good plate of borsch, the tea party as a pair of white crystal earrings worn by Mrs. Agar, the dispute with his brother as something shared by Leonardo, and the final regrettable incident with Fanny as the outer sheet of *The Times* newspaper.

The luncheon with Nell and her young man began it.

Nicholas had stopped Nell one evening and, moved by very real affection, had put his arm lightly about her and, drawing her a little closer to him, said: "Nell—I'd like to meet your young man one day. Can't I?"

"Why, of course, Uncle Nicholas," she had said.

"What about a meal? I've made a bit at bridge. I'll treat you both to a lunch."

So, on this 19th of October, they all three met at the Basque restaurant in Dover Street. This is one of the best restaurants in London for a quiet little gossip, because the inner room is all corners, the lights (the room must be lit all day) are low, the attendance is polite, swift, unobtrusive, the food is excellent. They had a table in the far corner *round* the corner. They were as remote as though they were in the middle of Glasgow.

Nell's love had matured her in a few weeks, so that she was a child no longer but a woman, ardent, courageous, all-generous, lit with a spiritual as well as a physical radiance. Something too had happened to Hector. He no longer considered as to whether he might not be, with a slice of luck, the greatest poet of the age. He wanted, more than ever before, to write great poetry, but it was poetry now that would be laid at Nell's feet. Like all poets freshly in love he thought his mistress compact of divinity and, as day succeeded day, he found her ever more divine. For these things with every hour move upward until the easiest peak is reached. It is the great question then whether the descent will begin or the difficult climb to a peak hidden in clouds whose conquest is hazardous and uncertain.

Hector had great good fortune in this, that Nell Carlisle was of fine quality, brave, honest, and clear-sighted, with a heart inherited from her mother. This was his good fortune and not his merit, although he was himself a nice boy. But he was, when Nell found him, at the parting of the ways. Another year with his wife and the rot would set in. Which is only another proof of the intricate complexity of all moral questions.

Nicholas, looking upon them, enjoying the experience, recently forbidden him, of acting host again, touched by their youthful ardour, gave them his blessing and thought that the sooner they were in bed together the better. Moral questions did not seem complex to him at all. Then he liked Hector at first sight. He could see that he was a poet, and poetry, as we know, was one of his passions. He had also a natural sympathy with any young man who wished to deceive his wife.

"Now then, you two, what are you going to eat?"

They chose borsch and then other things. They chose the same things, which was, Nicholas thought, very sweet of them.

It was not long, of course, before they were deep in the complexity of their affairs. They told Nicholas everything. Hector, after a cocktail and some very excellent Grave, decided that Nicholas was exactly the man-of-the-world he needed.

And Nicholas was perhaps happier than at any time since that April day of his descent on the Westminster house. Happier and more benevolent. This was how he would always like to be, how, when he was tender with himself, he saw his soul—a bright, thin, shining soul like a sword, but on its sheath carved the figures and patterns of strong benevolence. The two cocktails that he had had, the Grave that he had absorbed, the extraordinary rough richness of the borsch, the knowledge that he would, that afternoon, have tea alone with Mrs. Agar—yes, and something behind these things, as though he were aware, without being actually aware, that today was an important one in his history—all this led him to gaiety, a sort of golden trumpet splendour, a herald of the new world blowing his challenge to the old mildewed castle of dead convention.

"You shouldn't," he said, smiling at them both, "miss your chance. You don't know how suddenly you'll find yourselves old."

Nell looked up at him. Her glance was sharp, even critical, and he had a sudden queer realization of how much of a piece they all were—Fanny, Grace, Matthew, and the two children—forming together a block of shining, innocent, glittering crystal, simple, clear-cut, beautiful if you liked, but irritating in its virtuous purity. He should have been the same block and wasn't.

Nell said: "I've been reading a book. Oh, I know you and Hector will think it most awfully old-fashioned. It's

The Wings of the Dove, by Henry James. I know—it seems older than the Brontës or Jane Austen."

"Where on earth," began Hector, "did you find it, darling?"

"I found it in Ella Parsbury's flat. I asked her if I could borrow it. 'Oh, that old thing,' she said scornfully. Funny, isn't it, when only thirty years ago it was considered the very last word in modern brilliance? I took it home and read it. I couldn't put it down as a matter of fact. But never mind whether I liked it or no. The point is, its subject."

"James's subjects!" Uncle Nicholas said. "He hadn't any—what Wells called a hippopotamus picking up a pea."

"There's one in this book, though. Two lovers tell a lie," Nell went on (she felt that they were both laughing at her, but she didn't care), "and the lie kills their relationship. The consequences of it stand always, afterwards, in their way."

"A very sentimental theme," said Nicholas.

"No," went on Nell gravely. "But the point of the book is that it makes you wonder whether fine conduct isn't worth *everything* else—worth more than *everything.* I know it's priggish now to talk about high conduct at all, but perhaps that's just what's wrong with us all."

"Well——?" asked Hector.

"Well," Nell answered, suddenly smiling rather shyly, "all the time that I was reading *The Wings of the Dove* I was thinking of us. Perhaps if we're shabby and secret over this we'll destroy our love for one another. It won't ever be the same after. *We* won't be the same. Henry James makes you feel that acting nobly is the *only* thing to try for—I expect it's the same now as then."

"Darling," Hector said, "aren't you being a bit sentimental?"

"I don't care," Nell answered defiantly. "It's easy to call names, Hector, and ordinarily I'd be shy of talking like this. But I'll risk your laughing at me. I feel as though we were in for a sort of duel—a duel with someone or something. After all," she went on, raising her head and challenging Nicholas, "you said, Uncle, just now that we might grow old and find that we've missed everything. But what's the fun of having *anything* if you grow cheap and mean and shabby in the process?"

Hector laughed and, putting his arm round her, drew her close to him.

"You're sweet. . . . You're like one of the Della Robbia angels. You're——"

But she drew, almost angrily, away from him.

"No, Hector, I mean this. You can both tease me as much as you like. I'm *sick* of all of us not believing in anything, being so sure that there are no standards any longer, just grabbing at anything, hurting anyone so long as we get what we want. And how are we after it all? Pretty rotten. Look at Ella or Bobby Campbell or Barbara or St. John. . . . And I would have been the same, Uncle Nicholas, if I hadn't fallen in love with Hector. I'm not a bit better than the others, but when you're in love—like this—then it's funny—you don't want to lose the fineness——"

The waiter just then brought the chicken, and it was a good thing because they were all a little embarrassed. Hector had never seen Nell like this, and Nicholas felt (although obviously without reason) that it was in some way a challenge to himself. Nell was showing some of that obtuseness to reality so evident in her mother, her aunt, and her uncle. What *was* this strain in them that was for ever antagonizing him? Anyway he took up the challenge.

"Why should you think we'd laugh at you, Nell?" he said gently. "The question *is* about conduct. It always is. Of course I'm an old ruffian myself," he went on, laughing, "but even I have my rules. But in your particular case, as I see it, it is just what you say. How are you both going to behave so that you get the finest possible thing out of it."

"There, you see!" said Nell triumphantly to Hector. She wondered, as she looked across at her uncle, with his brightness and honesty and kindliness, how she could ever have distrusted him!

"Yes," Nicholas continued. "But Hector's right, too. You mustn't be sentimental."

"I'm not!" Nell broke in.

"No, *you're* not. But Henry James and his pre-war collection of old women were. We really *have* moved on, I think. We—or rather *your* generation—refuse to be hypocritical any longer about sex or anything. You're courageous, open, honest. You don't lie, you can't—because you hide nothing."

"That's just what I say," cried Nell. "We must go to Lottie and say to her—'Look here, Lottie, Hector and I are in love with one another. We're very sorry, but there it is.' Then we must discuss it, quietly, the three of us."

"Quietly!" Hector said. "You don't know Lottie. That's what I'm always telling you. She doesn't want me so long as no one else does. But once you try to take me she'll hold on for all she's worth."

"But she can't," Nell said, "if you don't love her any longer."

"Ah, but she will. She'll make everything as difficult as possible."

"Then we must just go away," Nell said, "until she realizes how things are. We're doing her no wrong. She doesn't love you a bit."

"Yes, and what do we go away on?" asked Hector. "I haven't a bean."

"Oh, we'll get a job," Nell said confidently. "I don't mind what we do."

"There's one thing," Nicholas remarked quietly, "that you seem to have forgotten. There's your mother and father. They don't belong to your generation, you know."

"Mother understands," Nell said eagerly. "She's wonderful, the things she understands."

"I don't believe she'd understand this, all the same. And, anyway, just because they love you so much they'll want to save you from, as it will seem to them, certain unhappiness."

"I don't care," said Nell, who felt that she was being cornered. "I know the right thing is to be open and honest. There's nothing to be ashamed of. Lottie doesn't love Hector, and Hector doesn't love Lottie. It's obviously wrong for them to stay together when Hector loves someone else. There are no children. There's nothing in the way."

"Wait," said Nicholas. "Wait for a while. See how things go."

"The trouble is," said Hector, "that it's diffcult for us to wait. We love one another so much."

"I don't know," Nicholas said. "I've told you already that I'm an old ruffian—but surely that's old-fashioned morality. If you *do* occasionally spend a night together is anyone the worse? Lottie might be if she loved Hector, but she doesn't. And it seems to me that if you hold yourselves in, you two, you'll be doing yourselves more harm—*I* don't know. I mustn't advise you. But that's how I see it."

"It would be secret, underhand, furtive," Nell said. "I don't *want to* be secret about this. I'm proud of loving Hector."

"Yes, that's all very well, my dear," Nicholas said. "But if you tell all the world about it you'll hurt everybody—your mother, your father, yourselves. Of course you *can,* if you like, decide never to see one another again!"

"Oh, can we?" said Hector. "Not if I know it!"

Nell was silent. She had been caught. Uncle Nicholas had an influence on her, steady, strong, determinate. He knew so much about life. He was wise, he was considerate.

Worst of all was the fact that as Hector took her hand her love for him enveloped her, caught her heart and dimmed her judgment. Could she leave him, never see him again? No, she could not. She turned to him with a look, strangely baffled, almost beseeching, infinitely loving.

Uncle Nicholas ordered the bill.

When he left them and went to Mrs. Agar's flat he felt an uncertain twist of annoyance that discomforted him. He was the last man in the world to be sentimental about fine feelings, but Nell's final glance at him had in some way reproached him. He did not believe in consciences—that seemed to him a week-kneed excuse for emotional narcissists—but he *did* believe in anything that happened to himself. He seemed to realize that, in a very short time, he would be forced to make some serious decision. The way that he went then would determine the rest of his life, for he was forty-four years of age and fate could not have the patience to continue for ever offering him choices.

This moment here and now was, in fact, the crisis of his whole life. And Nell's eyes had asked him a more important question than she herself knew: "Uncle Nicholas, are you going to clear out and leave us alone—or—will you remain?"

A quarter of an hour later he was asking Mrs. Agar that question. As soon as he came into the quiet hushed room and saw her with her feet up reading a book and, of all things in the world, with a lace shawl over her shoulders, he knew that he wanted to—that indeed he must—make love to her.

She surrendered at once. She had known, of course, that this was the way that it would go. They spent together a very passionate hour—the little clock was striking four as they came back into the sitting room again—and in the course of that hour Nicholas said a great many excited and foolish things. He asked her—as he had asked very many women before her—to go away with him. He said that she was eating into his blood, that he thought of her night and day (which was quite untrue), that she had the loveliest body in the world, and many more things. Like most sensual men of middle age who have loved women from the age of ten or thereabout, he lost his head in a kind of practised, accustomed manner. In the middle of his most passionate ardours he was aware that he had been abandoned, in just this fashion, a great many times before. Only, a little later, there was, for the first time perhaps, the malancholy little cry of the ageing sensualist: "How long, O Lord, how long? . . ."

And then, when they were quietly seated in front of the fire again, he knew that he had, for ever and ever, sunk one stage lower in the slow remorseless degradation of life.

"And now, Captain Nicholas Coventry," Mrs. Agar said, arranging her shawl about her shoulders and smiling at him very sweetly, "in five minutes you must go. I am so sorry, but I have another visitor who likes me best alone."

He bent forward and kissed her. Their kiss was weary with satiety. He got up.

"You *have* been good to me," he said. "When shall I see you again? Tomorrow?"

"Yes. Perhaps. There are one or two little things I want you to do for me if you will. Oh! nothing important—we'll talk another time."

Suddenly he wanted to get away, to get far away—back to Jamaica, perhaps—somewhere safe.

"Do you know," he said, "I'm not sure whether it would not be better for me to leave England tomorrow—shall I?"

"Certainly—if you think it better."

"I haven't a bean, though. I got twenty pounds out of my dear brother-in-law yesterday. But twenty pounds—it soon goes."

She laughed. "Yes—it does, doesn't it?" Then she said: "Do you want to be put in the way of making quite a lot of money?"

"What way?" he asked.

"Oh, there are lots of ways. If you are clever it's very easy to make money."

It was difficult for him to realize that, only twenty minutes before, he had had her intimately in his arms. But this experience too was no new one.

"Yes—but I don't want to go to gaol," he said, laughing. "Remember that I belong to a very respectable family."

"Risks are the salt of life," she answered, stretching her arms and smiling reflectively. "And really there are so many people who deserve to be plundered—so many conceited, stupid people. Besides, you need never go to gaol. You can always slip out of life—much more easily than you slipped into it."

"Yes, I suppose so. But—it may seem strange to you—I don't want to die. I love life. If only an old lady would adopt me, look after me, give me security, what a good young man I could be!"

"Yes," she answered lazily, "but being adopted isn't such fun as you'd suppose. I've tried it and I know. Very tiresome. After all, nobody gives you anything for nothing. Why should they? I've tried all the alternatives and my way is the best."

"What *is* your way?"

"You shall see if you care to."

He said good-bye. They did not kiss again.

He knew, as he boarded a bus for Westminster, that he would now give a very great deal never to have met Mrs. Agar. That regret—and that fear—put him into a malicious, irritable humour. It was not, he told himself, that he was weak but that one thing led so damnably to another. He was exasperated at the placid safety and good fortune of the family to which he was returning. What had *they* done to revel undisturbed in their smug complacency? He was as good as they; better, because he saw life with clear, honest courage while they cheated. He was a dangerous man as he let himself into the Westminster house.

It was striking a quarter to five as he climbed the stairs. As he turned towards his room he saw Matthew.

"Hullo, Matthew!" he said gaily.

Matthew appeared embarrassed.

"Look here, Nicholas. Have you got a minute?"

"Why, yes, of course."

"Would you come up to my room?"

"Certainly."

The sense that he had had all day of a developing crisis grew on him. He had never been in Matthew's room and, as he entered it, and saw the Leonardo, the orderly bookshelves, the quiet decency of it, he felt that Matthew had an advantage of him. What a quiet old humbug the old boy was! The only one now of the whole family over whom Nicholas had not some hold, and if the truth were known *he* had a mistress hidden somewhere—or even a worse skeleton. Bachelors were queer cattle one way or another.

But the important thing was that this little meeting would suit his mood, for Matthew was the only one of the family whom he thoroughly disliked, had always disliked since they were tiny children together rolling about on the floor of the nursery. Matthew was a year his senior—that had always annoyed him. Matthew was calm and imperturbable. Matthew was (as far as one knew) good. Matthew was religious. Matthew was really detestable.

He tumbled into one of Matthew's armchairs, took out his pipe, stretched his elegant legs, and looked at his brother most lovingly.

"Well, old man, what is it—and, do you know, I've never been in your room before?"

"No, I know you haven't."

"I've always been afraid to. What do you carry on in here so quietly—private orgies or something?"

"No, nothing so exciting, I'm afraid," said Matthew, timidly smiling. He was afraid of his dashing scornful brother and, realizing his fear, was ashamed of himself.

"We all want to know," said Nicholas lightly. "I myself have seen some of the oddest people coming up the stairs, an old man like a prophet, a young man like a prizefighter. . . . You know," he went on, "this *is* a comic house! There can't be another like it in London—the way we all go on leading our own lives. . . . Why, I've been here since April and we really haven't had a talk, you and I, although we're brothers, all the time I've been here."

"No," said Matthew. "And that's the reason I asked you in now. I've been shy of inviting you."

"Shy—of me!" said Nicholas, laughing. "Impossible! Why, old chap, no one could be shy of a lazy good-for-nothing like myself!"

"I've always been shy of you, I think," said Matthew, "all my life long—and you know I have."

"Well, we haven't seen so much of one another, have we?" said Nicholas. "I've been abroad such a lot."

"Yes, you have—and for ten years never gave us a sign of your existence."

"I know," said Nicholas, giving his legs a cheerful little kick. "That's just like me. I'm a most awful rotter. And I'm so fond of you all. And yet I let all that time pass."

"And what are you going to do now?" asked Matthew.

"Now—why, what do you mean?"

"How long are you going to stay with us?"

"Oh, I don't know." Nicholas stretched his arms and yawned. "Why—are you tired of me?"

"Yes, I am," said Matthew.

After that there was a long pause. Nicholas looked at Matthew from his head to his feet, at his plump cheeks, his square body, his broad thighs, his small feet.

He said at length:

"Of all the damned cheek!"

Matthew sighed. "Yes, I suppose it *is* cheek. I hated saying it. I've been days and days making up my mind."

"Making up your precious mind to what?"

"To asking you to go. You see, it isn't really my place. It isn't *my* house. So long as Charles and Fanny like to have you here it isn't anything to do with me, especially as we scarcely ever see one another. All the same I do ask you!"

Nicholas drew a deep breath. Then he laughed. He repeated: "Of all the damned cheek!" Then, as though to himself: "Never mind. Let's see what this means. What *does* it mean, my dear brother? Is it simply personal? Of course we've always loathed one another. That's why we've kept out of one another's way. So that if it's simply personal, it's nothing new. But *is* it? Is it only your own idea?"

"I don't know," said Matthew slowly. "I don't want you to take offense at this. I don't see why you should. All our lives you've completely disregarded me. I don't see why we shouldn't quietly discuss it. I think you're doing a lot of harm here. I don't suppose you mean to. I don't think you ever *do* mean to do harm. All the same—please go away. You aren't our sort. You never were. You're making a lot of people unhappy."

"Oh—and whom do I make unhappy?"

"Fanny, Grace—soon Romney, and Nell and Charles."

Then Nicholas burst out laughing. He slapped his knee.

"Matthew, you're priceless! You always have been, you always will be. You're the most hopeless old-womanish prig and sentimentalist the world has ever seen. And so you always were. Do you remember when those boys came over from Donnington once and we had the rat-hunt? Do you remember how sick you were? And do you remember when I whacked your behind for sneaking to Mother about the apples?"

"I don't think I did sneak," said Matthew quietly. "But never mind. It's a long time ago."

"No, of course you didn't sneak *really,* but the results were the same. That was you all over. You were always better than everyone else, afraid to swear lest God should hear you. You wouldn't kiss a girl because it was wicked and you wouldn't bet because it wasn't fair and you wouldn't drink because you were ill if you did——"

"Anyway," said Matthew, laughing, "you can't hold that up against me, Nicholas. It wasn't my fault if it disagreed with me."

"Oh, but it *would* disagree with you! Anything sporting always did. . . . And now this is just like you again. *You* want me to leave the house, *you* inform me, quietly and in the secrecy of your chamber, that I'm an offense to the family! As a matter of fact if you ask them you'll find that they like me very much indeed."

"Yes," said Matthew, who discovered that his fear had left him. "Of course you're charming. You can charm anyone. That's why I've kept you out of my room. I didn't *want* to be charmed by you."

"Well, you're not going to be charmed by me now," said Nicholas. His voice had changed. It was hard and chill—even a little exasperated. He was determined *not* to lose his temper, but he really did detest Matthew and would not mind at all kicking his too large behind even as he had done in childhood. The sense of this made control more difficult.

"I tell you straight, Matthew, you're a meddlesome humbug just as you've always been. You sit here in your room like an old woman—God only knows what you are *doing* with your prizefighters and prophets!—and when you come out into decent daylight you blink like an old owl. Meanwhile we're all very happy and jolly and comfortable, thank you."

"So you're going to stay?" Matthew asked with a sigh.

"Yes, I'm going to stay."

"I'm sorry——" Matthew rubbed his nose with his forefinger. "Because in that case I shall do everything I can to see that you don't."

"You!" Nicholas cried scornfully. "What can *you* do?"

"I can show Fanny and Charles what you're like. They haven't the least idea."

"What I'm *like?"* Nicholas was scornfully amused. "My dear Matthew, how do *you* know?"

Matthew knocked his pipe out against the fireplace. "I'm not such a fool as you think, Nicholas. I never was. That was always your big mistake. I'm not clever in *your* way. I believe in the things you don't believe in and so you think me a fool. But you're an ass in your own way, you know——"

Nicholas laughed. "You're not worth being annoyed with, Matthew. Of course I'm an ass—it doesn't need you to tell me. If I weren't should I be here amusing the family for my bread and butter? Do you really think that that's the most amusing thing I could find to do? But there is at least this difference between us: I'm honest. I know the world to be a swindling sham. I know that my next-door neighbour's probably worse than myself and I'm bad enough. And thank heaven the rest of humanity's coming at last to my way of thinking. God's finished, even though it's taken two thousand years to finish Him."

Matthew puffed at his pipe. "I said just now that you're a fool, Nicholas, and so you are. How do you know anything about God? You've never been on speaking terms with Him, nor ever tried to be. It's as though you said the Taj Mahal didn't exist simply because you've never been there."

Nicholas leant forward. He looked at his quiet pipe-smoking brother for the first time with intentness.

"Now that really interests me, Matthew," he said. "Forget our personal dislike of one another for a moment. Can you seriously tell me, as a grown man with his wits about him, that you believe in God?"

"I do."

"Well—I'm damned! I'm being quite sincere in this. I didn't conceive it possible that in this year nineteen thirty-two there was any man anywhere with brains and education who seriously believed in God."

"But you know there are," Matthew answered. "Plenty—Roman Catholics——"

"Oh—it's their job. Will you tell me that any of these professing Christians, when they're alone with their naked selves in their bedrooms, believe in God? Really believe, I mean—believe in Him as they know that two and two make four."

"But certainly," Matthew answered. "No one is *certain* that two and two make four. You may wake up tomorrow morning and find that two and two make five. But a great spiritual power working in us to increase us in wisdom, beauty, holiness, generosity—*that's* more certain than any mathematics."

Nicholas nodded. "I won't contradict you. To me it's as though you were repeating the sort of nonsense we learnt as children—'The cat is on the mat'—'I have the pen of my aunt.' To me, Matthew, you're like a little round funny kitten who thinks the world one large saucer of milk. But you can take this from me—there *is* no spiritual world. Men are animal, chemical, mineral, what you like—spiritual—bosh! And we're talking like a pair of schoolboys. Don't let's waste our time."

"No, we won't," Matthew said. "But I'm glad that we've said what we have because now you must see why one of us has got to clear out of this house. It's more than a personal difference of opinion between us two. The whole world is divided as we are. And now it's a fight in the open. You and the others like you think meanly of men, you pride yourselves on your cynicism, your grasp of reality, your humour, your refusal to be humbugged. You'd pull everything down and build up some sort of scientific machinery. Everything that we ever regard as essential you despise. You think that we are humbugs when we say that we believe in God and a spiritual world, that we are sentimental when we say that men are noble and must think themselves noble, that we are silly children because we think Heaven a practical possibility. It *is* an open fight now, however concealed it used to be. You give yourselves the right to say what you like when you think, but if we open our mouths you call us impertinent."

"Here endeth the Lesson," said Nicholas.

"I don't care. You can laugh at me for preaching. But your time of going about unchallenged is over."

Nicholas got up.

"My dear chap, *I* don't mind you having your beliefs. You can shout your gospel all over the place for all I care. It doesn't harm *me*."

"No, it doesn't," Matthew cried excitedly. "Not until it touches you. But now it does touch you. It interferes with your daily life and will interfere more and more. It isn't a theory any longer. It's an active question of conduct. You come into this house and, because you believe as you do, begin to break everything up. You can't act otherwise. When you think our love for one another an absurdity, our belief in one another romantic nonsense, our ideals sentimentality, Fanny and Grace two silly old women, Charles and me two idiotic old men, the children ignorant, waiting for your wisdom—of course you, being restless, conceited, idle, unscrupulous, set to work to destroy us. It's quite natural. I don't blame you a bit. But I'm going to fight you, Nicholas. I'll throw you out of this house one way or another——" He banged his pipe on the side of the fireplace again and it snapped. "Oh, dear—that's my favourite pipe."

Nicholas looked down at him, almost with affection.

"Why, I've never seen you excited before! I didn't know you could be! Poor old Bottomley in his prime couldn't have done it better."

There was a long silence and, during that silence, both realized that there was something *actual* in this—that it was not merely a discussion or a quarrel. There was a deep fundamental antagonism here and a declaration of battle.

"Do your damnedest," said Nicholas. "I'm comfortable here and I'm staying."

Matthew looked at the two pieces of his pipe ruefully.

"Perhaps Charles can mend it," he said. "I mean what I say, Nicholas."

"Oh, go to hell!" said Nicholas.

Back in his own room and dressing for dinner the sense of wanting to hurt someone grew with every moment. The events of the day had hit his pride: Nell, mysteriously and without herself knowing it; Mrs. Agar, because she had humiliated his personal conceit; and now Matthew, because the silly old fool had shown him a real fighting opposition.

"He'll kick me out, will he?" he murmured as he fitted his studs into his shirt. "I'll show him."

And the climax of the day was a quarter of an hour later. He was first in the drawing room, and Fanny was second.

She came up to him, flustered, excited, her face like a child's, eagerly expressing her distress.

"Oh, Nicholas, you shouldn't," she cried.

"Shouldn't what, my dear?" and he kissed her.

"No, I don't want you to kiss me. I'm cross with you. Oh, dear, how I hate these things happening."

"Now, Fanny, what *is* the matter?"

"You've borrowed from Charles again. That's the third time! Oh, I'm so ashamed! You're my brother—I've been so happy to have you here. I've been so proud of you. But this spoils everything. Don't you see that Charles hasn't got it, the money, I mean? He's so good and generous. He'd give his shirt away. But that's all the more reason why you shouldn't ask him——"

"Now look here, Fanny——" he began.

But she was too deeply moved to stop.

"No, I mean it, Nick. That first fifty pounds you said you'd pay him back at once, that you had money in Paris. But you haven't attempted to. And then there was thirty —just before we went away in the summer. And now this. It's too bad. It really is."

His lips tightened. He stood leaning with his hand on the mantelpiece.

"Aren't you making rather a fuss about nothing, my dear? It's only a hundred in all. Charles shall be paid the whole lot in a month's time. Incidentally I thought the thing was in confidence between Charles and myself: I didn't know he was going to blazon it all over the house!"

"How silly! He isn't blazoning it. He tells me everything."

"Oh, does he?" Nicholas looked at her.

"Of course he does."

"Well, that's what *you* think!"

She looked at him fiercely, as though Charles were there in the room with them and she had her protective arms around him.

"What do you mean? Of course he tells me everything. You're always hinting at things, Nick."

He blew the ash off his cigarette into the fire.

"Oh, no, I'm not." Then he smiled. "Now look here, Fanny, you're making a fuss about nothing. Charles and I understand one another perfectly."

She looked up at him pleadingly.

"Nick—promise me—promise me that you won't ask him for any more money. He's a child about money. Come to me and talk things over if you're in a hole——"

He put out his hand and took hers.

"All right, Fanny dear. I will."

But she still looked at him anxiously.

"Nick—don't you think—oughtn't you to be getting a job of some sort? You said you would. You're so clever."

He withdrew his hand.

"Ah, I'm outstaying my welcome. . . . All right, I'll go."

"No. No. Of course I don't mean that. The children love your being here. So do I, of course, but—all the same——"

"Yes, I quite understand." He sighed.

She put her hand on his shoulder. "I'm so sorry. I've been as usual perfectly tactless."

"No—it's all right. You're a brick to put up with me."

But, at that moment, he made his resolve.

His own brother, his own sister! And he'd done nothing but amuse them for months. He'd made this dull house a different place. And that was all the thanks he got! They wanted to turn him out. . . .

Well, they should have their lesson. He'd show them! Looking into the fire, he thought of the letter, Charles's letter. He thought of Grace, Nell with her love affair, Romney and his desire for instruction. . . . The old woman upstairs afraid of death. . . .

He had this house in his hands. He could do with it what he wished.

They all came in—Grace, Romney, Nell, Matthew, Charles. The gong sounded. He caught Grace's arm.

"Come on! Dinner! I'm famished. Now, Grace—we'll head the procession!" And then, as they reached the top of the stairs, he whispered gaily in her ear:

"Been writing any more letters lately?"

END OF PART II

PART III

THE LETTER

THE LETTER

IT WAS now that Nicholas achieved his powerful domination over Nell and Romney. It was as though he had not really tried his strength until now. And yet, even at that, he need not put out his strength exceptionally. His conquest was very easy.

He achieved it in all sorts of ways, but mainly in two—his love of the Arts, his vision of London.

Romney and Nell also loved the Arts, but they possessed no friend as humorous and as justly critical as Uncle Nicholas. He seemed always to put his finger on the right spot. They were, for instance, discussing the novels of Somerset Ball, who was often roughly treated by the younger æsthetes. "It's absurd," said Romney, "to pretend they're jealous of him. There's nothing to be jealous of. What exasperates them is his shamness. His work is all iridescent, false in colour, brittle like those awful Moorish rooms you see in Turkish baths. It's even more glittering than the real thing and *all* sham from ceiling to floor."

Nicholas said: "Now that's just it. The young always go halfway and stop there. Ball's novels *are* shams—a sham world—but something saves them, a real sense of terror, of apprehension. He was frightened some time—you wouldn't think so to look at him!—but he was, and there's *real* terror in his Turkish bath—something hiding behind the lattice screen. Never mind how many pieces of coloured glass there are. He knows what it is to be frightened—unlike all your splendid modern young Siegfrieds who go cynically up the mountain although they know the fire's false. Ball knows the fire's real. He was burnt once."

He gave himself up to them now with a freedom and a gaiety that was enchanting. He was as young as they and infinitely wiser. His passion for reciting poetry, that would have been so boring in another, was only natural in himself. He would gave them a poem of Baudelaire's in Piccadilly and then make so enthralling a story out of that unhappy man's life—his Œdipus complex, the awful Mme. Aupick, his passion for his mother, her love for him which nevertheless allowed her to keep him in penury most of his days, the appalling Black Venus, Jeanne Duval, the day when he gave his lecture in Brussels and because of some allusion to "virginity" in his opening sentences emptied the hall completely save for one young man, of whether he were impotent or no, of his lonely and piteous death—made, yes, so enthralling a picture that they walked, all three, to Sloane Street with Baudelaire and Hugo and d'Aurevilly in their company, coming at last to earth with a bang into the society of a blind man with a tin cup, a raucous young lad selling the *Evening Standard,* and a pastry cook's window.

It was, in fact, London that he created for them in those weeks.

Whatever else they will think of him, this at least they will never deny—that he joined his genius to London's genius, and the two together were something new, never seen by anybody before. For he *had* genius, Nicholas had, when he was happy and free. That was his tragedy—that he wasn't happy and free enough. Just this week or two with Nell and Romney before he passed on to other things, not quite so meritorious. . . .

They adventured all over London during that time. Looking back, Romney will always see it as moving in and out of grey cloud and fog, cloud lit with red streams of light, of sudden cold crimson suns like fragments of lacquer; the town moved like a gigantic ship. All London was London River because the sky made it so. Hotels seemed like liners, and he would never forget the hungry blank-eyed warehouses in the glass of whose staring windows a revolving light of some sky sign would spring to life in a grand flashing contempt and then spring away again.

They enjoyed the Fragonards at the Wallace and the little Watteau called "The Fountain" which, although they had both been to the Wallace several times, they had never noticed before.

"Just imagine!" said Romney. "I'm supposed to care about pictures and this is the first time I've seen that gold statue and the woman in white!"

They went to the police courts and were, in turn (so ardent were their sympathies), a couple of lovers who had made the Park their paradise, an old lady with a recalcitrant daughter, and a young woman who appeared, for the thirty-eighth time, on the score of soliciting. They went to the Zoo and liked the Aquarium best, for here bubbles of light broke, like golden rain, into the heart of translucent water, and there was the king crab whose shell is armour-plated but whose stomach is a paper napkin. (Others have observed this besides Nicholas.) They had luncheon in a very grand hotel where everything was counterfeit except the anxious eyebrows of the waiter and the Crêpes Suzette. They went on an omnibus up the Old Kent Road where, outside the Methodist Chapel, there is a sentence in big black letters on a white board—"God rewardeth the humble"—and the humble waited patiently outside the butcher's shop and searched in the gutter for cigarette ends. They went to a Literary Party and found the struggle for existence to be very bitter, but in Fortnum & Mason's, among the jellied tongues, the comfortable pies, and the bottled fruit, everything was tranquillity.

How did all these incongruities mingle? What do you make of them, you disordered, sprawling city? London is the boarding house of the world. Upstairs the iron bedstead, the looking-glass with the chipped white-painted frame, the strip of shabby carpet, the text "Thou God Seest Me," but downstairs lives an old bachelor who has in his wide spacious rooms a Gainsborough, a Tang horse with a green saddle, butter dishes of George II with handles like rosebuds, and the most beautiful Chippendale chairs. And from his windows *such* a view—bridges like spider webs, skies of rose and amber, bronze lions set about a fountain, and a church with a dome as big as the moon, pearl-grey cliffs with pools of the faintest green. "No Noise Here. No Organ Grinders Allowed." But the street is rent with electric drills, and great buildings fall, in showers of dust, between scaffoldings of gleaming iron.

A policeman lifts his hand. The world stops.

Nicholas had, of course, the greater power over Romney just at this time because of Romney's unhappiness.

The evening came when Romney took Nicholas out to dinner and Nicholas took Romney out somewhere afterwards. This was an important evening in Romney's life.

He chose a small restaurant in Albemarle Street because it was very expensive. He knew that his uncle wanted the best. The room itself was simple enough. There were not more than half a dozen tables in it, and the waiter who cared for their needs was so quiet that you heard his heart beat like a clock. He was very firm about what they ought to have. The food indeed was excellent but very quiet, too. The windows were hung with dark purple curtains, and on the white walls there were some highly coloured drawings by a Chinese artist. Between the windows there was a cuckoo clock which was homely and reassuring.

In this quiet place Romney told his Uncle Nicholas everything just as he had told his Uncle Matthew everything—but he was very much more at his ease with Uncle Nicholas, who was certainly not shy and did not believe in God. He explained to Romney what life had taught him about love—exactly as one man to another.

"You see, I'm a little handicapped about your story, Romney, because I've never known any tender emotion towards my own sex. It's been women with me all my life. Frankly any sentiment about another man seems to me silly—a little out of drawing if you understand what I mean. Men are physically very unattractive. I'm sure you feel that yourself. What *you* were experiencing was a sort of "Parsifal" business. Most boys go through it at school. You came to it rather late, that's all. Although how you *can* have seen the Holy Grail in that dull clodhopper you've described to me I altogether fail to understand."

Romney laughed. "Well, I don't now," he said. Yes—how *could* he? He saw Harry now as a pair of golf stockings, a pipe, and a leather armchair.

"Oh, well—we all go batty sometimes. I remember a woman once . . ."

He explained his philosophy about women. Women were realists. They wanted only one thing at a time, but what they wanted they wanted like hell!

The thing to do then, if you liked them enough, was to give them what they wanted and then, after mutual pleasure had been taken, go away.

"That doesn't account for people like Mother," Romney said.

Ah, no, Nicholas agreed. Sentimental women were different. They needed sentimental men. But he, Nicholas, wasn't a sentimental man. He abominated sentiment. All the evils in the world came from it. All the bad art, all the bad thinking, all the mush and the tosh and the slime of life came from it! Nicholas hoped that Romney wasn't a sentimentalist. He didn't think he was. *If* he was, then he must find a sentimental woman as quickly as possible, marry her, have a lot of children, and live happy, like a fly in sugar, ever after.

"But aren't there," Romney asked, "people in the world who meet, love one another devotedly, and yet are not sentimentalists?"

Yes, Nicholas admitted that there were. But these became companions of the most realistic kind. And they were rare.

"Mind you, I say nothing against your father and mother, Romney; I'm delighted, of course, that they are so happy. But I have to admit that they are sentimentalists. And they belong to another age than ours. At last," he went on, enjoying his excellent wine, "we are beginning to understand that physical delight between men and women is something by itself—to be enjoyed to the full but never to be confused with the domestic virtues. See things as they really are and life will be worth while. But litter it up with sham mysticism and a God like a spiritualist's tambourine and you're better dead. Take warning from your Uncle Matthew."

Without being at all sentimental he was compelled to feel a kind of tenderness for young Romney. The boy was just emerging from the shell. It was amusing and rather touching to witness. He was *not* touched by the fact that Romney was unhappy. That would be good for him and help him to get to grips with life. Moreover that unhappiness would vanish after he had made love to a woman or two. The boy was good-looking and intelligent and would be attractive to women.

Here also was a further charm, for this education that he was giving Romney would lead him finally from his mother's apron strings. To give Fanny a shock or two—for had she not been tiresome and interfering?—was not an unpleasant amusement.

She had kept Romney altogether too close to her. He was too much of a mother's darling.

The little bird sprang from its wooden door, cuckooed nine times, and returned to its home with a whir of satisfaction.

"You see, Romney," he said, "the great thing is not to be humbugged away from reality. See life exactly as it is. Don't think that everything is different from what it is. That way lies perdition."

"Yes," said Romney a little uncertainly. "But what about people like Blake and Emily Brontë?"

"Oh, *Wuthering Heights!*" Nicholas answered in disgust. "I'm sick of all the flim-flam about that overpraised work. The madness of a besotted boy. Because Bramwell wrote most of it, you know. Nothing but fustian."

"Well—there's *King Lear.*"

"Oh, *Lear!* Magnificent of course. But never was there a completer exposure of sentimental nonsense. Lear is a sentimental vain old man, and Nature whips him for it. Gloucester's another, and doesn't Shakespeare enjoy gouging his eyes out! . . . Well, we must be getting on. We're going to visit some old friends of mine."

He had telephoned earlier in the evening to Dinah Brown, who lived with her friend Florence Kirby in a nice flat in Knightsbridge. They had said that they would be at home. He had met Dinah in Paris some five years before and had promised her then that he would visit her some time in London. This seemed to him a good occasion.

Dinah and Florence were waiting for him. Their room was very gay; there was a large doll in black silk on the crimson sofa, there was a small white dog with a blue silk ribbon, there were pictures of naked ladies on the wall, a roaring fire, many silk cushions, drinks, and a gramophone.

Dinah was thin, flaxen, and talkative. Florence was dark, plump, silent, and smiling. Nicholas was at once at home with them and sat on a sofa, one arm round each. Romney sat on a chair, feeling most uncomfortable. Dinah shrieked and laughed and shrieked again. After a while she took Nicholas away into another room to show him something.

Romney and Florence stared at one another and said nothing. Then, quite suddenly, Florence sat on his knee. In a soft husky voice she said: "Tell me all about yourself, darling boy."

Romney told her a little, and after a while she suggested that they should try the sofa. Romney longed passionately that Nicholas would return. . . .

Florence was very affectionate. She told him that he was the dearest, dearest boy. Her affection grew with leaps and bounds, and he, in a misery of frustrated desire, behaved as he supposed a gentleman should. The little white dog scratched itself in front of the fire. The room became as hot and confined as Hell must be.

After a long time affection languished and polite manners returned. Florence, straightening her hair, said:

"Oh, it's a lovely piece. A gentleman friend took me the other night, but I could see it again. I really could. What about stalls one evening?"

Nicholas at length returned and, in a quick aside, suggested that Romney should put a five-pound note on the mantelpiece, which he did. Dinah kissed Nicholas. Florence kissed Romney.

In the taxi, Nicholas said:

"Well, my boy. Had a good evening?"

"Yes, thanks," said Romney. But he was moving in the black circles of despair. Gone for ever, yes, for ever and ever, was the Holy Grail. No hope for him anywhere now. Not that he had sinned—anything so grand as sin was surely not in question. But the world of beauty, the world of his little sculptured negress, the world of the spring evening that spreads its lovely cloak over the homely misshapen body of mankind, was denied to him now because he was not worthy to behold it.

"We must think nobly of ourselves," Uncle Matthew had said.

"They are not bad girls," Uncle Nicholas remarked. "Kindly and all that. They have a pretty stiff time, I shouldn't wonder."

"And so do I!" Romney thought. "This hateful world!"

2

After Janet's taxi had disappeared around the corner of the church, Fanny had felt a quite desperate shock of being abandoned. Their last words had not been very eloquent:

"Why, why, why, Janet . . . ?" Fanny had asked. The tall bony woman, in her Sunday clothes that fitted her as they might a waxwork, said, looking fiercely from under her grey eyebrows: "I think it better, mum."

"But *why?*" Fanny repeated. "The Captain has apologized. We shall miss you dreadfully. You won't find it too amusing, you know. If you'd only give me an idea. . . ." And then she added what she would not have added two months earlier: "The Captain won't be staying here for ever."

Janet said nothing. She simply stared obstinately in front of her, her hands folded over her umbrella. Then Fanny felt that her underlip was trembling, so she went on hurriedly:

"Don't you understand, Janet? You can't be so stupid. . . . I can't—I shan't be able to get along without you. I depend on you for everything—I——"

"I shan't be far away," Janet said.

Then Fanny understood that Janet was doing this for a purpose, that she had no intention whatever of abandoning the house and the family for ever. She was expecting that something would happen that would call her back. But what? What *could* happen?

"You'll come back," Fanny said. "I feel it in my bones."

"Maybe," said Janet, staring in front of her. Fanny kissed her, and off she went with a large brown trunk studded with brass nails, a big worn hold-all, and a pile of grim-looking black-bound volumes of *Good Words.*

So the taxi turned the corner and Fanny was desolate. Of all things, that was the last to be expected, that Janet would leave her. But she hadn't left her. Fanny felt exactly as though Janet were just round the corner with her brown nail-studded box, her umbrella, and her volumes of *Good Words* waiting for the catastrophe to occur. But again, *what* catastrophe?

Then there was a new unexpected element in the situation. Matthew stepped forward. Fanny and Matthew had been always great friends—they had, from childhood, loved one another—but they kept, on the whole, apart. They were both shy persons. They were shy of one another. And now, for a long time, they had lived in the same house, eaten together, talked and parted. It had been an excellent arrangement. Fanny's idea of Matthew was that he was a darling and a saint, but that his close companionship with God made him rather a difficult companion for anyone else.

But now, quite suddenly, he was changed. One night he took herself and Charles to the theatre, giving them supper at the Savoy after. When he met her on the stairs or going out of the house he said: "Hullo, Fan! Is there anything I can do?"

He realized, she supposed, how deeply she would feel this departure of Janet's. One thing he knew about her—that she was quite helplessly dependent on human affection. She needed love as a flower needs the sun—not a new metaphor but exact in her case. She drooped, she failed, she lost all heart before hostility, criticism, unfriendliness.

Then she was frightened. Was it because he saw that those she loved were withdrawing from her that he came out now to help her? Were they withdrawing—Charles, Romney, Nell, Grace, Janet? Janet had left. Were the others going to leave her, too? Did he foresee that?

An afternoon came when he volunteered to go with her to a meeting about cruelty to children. This was held in

Mrs. Pontifex's house, and the distinguished novelist, Somerset Ball, was in the chair.

Mrs. Pontifex had never been the same to Fanny since the evening of the unhappy dinner party—*nothing* had been quite the same since that evening—but cruelty to children was so terrible a thing that one must do all one can and sink Mrs. Pontifex in the general cause. Moreover, Fanny was a child at heart and thought that it would be interesting to see Mr. Ball.

Mr. Ball must have been taking chairs since his bassinette days, so exactly suited was he, by physique and temperament, to that honourable calling. He looked, as Matthew observed, quite incredibly "right." He was robust, red-faced, had a large shining forehead and precisely the correct manner—friendly, modest, cheerful, a little assured but a little shy, too, a little humorous and a little serious, an English gentleman through and through —and, as so many of the ladies present felt, so very few novelists today *are* gentlemen.

He introduced the principal speaker of the meeting—a small, rather shabby woman to whom cruelty to children was an actual, positive fact that had nothing at all to do with whether you were a gentleman or no—in exactly the right manner. He told a funny (but friendly) story about the Bishop of London, he alluded, deprecatingly, to the folly of a man so stupidly ignorant of the facts being in the chair (but showed that he was pleased to be there), gave his voice, that had been jolly (almost schoolboyish) and we-are-all-friends-here-together, a note of true seriousness when he said that, however wars and conferences might come and go, this awful child cruelty was always with us—and then introduced Miss Ellen Parker.

Miss Ellen Parker told such terrible stories (and they

were clearly nothing to the stories that she *could* tell) that Fanny felt quite sick, seeing, as always, her own dear Edward in these situations and herself powerless to help him. Before Miss Parker sat down Fanny had resolved to devote her every spare penny to this splendid cause, but then Mr. Ball spoke again, and he was so reassuring, so comfortable, so friendly, that Fanny felt at ease once more. It was as though he said: "I'm not much of a fellow, although you may think I am. These things that Miss Parker has been telling you are *quite* awful, and no one feels them more than I do. All the same, so long as I'm here, things can't be so dreadfully bad."

Pursuing the rather drab little byways behind Victoria Street, on their homeward course, Matthew remarked: "Now, if I ring the bell of Number Nine and say, 'Please tell me what you think of cruelty to children, your notion of God, your true conception of the universe,' they will call for a policeman."

"Of course," Fanny said, "life couldn't go on if we behaved like that."

"Why not?" Matthew asked sharply.

"Oh, well—it couldn't. We have our daily jobs. If you kept a barrow with oysters and winkles, Matthew dear, you wouldn't be able to think of God as much as you do."

"Yes, I would! Yes, I would!" Matthew said, quite excited. "I don't go after God—God goes after me."

"Well, then," said Fanny rather wistfully, "why doesn't He go after everybody?"

"He does, but they have to give Him a chance." He shook his round head. "I didn't like that fellow Ball. He's done it all too often."

"Perhaps," said Fanny, "he dislikes his public manner very much. I've noticed with all public men that they *have* to have a manner. I daresay they are ashamed of it when they are alone."

A thin fog, through which the autumn sunlight in cold sullen splashes tried to break, crawled about the houses, the children playing, and a policeman writing in a little book.

"Fanny," said Matthew suddenly and taking her arm, "I want you to do something."

"And what is that?" asked Fanny, who walked with her head up, her eyes shining, her hat a trifle askew, wondering whether she would be home in time to give Edward his tea.

"I want you to ask Nicholas to take his leave of us."

He felt her arm stiffen under his. She turned to look at him.

"Why—don't you like him?" she asked.

"No. You know I never did. But that isn't important. Brothers often don't understand one another, and certainly Nicholas and I *never* could. That has *nothing* to do with it. I would never have said a word had I not been sure that he is a danger to all of us, that he is going to make us all very unhappy."

"Oh, Matthew—do you really think so?" she asked.

"I do. And there's no time to lose."

"Why—what is he doing?"

"He's breaking us all up. He's setting us all against one another. I know I've no right to speak. I've kept to myself so much and led my own life. I've been selfish, I suppose, although I didn't think so. But I *mean* it, Fan. Nicholas has no morals, no scruples. I don't say that he means to do harm, although I think that sometimes he does. He can't help himself. He has no rules to go by. All he wants is to be fed and kept, and he has a kind of malice, a sort of humorous malice——"

"Matthew!" Fanny said. "I've never heard you speak against anybody before!"

"I'm not speaking against Nicholas now. I'm simply speaking of him as he *is*. I don't blame him. That's how he's made. But we've got to look after ourselves. We've got to look after the children. Soon, if you don't look out, he'll have broken us all up, spoiled our love for one another, ruined our lives perhaps."

Fanny felt that he was trembling.

"And there's no time to lose, either. He's hard up. I don't believe he has a penny. He has nowhere to go. He won't work. All this puts him in a bad humour. He'll vent it on us, and especially, Fanny, on you."

"What do you mean? What have you heard?"

"Never mind. I know he's plotting something. He despises the lot of us, and in a way he's right, because he's much cleverer than we are. But you and Charles can get rid of him. And you must."

"But Charles likes him. He didn't at first, but now he does. And Romney and Nell like him. And Granny. And Edward."

"All the more reason to get rid of him. That means he has all the more influence. Can't you *see,* Fan? Can't you see how you and Grace and Romney and Nell have all changed in these last months?"

"Have we? Have *I* changed?"

"Of course you have. Have you been happy lately? Ask yourself."

"It's only Janet going and——"

"And why has Janet gone?"

"Yes, I know. But that's only her tiresome obstinacy. Nick apologized to her most handsomely."

"More of his cleverness."

They were at the door of the house. Inside, before they

went upstairs, Matthew put his arm around her and kissed her.

"Get rid of him," he whispered.

Fanny was greatly disturbed, but there was more trouble coming, for as she stood in front of the glass taking off her hat, Charles put his head in through the door.

"Can I come in?" he asked.

"Why, of course." She smiled round at him, delighted to see him, as she always was.

Then she saw that he was cross. He stood in the middle of the floor, his hands in his pockets, his broad body swinging slightly on his stout legs.

"Look here, Fan. What the devil did you speak to Nicholas for about my lending him that money?"

She sat down suddenly.

"Oh, dear—why shouldn't I?"

"Why shouldn't you? What business is it of yours?"

"It *is* business of mine," she said, almost fiercely, swinging round towards him. "It isn't *right* that you should go on lending Nicholas money."

"Is the money mine or isn't it?" he asked, advancing towards her.

"Of course it's yours, but Nicholas is my brother. It's my responsibility that he's here."

"Well, what of it? I'm his brother-in-law, and if I choose to lend him money, what the devil has it got to do with you?"

They looked at one another and like people who, knowing one another very well and loving one another very deeply, see a quarrel inevitably approaching, they were both frightened.

Fanny turned back to the mirror.

"Oh, of course it doesn't matter. If you want to lend

Nick money, it's your own affair. In my opinion it's time he got something to do and went elsewhere."

"Upon my word——!" Charles pulled himself in to collect himself. "I don't call that very gracious, Fanny. It isn't his fault he hasn't got a job. He's been trying. As a matter of fact the house has been twice as amusing since he's been in it."

"I'm sorry you found it so dull before," she said.

"What's the matter with you? Why are you so cross?"

"I'm not cross."

"Oh, yes, you are. You haven't been yourself lately. Everyone's noticed it."

She turned round again. One of her tempers was rising. She could see it approaching like a white-capped wave across a sullen sea.

"Oh—who says I've not been myself?"

"Oh, nobody exactly, but——"

"No. I want to know."

"Well—Granny and Romney——"

"Romney?"

(So her own son, her child whom she had carried in her womb, her little boy—he had also criticized her!)

"Oh, nothing much——" Charles was of course uncomfortable. "You're playing the game you always play—shifting the subject. I came in here to say it's not *your* business what I do with my money——"

She ducked her head in the rising, towering temper, felt the crash, heard the roar, emerged breathless to a quiet but very hostile contemplation of Charles.

"*Of course* you're to do what you like with your money. Give it all to Nicholas if you want to. Only—would you mind telling me?—you seem to be in his confidence—*how* much longer is Nicholas staying here?"

Then Charles was uncomfortable. He loved Fanny so

much that even when he was angry with her he hated to see her unhappy.

"Oh, look here, Fanny. Don't be cross. I didn't mean to be. I didn't really. Only—I can't understand what's happened. When Nicholas came you were delighted. I remember that first evening when Gran and I were rather doubtful about it you were quite angry with us."

"On that first evening—that spring evening," she murmured, "everything was different."

"It isn't," Charles went on, scratching the back of his neck, "as though Nicholas has been tiresome or anything. Neither he nor his girl have been the least bit in the way. I must say he's awfully good company."

But she was still exasperated. Men! Their stupidity, their bovine complacency, and the dull herdlike way they stuck together!

"Defend him as much as you like," she said. "Of course I love Nicholas, but allow me to remark that I've known him a great deal longer than you have. Matthew's right. He's the laziest man on the face of the globe."

"Oh, I see!" Charles cried, suddenly furious again. "Matthew's been putting his finger into this, has he? What the hell has Matthew got to do with it?"

"Nothing," said Fanny, "except that he's my brother and doesn't like to see me unhappy."

"And I don't care a damn, I suppose?" Charles shouted.

"You needn't shout, Charles. I can hear perfectly well."

And in answer to this Charles, quite properly, went out, banging the door behind him.

Fanny sat in front of her mirror and cried. She never loved Charles so much as when she had quarrelled with him, behaved abominably, felt herself to be in the wrong but was determined not to say so. Thus it was now.

She bathed her face, brushed her hair and went to see Edward. Here things were no better. Edward and Lizzie were bending, their heads close together, over a book. Edward was also in the middle of his tea. He looked up when he heard her come in, and his mouth was stained with strawberry jam. Then he shut the book. Fanny's curiosity was strongly aroused. Lizzie gave her one of her grown-up, superior but friendly glances. She and Lizzie had been friends for some time now, but rather as the missionary is friends with one of the wildest and most uncertain of the native tribe.

"I'm so sorry I'm late, dear. Father came in and kept me. What's that you've been looking at?"

"Nothing, Mother." (Couldn't she understand that when he and Lizzie had some amusing thing between themselves they wouldn't want to share it? Besides—it was Lizzie's affair. It was Lizzie's book.)

But Fanny did not understand. She was certain that the book had improper pictures. She advanced.

"Let me see, darling," she said.

But Edward laid his hand on the book.

"It's Lizzie's book," he said sulkily.

"May I look, dear?"

"Why, of course, Aunt Fanny."

It was not in the least improper. It was a very fine French volume about Marie Antoinette's court, and there were many coloured illustrations. Fanny found herself looking into the unpleasant features of Cardinal Rohan. She felt foolish, and that Lizzie was laughing at her.

"I was telling Edward about the Diamond Necklace," Lizzie said.

"I see," Fanny said. "That's very interesting. Wipe your mouth, Edward. Have you finished your tea? Then ring the bell."

She went out, dignified, her head up, but feeling more desolate than ever. How very, very different was this from the old teas when Edward cut the top off his egg and told her all that had occurred during the day.

On the way to the drawing room she put her hand to her forehead and for a moment paused. "What is happening? Why is everything going wrong? Matthew was right. Something terrible is preparing."

And then, on opening the drawing-room door quietly, expecting to find them all at tea, she saw instead a queer sight. The tea was over—it was later than she had supposed. But Nicholas was there. He was standing in front of the spindle-legged table with the glass top that contained small bijoux—the jewelled crucifix, the silver snuffboxes, the miniature with the pearl border, the gold snuffbox with the picture of the hay-making on the lid. . . .

The glass top was open. Nicholas stood staring at the contents; in his hand was the gold snuffbox and, even as she came in, he had slipped it into his pocket.

"Nicholas—whatever are you doing?" she cried.

He turned. He took the box out of his pocket. He was perfectly composed.

"Do you mind, Fan darling, if I take this and look at it? I'll only keep it an hour or two."

"Why, no—take anything you like——"

He turned it over in his hand, looking at it.

"It's so lovely. . . . One never can see things in a case." He smiled at her. "You didn't think I was stealing it, darling, did you?"

"Stealing it! My dear Nick——!"

"Oh, no—you might. I wouldn't blame you—I do steal things sometimes—if they're beautiful and neglected by their owners. After all, everything lovely ought to be with someone who appreciates it."

"Yes, I suppose so." (She was thinking: "I believe he *was* stealing it. He knows that I think so.") She turned back to the door. "I must be getting on. I've a thousand things to do before dinner."

But he came up to her.

"Fan—what have I done? Is it taking that money from Charles? I hate you to think badly of me."

So when they were children he had come to her, exerting his charm, begging for her sympathy when he had done something disgraceful. And she had given it him always.

But now she was too honest. Matthew's words were still in her ears. There was the quarrel with Charles. And there was the gold snuffbox. She looked him full in the face.

"Yes, Nick . . . I think you've stayed here long enough."

"I see. Well, of course, if that's what you think——"

She was tempted, as she always was, to soften. But she remembered that Janet was gone, and she saw the heads of Edward and Lizzie bent over the book. . . .

"But if I *don't* go, Fanny dear . . . Charles wants me to stay."

"Of course," she said quietly. "So long as Charles wants you to stay, that's settled."

He brushed past her and went out of the room.

He had a capacity for hatred, and now, in the next quarter of an hour, he indulged it. Lizzie was on her bed, reading.

He stood in front of her.

"Your dear aunt wants us to go."

"Then we'd better," she said without looking up.

He removed the book.

"Attend to your loving father. . . . We're not going."

Lizzie slowly got off the bed and walked to the window.

"Well—tell me—do you want to go or not?" he asked.

"I'm happier here than I've been anywhere else," she said, "but everyone always wants us to go."

"It's only your aunt who does—and your dear Uncle Matthew. That's why we're staying. One part of the family against the other."

But she spoke of something different. "Abel stopped me in the street and spoke to me today," she said.

"Oh, did he? What did he say?"

"I was to tell you he wanted some money."

"And what did *you* say?"

"I said I'd tell you."

Then she began, quite passionately:

"I hate him to speak to me in the street, Papa. You always said he mustn't. And Edward was with me."

"Oh, he was, was he? How was that?"

"I go sometimes and meet him when he comes from school."

"Oh, you do! Quite a pretty friendship."

"Yes, I like Edward. And he wondered who Abel was and why he spoke to me. Please, Papa, you must stop him speaking to me. I hate him. I'll slap his face if he does it again."

She went back to her book.

In his own room he took out Charles's letter. He read it through again—then, looking up, he was startled. Curled up on his pillow, fast asleep, was Becky Sharp. The cat was a small black cloud on the whiteness of the pillow. It was as though something had grown out of the bed and belonged to it.

"Shoo!" he said, "Shoo!" waving the letter at it. It did not stir, and he was conscious of a strange reluctance to touch it. But he picked it up, and it moved silkily, stretching itself like a snake. He put it on the floor, opened the door, and it slipped out.

He looked at the letter. Well, why not? He had always had something of the kind in his thoughts.

His curiosity was warm in him like a wakening vice. What would Fanny do? How would Charles behave? This would shake some of dear Fanny's complacency. Her brother was not good enough to remain under the same roof with her. He had an impulse of intense self-pity. For once in his life he had tried to behave decently—he had been kind, thoughtful of others, he had brought pleasure and fun and excitement into this house that had been drab and bored. He knew that Charles had been bored; if it were not so he would never have written letters like this one. They were all fond of him save only Fanny and Matthew. Were it not for Fanny he might find some little job in London—not too arduous—and settle down here in the house. But Fanny and Grace and Matthew—what a heavy-footed psalm-singing trio! It would do Fanny good to realize that Charles was not always her good devoted slave, would take her down. . . . She would be kinder to others perhaps if she suffered a little herself. . . .

And, after all, there was little harm in it. Only a joke. Charles would explain, Fanny forgive. Would she? It was that that decided him. *How* would Fanny behave? Would she keep it to herself? She might. You never knew with these sentimental women!

He went out, knocked gently on Fanny's door. He looked in. There was no one there. On her little writing table he saw a pile of papers, bills, receipts, odds and ends.

He slipped Charles's letter in amongst them.

3

It happened on that particular evening everything was very gay. The family had not been in such high spirits for a long time.

This was due to Nicholas, who was at his very funniest, kindest, and most considerate. How kind indeed he always was when he was happy! He committed crimes only when he felt that he was a prisoner! Tonight he shed his monkey-self, and Matthew, watching benevolently and even, rather clumsily, joining in, confessed to himself—"Were Nicholas only always like this."

Happiest of all was Fanny. After the discomforts of the day it was wonderful to find, so unexpectedly, this radiance. Her principal happiness came from the thought of her approaching reconciliation with Charles. Reconciliation! That was almost too big a word. Their quarrel had been *such* a little one.

But she knew that he also was thinking of it—the touch on the shoulder, his arm, strong beneath his pyjama sleeve, coming round to her, drawing her nearer, his kiss, so familiar in its roughness and strength and lingering affection, close upon her mouth.

After dinner Nicholas proposed Charades.

"But, Nicholas——" Grace protested.

He saw in her large frightened eyes that she suspected that he would use the charades to make fun of her. He went up to her and put his arm around her fat shoulder.

"Come, Grace dear, you and I shall be in the first charade. You and I and Charles——"

"Oh, I *can't* act, Nicholas. You know that I can't."

"Wait and see. You'll be marvellous."

And so she was. She was exactly herself. She came in

across the drawing-room floor, dropping her bag, her handkerchief, and keeping up a stream of chatter. . . . Nicholas, in an absurd cap and with an eyeglass, proposed marriage to her, and she was fluttered, agitated, happy just as in real life she would have been. He was kind that night. He frightened her only once.

"Euphemia, Euphemia, I know you love me—you write me such *beautiful* letters!" and everyone laughed because of course everyone knew how dear Grace received letters from her gentleman in Winchester.

Charles was just himself, a big kindly St. Bernard sort of a man who discovered that Nicholas was married already, struck him to the ground, and carried Grace off in triumph. Fanny, in the audience, thought that he had never looked so splendid and that the wrinkles about his eyes showed his goodness. It was absurd perhaps for two old plain people to love one another so dearly, but there it was. Love, gathering strength as it goes, outruns Venus and Adonis.

Then Nicholas made Fanny, Nell, and Matthew act with him. Fanny was the postmistress in a rural village (*very* rural), Matthew Nell's father, Nicholas Fanny's gay and philandering husband.

Fanny was emotional enough and excitable enough to throw herself, heart, soul, and body, into a thing like this. She acted splendidly, inquisitive about the letters, sharp with the flirtatious Nicholas, kindly with the rather stupid Matthew—and Charles, watching her, beamed with content.

"Is there any woman in the world like her?" he thought. "A little childlike at times. She's never grown up entirely. That only makes her the more lovable. These clever, sophisticated women must be the devil to live with."

Fanny herself tried no longer to resist Nicholas's charm.

He was her old dear Nick—the *real* Nick, she told herself, kind, generous, impulsive. She would be more generous herself in her view of him. . . . At the end of the charade he kissed her.

"Fan dear, you're a born actress."

"Oh, am I?" she cried, delighted.

"You're marvellous. If Charles loses his money there's a career waiting for you."

Everyone praised her. Charles, a little stiffly, a little shyly, said: "I didn't know you could act like that, Fan."

But the true reconciliation was yet to come.

She delayed it. She sat, in her little room, brushing her hair. The door into their bedroom was open. He called once:

"Coming, Fan? I'm in bed."

"All right. In a minute," she answered.

She moved, fussing with the things on her writing table. She turned over some bills. "Oh, I'd forgotten that one," she thought. "What a bore!"

Then she found something in Charles's handwriting. At first she thought that it must be one of his old letters to herself, escaped, in some way, among her papers.

She read:

"*. . . Of course I know that these early morning hours are bad for truth. Nothing is real, daylight-real. And yet this* is *real I think—that I hunger for you as though I were a boy of twenty, to hold you in my arms as though you would never leave them again. The folly of an old married man! But I did not know, until now, what it was that all my life I had missed. This love is different from any other that I have known and I am the wiser, the richer . . .*"

She stared at her face in the little gilt mirror. Then she hung her head. She shivered so that the rings on her fingers rattled on the gleaming glass of her dressing table. She read the letter through again with the glaring attention of a lunatic, as thought every word had a secret meaning. There was no woman's name in the letter. No address. It might have been written years ago. Then she remembered a sentence: *"When my wife comes back from her cruise . . ."*

She put the letter in a drawer in the table and locked the drawer.

At last she went into the other room. She saw with thankfulness that Charles had turned on his side and was quietly sleeping. With very great care she crept into bed and lay there, not touching him, staring with hot eyes into the dark.

4

Hector, Nell's young man, dressed from head to feet in black tights, over his eyes a black mask, bent forward as though he were rowing, and shouted, in chorus with seven other young men, "Seventeen." Bent back, crying "Eighteen," forward again, "Nineteen." As he moved, a fat woman, also in black, beat on a drum. A tall thin man in red tights and with a red mask came to the front of the stage and called "Finish!" The curtain came down. This scene represented "Flight from Satiety."

Inside the dirty dishevelled room where he dressed with the seven other young men, Hector was attacked by Hamish Bennett, who, stripped in front of the ugly little looking-glass, rapidly took the paint from his face.

He was a strong broad-shouldered man and his chest

was covered with hair, so that it was unexpected to hear him cry in a shrill voice: "Oh, damn and blast these Americans! It's they who're responsible for all the bloody mess! *Why* don't they think of someone but themselves? And look at them! Despised by the whole of the world! My God, if they could *see* themselves!"

Hector, who liked the Americans, said: "Why should they bother about us? Do *we* bother about anyone else really? Of course we don't. We're all the same. America has to fight for her life just as we have for ours. We're all fighting and we'll go on and on until . . ."

"Until what?" said Hamish sarcastically.

"Until we believe in God again."

"God?" said Hamish. "I didn't know you'd turned religious, Hector."

"I haven't *turned* anything. Only I'm not just a damned microbe. You're not either, Hamish, although you look one. We're both immortal. When everyone everywhere gets a sense of values we won't want to quarrel about bread, gold, and all that nonsense. There'll be more important things to think about."

"I've got to live, haven't I?" said Hamish, pulling his shirt over his shoulders.

"Of course. You'll always live whether you want to or no."

Hamish danced down the room, naked save for his shirt.

"I've got to live! I've got to live! I've got to live!" he shouted. Then stopped in front of Priestley, the wealthy member. "Tom, lend me a quid until Monday."

It was a matinée, and Hector went through a biting driving wind to his home. He was thinking of two things, his poetry and Nell—and they were both the same thing. In his poem he had reached the section that he called

"Interlude in Heaven." Here, in a land like a Toy Village, God the Father, St. Peter, Dante, and an old village woman took tea together and played at bowls. The greensward stretched like glass in front of them, bells rang the hours, the shepherd cared for his sheep on the hill. God the Father played bowls and allowed St. Peter to win because he cared so much about winning. The moon rose over the clover-scented fields.

In and out of this scene Nell moved. He could not keep her away. That luncheon with her uncle, he reflected, had been the decisive factor in their action, for now they had been for three week-ends to a village near Lewes. They considered themselves now to be man and wife. They loved one another with every day more dearly, but she was, he knew, not happy. The deceit troubled her. At her home she had invented a family with whom she went to stay, and because they all (except her Uncle Nicholas) believed this absolutely she was the more unhappy. Also she was *most* unhappy about Lottie. She wanted to tell Lottie everything because she said Lottie liked and trusted her.

Hector, who knew his Lottie, was not sure that she either liked Nell or trusted her. How much did Lottie know? What did she suspect? Oh, hell! what a world this was! How simple it ought to be. He did not love Lottie, and Lottie did not love him. He *did* love Nell, and Nell cared for him. Well, then! He never went to the flat now without thinking: "Tonight I will tell Lottie everything. We'll have this out. We'll clear this up." But it was not so. Lottie was too clever for that.

What a jumble! God and St. Peter, Nell and Lottie, and this rotten, rotten play that ran on and on for no reason at all. His beautiful poem and Lottie as he saw her tonight lying on the sofa, eating chocolates out of a bag and saying:

"Hector, darling, take me to the pictures tonight."

"Oh, let's stay in. . . . I want to work a bit."

She did not protest. She sat up and looked at him.

"I've been spending the afternoon with Nell and her nice uncle."

"Uncle? Which uncle?"

"The new one—the wicked one."

"How do you know he's wicked?"

"One can see it with half an eye."

"What did you do?"

"We went to the pictures."

"Oh—then you can't possibly want to go to them again tonight."

"Of course I can," said Lottie. "I could go to them all day." She bit into a chocolate. "I love Nell. She's so sweet."

"What did her uncle talk about?"

"Oh, nothing particular. He will, though. When we know one another better he'll tell me all sorts of things."

"What things?"

She leaned forward and looked at him.

"Wouldn't you like to know?"

Later he sat with paper on his knee near the smouldering fire. He had given in. He was to take Lottie out at nine. Meanwhile God the Father, watching while St. Peter trundled his wood, looked down on the little earth. It was now a wild garden thronged with thirsting plants, and the faint sound of its running water came up like the murmuring of summer flies. His new creatures with whom He was experimenting were lonely. They were lost children without their Father.

It was His turn. He took the brown smooth ball in his palm and bent forward. . . .

On the following afternoon Hector and Nell had tea together in a funny underground café off Bond Street. The café was called "The Good Companion." It consisted of three long thin rooms, and it was always lit by lights that gloomily failed to give enough illumination. The walls were of a sombre dark green. It was a perfect mausoleum of a café; two ladies conducted it. They were plainly nice ladies, but they were harassed, anxious, and unpunctual; they smiled continually, but their sad thoughts were far away from their smiles.

Nell detested this atmosphere of secrecy in which herself and Hector were now constantly involved. She hated it and was determined to end it. Nevertheless she could think of nothing at first save that she loved Hector so desperately. They sat on the same side of the table and held hands, which is a childish thing to do perhaps, but a help when you are frightened. In their golden fairness, youth, and slenderness of body they must, it seemed, to two female Argus-eyed tea drinkers close by, be certainly brother and sister. Then said one, in a hot whisper: "They are holding hands." They were therefore not brother and sister.

"Hector, I want you to know," said Nell, "that I shall always love you—whatever happens it will never change. I wouldn't have said this before because I know how love changes. But now I'm quite certain—whatever happens."

"Why do you say," Hector broke in rather crossly, " 'whatever happens?' Don't you see that *nothing* can separate us now? What an awful thing to keep saying!"

She pressed his hand. Here was the tea in a teapot with roses and a cracked spout, and there was a toasted bun, dry and hostile. They could hold hands no longer.

Nell sighed. "Things can't go on like this, can they?"

"I don't know," said Hector. "They probably will for a bit." Then he added: "Your Uncle Nicholas has been meeting Lottie."

"I know. I was there."

"Isn't it rather dangerous?"

"Everything's dangerous," she answered quickly. "Do you know what's happening at home?"

"No. What?"

"I don't know either. For one thing something's happening to Mother."

"More hot water, please," Hector said to the lady.

"Oh, yes," said the lady and went away, not to return again for many a day (or so it seemed).

"Something has happened. Mother is one of the bravest, most generous, finest people in the world."

"Yes, I know, I know."

"She's had a dreadful shock. No one has noticed it yet but myself. I know her so much better than the others—even Father. At first I thought she might have found out about us. But it isn't that. Then perhaps that she was missing Janet so badly, because certainly everything is changed since Janet went. But it isn't that, either. She is doing everything she can to appear the same. She laughs and talks as though she were acting."

"What do you *think* it is?" asked Hector.

"I can't imagine. She's shy. She's still very young in lots of ways—much younger than me very often. And I've often imagined her saying to herself: '*Everything's* all right however upside down the world's getting so long as Charles and the children love me.' Yesterday I thought Romney had done something. He's changed, too, very snappy, snarls like a dog if you ask him to pass the butter. I thought it might be Romney. But it isn't. It's something worse."

"I tell you one thing that it is," Hector said, catching Nell's hand again. "The world being unsettled makes private lives unsettled. No one is secure any more. They don't know what will be happening to them in six months' time. Perhaps your mother's worrying about money."

"Oh, no, it's worse than that. She wouldn't bother, so long as we had enough to eat, if she lived in a basement off the Old Kent Road. She's one of those women who build their whole lives round one or two whom they love. If that goes everything goes. But why should she worry? Father isn't changed. We're not changed. She knows we'll always love her."

"You must help her," Hector said.

"Yes, I'm going to. She'll have to tell me. I'd do *anything* for her—except give you up."

"If it *were* that," said Hector slowly—"if she knew that we'd been living together, and if the only way to make her happy *was* for you to give me up—would you?"

Nell shook her head. "No. . . . She'd have to see that I couldn't. I think she *would* see."

"Maybe," Hector said, "your uncle has done something?"

"What—Uncle Nicholas? What could he do?"

"I don't know—I scarcely know him. But I have the idea that he could do a lot. That day when we lunched with him influenced us, didn't it?"

"No, I don't think so."

"It did. Not directly. He just gave us a little push along the way we wanted to go."

She shook her head.

"I don't think Uncle Nicholas has anything to do with it."

Then they parted. They rose out of the basement into the upper air, and when Nell climbed onto an omnibus

Hector looked after her as though never, never would he see her again.

Nell, inside the omnibus, thought for a little while of Hector, holding him in her slender arms, pressing her cheek against his, then turned her mind towards her mother.

She saw things very clearly, as clearly as the stout fishy-eyed old gentleman in the blue suit sitting opposite her. He looked at her as though he would very much like to be her friend. Once when, by accident, their eyes met, he smiled. How hateful almost all men were! Only Hector was perfect. She was aware that she was faced with two urgent problems, both of them old ones and very familiar to her in the pages of fiction. In real life they were different. They were problems with which her generation was supposed very effectively to deal. The sexual one she had known, of course, from her childhood. No more nonsense for her generation about marriage; if you loved a man you went to him. But in actual practice, it did not work out like that. She had no conviction of sin, for she was, so far as she could actually see, doing Lottie no wrong. Nevertheless she was now, in every hour, betraying her sincerity, her honesty, and, worst of all, her courage. She had always supposed that if ever this situation arose she would treat it bravely. As it was she was anything but brave. She wondered whether after all the old rules had not something to be said for them. She frowned at the old man in the blue suit and, for the moment, dismissed problem number one.

Problem number two—mother and daughter. All the modern novels were concerned with the struggle between parents and children. Children went their own way, parents complained and grieved. But now, in her own case, there was again a difference. She almost worshipped her mother. It had seemed that they could discuss anything together. But now there was some real trouble, and Nell discovered that she was much younger than she had thought that she was. They—she and Romney—had always patronized their mother a little. Such a child, so impetuous, so unsophisticated! But now Nell realized that her mother had lived, had known birth and death and enduring love and loneliness and companionship with a reality of experience that Nell, herself, had not begun to know. Never mind the generations! Here it was a matter of living, of fidelity and courage and patience. How could Nell share her mother's trouble as she wished to do? For the first time she was convicted of her own youth; for the first time she saw something, if only a glimpse, of the courage that women need if they are to arrive, undefeated, at the other end.

In the drawing room she found that Mrs. Frobisher was approaching the end of what had evidently been a lengthy call and that her mother and Aunt Grace were assisting her to do it. Mrs. Frobisher had just performed that most maddening of all acts in a caller—she had risen and then sat down again.

"Why, there's Nell!" she cried. "I haven't seen you for ages, dear. How well you're looking! And so I said to the doctor that Cyprian had been ever so much better when he was drinking Contrexéville. Of course it's expensive—one and three a bottle—but it really *had* done the boy good—no doubt of it at all—but would he listen? Not he. So I changed the doctor, and the new man is *very* clever, very clever indeed. He has started Cyprian on a diet of worms."

"Worms!" Grace cried, quite horrified but fancying that the phrase was, in some way, familiar to her.

"Oh, not the ordinary worms of course. They are special pink ones to be found only in the South of France—near Nice somewhere, I believe. You take them in a paste and they don't taste too bad. I tried some myself just to encourage him. He's *so* good, Cyprian! He does everything he's told without a murmur."

Fanny said something.

"Well, I must be going. We're dining early and going to the Queen's Hall. I adore music—almost any music. After all, if they play a dull piece it is such a splendid quiet chance to think of other things."

She departed, and Grace went, too.

"Well, dear," Fanny said. "Have you had a nice afternoon?"

"Yes—very."

"What have you been doing?"

"I had tea with a friend in Bond Street."

There was a pause; then Nell said:

"Mother dear, you look tired."

Fanny smiled. "Yes, I have a little headache."

"Look here, darling. Have your dinner sent up to you. I've noticed you haven't looked so well the last few days."

"Have you?" Fanny said sharply. "I don't know why, I'm sure. There's been nothing the matter."

Nell caught her hand.

"Mother—there *isn't* anything the matter?"

Fanny took her hand away.

"Matter? No, of course not."

(She was thinking as for three days now she had been ceaselessly thinking: "Tonight I will tell him about it. Tonight I'll challenge him.")

Nell turned away.

"That's right. I'm awfully glad." She walked a little

about the room. She stopped, idly, looked down at the glass-topped table. "Why—where's the gold snuffbox?"

"Isn't it there?"

"No."

"It's being cleaned, I expect."

Fanny stayed by the door.

"Yes, I think I *will* go to bed. Explain to them, darling, will you?"

In the silent room the echoes of many secret things seemed to linger. The Japanese screen, the Bonington, the little silver boxes—*they* knew what Nell didn't know. They were old, they were wise. Nell was young, ignorant. Life seemed to her suddenly to be terrifying with its hidden underground movements, its disregard of human suffering, its mocking of tragedy. Nell set her shoulders. "Well, it shan't beat *me!*" she thought.

5

And now, as events developed, Charles Carlisle received the shock of his life.

Coming down from his carpentering shop to search for a hammer, he saw that a small bed had been put up in Fanny's dressing room. There it stood, white, chaste, aloof, scornful, and stared back at him.

Fanny was at her table, writing. He shut the door behind him. He could scarcely speak for astonishment.

"Fanny, what *does* this mean?"

She turned, holding a pen aloft, meditating. "Monday would do," she murmured. "Monday afternoon." Then she said very calmly: "What is it, Charles?"

He did not know that her heart was hammering, that she had been anticipating this moment with a frozen horror of what this interview might be, of the things, fatal perhaps to both of them, to which it might lead.

For now surely she would tell him. She had thought it all out down to her minutest action. The letter was in the drawer. She would extract it, hand it to him, and say very quietly: "This is the reason, Charles." But she did not move. She sat there, the pen poised in her hand.

"Why——" he stammered. "This bed . . ."

She looked at him. His gaze faced hers without flinching. He did not *look* a guilty man.

"Oh, yes—I've not been very well lately. I thought that—for a little while—I would sleep in here."

"Not been well—what's the matter?"

"Oh, nothing. I haven't been sleeping. I've been bothered by the fear of being restless and keeping you awake."

"Keeping *me* awake? Nothing keeps me awake. You know that." He came close to her, put his hand on her shoulder. "Fanny—you're not still angry? That ridiculous little quarrel——"

"Oh, no, of course not." She was trembling. She bent forward over her letter.

When he felt her trembling he tried to draw her towards him. She resisted.

"Fan, there *is* something the matter! You're trembling. What is it?"

Now was the time! She knew it. She faced it as though Fate, a dark silent watching figure, stood before her. Had she spoken! But she did not. She was a coward about the consequences. And something more than that. A new foreign element was entering into her, some creature bred of jealousy, unhappiness, and a sudden sense of power.

Charles would be unhappy now. His uncertainty would disturb and bewilder him. He would have to think of her as for years he had not. His conscience, which must now be awake like a wound, would ache in him as she herself was now, with every minute of the day, aching.

So she pushed the moment aside, not realizing that nothing stands still.

She began again to write her letter.

"It's nothing, Charles. Only I haven't slept for three days."

He bent forward and kissed her cheek.

"Poor dear. Only—the first time since our wedding night. Couldn't you . . . ?" A new shyness, delicacy, prevented him. He kissed her again and went away.

But now indeed Charles had something to think about. He forgot that he had come down for a hammer. He slowly climbed the stairs and sat down in his happy attic on the old horsehair sofa with the hole like a fungus in its middle. Around and about him stood all his friends—the table that he had carved, the chairs, a little wobbly on their legs, the long bench with his tools, an old sword and two guns hanging on the wall, the wide attic window that embraced that familiar beloved view of roofs and chimneys and the changing restless sky. But he saw nothing. He sat forward, his hands between his knees. *What* was the matter with Fanny? He had asked himself that several times of late but never so urgently as now. Separate beds! But there must be something serious in it for her to take, without consulting him, such an action. If she was unwell, had not been sleeping, why had she not talked to him of it? *What* was it that had grown up between them of late?

Amazingly he did not fly to the proper cause. He did, for a moment, think of that spring affair, but immediately dismissed it. He had forgotten that mislaid letter. The whole episode was to him like a coloured painting in some house that he had once visited. He did realize that it had been the last kick of his youth. He welcomed it. He was glad that his youth was ended; he saw, very clearly, that there had been something comic, absurd, in his moment's ardour. He fancied now that, from first to last, she had laughed at him—kindly laughter (for truly she had been kind). During these last six months he had been happier with Fanny than ever before. It was as though that episode had been needed to show him how fundamental, how unique, how all-embracing, all-important his love for Fanny was.

And because he knew how faithful to Fanny until death he now would be, he never for an instant supposed that she did not know it also. Moreover it was impossible that she should be aware of the affair.

So he cast round for something else. He was not either by nature or training at all subtle about his fellow human beings. He was one of Weininger's rare instances of the complete male.

Nevertheless, like all Englishmen who are completely male, he was mainly boy. He still reasoned as he had done at school, still cherished as fiercely irrational prejudices, was still enchanted with the victory of his own side at cricket or football or tennis, could still be amused for hours by trifles that would seem to a grown man of another country proper only for the nursery.

He had, also, as befits the Tom Brown type of Englishman, a warm generous heart, very easily moved; he believed emphatically in England, the public-school system, and Mr. Baldwin.

It was part of his character, too, that he could not bear to see others unhappy.

When he was unhappy himself he suffered acutely, for he had still something of the child's sense of limitless torture—a bad toothache and Fanny had to remind him that it would soon be over. And so, because he suffered himself, he felt that others must find things unbearable. He wanted everyone to be happy, and now, when there was so much unhappiness in the world, he moved about, puzzled, bewildered, as he did when he read in one of the more vicious of the Sunday newspapers about the torture of some child.

So that now, sitting on his old sofa, absent-mindedly whittling away a piece of wood with a pocketknife, he was deeply distressed. Fanny was unhappy; she had been unhappy, he now saw, for a long time. Why? Was something wrong with one of the children? He was not aware of anything. It was true that Romney seemed a little out of sorts. He sighed here. He wished that he had more of that boy's confidence. He was in a mess, maybe about some girl, and was shy of telling his father about it. But fathers now were companions for their sons; that was one of the few advantages of these modern days. And yet he himself was shy with Romney. Come to think of it they never did anything together, went out of an evening, or watched a cricket match. Romney would not care for cricket matches, and this was perhaps the heart of the trouble—that Romney's taste was not his father's. Charles, although, like most modern parents, he had learnt to be cautious with his children, could not understand those queer paintings and carvings that his son preferred. And yet he was proud of Romney's taste. How could an old buffer like himself be right about modern art? He still enjoyed music with a tune, a novel with a story, a picture with real scenery and people like life. But he understood that things must move on, that Romney's world could not be his world. Until lately he had thought that they had found a compromise, but now he was more shy of Romney than he had been. . . .

Realizing that, he was suddenly afraid. Fanny, Nell, Romney, even Grace. He was not at his ease with them as he had been six months ago. And, as he had done so often in the past when he was troubled about something, he went downstairs to see his mother.

That old lady was now applying all her energies to fighting her disabilities. Do what she would, assert her pride, fiercely try to maintain her old proud independence, her weakness—physical weakness, not spiritual—increasingly invaded her.

Today she was in bed, and when Charles came in she tried to conceal her excessive joy at the sight of him. But she could not help herself. Her eyes filled with tears; her dry bony hand clutched his, and, as he sat at the side of the bed and she saw his thick strong body, looked with maternal love at his kind, ugly, beloved face, she wanted to hold him there, to keep him beside her for ever and ever because it was only with him that she felt really safe.

She found now that it took almost all her time and strength to control her pain, and this was the harder because she had had, through her life, so little experience in this. The pain was not severe, but it visited her in many forms, now a cramp in the left leg, now a thick pressure on the heart, now neuralgia above her left eye; it was as though there were some actual person there, some enemy who took delight in torturing her—not severe torture but a sort of threat to her of what he could do if he tried. And behind everything was the constant fear that, in a little while, the tortures would be more severe, that they would beat her down, subdue her pride, and make her one of those whining, complaining old ladies whom she had, all her life, so thoroughly despised.

Charles sat beside her. He put his arm around her,

and she leaned up against him, feeling the strong bulwark of his chest, the steady beating of his heart.

"Well, Mother—has Moffatt been?"

Moffatt was the doctor whom Mrs. Carlisle tolerated best, but she didn't tolerate him very much.

"Oh, yes—he's been."

"What did he say?"

"What would he be likely to say?—'Oh, you're getting along nicely, Mrs. Carlisle.' Nicely! I wonder how *he'd* feel if he had my leg!"

Charles laughed. "You can't expect doctors to be soft-hearted. They meet too many legs!"

"Oh, *I* don't want him to be soft-hearted. Only not to tell me lies. If I'm dying why doesn't he say so?"

"Of course you're not dying, Mother."

"Oh, no—I'll beat them yet. I'm good for another ten years." She held his hand very tightly. "Charles, you do think that I'll get well again, don't you?"

He bent forward and kissed her forehead. "Of course I do, Mother."

"I slept better last night."

"That's good."

She looked at him sharply.

"Charles, what's the matter?"

He looked at her, smiling.

"Nothing."

"Yes, there is! Fanny being tiresome?"

Then he burst out with it; he could not conceal it if he wished. It was exactly as it had been when, a little boy in knickerbockers, his ship had been broken by Tommy Brook, the boy in the neighbouring house. She saw that and was at once delighted, forgot her pains, her fear of death, did not care so much what his trouble might be so long as he should tell her of it.

"No, Fanny's not tiresome, of course not. She never is. But she's queer." He shook his head. "What do you think she's done, Mother?"

"I don't know," she answered triumphantly. "She's been queer for a long time."

"She's put up a bed for herself in her own room."

Mrs. Carlisle's hand tightened on his.

"All these years——" Charles's voice shook a little. "The very last thing in the world I'd have dreamt of!"

"What reason did she give?"

"Oh, she said she'd been sleeping badly and was afraid she was keeping me awake. But that's all nonsense. Nothing keeps me awake!" (He was proud of this.) "Over and over again one of us hasn't slept well, had a cold or something, but we've neither of us minded.

"And it isn't only what she's done but the way she looked at me when I asked her about it—almost as though we were strangers."

"How very odd!" said his mother. She could not quite keep the satisfaction out of her voice. She liked Fanny of course—a good woman, a *very* good woman—but for years she had been jealous. She had fought her jealousy with much bravery and common sense, but she had not killed it. She had not even wanted to kill it. And she had all the pleasure now of finding a virtuous person in the wrong.

"I think it's monstrous of Fanny," she said, settling herself a little more comfortably against Charles, as though she felt that she owned him now more completely than she had done five minutes ago.

"Monstrous! Of course it isn't! Fanny must have her reasons. She always has." For a moment once again the spring episode of his infidelity flashed through his mind, only at once to be dismissed.

His mother, although she knew nothing of it, was thinking the same thing. There was only one cause for good wives to move their beds, and that cause was sex. She looked at Charles. But no. He *could* not be unfaithful! She had of course never wanted him to be, but she had, once and again, wished that he would give Fanny a little shock!

"Have you been quarrelling, dear?"

"No. Not really. We had a few words the other day about my giving Nicholas money."

"Ah—Nicholas. He seems to come into everything."

Charles considered Nicholas. Then he shook his head.

"Oh, no, it could be nothing to do with him. The only trouble he's made was over Janet. Of course that made Fanny unhappy, but the old woman has been getting above herself lately—thinking she runs the house."

"Ah, well!" Mrs. Carlisle sighed with satisfaction. "My advice to you, Charles, is to leave it alone. Fanny will soon come round. She's got some silly idea in her head."

"No, but she's unhappy. I *hate* her to be unhappy."

"You're too soft, Charles. You always have been. You give in to Fanny over everything. You can't say that I've ever interfered, although I've often wanted to. You know that I'm very fond of Fanny—very fond indeed. But I do think she's a little self-righteous. She's no right to do a thing like this and give you no reason. And you've been so good to her all these years."

No, by Jove, she hadn't. His mother was right there. Fanny couldn't do a thing like that and leave him in the dark. That wasn't playing fair, and for Charles, in spite of the spring episode, to play fair was simply the rule of life.

"No. I agree. She ought to tell me," he said, and his

mother had joy in her heart, for this was the first time that Charles had ever complained of Fanny to her.

She patted his hand.

"You leave it alone. Fanny's a sensible woman. She's got some idea in her head—nonsense, I don't doubt. Women are funny creatures. When they want something they'll take any steps to get it."

"But what *can* she want?"

"Who knows? More power, I daresay. She thinks it's time she had you under her thumb."

"Oh, absurd!"

"It isn't absurd a bit. I felt just the same about your father at one time. Oh, I behaved abominably!" (She remembered it with satisfaction.) "I plagued him and worried him until the poor man didn't know where he was. Women are like that from time to time, especially with anyone they love. It will come right, you see." (She hoped it wouldn't come right *too* soon.)

He bent down and kissed her. "You're not to say a word to anyone."

"Of course not. As though I would!"

He got up. "How are you feeling now?"

"Oh, much better, dear, thank you. Your talk has done me ever so much good."

"I'll come in and see you soon again."

"Yes, dear, do."

She turned on her side with a little light breath of pleasure. Her leg wasn't hurting her at all. She might get up a little later.

There was one strange part of this house that has not yet been described. This was the conservatory. It had been constructed in Victorian days: there had been a time when all over the country the Crystal Palace had been the cause of panes of glass that flashed in the sun, and gardeners' pots in smirking rows, strings of little green tomatoes and maidenhair ferns as delicate as spiders' webs. Somewhere about that time this conservatory had been appended to the Westminster house. It had never belonged to the house, and that was perhaps its grievance—is the grievance of so many conservatories.

Someone had come who cared for flowers and had done what was possible, but the light was wrong, the glass was smoked by neighbouring chimneys, the tomatoes perished, the chrysanthemums wilted, spiders wove their webs in the dusty corners. Only one large, hideous triumphant palm with leaves like dusty green blotting paper prospered and was, it seemed, immortal. From time to time someone said: "Let's destroy the conservatory," and when a child had lost its ship or its horse someone said: "Look in the conservatory." Romney, aged eight, after being beaten by his father, stayed there for six hours and caught a cold from the heat. There was an old blistered watering can, three numbers of the *Illustrated London News,* and the legless body of a negro doll. No one went there now, and the light, under the grimy glass, was London in a perpetual fog. It smelt of mice, the palm, a laundry, and the desert. When the door opened, little spirals of dust, from the empty boxes, blew in the air.

But Charles, passing it now, saw that the door was open and, looking in, found, through the dusty murk, the surprising figure of Grace busily engaged on one of the boxes.

He was amazed. When she heard him she jumped.

"Oh, Charles—how you startled me!"

"Why, Grace—what on earth are you doing here!"

"I'm planting seeds."

He was close to her now and could see that her forehead was grimy, her hair dishevelled, and there was a streak of grey on her cheek.

"This is a new adventure," he said.

"Would you mind shutting the door?"

He closed it.

"I know you'll think me very foolish, Charles, but I can't help it, and it does no one any harm."

"No, of course not."

"You see, I was passing one day and I looked in and it was so deserted. No one's bothered about it for years and years, and I thought it was nice to have some flowers again. It's all gone dusty just as I have!"

"My dear Grace!"

"Oh, yes—you know I have, Charles. And one great interest that I had—well, I haven't got it any longer. Of course there *are* things I could do, like visiting children's hospitals and housing and things like that. There are *lots* of things want doing, of course! But work like children's hospitals means going among a lot of people who, I'm sure, don't want you and look down their noses. No one wants an old woman like me."

"Nonsense, Grace. *You're* not old!"

She nodded her head vehemently.

"Yes, I am. Suddenly. Something's happened——" She stopped. "Never mind that. But I was very upset about something, and then I had this idea about the conservatory. Flowers can't watch you and laugh at you and hold something over your head."

He put his hand on her arm.

"Grace, dear—what *are* you imagining? No one's watching you or laughing at you."

"Oh, yes, they are though! If I were younger and had more energy I'd be able to deal with it, but I can't. I've been very nervous lately, and the conservatory's safe anyway."

What on earth was the matter with her? She was looking at him almost maliciously.

"Well, anyway," she went on, "women don't have much of a time, Charles, and that's a fact. But flowers—there's nothing much wrong with flowers. I've planted seeds in all these boxes and there'll be a fine show one day, you'll see. I do hope you don't mind."

"Mind! Why, of course not! But, by Jove, it's hot in here!"

"Yes, it is, isn't it? But you soon get used to it. It's not at all a bad conservatory, only nobody's taken any trouble with it for years and years. I'm sure it's delighted that somebody should."

"You must let me get you some plants and things."

"Oh, no," she replied eagerly. "I want to do it *all* myself! I've got several books and there's a man in the shop where I get the seeds who's most helpful." She went on with her work, taking up a little paper packet, then planting the seeds with the utmost care, bending over the box with absorbed, concentrated attention.

He watched her for a little and felt, although he was anything but imaginative, as though the place really had some kind of a life, as though the palm and the rows of dusty boxes waited, saying: "Now you're not to interfere. This kind lady is bringing us to life again."

"It's a bit musty," he said. "Don't you mind the smell?"

"No, I don't," she said. "I like it."

So he left her to her work, a green shadow in a green shade.

But this was a queer day for him, and he was not accustomed to queer days.

The next thing that happened to him was that on the landing he encountered a man. Matthew being what he was, Charles was accustomed to finding unusual people on the stairs, but this man was indeed *most* unusual, for his hair was so black, his face so brown, and he wore a shining black suit. He was, of course, a foreigner. He was about to descend, but instead he stopped and smiled.

"I beg your pardon," Charles said.

"Oh, not at all." The little man had something of an American accent. But he was not an American. He was quite clearly, in Charles's opinion, a dago. It was probable that he had been stealing something.

So Charles said: "Is there anything I can do for you?"

"Oh, no, nothing at all, thank you. I have been to pay a visit to my friend, Captain Coventry."

"Oh, yes," said Charles.

"Thank you very much. Good-afternoon," and the little man went on downstairs.

Charles had never quite approved of the fashion in which strangers went up and down the stairs of the house, but, after all, Matthew shared in the expenses, and Romney had his own friends and Nell had *her* friends. But this was the oddest one yet.

He heard the hall door close. The man was out of the house. Then, after hesitating, he went and knocked on Nicholas's door.

"Come in," said Nicholas.

Nicholas was lying, stretched out on his bed, dressed only in shirt and trousers, looking up at the ceiling.

"Hullo, Charles!"

"I say, Nicholas, that's a funny friend of yours just gone out."

"Yes, isn't he funny?" said Nicholas, "and damned

funnier than you know, Charles my friend. The little bastard's in a hole and I've been helping him."

"Oh, that's all right," said Charles, "only I thought he might be someone stealing the spoons."

Nicholas sat up.

"Oh, he *would* steal them if he got half a chance! I've been taking his skin off for coming here. He won't do it again. I knew him in the West Indies. He's up against it, and I did what I could, but I'm a likely one to help anyone, aren't I?"

"Excuse my coming in like this," said Charles, moving to the door.

But Nicholas stopped him.

"Don't go for a minute. That chap put me out, daring to come here like that. He's part of my bad past." Then after a pause, he said, smiling: "Have *you* got a past, Charles?"

"I?" said Charles. "No, of course not."

"No mistresses or anything?"

"Why, no. What an idea!"

"Well—I wondered. It's you quiet devils who are the worst." Then he went on: "Look here, Charles, let me have another thirty quid. I swear it's the last time I ask you."

Charles looked uncomfortable.

"I'd rather not, Nick. You see——"

Nicholas laughed.

"Fanny been lecturing you?"

"No. It wouldn't matter if she had."

Nicholas nodded.

"I quite understand. Of course if you haven't got it ——" Then he said cheerfully: "What a row Fanny would make if she thought you *had* a past! Lucky you haven't. . . ."

Charles slowly coloured.

"Let's leave Fanny out of it."

"All right. Only I know why you won't lend me any more money. You can't kid me." He went on chaffingly: "I shall go to Fanny and tell her you've got six mistresses. One in Bayswater, one in Chelsea, one in——"

"Oh, chuck it!" Charles said. "I'm going to count the spoons to see whether your dago friend——"

"Charles," Nicholas said softly, "please lend me another thirty. I'm in an awful hole, but any time now that Spanish job will be settled and then you shall have all your money *with* interest. I won't tell Fanny," he added.

"Oh, damn Fanny!" Charles said. "*She* doesn't run me."

They looked at one another.

"All right," Charles said suddenly. "You shall have it. But it's the last time, remember."

Nicholas lay down on the bed again.

"You're a damned good sort," Nicholas said. "Even though you *have* got six mistresses!"

6

The result of the little conversation with Nicholas was that Charles resolved that not another day should pass without a full explanation from Fanny.

At what had Nicholas been hinting? Why had he, Charles, quite suddenly given Nicholas the money when he had been firmly resolved to give him no more? Nicholas could not, of course, have known of the spring episode, and yet it was because of his own guilty consciousness of this that Charles had given him the cash. Well, he would have a guilty conscience no longer.

And yet—what courage it needed! Fanny had said quietly "Good-night" (they had not kissed) and then had closed the intervening door. He had lain in his bed realizing for the first time that this coming conversation might very easily be a crisis in their lives. How was it that until now he had been so blind as to the effect on Fanny of what he would tell her? Perhaps already she knew! No, but she *could* not. Perhaps there would be some simple, trivial explanation and he need not tell her. And all through this he lay flat on his back, his ears straining for some sound, his heart hammering, his head hot, his feet cold.

"Now!" he said to himself, and he got out of bed. He stood listening (but for what he did not know). He heard the clock ticking, as though it had been asleep all day and lived only in the night. He was a coward. He was trembling.

He put on his dressing gown and slippers and went into her room. Here he stood (remembering vaguely Othello), and heard no sound but the beating of his heart and Fanny's gentle, regular breathing. He knew, though, that she was not asleep, that she was aware that he had entered the room, that her heart was hammering even as his.

"Fanny!" he whispered. "Fanny!"

There was no answer.

He went to her bed, sat down on it, and touched her arm.

"Please, Fanny," he said. "I want to talk to you."

He switched on the light above the bed. He saw then that she was lying on her side, with her face to the wall. He touched her again and she turned round.

"What is it?" she said. Her eyes were filled with tears, and as he looked at her one tear rolled down her cheek.

That moved him so deeply that he bent forward and caught her in his arms, held her closely against him, crying:

"Darling. Darling. Don't cry. You mustn't. What is it that is hurting you? *What* is the matter? What have I done?"

She wiped the tear from her cheek, moved gently but with determination out of his embrace, sat up:

"No, Charles. Please," she said. "I'm tired."

He moved away from her, angry at her repulse.

"I'm sorry, Fan," he said. "But we've got to have this out. You're not going to sleep away from me like this without a very good reason."

"I've told you my reasons."

"What—that you've a cold or something! And that's why you're crying, I suppose."

She made no answer.

"Now look here," he went on, "I won't touch you. I won't come nearer you than this. But also, I won't go away. I have *got* to know. I'll stay here all night if necessary."

She looked down at her hands, which were tightly clasped in front of her.

"There's nothing to explain," she said.

"There's just this to explain. For more than twenty years we've been happy. We've never had a quarrel that mattered. Do you remember? We settled years ago that we would never let the day end without a reconciliation if we *had* been at odds. And we never have. That's the truth. Until a few days back, we never have. And now, quite suddenly, without a word of explanation, you separate yourself from me. Don't you *know* that I love you, that I love you more every year, that without you I'm a lost man——"

"That isn't true!" she interrupted. "That isn't true!"

"But of course it's true! It's the one thing that *is* true about me!"

She looked at him, then away from him across the room. She waited, staring in front of her.

"Very well," she said at last. "I'll show you why it isn't true."

She got out of bed without touching him, walked quickly across the room to her desk, opened a drawer and took out a letter. She gave him this, then sat down in an armchair near the fireplace, looking away from him.

"My God!" he said at last. "So that's it!"

When she heard that, she knew that he had written the letter. She had, of course, always known, and yet, through these days, she had had mad hopes that it might be a forgery, a joke, a . . . she did not know what!

"Yes—that's my letter," he said.

She turned half towards him.

"Written this year?"

"Yes."

He sat staring at it.

"I was going to tell you—I—I came in to tell you now."

"Then you knew that I had seen it?"

"No. Of course not."

"Then why didn't you tell me before?"

"I had forgotten all about it. You mayn't believe it, but it's true. Something Nicholas said today made me suddenly wonder whether it was *that* that was making you so unhappy."

"Who is she?" Fanny asked.

"Here—come back to bed, Fan," he said. "You're cold. You're shivering. Come to bed. I'll sit in the chair."

She made no answer and no movement. He took the eiderdown and put it over her shoulders.

"Who is she?" he repeated. He was reading the letter. It appeared to him quite incredible, and he realized now, with a shock of almost terrified dismay, how it must seem to her.

He pulled himself up. He must be cool, concentrated, collected as he had never been in his life before.

"She's nobody. She's nothing," he said. "I haven't seen her for months. We parted once and for all in—when was it?—in April."

She said nothing. He went on:

"It was a crazy thing. It meant nothing at all. It was when you were on that cruise. I met her at the theatre; she was a woman in a flower shop, a decent, kind sort of woman. Quite ordinary."

"Did you live with her?" Fanny asked.

"I went to her flat in the evenings. I slept with her—if that's what you mean. It was entirely a physical thing. The one and only time I have ever been with any woman except yourself since our marriage."

He paused, but she said nothing.

"You've *got* to understand this, Fan. You've *got* to. I know that the things in this letter are monstrous. They seem so to *me* now. I can't believe that I ever wrote them. But still, there they are. I can't deny any of it. What's more, I can't explain it, either. It wasn't as though she was beautiful or clever or anything—except that she was kind. She wasn't in love with me herself a bit—in fact, on looking back now I think that she must have laughed at me. She was a woman who thought those things unimportant. It isn't pretty, I know, but what you *must* understand, Fan, is that it doesn't mean anything. It was a moment of madness I had, and then in a few weeks it was over."

"How can I tell that it's over?" Fanny said. Then she added to herself: "Last April—that lovely day."

"How can you tell? You can only believe me if you try to understand me. It was a kind of illness. I caught an infection."

"At the time," Fanny said, "while it lasted, you believed in it."

"Believed in it? Yes, for the moment. One believes in a fever while one has it."

"How did it end?" Fanny asked.

"Quite simply. I woke up. I realized that I didn't care in the least about her, except that I was grateful because she was so kind to me." He was simple-minded enough now to praise her. "She was never kinder than that last time. We had tea, she gave me back my letters, we said good-bye."

"Not all your letters," said Fanny.

"No. I told her then that I had lost one, and she said that she wondered that men could be so careless. She really *was* kind and generous, Fan. She said you must be splendid——"

"She *dared* to speak of me!" Fanny cried.

"Oh, well—she had seen long before that I loved you and only you——"

Fanny interrupted:

"I don't want to hear about her! I don't want to hear about her!"

He got up and stood near to her, not daring to touch her.

"Fan, *don't* let this make any difference. *Don't. Don't.*"

Fanny looked up at him, bewildered unhappiness in her

eyes. It was as though she were asking him to help her out of this and yet could not trust him to help her.

If Nicholas had seen them, he would have thought them quite unwholesomely sentimental, getting out of the scene all that they could, enjoying their own self-pity. And he would have been quite wrong. They were, both of them, much too simple-hearted to think of anything except the danger that they were running—the danger that they would not love one another any more. If it was sentimental for them to realize, as one of their deepest experiences in life, that there is nothing so fine and so valuable as trust, love, and confidence between two human beings who have lived long enough to know what life is, then they were sentimental. But there is nothing nearer to God than love of this kind. So "sentimental" is the wrong word to use about those who are in fear of losing it.

"Well, Fan?" Charles said at last.

She tried to smile.

"Well, Charles?" Her face, as a rule so rosy, was white and marked with shadow. Her broad, heavy figure, the eiderdown draped untidily about it, was hunched up in the chair. He, with his grey, tousled hair, his eyes anxious but loving, gentle, simple, his brown dressing gown with a torn pocket—they were not perhaps a romantic pair. But they were in most serious distress.

"You've been very honest," she said at last. "If I could understand it better . . . But—how can I? I've never trusted anyone in my life as I have you. I've built my life up on trusting you. I've always said: 'Well, anyway there's Charles.' Nicholas said not long ago that one is wrong to trust anybody. I see now he's right."

She twisted and untwisted her hands.

"I remember—in the spring—one day when I was shopping, there was a woman I was talking to. When I told her how we all lived together, she said that couldn't last—not in these days. I laughed at her. I thought she little knew how united a family we were. Well, she was right, too. We're not united. In these last few months we've all broken up. We're none of us happy any more. We don't trust one another any more. I've seen this, I've known it, but I've always said as long as you were there, Charles, nothing could really be wrong."

"I *am* there, Fan," Charles said.

He was dreadfully distressed. Always before, when she was unhappy, he had been able to put his arms round her and comfort her.

"No." She shook her head. "Not as you were. You can't be again. I expect that that's my fault. I ought to be a modern woman. Every book, every play, every paper—they all say the same thing now—that married people ought to take infidelity lightly. But I'm not young. I can't change from believing the things I always believed."

He broke in: "Yes. Yes. I don't *want* you to change! We're neither of us modern, and what's more, the things we believe in are *real* things, Fan. What I want you to see is that I haven't been unfaithful to *you*. It was only my body—for a moment. As though I'd gone off on a drunk for a week——"

"Yes," Fanny said. "But if you had it wouldn't be *you*. Just as this isn't *you,* not as I've always thought you were. I don't hate you or despise you. But you've done this once—you may do this again——"

"No. Never, never, never!" he cried.

"Yes, but you may. Perhaps all men do. I don't know. I know so little about men. You're the only one I've ever loved. For a few weeks you loved her as you've never loved me, even at first. You never wrote me a letter like this."

"It was better, finer—altogether different—with us."

"Perhaps I'm jealous," she said slowly. "Perhaps I've wanted what that woman had."

Then she cried, her head in her hands.

He tried to comfort her, kneeling beside her, holding her with his arm. But he could not. Nothing that he could do just then could touch her. So at last he kissed her.

"Go to bed, Fan. Fan, darling—I love you so much more than I ever did."

But he could not come near her. He fancied that she did not even hear him. So, very miserable indeed, bewildered even as she was, he went back into his own room.

7

Young Romney, during these events, was regarding himself as an exile from the common life of the human race.

He was not alone among his generation in thinking of himself thus. Only last year Eddie Battin had tried (not very successfully) to commit suicide, and had explained afterwards that his act had been in protest at the atrocious conduct of the late war by his elders.

Gordon Gummeridge, two years ago founder of the Byron Club at Oxford, wrote frequently, for the daily journals, articles of the deepest pessimism, simply saying that everything was in ruins and it would be better to end it all. The generation younger than Romney's (now honouring the upper forms of the public schools) thought this all rather silly, when a new kind of aëroplane was invented almost every day and motor-racing was every Sunday faster than it had been the Sunday before—but their time was not yet.

Romney's unhappiness was quite real. He felt himself degraded and repulsive. He had failed with Harry, he had hated those women introduced to him by Nicholas. His hatred of them was not normal; on the other hand, he had no friend now anywhere. He wanted neither mistress nor friend, and his loneliness was appalling.

It was natural, therefore, that Nicholas's influence over him should now be very powerful, for there was no one, besides his uncle, who understood his trouble. Moreover, Nicholas was exceedingly kind to him. Nicholas showed in his relationship to Romney an understanding, sympathy, and generosity that he bestowed on no other member of the family. Here at least he was unselfish, for Romney, at this time, was not at all entertaining. But they were, Nicholas explained to him, in a way, both outcasts from the family.

"You can't talk to either your father or your mother frankly, can you? Well, neither can I. Something stops us. They are not close to real life. No one *is* in our family except you and I—and possibly the Old Lady ill upstairs. We're different. Oh! I don't mean sexually. You must put it right out of your head that you're abnormal, Romney. You're not a bit. But we're artists, both of us. Beauty means more to us than anything else in the world. I think your father and mother are the best in the world, but they don't care for beauty, do they? One can't pretend they do."

No, one couldn't, although Romney had never quite thought of it in that way before. He began, without knowing it, to take sides with Uncle Nicholas against his mother. Of course he loved her, but the trouble was that she didn't understand modern life. It was only since Uncle Nicholas had been in the house that he realized it. Then Uncle Nicholas borrowed small sums of money from Romney—nothing very much, but Romney was proud that he should ask him. Uncle Nicholas was very frank about himself.

"I'm a complete rotter, my boy. I don't say that it's altogether my own fault. Things have been against me a bit. But a rotter I am and a rotter I shall remain now, I suppose, until the end. I can't keep my word. I borrow money (I'm too damned good-natured), and worst of all, I see things as they are. It's my passion for honesty that keeps me crooked. I see things so clearly. Most people are such humbugs about religion and morality and affection. I'm not a humbug, but I *am* a rotter. I love women, I borrow money, I can't keep a job. What's to be done about it, my boy?"

And so Romney grew very fond of him. He was the only friend just now that he had.

Only one thing distressed him a little, and that was that his uncle had seen the little carved negress in his room and had gone into ecstasies over it. And then he had borrowed it. "Only for a day or two. Just to look at it." And Romney missed it, missed it most terribly. And he hadn't the courage to ask for it back again.

He was growing, too, very worldly-wise under his uncle's instruction. He was becoming a first-rate business man and sold pictures twice as well as he had done. If they were not always very good pictures, what did that matter?

And then, early in December, there happened to him a very queer little adventure. He was returning to the house about four in the afternoon, when he saw Lizzie emerge and start walking quickly down the street. Lizzie was a child with whom he had made no terms at all. He was himself too self-distrustful to make friends easily with children, who like their elders to be confident; and then she was so silent, so old for her age, and, he was sure, disliked him. Now for some reason—to rid himself of his dreary self-preoccupation, perhaps—he decided that he would follow her a little way. It was not curiosity that drove him, but possibly something touching in her childishness and even in a suggestion of loneliness that corresponded with his own.

Lizzie turned the corner, passed into Dean's Yard, and then waited at the school gate. Romney quickly caught her up.

"Hullo, Lizzie!" he said.

She was wearing a simple grey frock and a rather large grey hat with a blue ribbon. The hat looked too young for her. She did not appear to be at all surprised at seeing him, but gave him a quiet, polite, and distant smile.

"What are you doing here?" he asked.

"I'm waiting for Edward."

He was surprised.

"Why—have you some message for him?"

"Oh, no. I often wait for him. We go for a small walk before his tea."

"Does he like your waiting? I should have thought the other boys might laugh at him."

"Oh, yes—at first he did not like it at all, so I would wait in the door of the church there. But now I know many of the boys. They are so very odd in their dirty tall hats."

Romney was greatly interested.

"Then you and Edward are great friends?"

"Very great," she said, looking at him, he thought, rather contemptuously.

He felt that he ought to go—that she did not want him to remain there at all—but this was the first private talk that he had ever had with her. She was so quietly composed that he felt ashamed of his own complainings.

"Have you liked staying with us?" he asked her.

"Not very much," she said. "Except for Edward and Aunt Fanny."

"Where do you like most to be?"

He felt that his questions were extremely silly and that she thought that they were.

"What I should prefer," she said, "would be to be *quite* by myself. I wouldn't mind Edward," she added.

"And your father?"

At that she withdrew entirely inside herself, as though she had entered the grey stone wall of the school and disappeared.

"My father? Oh, he is different," she said.

There followed then an awkward silence.

"My God, how she dislikes me!" Romney thought, and felt that he was spying on herself and Edward and that he had better go home. But he said:

"Would you come with me one day? We could go and look at some pictures."

She came out of the stone wall and gave him a most unexpected smile.

"Thank you very much."

"Do you like pictures?" he asked.

But she didn't answer, because the boys came out with a rush. They paid no attention to Romney and Lizzie. Edward appeared, and with him a lanky freckled boy who knew Lizzie, talked to her as though they were very old friends, and vanished. Edward did not appear overjoyed to see his brother.

"Well—I must be going," Romney said.

"You can come with us, too," Lizzie said. "Can't he, Edward?"

"Right-oh," said Edward indifferently and began at once a long narration:

"It was just what you said, Lizzie. Baldwin offered to swop the dog if I'd let him have the watch as well, but I said no bally fear—I knew it was the watch he really wanted, and if I work it I can get another for Christmas, but the tools and the watch was a bit too much, so I said he could have the hammer and the chisel *and* the watch, but not the other things. He's awfully mean, Baldwin is—his father's a Jew or something—and he didn't half like it, but just as you said he wanted the watch no end, and after all it's only three weeks to Christmas—so now I've got the dog!" he ended breathlessly.

"Oh, Edward—I'm so very glad!" Lizzie said.

"What dog's this?" asked Romney.

"It's a terrier Baldwin's got, and his father doesn't want him to keep it."

"Your father won't want you to keep it, either!" said Romney.

"Oh, that's all right," Edward said. "I was with Mother in Bond Street and we saw a dog in a window and Mother said I could have it if we'd got money enough, but we hadn't."

"How are you going to exercise it?" Romney asked.

"That's easy," Edward said. "I'll run it out in the morning and Lizzie will have it in the afternoon and we'll both have it at tea time. That's enough for *any* dog!"

"But Lizzie won't be here always," Romney said.

"Perhaps she will," said Edward with that calm command of fate that was always to be especially his. "You never know."

"Where are you going?" Romney asked. "Mother will be expecting you back."

"Mother's gone out to tea this afternoon," Edward said. "She said this morning that Lady Congreve had a tea party."

"Oh, Lady Congreve!" said Romney.

"Yes, isn't she awful?" Edward remarked. "When she sees me she says: 'And is this *your* little boy?' every time, although she knows I am, and I'm not little anyway. I *hate* her!" he ended cheerfully.

"And where are you going?" Romney asked.

They were at the beginning of Victoria Street. The sky that stretched here, in a wide expanse, over the ivory-grey of Parliament and Abbey, was flecked with colour above a triumph of stone that has the snowy whiteness of seagulls' wings. There seems, at that moment, no height to which these towers might not soar. The Square in its movement whirls the traffic round its circle as a croupier turns his wheel, but the sky and the towers invest the rhythmic movement with their own shining pallor. The moment before the lights come out, before the sky darkens into repose . . .

Romney looked up and, in that brief time, saw the sky gather the coloured fragments of cloud, turn them into feathers of rose that, in the cold still air, had the radiance of fire. It was one of those moments in London's life when she chooses to forget her business and give herself, for an instant, to the creation of beauty. In another whisper it will be gone; seize it or not as you please—but for that instant everything is in perfect accord. The sky is pale as the buildings are pale, but it is a translucent pallor as light placed behind crystal.

"Where are you going?" he asked again.

"I'm going to buy Mother some flowers," Edward said. "I've got four and six. That's enough, isn't it?"

Romney was surprised. Edward was not at all the

sweet sentimental type of boy who bought flowers for his mother.

"She's had headaches every day lately," Edward went on. "Gosh! I think that's awful, so Lizzie and I think some flowers might cheer her up."

They started down Victoria Street, and Romney was surprised to find that the expedition was an adventure. Edward talked without ceasing and treated Romney as a sensible companion, which he had never, in Romney's memory, done before. Also he appeared to consider Lizzie an authority upon everything. Lizzie was quiet but observant, and was clearly enjoying herself.

"Do you suppose," said Edward, "if you got on a bus and then changed and got on another bus and changed and then *another* bus you could go right round London for sixpence?" Then, without waiting for an answer: "Temple Minor's got a brother who's an awful cheat. He gets on a bus and pays a penny less than he should, and after a bit he changes his seat and the conductor forgets where he's been sitting and thinks he's paid the whole lot. I should think you could be sent to prison for a thing like that. But Temple says his brother wouldn't care. He says it would be an experience."

Once and again, Romney noticed, Edward put out his hand and protected Lizzie, who walked quietly forward as though she were above the world, from running into someone. That was very charming, Romney thought. They had also private jokes which showed that their intimacy was now a deep one. Edward called things by strange names that had, Romney thought, an Italian origin, and, when Romney enquired, Edward nodded:

"Lizzie's teaching me Italian," he said in his most off-hand manner.

They came to a flower shop and went inside. It was a

blaze of glory, and the glory was chiefly chrysanthemum. Here Lizzie, too, was glorified. Her coat with its cheap fur collar was shabby, her hat was the wrong shape, but her eyes beamed, and Romney noticed that she had beautiful hands; for she had taken off her gloves, and her hands moved toward the flowers, touched them, withdrew, seemed to draw the gold, crimson, amber into her own small body.

Edward was severely practical.

"Those are a shilling a bloom," a lady like a governess in one of the best of England's families told him. And indeed they were glorious, their shaggy petals whiter than the moon.

Some of the chrysanthemums, sturdily independent, were in pots.

"She'd like that one, I think," said Edward, pointing at a plant that burnt like a sun on an autumn day.

"That's the one I like," said Lizzie.

"How much is that one?"

"Five shillings," said the governess.

"Will you lend me sixpence?" Edward asked. "I'll pay you back Saturday week if you can wait till then."

The pot was wrapped up, and they turned homewards. Edward carried it almost sacrificially, and Lizzie was as anxious as he.

All was well; they were home again.

A very terrible scene followed. Fanny was in the hall, and they all were at once aware that here was tragedy.

"Where have you been, Edward?"

He placed the chrysanthemums carefully on the table.

"It's all right, Mother. I've been——"

"It isn't all right," she broke in. "I've been in a dreadful way. You should have been at home an hour ago." She turned on Romney. "Romney, it's too bad of you letting the children stay out like this. Couldn't you realize what I've been feeling? I thought Edward was run over or stolen or——"

To Romney and Edward this scene appeared quite absurd. Lizzie understood it perfectly. But they were aware, all three of them, that Fanny was terrified, and her terror affected themselves. But why? Romney was greatly annoyed.

"Mother, this is ridiculous. What *could* happen to Edward? We only went for a little walk——"

"Ridiculous! I don't think that's very polite, Romney, You don't care what you say these days——"

"Oh, damn!" He was furious. As though it was *his* fault. "It *is* ridiculous, Mother," he went on. "I'm damned if I'll be ranted at for nothing at all."

He looked as though he hated her. Then he started upstairs, the children following him.

The chrysanthemums were forgotten.

8

The room where Matthew and his friends met was a very ordinary one. The furniture was hideous; there was a bookcase, simple and practical, but one of the growing kind. You add a shelf when you have a pound to spare, and the books, imprisoned behind glass, lament their fate. There were two cheap gate-legged tables, and the chairs, the sofa, and the two armchairs quite clearly hated human beings. There were two pictures, one an excellent copy of Manet's barmaid, the other an exciting representation of a ship in a stormy bright-green sea. The first had been presented by Matthew, the second by Bob Orange.

But the room was alive; it was alive because the people

in it were comfortable. Two ladies, Miss Murdoch and Mrs. Bell, were knitting. One lady, Mary McTavish, was sewing. Bob Orange sat back in his chair, his legs stuck out, smoking. Sam Somerset sat forward staring, absent-mindedly, at Mr. McTavish. Many others were present. It was a very full meeting. There were Jack Henry, a policeman; Miss Clare Romanes, a young woman, very good-looking, once fashionable, now crazy about planting flowers in waste places like the hero of Maurice Hewlett's story; Samuel Cope, a grocer in Pimlico; Ramon Spender, a painter and an all-in wrestler; John Prentice, a young Member of Parliament. Of course Danny.

And more than these.

The differences between these human beings were so acute, their personal histories so varied, that it was remarkable that the room gave so strong an impression of harmony. But no one, entering, would have supposed that religion had anything to do with the gathering. There were no public confessions, no prayers for guidance and, above all, no hysteria.

A large black kettle was singing on the hob, and Miss Romanes had brought with her her Airedale, who lay at her feet fast asleep.

Mary McTavish was reading to the company. She had a beautiful voice, soft, gentle, distinct, with every word clear as a silver coin:

" 'Set not much by this—who is against thee or with thee, but so do and care that God is with thee.

" 'In every thing that thou doest have a good conscience and God shall defend thee: for him that God will help no man's overthwartness shall be able to annoy.

" 'If thou canst be still and suffer thou shalt see without any doubt the help of our Lord: He knoweth the time and manner of helping thee, and therefore thou oughtest to reserve thyself for Him.

" 'To God it belongeth to help and deliver from all confusion.

" 'If it seemeth to thee that thou knowest many things and are understanding enough, yet there are many more things that thou knowest not.

" 'Think not highly of thyself but rather acknowledge thine ignorance.

" 'Thou comest to serve and not to govern: know well that thou art called to suffer and to labour and not to be idle and tell tales.

" 'He hath great tranquillity of heart that setteth nothing by praisings or blamings.

" 'Thou art not the holier though thou be praised nor the more vile though thou be blamed or dispraised. What thou art, that thou art; that God knoweth thee to be and thou canst be said to be no greater. . .' "

"What's that out of, Mary?" Somerset asked.

"It's Thomas à Kempis's *Imitation of Christ*. This is an anthology." She held the book up. She turned the pages and began to read something quite different:

"O'er the broad nest her silver wings
Shook down their wasteful glitterings;
Her brindled neck high-arched in air
Like a small rainbow faded there;
But brighter glowed her plumy crown
Mouldering to golden ashes down;
With fume of sweet woods, to the skies,
Pure as a Saint's adoring sighs,
Warm as a prayer in Paradise,
Her life-breath rose in sacrifice!

The while with shrill triumphant tone
Sounding aloud, aloft, alone,
Ceaseless her joyful deathwail she
Sang to departing Araby.
Deep melancholy wonder drew
Tears from my heartspring at that view.
Like cresset shedding its last flare
Upon some wistful mariner,
The Bird, fast-blending with the sky,
Turned on me her dead-gazing eye
Once—and as surge to shallow spray
Sank down to vapoury dust away!"

After Mary's voice ceased there was silence. Then Jack Henry, the policeman, said: "They're very pretty words, but I'm blowed if I understand what it's all about."

McTavish began to explain to him concerning the Phœnix, but Henry wasn't interested: "I'm a townsman myself," he said. "First Shoreditch, then Elephant and Castle, now Albany Street. I've never known nothing about birds except it seems to me it's a damned shame to keep them in cages." He went on, however, to the thing that interested him, which was that God had seemed to him lately like a balloon, a large balloon full of fire and moving in the sky. This, of course, would appear quite crazy to everyone except his friends here in this room, and that was why he mentioned it now. When he was on night duty, walking up and down dark and solitary streets, this notion of the fiery balloon was somehow a very cheering thing. He didn't, of course, mean that there *was* a balloon there, but still a kind of brightness moved where *he* moved. . . . He had a friend in the Salvation Army who said this was nonsense. It wasn't a matter of fire in the sky but of salvation. Was Jack Henry saved?

Now by what Miss McTavish read just now, one wasn't to think oneself better than one's fellows, but if you were saved and the man next door wasn't, then you *did* think yourself better than your fellows. . . .

Tea followed.

Matthew, this evening, was sitting a little apart. This was not his usual way, for he was extremely popular and was innocently pleased that they liked him. Moreover he knew the personal histories of everyone here and, at these meetings, there were many new chapters to be added.

But today he was very unhappy and sat apart. A dreadful thing had come to him. He hated his brother. Hatred comes always like a cloud slipping low down over the mountains, covering everything with a wet mist, cold and drenching. Malevolence strangles, and now Matthew was, for the first time, malevolent. He wished every possible ill to his brother, and so God was excluded. The words of à Kempis seemed to him today to be platitudinous nonsense and "Nepenthe" nothing but florid affectation. He was *blinded* from his friends and knew, to his horror, that he was seeing them as Nicholas would see them. For the first time he regarded Jack Henry with actual dislike. As though policemen could possibly think of God as a balloon! This was a pose that Henry had acquired in order to be more interesting to these friends of his!

"A bit priggish, aren't they all?" he could hear Nicholas whispering in his ear—and so perhaps they were. This business of intimacy with God put you above your fellows, and at once there crept in superiority, self-conscious virtue, pomposity. And yet hitherto he had not thought these people pompous or priggish or self-conscious. He had often wondered at their simplicity, at the naturalness with which they all, so different in taste, education, training, met time after time and were happy.

That was enough, he had thought, of itself to prove that the world to which they belonged had some special properties of beauty and understanding and kindliness. But tonight he saw the elegant figure of Nicholas moving among them all. They were gathered about the table, drinking tea and eating cake and bread and butter. He could see now that they felt that they belonged to a moving, growing organization. From the person of each one stretched a chain of other persons. The family was spreading into Europe, and yet, very marvellously, it was still not an organization, had no rules, no documents, no finances save the very simplest. He watched Danny with feelings of almost passionate envy. Here was a very simple old man. Could *he* hate his brother? Matthew knew that if such a plague came to him he would cut off his right hand rather than continue under it. But that was because Danny was so *very* simple. He would not be able even to conceive of the complicated emotions, fears, distresses that now inhabited the Westminster house.

If Nicholas met Danny he would like him, but would consider him as of a different order. "Religion is for such a man," he would say, as you might say, "Dog biscuits are good for a puppy." Then Matthew forgot his present company and became involved in Nicholas as though Nicholas had wrapped him round with a cloak. He thought all day of Nicholas, of how he could force him out of the house, of how he could confront him and insult him so that he would be compelled to go. He had done what he could and he had utterly failed. He felt himself so weak and useless that all his confidence in God was a mockery. Easy enough to say that you believed in God when everything was comfortable and easy, but now at the first real test God could do nothing for him, nothing at all. God did not then, after all, exist? All this sense of contact was a sham, a self-hallucination, as so many clever people said that it was. What a mockery was this gathering in this room, and he had the temptation to shout out: "Listen, all of you! I who am responsible for your being here tell you that this is hallucination. There *is* no God, no law of love; the struggle towards nobility is a sham. We are fleas hopping on a dying cinder, jumping to annihilation!"

But more definite and actual than any speculation was his hatred of Nicholas. It appeared to him now that his hatred had threaded his whole life. Nicholas, as a baby, stealing his bricks, Nicholas taunting him because there was a cow in the field, Nicholas mocking him at a party, Nicholas twisting his arm in the barn across the road . . . and yet, for years and years, he had been free of Nicholas, had not thought of him!

Old McTavish with his huge spectacles and cadaverous face came over to him, carrying two cups of tea.

"Here, Matthew, take a cup."

Matthew took it.

"I'm going to be married," McTavish said.

Matthew congratulated him.

"Aye. She's a very decent body, with two children of her own. She'll be coming with me here in a week or two. She's that timid she's afeard of her own shadow, so this will do her a power of good."

Then he said, laying a bony hand on a bony knee:

"You're out of sorts tonight, Matthew."

Matthew nodded.

"Maybe thinking this is a lot of humbug."

"No," said Matthew. "Not this. But myself."

"Aye," said McTavish, pouring his tea into his saucer and breathing on it. "I'm that way myself at times. But it passes. Maybe it's the liver."

But in a little while Matthew slipped out. He could not endure it any longer. It was a dark winter night. The clouds rushed overhead and the traffic roared on every side of him. The whole earth seemed to heave at his feet, and around him all faces were white, windows were darkened with secrecy, the picture houses flamed.

In the stillness of Westminster, under the driving sky, ghosts walked, ceaselessly passing and repassing without sound upon layers of sodden leaves.

As he fitted his key in the door of the house he thought:

"I would be glad if he died! We could be at peace again then."

9

Nicholas sold the gold snuffbox four days before Christmas. It was characteristic of him that he should sell it when he had no real need to do so. Just then—because of lucky cards, because of loans from Romney and Grace—he was not penniless. But it was characteristic of him also that he sold it to give everyone presents at Christmas. Christmas, anyone might be surprised to hear, was one of Nicholas's festivals. A pagan festival, of course. The myth that created it was so ancient that its origins were hidden among the stars. But it was, he always thought, a pretty story with its contrasted kings and shepherds, gold and frankincense, dung and straw, cattle and angels, its starshine, its hilly freshness, its pretty baby fantasy.

But he liked Christmas. He liked the air of license, of kiss-and-never-mind; he liked the present-giving and -receiving which the young considered such a bore. He liked his own popularity, for he was never more successful than when he was organizing games and acting, quite easily, the part of a character out of Dickens.

For the rest he was content. He was, perhaps, more fully involved with Mrs. Agar than he wished. He had helped her in a little plan or two—oh, nothing criminal, only his social company when someone or other needed reassuring! And to Abel he was thoroughly accustomed. He never conceived now of bidding him be off. He found him, indeed, rather useful, saw him every day, and gave him money every once and again.

Of the house itself he was now Commander—and it was this especially that determined him to have a very happy Christmas, and to make everyone round him happy. Having disturbed them a little, his cleverness (oh! how he enjoyed his cleverness!) would now be directed to cheering them up. He really liked them all extremely save only Fanny and Matthew. Against these two he had what must be ancient, slumbering grudges. Grace was too foolish, poor thing, to stir him to anything but kindly contempt. Fanny he frankly detested, and one day he would tell her so. There was a certain pride and obstinacy in Fanny which exasperated him. In her heart she thought herself as good as he, nay, better. Well, he would show her. . . .

He was indeed already showing her, for he knew that she had given Charles the letter. The two were very quiet. To the ignorant they gave no sign, but Nicholas knew.

As for Matthew, he would deal with him faithfully also. The sly priggish preacher with God in his pocket!

And Nicholas was especially irritated with these two because they made him feel malevolent. He did not wish to feel malevolent. He enjoyed the world and everyone in it so long as he had some money in his pocket, pretty women not too far away, a stomach in good working order, Lizzie contented, and one or two beautiful things to look at and handle.

It was a shame to sell the snuffbox, only because it was beautiful, not at all because it wasn't his. It was in fact his quite as much as anyone's. He could remember it in the old drawing room at home. Even as a baby he had wanted to handle it. If Fanny asked for it what would he say? He would say that he had replaced it and they would blame a servant. And as to its beauty, he did not now mind so greatly, for he had the little carved negress to look at—the negress that, he was determined, should never again leave him. If Romney demanded it he would pay him for it. He would borrow the money from Grace, who would now do anything for him. The thought of that amused him.

So, in the best of tempers, he went out after an early tea to sell the snuffbox. It was after five, but the shops remained open late in Christmas week. Christmas was in the air. There was a sense of pleasant hurry, the stars were coming out in the sky, and, imaginatively, he could sniff the cold purity of mistletoe, the odour of baked meats, the thick consistency of raisins, sugar, and flour. He dropped down from Piccadilly into the quiet bachelor security of Duke Street.

Here he saw the very shop that he required. Over the dark-blue door there was printed in big gold letters the one name: ZANTI. The window contained only one or two things—a Limoges panel of the Nativity, rich in deepest blues and crimsons, a carved ivory box with huntsmen and dogs and a wild ferocious boar, a necklace of crystal beads and a jade cup. These were arranged on a platform of grey velvet. They were exquisitely lit.

He went in. A pale young man behind a table bowed.

Nicholas produced the snuffbox.

"Can you give me any idea," he said, "what this is worth? I should like to sell it."

The young man took the snuffbox and examined it carefully. Nicholas looked about him. There was only one glass case in the room, and this contained only a few things, but Nicholas could see that they were of superb quality. A miniature especially attracted him—a young girl in eighteenth-century dress. It was framed in pearls and diamonds. The dress was the palest rose-pink, her hair was powdered, and she had a young eager smiling countenance. Oh! but he would like to possess that miniature! He must have it in his hands.

"May I look at that miniature a moment?"

The young man, eyeing him very carefully, opened the case and gave him the miniature.

As his hand closed about the exquisite thing his heart began to beat thickly. His hands trembled. He could have put it to his lips and kissed it. And he had an almost irresistible impulse to slip it into his pocket. That way madness lay. So, with a charming smile, but feeling as though rough fingers had taken his heart and pinched it, he returned it to the young man.

"How lovely!" he said.

"Yes. If you will excuse me," said the young man, "I will ask Mr. Zanti . . ." He pressed a little bell with his thumb. A door opened, and there came in quite the fattest man that Nicholas had ever seen in his life (and he had known some fat men in his time!).

Mr. Zanti must be old, and yet his hair was still jet black and fitted, like a skullcap, his ancient yellow, many-chinned countenance. From the landscape of this large face his black eyes sparkled as though two holes had been made in a map and a young child peeped through. His body was short and immensely broad. His vast stomach spread like a bolster. And yet he was not unpleasant to behold, Nicholas thought, for he was most beautifully clean, like an ivory statue yellow with age. He had small fingers, slender for so stout a man. He wore a neat black suit. He was alert and alive.

"And what can I do for you, sir?" he asked.

Nicholas told him. He took the box and examined it, at first with indifference. He was suddenly excited.

"Excuse me. Please, sir, will you come with me inside?" He opened the door at the back of the shop, and Nicholas followed him into an untidy and messy little room. There was a table piled high with scattered papers. On a rather faded wall paper there was only one illumination—a faded yellow photograph of Penzance. There was an old armchair with a hole in it. Mr. Zanti sat down at the table and examined the box with a large glass. His black eyes jumped at Nicholas's face.

"Excuse me, sir, this is a very valuable box."

"Indeed?" said Nicholas.

"You did not know? Ah, well. It is the work of Pietro Taquisance, an Italian artist of the early eighteenth century. He was a very wicked man and a very fine artist. We know zomezing about his wickedness, very little about his art."

"What did he do?" asked Nicholas, who was interested in wickedness.

"He tortured old women to get their money, he poisoned his zister—and he had all ze vices. But there are not many examples of his work. I have not had one in my hands for a long time. I will give you two hundred pound," he said suddenly. "Pardon me," he added. "You cannot tell me the history of this box?"

"No," said Nicholas, who was greatly excited at the unexpected nature of this news, "I'm afraid I can't. It has been in my possession ever since I can remember. My mother had it. I played with it as a baby."

He was trying to collect himself. Two hundred pounds! Neither Fanny nor Charles had the slightest idea of the value of it. Had he any right . . . ? Oh, nonsense! He needed the money very much more than they did.

"I will give you a check—now," said Zanti. He added: "It is a pity for you to sell it—is it necessary?"

"Very necessary," said Nicholas, laughing.

"Excuse me," Zanti said. "Perhaps you regard this as an impertinence in me. But I have lived too long to care much for impertinence. But—it may be—your selling this—zomezing you will always regret. We do zomezing without thinking—and our whole life changes. This might be for you the wrong action which you will always regret."

What an extraordinary old man! But Nicholas liked him. They were brothers, for in both of them was this same passion—a love of beautiful things.

"I never regret any past action," Nicholas said. "I think I care for beautiful things as much as you do. In your shop there is a miniature—the loveliest thing I have ever seen. I would do anything to possess it. I would steal it if necessary. But then, on the other hand, one must live—to enjoy these things. And so, I'm afraid, I shall have to take your check."

Zanti looked at him closely. Then he said, almost casually:

"You did not see, in my window, a very fine rose-coloured bowl?"

"In your window?" Nicholas considered. "No. I'm quite sure there was no rose-coloured bowl in the window."

Zanti paused. "Ah, well, perhaps not."

He wrote a check.

As they went back into the shop Nicholas said:

"What wonderful things you have! How I envy you living with such things. It is just the life I should have chosen for myself."

"Yes?" The old man smiled. "Once, hundreds of years ago, I had a little bookshop. Before that I was in Cornwall. Also in Spain. I look old really, but I am not so old. I fought in the war for my country—Italy."

"You fought in the war?" Nicholas asked incredulously.

"Oh, yes. At the last they took anyone who would go. I was known as old Papa Zanti!" Then he bowed. "Good-afternoon, sir."

Two hundred pounds! What luck! What wonderful amazing luck! On his way home he passed a sweet-shop, and against its windows three small children, two boys and a girl, pressed their noses. He took them inside and bought for them as many sweets as they could carry. He enjoyed hugely this pleasure.

10

On this same afternoon from another side of the house a new perception of life came to a member of the family. Nell moved forward.

She was on her knees in the dining room looking in the lowest shelf of the bookcase for Samuel Butler's *Notebooks.* Romney had told her it was there. But, no. Here are the forgotten, disregarded shepherds and shepherdesses of the Arcadian age. She made a little pile on the floor beside her. *Scenes and Characters,* Charlotte Mary Yonge; *Red as a Rose Is She,* Rhoda Broughton;

Festus, A Summer in Skye, Dreamthorp, Keynotes, and, last but surely not least, *The Heavenly Twins.*

She was in a sentimental mood, perhaps, for Hector last afternoon had shown her (she said to herself) his very heart in the centre of the London Museum. So she looked at the little pile with tenderness. Once they had made people happy, once they had seemed fresh and wonderful and even (dear Rhoda!) bold. They would now, possibly, never make people happy again. Going, going, gone. . . . And yet who could tell? Would not some wise 1980 young man put on his spectacles, fly in his midget aëroplane to Miss Broughton's birthplace perhaps? Would not *Nancy* and *Cometh Up as a Flower* seem then the oddest, quaintest, most beautiful witnesses to kind hearts seeking for coronets? Squatting there and feeling that Charlotte Mary and Rhoda together had said "Boo!" to Samuel Butler, so that she no longer wanted to find him, she realized that her mother was at her side.

"What are you doing, darling? We *must* turn those old books out. I've been meaning to for ages." Then Fanny said, with that rather shy eagerness that was her own property: "Nell, are you busy? I thought—why shouldn't we go to the pictures?"

Nell jumped up.

"Yes, darling," she said, brushing her dress. "It would be lovely. What a good idea!"

She knew well her mother's capacity for finding happiness in very little things, and it pleased her greatly now to see that Fanny had some of her once-on-a-time happiness in her eyes; she was almost like her old self, her tall beautiful body strung up with a kind of eager tenseness.

"I'll go and put my hat on," Fanny said in a half-whisper.

Nell, waiting for her in the hall, thought: "I wonder whether she will tell me anything—I wonder whether that's why she has asked me."

The house's silence struck her now as it so often lately had done. It was not only the consciousness of her own secret that oppressed her but a growing awareness of the nerves and unhappiness and apprehension attacking them all. It was, in part, surely Granny's illness that was making this Christmas different from any other. Uncle Nicholas was the only one of them who was enjoying it. He alone was full of plans and little plotting surprises. Her anticipation of some unhappy event that would concern them all swallowed up, just then, her consciousness of her own problems. *They* were bad enough! With every day she seemed to be pushed into worse deceit and more furtive manœuvre. But, as she waited, her whole mind was on her mother. How could she help her, how discover what it was that had changed her so?

Looking up, she saw Becky Sharp descending the stairs. With slow sleeky deliberation, a secrecy that removed her from all outside contact, the cat came from soft step to soft step. She gave Nell one glance out of her large green eyes, then disappeared along the passage.

Fanny came hurriedly and a little confused as she always did.

"Now, dear, what are we going to?"

"I've no idea what there is. I haven't been to the pictures for ages." (No, because Lottie might be there.)

"Well, there's one at the Cosmopolitan called *Wives and Husbands*. I thought that sounded interesting."

When they were in the taxi, Nell said:

"Isn't it funny? Becky Sharp's always in Granny's room now."

"Oh, dear, I hope she doesn't mind!"

"No, I think she likes it," said Nell. "But it's only lately—the last week. She's there all the time."

Fanny took Nell's hand into hers.

"This *is* nice. I must say I like the pictures, but I haven't been for a long time. Every afternoon's engaged, although I'm sure I don't know what with. I remember when I was a little girl we used to go to magic-lantern shows. They were *wonderful.* I often think it doesn't matter what the thing is so long as you enjoy it. What I mean is that of course everything is so *developed* now, but we enjoyed that magic lantern in the village schoolroom just as much."

She held Nell's hand very tightly and said:

"Dear, I went and paid Janet a visit yesterday."

"Oh, no—did you? How was she?"

"I had to take her something for Christmas. It wouldn't have seemed right if I hadn't. It was *lovely* seeing her again. We both enjoyed it so."

"What did you talk about?" Nell asked.

"Oh——" Then Fanny stopped. "You know—old times. Anything. Janet had a grand tea for me, and of course I didn't want to eat it, which she very well knew. She took a grim pleasure," Fanny went on. "Janet is more to me than anyone except all of you of course."

"She shouldn't have left you," Nell said quickly.

"She hasn't left me. She's only waiting until——"

"Until what?"

"Oh, well, you know that she didn't get on with Nicholas. She's only waiting until he goes."

Nell laughed. "I don't think he'll ever go! He's with us for evermore. He's amusing, isn't he, Mother? But, all the same, it's nicer by ourselves." She was then on the very edge of telling Fanny everything. The thought of her uncle restrained her. *What* a silly thing for her to do, he would say! But in any case, Fanny gave her something else to think about.

"He is going—almost at once—after Christmas!"

"He's going!" Nell cried. "Why, wherever to?"

"I don't know," Fanny said. "But he's going." Her voice was low, vibrating, full of suppressed emotion. "It isn't right for a man to stay idly like that doing nothing. And I don't think his influence on you children is good. Romney is quite changed and will hardly speak to me. Lizzie dominates Edward. Your father—— But here we are! Yes, there it is—*Wives and Husbands*. Norma Shearer and Clark Gable. Do you know them, darling?"

"Well, not personally," said Nell, laughing. "But Clark Gable's a pet."

They sprang out. Fanny paid the man, giving him sixpence as a tip, simply because she was so thoroughly determined to enjoy herself and he was an old man with a grey bulbous nose and his neck was wrapped in a very dirty woollen muffler. He seemed grateful for the tip, and she said to Nell as they went in: "I never can understand why they say taximen are so rude. They're charming." Because she was herself so very unhappy she was beating everything up to its highest, forcing herself into excited enjoyment that like an illuminated turnip lantern was hollow inside.

They had the very best places in the front of the dress circle and, seating themselves, were caught up into a crowd of footballers, thousands strong, and cheering madly; a succession of motorbicycles charging wildly round corners; and Mr. Runciman standing behind a table and a glass of water, explaining something very carefully. They were hemmed in with violent noises, crack and roars and shouts and yells—and yet a lady behind them eating chocolates was the loudest of them all.

Then the news of the world passed as it always must into limbo, and a vast organ, decorated in the very worst of taste, rose from the bowels of the earth; a pale thin young man, bound to the organ like a victim in a heathen sacrifice, bowed to them all and offered them in frantic succession M. Gounod, M. Bizet, and M. Saint-Saëns. Then, quite rightly, he was swallowed up into the earth again.

There followed a farce in which a fat man called Hardy argued with a thin man called Laurel. But in spite of their arguments they were friends. Their friendliness pervaded the vast building. They fell downstairs together, ate custard together, and were both of them abused by a large fat woman. They were friends in spite of everything. And so to *Wives and Husbands.*

Nell, in spite of her modern sophistication, in spite of the fact that the most intimate of domestic crises were developed in halls as vast as Eblis, was caught into the drama. For here were two wives and two husbands. One wife was elegant (Norma Shearer—oh, how elegant!) and one wife was shabby (a little mouse of a thing). One husband was handsome and slim and fiercely charming (Clark Gable), and one husband was clumsy and ill-dressed. Norma Shearer was the wife of the clumsy one, Clark Gable the husband of the little mouse. So of course things went wrong.

Oh, what a smart party Norma Shearer gave! There were thousands of guests all in evening dress that was too good to be true. They threw balloons at one another and shrieked and drank champagne standing on tables. But in spite of this and in spite of a butler who bowed every time he saw anyone, things went wrong. The clumsy man found a letter in his wife's bureau, and Clark Gable took a lady to a restaurant where, by a very odd coincidence, the little mouse happened to be dining all alone. Will it come right? Oh, will it come right? Surely they will not be so foolish as to allow true love to be strangled? Surely, surely . . .

It was then that Nell, absorbed in the story, felt something warm on the back of her hand. Her mother was crying. There was no sound, no movement. The touch of that tear on her hand moved Nell quite desperately. Once again she felt the impotence, the unresourcefulness of her youth. Her mother was easily moved. It might be the drama of the story. But she knew that it was more than this.

She put her arm around her mother's waist. They sat closely together, side pressed against side, while the strange American voices came to them out of space, and that other story, now for both of them altogether unreal, moved to its conclusion.

II

Two days before Christmas and London was plunged into an ecstasy of present-buying. "This is surely the worst kind of hypocrisy," said the young men and women to one another. "Everyone knows that Christmas had its origin in the wild orgiastic sacrifices of the Neanderthal man. With our cards, our holly, and our carols we are now celebrating the savage bestiality of the Stone Age."

Behind Nicholas at the Sunday performance of the private film society one young man said to another young man:

"Isn't it awful—this Christmas idea?"

And the other young man said:

"Simply too ghastly."

Everyone everywhere protested that this present-giving was a farce and an imposition, that they would never give presents again, that they would not give presents *now* were it not that presents would be given to *them,* and that it was nothing else but sinful in these days when no one had any money at all and there were all these unemployed. . . .

Nevertheless the sun shone, London was happy, the streets were packed with excited purchasers, along Holborn the hawkers covered the pavements with little toy policemen and black dogs with scarlet coats and green men running up sticks and balloons of every shining splendour; in Gamage's little boys breathed deeply and watched Father Christmas, and the jewellers in Bond Street sold diamonds to young men who were gallantly overdrawn at the bank.

It would be a sad exaggeration, of course, to say that Piccadilly blossomed into Christmas trees, but Fanny, who had a child's imagination and walked in Edward's company down the Circus to Hyde Park Corner, had only to shut her eyes and she saw a forest of lovely trees, blazing with lights, while along the broad avenue, carpeted with fir cones, the feet of the reindeer softly padded and the sleigh bells rang out on the cold frosty air. (In fact the sun shone and it was warm.)

Edward too, at her side, was very happy, for now he had his dog (exchanged for the watch and named Crusoe). He faithfully hoped, moreover, that on Christmas morning a new watch would lie ticking beside his Christmas sausage and bacon. It would not be *his* fault if it did not. . . .

Do not imagine, however, that Edward, at this happy Christmas time, was like a little boy in one of Mr. Mullinger's pretty stories. As he walked beside his mother he was one of the plainest and most matter-of-fact small boys in London.

As history goes, this day was as important to every member of the Carlisle family as 1066 was to the Conqueror. History was made on this day.

In the first place, before evening Romney and Nicholas suffered two extremely important encounters. Both were fortuitous.

Romney's was in this wise:

Romney was in the depths. Christmas meant nothing to him save that it was an impertinent jest at the expense of his own feelings. He had developed, in the course of these weeks, a concentration on his own weaknesses which would have delighted any psychoanalyst, and provided him with at least two years' earnest and responsible employment. And with this self-contempt went hostility towards all the outside world and especially his own family. It was as though his spiritual skin were raw and first one and then another tortured him by touching it. Especially his mother, who seemed to him to blunder with every word. There wasn't one of them he could endure save only Uncle Nicholas. And with all this he was lonely as he had never been before, longing for affection and repulsing it, seeing himself whom every man must despise and despising them himself in return. In addition to all this, business was bad. Partly because of his own enthusiasm they had opened, three weeks before, an exhibition of the paintings of a young Spaniard, Señor Cervantes. Señor Cervantes was, in spite of his name, no success. His pictures were charming when you could understand them. They were Apocalyptical and connected, in a dark misty way, with the Last Judgment. Not a single one was sold. People did not want the Last Judgment at Christmas time.

So, on every side of him, darkness. His only light was his uncle, who appeared to him now as a genius of wit, intelligence, and scornful opinions delivered in the kindest, jolliest way.

And with his admiration there was fear. He did not dare to ask him for the return of the negress; he slipped, unobserved, sometimes into his uncle's room to take a look at it.

And then he had this encounter. On this afternoon, two days before Christmas, he made his way into the English Book Club. There was a new book about Dostoieffsky. That ferocious Russian genius would make him, he felt, good company during this intolerable Christmas season.

He climbed the stairs and found himself struggling in a sea of women. It seemed that all the ladies of London were changing their books, stout ladies, thin ladies, young ladies, old ladies, all wanting works of fiction. A kind of disgust filmed his gaze as he perceived these rows and rows of novels, all so alike, all, he was convinced, so unnecessary, and these ladies, fire in their eyes, their hands curved to clutch, crying names of authors, titles of books, as though this were the last hour of all the fiction in the world.

"Give me," he imagined a stout lady, her elbow in his waistcoat, crying, "*The Forsyte Saga* or I die!" "No, no," a tall thin one with a hat like a sea shell was screaming surely. "The Forsytes for *me! A moi* the Forsytes."

He moved disgustedly forward and, propelled from behind, almost fell over a young lady at a desk. The young lady was in black; she looked very, very weary.

"Excuse me," he murmured. (He felt a dark shame at his importunity.) "I want Mark Lemon's *Dostoieffsky.*"

She found his card, slipped her way through the struggling mass, and with miraculous swiftness returned, the book in her hand.

They were in a corner of the room and it happened that, just then, the tide ebbed, the sea's murmur beat against other rocks. There was a sudden quiet peace.

She gave him the book with a weary smile. He smiled in return, the first time, he was sure, that he had smiled for weeks.

"This is pretty awful," he said.

"Yes, it is," she answered sharply. "And I'm sick of it."

He glanced at her and saw that she looked about seventeen, so young in fact that she had no right to be there. In her black dress, her face pale with fatigue, she touched his sympathy.

"You look pretty tired."

"So'd you be," she said, looking not at him but at the card index. "I never want to see a book again. I lie awake sometimes thinking how *wicked* it is that there are people all over the country writing *new* books. They ought to be gaoled." Then, suddenly staring up at him, she added: "The sad part of it is that I took this job because I *loved* books. Now I hate them."

She was certainly not pretty. Her nose was too short, her cheeks too thin, her hair was not as tidy as it should be.

"If only they'd know what they want. They *never* know. They don't seem to care. Some of them change their novels every day. But it's the novelists ought to be ashamed. They come in here sometimes just to see how their books are getting on, and don't I long just to tell them what I think!"

"Why don't you?" asked Romney.

"It wouldn't do. Novelists are the most touchy creatures. They go sniffing along the shelves under their initial, pretending they're looking for something. But I oughtn't to be talking to you like this."

"It doesn't matter," said Romney. "They're fading away."

"Yes," said the young woman. "We'll be closing soon, thank God."

"Why do you do it," asked Romney, "if you hate it so much?"

"One must do something. I haven't a bean. I'm a poor little orphan. Oh, dear!" She sighed. She smiled at him again. "There—take your old *Dostoieffsky* and go."

He felt a strange emotion in his age-weary heart that he had never known before. It was almost as though he had found Harry again.

"You aren't more fed up than I am," he said.

"Why—what's the matter with you?"

"Oh, everything—things have been going wrong for ages. Business, for instance."

"What do you do?"

She was looking at him, he was aware, with considerable interest.

"I help to run a picture gallery."

Her eyes gleamed.

"I love pictures."

"What kind of pictures?"

"I don't know. I haven't any idea. Sometimes I go to the Tate with a friend. Do you know which picture I like best?"

"No," he said.

"That one of Chatterton dead under the window. I think that's lovely."

He was disappointed but didn't say so. What he did say was:

"Look here! Couldn't we meet again?"

She gave him a long straight look.

"Yes—if you like."

"When?"

They settled a time and a place. Her name was Mary Benson.

Nicholas's encounter was also in the centre of a human whirlpool. This time at Fortnum & Mason's. He had been taking his Christmas presents very seriously. He thought that he would buy *foie gras* for Grace, and it amused him to remember that, had it not been for the gold snuffbox, he would probably be buying it with Grace's own money.

He was in the highest spirits. The two hundred pounds had altered everything, and now he thought that he would settle down for the rest of his days with the family. Why not? He had them all at heel. Many sources of income were opening out before him. Mrs. Agar was an agreeable excitement, Abel just dangerous enough to be amusing. Fanny and Matthew and Grace would be there for him to tease. Charles was not a bad old sort and might be tempted into one or two profitable little financial adventures. . . .

And—believe it or no, this was one of the strongest reasons for his remaining—Lizzie was happy here, happy as she had never been before in all her life. Yes: the Westminster house should be his home for the rest of his days!

That being settled, he felt most kindly towards them all, yes, even Fanny and Matthew. He enjoyed the Christmas-present buying like a child. But, in Fortnum

& Mason's, what a struggle! As a rule it was the temple of calm. So efficient a place was it that you might buy a tongue, a set of chessmen, a bathing suit, and a pair of shoes all within ten minutes! Not so today! People almost snatched jellies and hams out of one another's hands, and Christmas hampers, their apples bursting and their plums sweating, fought with one another for attention.

"Oh, dear! Oh, dear!" said a lady to Nicholas. "Where is Lucy? I have lost Lucy." Her cry was as heartfelt as any poem by William Wordsworth, and in her agitation she appealed to Nicholas as though she had known him from his cradle.

He had, however, never seen her before. She was tall and stout, with a round red face and soft appealing eyes. She was dressed in admirable taste, and that he appreciated, for she had so much to dress. He summed her up at once as stupid and kindly. She had a galantine in one hand and a small gold pencil in the other.

"I beg your pardon——" he said.

She looked at him with almost frantic despair. She did not care whether she knew him or no. All she wanted was assistance.

"It's my little girl. I said to her not to move, but she can't resist the sight of so much food. She's wandered away twice already. Edward said that it was mad to take her, but Miss Spence had to do the invitations. It was this morning or never. . . ." She realized that he was a stranger. "I beg your pardon. This is perfectly dreadful."

"Not at all," said Nicholas, smiling. "If perhaps you could describe her to me——"

"She's wearing a red hat and has an orange in one hand——"

At once he departed, edged his way through the mob,

and soon discovered a fat little girl in a red hat and holding an orange, her eyes fixed, in a sort of trance, on glistening piles of candied fruit.

"Excuse me," he said sharply (he did not care for little girls). "Your mother wants you."

With a sigh, as a lover is torn from his mistress, the little girl turned away. She went with Nicholas as though she, too, had known him all his life.

"Extraordinary thing," Nicholas thought. "I must have met this family before somewhere."

The stout lady, who had now resigned the galantine to a pushing assistant, clutched her daughter.

"Thank you so much," smiling sweetly, helplessly. "It's too good of you——"

"Not at all," said Nicholas.

"It's fearful, isn't it, at Christmas time? Why does one leave everything to the last? No, dear, you can't have any ginger. She's crazy about ginger, which I can't abide myself. But what was I to do? I promised Helen Vincent in Mentone that she should have a galantine, and of course it's too late now, but it'll do for the New Year——"

"Do you mean," said Nicholas, "the Vincents of Raquillant? I was staying with them last winter."

"No!" cried the lady. "Were you really? Helen and Bob and Martine—but that's too extraordinary. How small the world is!"

Smiles broke out all over her round face. Nicholas realized that she was one of those women to whom all the minutiæ of life were of thrilling importance.

"Isn't it?" said Nicholas. "I had a delightful week there with my little girl. They had just completed the new bathing pool with the green tiles——"

"Why, isn't that *too* extraordinary! Do tell me your name."

"My name is Nicholas Coventry."

"Of course! Of course! They've often talked of you! Helen says you're the best bridge——"

She stopped. The assistant was asking her address. She gave it. She continued to stare at Nicholas in a kind of dream.

"Do come and see me one day." A most elaborate and confused business in a bag followed. "Four Clarence Gate. And that's the country address—near Hereford. Perhaps you would come and play bridge one evening? I'm writing to Helen today. She'll be so *very* interested. . . ."

She was plainly impetuous, good-natured, generous, absent-minded—all useful qualities.

"You never know," thought Nicholas, putting the card carefully away in his pocketbook. And, as he went out into Piccadilly, he added, "How very strange the English are! So cautious and then, once you know someone *they* know, so incautious! . . ."

And now, while Fanny was thinking of reindeer, Romney borrowing *Dostoieffsky* from Mary Benson, Edward making plans about Robinson Crusoe, Nicholas collecting a new promising address, Nell and Hector were snatching a swift, almost desperate, meeting under the bare skeleton branches of the Green Park trees. They had but a moment. Hector had promised Lottie . . . Nell had promised Aunt Grace . . . So always now were their meetings. Every day the situation was worse. Hector was out of a job now. Lottie was very strange. Nell detested, more and more, the furtive deceit. And so, like shadows thrown by the flickering sunlight onto that screen of bare brown trees, grey walls, pale winter sky, these two met, clasped hands, and fled again. For Nell it was maddening because, hurrying along Piccadilly (they were to have just a quarter of an hour together), whom should she encounter but stupid, great, gawky, drawling-voiced Iris Tarbell who, dragging her dress about her as though she were a child in family theatricals, detained Nell most painfully, there right in front of the flower shop where they sell you one carnation for a shilling.

"Oh, darling, how *are* you? Isn't Christmas too perfectly frightful, and I've just been to such a ghastly luncheon. Honor Lighter's, to meet a Chinese poet. And there he was, my dear, four foot high and *frightfully* polite. He looks about eight years old, but he has ten Children in China. And you know how stupid Honor is. He said he'd had a letter from his daughter that very morning, and Honor said, 'Written in Chinese, I suppose?' What on earth did she think it *would* be written in? Where are you going, darling? You look perfectly sweet."

Nell, in an agony, watched a clock above her head race the seconds. At last she flung free of Iris who stood lost in Piccadilly and surely growing, with every moment, taller as Alice did after eating the cake.

"Oh, darling, I'm so sorry—and we have such a *little* time!" They kissed there where they were in the Green Park and didn't care who saw them. They sat down on two little chairs close together. "I would have been here five minutes earlier, but whom should I meet but Iris Tarbell? You don't know her. . . ." She held his hand. They looked at one another as though it were months since they had last met. There is no question but that difficulty and frustration are fine for passion.

"Darling, I've finished my poem. Last night. I did the bit about the Trumpets and all the angels rising like petals blown in the wind. You remember—God is watching from a great height, and He sees the earth open like a pomegranate. The Trumpets cease and He speaks. His voice is very quiet and still. . . ."

"You've finished it? Oh, Hector, I'm *so* glad! Now you won't be so worried. . . ."

"Well, I don't know. Lottie's got something up her sleeve. I can't get a job. It's all pretty beastly." Then his face lightened, he smiled. "I've got your present. I do hope you'll like it."

He gave her a very small parcel, and when she opened it there was a very small box and inside the box a very small ring and in the centre of the ring three very small pearls.

Nell was in ecstasy. "Oh, Hector—but you shouldn't! How did you afford it?"

"Never mind how I afforded it. Now, I'll put it on your finger." And so he did. It has been done so often, just like this, that it need not be described.

"They'll see it. They'll ask me about it," Nell said. "But I don't care. They can, and I'll just tell them. I'm sick of this secrecy. I'm *ashamed* of it. I should have told Mother long ago if it hadn't been for Uncle Nicholas. He *makes* one secret, I think. I don't know why. And now here's your present!"

Her present was an old silver-gilt box engraved with figures of shepherds and shepherdesses. Inside the lid it was stamped: "Hector from Nell. Christmas 1932."

He kissed her, and a very old man, wandering near them, looking for cigarette ends, gazed at them with rheumy eyes and, for a moment, out of shadows and pains and a hungry stomach, recovered his youth. He came towards them, murmuring. Hector gave him a shilling.

"And what now?" asked Hector.

"Directly Christmas is over you are going to tell Lottie to divorce you."

"Yes—and then?"

"Then we shall be married."

He looked at her, bent his head.

"Nell, I ought to tell you. I *must* tell you. You'd better give me up. I'm a failure. I shall never be anything else. This morning when I woke and thought about my poem I knew it. All the time that I have been writing it I believed in it. While I was working at it I thought that it was going to be wonderful. I saw it as it *ought* to be. My conception of it was as good as anybody's. Shakespeare and Dante and Milton weren't finer. But now I know that it's nothing—tenth-rate, worthless. It shrivelled away as soon as I wrote the last line. I'm no good. You mustn't stick to me."

She saw that his underlip was trembling, that, perhaps, he wasn't far from tears, and she loved him then as she had never done before.

She felt strong enough and brave enough to storm the ramparts of heaven. But all she said was:

"We've only got five minutes, so don't let's waste them, Hector darling. How funny men are! You give me a ring and then tell me to leave you! How *can* you fail when I believe in you as I do?"

"You *do* believe in me?"

"I wouldn't love you if I didn't believe in you."

The sun was falling, lights were coming out. They heard Big Ben, through the wintry air, strike the hour. They walked into Piccadilly, and she climbed a bus, waving to him before she disappeared.

She had grown in these last weeks. She was ready now for anything and, feeling her ring beneath her glove, faced life as though she were its only challenger. Nothing could defeat her. She smiled brilliantly at the conductor as she gave him her pennies.

12

The thin sunlight fell, now here, now there, about the house, touching the carpets, the stairs, stroking the pictures, flooding, in one last pale glory, the drawing-room walls, so that the Bonington caught a new brightness of blue sky and brown-striped field. Then the light died. Over all the house there was dusk. The drawing room was scented with the close richness of chrysanthemums; the holly, the berries like red buttons, clung in green shadow to the pictures, and a thick bunch of mistletoe drooped its head, hanging from the great chandelier in the hall.

Fanny, coming in with Edward, settled him down to his tea and, as she left the room, knew that he was hurrying about the great cupboard secrets of his Christmas presents. She sighed. She wanted Charles. She wanted him morning and night. She longed, with aching desire, to throw her arms round him, to press her cheek against his, to tell him that everything was well. She could not; it was not that she judged him, it was not jealousy. It was rather that the old Charles was accompanied now by a stranger, someone whom she had not yet learned to know, someone who might surprise her by a sudden, unexpected, devastating act. Her love was, in a strange way, increased, but her trust was gone.

Her loneliness was terrifying, and already she could

dimly perceive approaching her a crisis when she must make some tremendous decision. What reserves of force and power were in her nature? For so many years she had not needed to summon them, and now she did not know what kind of woman she was. Her own weakness, by her sudden discovery of it, might appal her. She distrusted herself as well as Charles.

Indeed now she distrusted everyone and everything. If Charles could fail her, then how easily might she fail herself! It would be an easy thing to tell Charles that she loved him and all was well again. How happy he would be! But she might then be in a relationship more uncertain and more dangerous than the present one. It seemed to her that she knew nothing *about* Charles now—how he would act, how think, how feel. She must build up a new test of character. Meanwhile there was no time; there was no pause in the house while Nicholas was there. She saw him now as something driving them all relentlessly forward. Unless someone held him in his course they would, none of them, ever recover one another again. With every day he separated them more completely. But who *was* there to stay him? For the first time she began to realize his horrible power.

She went up through the dim house. She found that she *hated* that it should have been Nicholas who had hung the holly. She and Nell and Edward had always loved to do it. . . . She sighed again and opened softly the door to see how the Old Lady was getting on.

The dark purple curtains were already drawn. The only light in the room was from the fire, which leaped wildly with sharp tongues of pale yellow flame and threw long live shadows on the wall. On the end of the bed Becky Sharp was curled asleep. Fanny stepped forward to move her, then hesitated. The Old Lady, lying on her side, was also asleep. Everything in the room slept save the fire, which was silent like a dream fire.

She stayed as though she herself were in a dream. Some alarm held her. Something was wrong here. With a quick fear and with an effort as though something were trying to root her to the floor, she very softly crossed to the bed. The Old Lady was breathing tranquilly, her eyes tightly closed, her upper lip fallen in, for her teeth were in a glass on the washhand stand. It was perhaps that, seen thus, she looked so very old, and only six months back she had been so lively, so dominating. Now she was helpless, and the shadows of the fire leaped above her head.

Uneasy, although she did not know why, Fanny stole from the room. In the passage there was a strong odour of chrysanthemums, and she saw, on a table above the turn of the stairs, a big bowl of white blooms whose furred edges, under the electric light, seemed to move. She thought that the scent of the flowers was too strong —it might penetrate into the room—so, in both hands, she carried the bowl downstairs.

While she placed it on the table in her room Charles stood in the doorway.

He watched her; she looked up and said:

"Charles, I'm uneasy about the Old Lady."

"Why?" He stood there, his hands in his pockets, looking, she thought, like a sulky boy.

"I don't know why. That's what bothers me. I went in just now to see that she was all right. She was sleeping. There was nothing the matter and yet I felt this. It may have been the chrysanthemums."

"The chrysanthemums?" he repeated stupidly. Then he continued quickly: "Look here, Fanny—how long is this to go on?"

"Is what to go on?"

He leaned his heavy body against the wall, hunching his shoulders, his head forward.

"I can't stand it. If you want to punish me, all right. That's your affair. But I shall go away. Anything is better than this."

She sat down. She looked at him, then quickly away. In a voice so low that he could scarcely catch her words, she said:

"You must give me time."

"Time for what?"

"Time to recover. Everything's altered."

"Why?" he asked.

"My trust is gone—not only in you, in everything."

He straightened himself up against the wall.

"Because of that one thing?"

"Yes—I suppose so."

"Do you think," he said, bringing the words out painfully, "that I wouldn't forgive you anything—anything in the world?"

"*Would* you? If I went away with a man for a month? *Would* you forgive me?"

He hesitated. "Yes," he said at last. "If you still loved me. But, you see, you wouldn't. You couldn't. You're finer, better, than me in every way. And it means more if a woman does it. It's much more significant. What I keep on telling you is that this *wasn't* significant. It meant *nothing.*"

"No," she said. "It didn't alter your own idea of yourself. I can understand that. No man is sure that he won't, at some time or another, be for a moment unfaithful. I've always known that. But I thought you were different, not better or worse but *different.* I've always thought that whatever else went *you* wouldn't. It's my fault that I believed that, not yours. And now it isn't a question of forgiveness but of getting used to a new idea. I must have time."

"So," he said slowly, "nothing will be as it has been before?"

"No," she said. "Nothing. We're all changed. We're not together any more."

"And you don't love me now, Fanny?"

"Yes, I love you. More perhaps than I did. But I can't depend on you. I've got now to depend on myself. I don't know that I can. . . . I'm not, probably, more dependable than you are."

After a long time he said:

"I see. That's clear. . . . It seems to me it's no use our living together any more."

She was terrified at that. She looked round, through the door into his room, so that he should not see how suddenly frightened she was.

"It must be as you think, Charles."

"Perhaps if I went away for a bit you'd see—you'd understand. . . ." Then he began furiously, the words tumbling over one another: "What I can't understand is that, just for this, only because of this, the past is all nothing—all our love, all that we've done, the children, our friendship. . . . But women are like that. Men have to keep *all* the rules *all* the time. All the rules that *women* think important, anyway—and if you break one once then it's all up, it's all over. The past doesn't count. Nothing matters. . . ."

"I haven't said that we must separate. I've only said that you must give me time. . . ."

"Yes—and we go on like this—miles apart. Polite.

Not sleeping together. Polite strangers. I'd rather go away; I can't stand it. It's your way of punishing me and you've succeeded. I'm more miserable than I've ever been. There! That pleases you, doesn't it? That's what you want. You've got it——"

Fanny interrupted. "No, no, not to punish anybody. But it's no use being false. If I came to you and kissed you, Charles, and said everything is all right . . . That would be easy, but it would be untrue. Since Nicholas came we've all changed. We aren't a family any more. I don't know how he's done it, but he's separated us."

"That's nonsense," Charles broke in. "You put it all down to Nicholas. You say that we've all changed—well, so have you. Do you remember how glad you were when he came, how you loved him, how you wanted to give him everything?—and now, in such a short time, you seem to hate him——"

"I want him to go!" Fanny cried. "He may be my brother. I can't help it. He despises me and laughs at me. He makes you all laugh at me, too. It's a fight between us. I can see that quite clearly now—and, what's more, I believe it always was. I believe that he's always disliked me. When we were children he used to laugh at me; on the way to church, I can see us now, going across the fields and Nicholas laughing at the way Matthew and I carried our prayer-books. I'm sure that he came here because he had nowhere better to go, but when he'd been here a little while our old relationship revived again just as it used to do. He thinks Grace and Matthew and me ridiculous, old-fashioned, religious. He thinks it fun to separate us all, to make Nell and Romney laugh at me, to make you look down on me. I wouldn't wonder if he doesn't know somehow about—about what you did in the spring. He knows everything, he can see everything at once. He always could. When we were children he would tease us for things we'd done which he'd discovered in some uncanny way. . . ."

Fanny raised her head.

"It's more than just you and me. It's home, all of us, whether we stick together or not. He's made me miserable. I've been weak about him. But I don't think I shall be weak any longer."

Charles shrugged his shoulders.

"You can put it all onto Nicholas if you like. But it's just one of those ideas women get in their heads. Nicholas is all right. He's a damned fine fellow. You're trying to pretend this isn't between you and me, which it is. I made a damned fool of myself for a week or two. You needn't have known a thing about it. Neither of us would have been a penny the worse if it hadn't been for that letter I was ass enough to lose. You can't put that down to Nicholas anyway!

"And now you've got the whip hand over me and you're going to let me know it. It's a grand game for women. They simply love it. Sulk and be on your dignity and graciously grant me a kind word once and again. Play with me as a cat does with a mouse. But you shan't do it. I'll go away. I've said all I could, that I'm damned ashamed of myself, that it was a kind of insanity, that it's made no sort of difference in my love for you. But I tell you what *will* make a difference. If this sort of thing goes on! *That* can kill love——"

He stopped. He was aware, as she was, of moving into country that was exceedingly dangerous, as though they might, both of them, be pushed by pride, egotism, wounded feelings, into a situation that would alter everything for ever.

Fanny said: "That's unfair. Because you say you're

sorry, you expect me to be just as I was. *You've* changed. How can I be the same?"

"Very well, then," he said. "You think me too awful to live with. Don't live with me then. You can keep the children. I'll go abroad. Anything you like. . . ."

"You can't love me very much—when you can go so easily."

He came a few steps towards her: "Look here, Fan. You can't play with me just to satisfy your vanity. You want me to go down on my knees, hang my head, wear sackcloth evermore. Well, I won't. I wouldn't do that for any woman alive—or man, either. This is the first thing I've ever done you could complain of. And if that's enough to kill all your trust in me, well, all I can say is that your love can't have been very real—and that's a fact."

Now they were thousands of miles, spiritually, apart. She got up. They stood close to one another, infinitely separated.

"You must do as you think right," she said. "I can't help it. I can't be different."

"You could," he said, "if you cared enough."

At the door he turned.

"Look here, Fan. This is terrible. Of course we love one another. We can't let a thing like this——"

"It isn't only this," she answered. "It's Romney and Nell and you—even Edward. But I'm myself. I'm someone apart from you all. I didn't know that until now. I thought I lived only for all of you. But I don't. I live for myself, too."

"Very well, then," he said angrily. "You shall have it your own way." And he went, banging the door behind him.

13

The Old Lady struggled up from an awful descent that she had made into icy clear-green waters. Her limbs were weighted as though damp, clinging clothes were bound about them.

"I *must* rise! I *must* rise!" she was crying to herself, and yet as she was drawn upward the terror that accompanied her increased. With a tightening of the breath, constriction of the heart, she reached the air, but it did not flood her lungs as it should have done.

Gasping for breath, she raised her head and looked about her. She saw the room very dimly: it was dark save for the leaping fire, but in that light she saw the black cat that was not now sleeping but stood, its back arched, stretching very softly its legs, first one then another. It stared at her with its green eyes. She hated it and intended to cry out, "Take the cat away," but to her horror no words came. Only the agony below her heart grew stronger as though a determined boneless hand were feeling its way about her flesh and soon, when it had discovered what it wanted, would squeeze and squeeze . . .

The pain was dreadful. There were drops in a bottle beside the bed, but there was no one there to give them to her. The room grew darker and the fire fiercer. The flames leaped on the wall and she thought that perhaps the room was on fire. Was she to be burnt alive here with no one to help her?

The cat moved quietly forward looking at her. It paused beside the bed, then, very gently, gathered itself together, jumped, and settled at the bed end, crouched there, watching her.

"Oh! Oh! Oh!" she cried within herself, but everywhere there was silence.

The door opened and Nicholas came in. She knew that it was Nicholas, and yet he did not move but stood beside the door, looking at her as the cat looked at her.

"Take away the cat, Nicholas! Take away the cat!"

But he did not move. He grew; he spread against the wall. The cruel hand paused, then, with a fearful determined clutch, squeezed her poor heart, and in that agony she died.

14

Later on Nicholas looked into the drawing room. Fanny was there.

"Is there anything I can do?" he asked.

"No. Nothing," Fanny said.

He looked at her and thought: "Now they are all mine. I shall settle here and stay till I die and do with all of them just what I like."

And Fanny, turning away to wind the clock which had run down, thought: "I shall have to fight for my life."

END OF PART III

PART IV

BATTLE FOR THE SPRING EVENING

BATTLE FOR THE SPRING EVENING

THIS was a terrible beginning to the New Year. The days were dark and cold, as though the town were invaded now with a dank forest, half seen, half heard, closing almost invisibly about roofs and streets, rain pattering down between the bare stems.

With this chill, this darkness, this sense of apprehension came the influenza. Not, everyone said, a pestilence as at the end of the war, but bad enough, for many people died, quite easily, with no attempt to resist, as though they well knew that it was hopeless, that everything in any case was against them. No one spent any money even when it was there, and America was in a mess, Russia was in a mess, the Japanese were really disgraceful, and the unemployed appeared quite ungrateful when people gave them sets of draughts and backgammon to occupy their spare hours.

Charles, who had never been good at cause and effect, went about now like a dog who is spiritually wounded by his master. He could settle to nothing. His woodcarving no longer gave him any pleasure. It seemed to him that soon he would have no money, no wife, and no children. Especially he was hurt and wounded by Fanny, with whom now he was not in touch. And the children were unhappy. And he missed quite dreadfully his old mother, whom he had loved more than he knew, who had thought him perfect. He was not perfect of course—very far from it. All the more comfort then that someone should think him so! Now no one thought him perfect. Everyone, save Nicholas, it seemed, disapproved of him.

So he fell, very thoroughly, under Nicholas's influence. He was humble about Nicholas. He thought it remarkable that Nicholas, so brilliant, so modern, so well read, should bother his head about an old duffer. For he *was* an old duffer. Recent events had shown him something of the attributes that he lacked. He must be a bore and, thinking this for the first time, was the more silent, the more confused.

He thought that he would discover what this new literature, this new painting, was about. He would (he was told that he must) look upon morals scientifically. Everything was Glands or Dreams or both. If Fanny would but consider this she would be more tolerant. . . .

Nell gave him first a novel by D. H. Lawrence. He found it most depressing and, in spite of all that he wanted to feel, altogether disgusting.

"I can't help it," he said to Nell. "I think sex is a private thing. I don't *want* to know how people behave sexually. I haven't enough curiosity, I suppose. And then this fellow says the same thing over and over. And then he's always unhappy."

So Romney gave him a gay story to read—a story by Essex Waters called *Stomach Pump*.

He reached page fifty-three. Then, seeing Nicholas come in, he looked up and said:

"Nick, what's the matter with me?"

"What do you mean?" Nicholas asked.

"Here's this novel Romney gave me. It's one of the

successes, he says—and I can't understand a word of it."

"Can't understand it?"

"No. I've read fifty pages and I don't know *what* it's about. They are all staying in the country together. They slide down the stairs on tea trays. Someone's going to have a baby. There's an awful description of some disease someone's got. There's a pet dog called Ramsay Macdonald. And that's *all* I've understood. What's the matter with me? Have I gone potty?"

"No, Charles. Of course not. It's only a convention you've got to get into."

"But if it's so clever, if it's what everyone is reading, then there *must* be something wrong with myself."

Nicholas laughed and settled himself in a comfortable armchair.

"Not a bit. But the Arts have got to move on. You wouldn't have everyone *still* write like Dickens, would you? People have discovered a lot about human nature since Dickens died. There's your subconscious, for instance."

"My subconscious?"

"Yes. You're not really thinking what you *think* you're thinking. You're not really doing what you *think* you're doing. You work in layers. In the old days writers dealt only with the top layer. Now they go down and down—ever so low."

"But I don't want to go low."

"Ah—that's because you're afraid to face the truth. You don't want to see what you're really like."

"No. I don't think I do," said Charles. Then he asked rather pathetically: "But, Nicholas, are there never going to be any jolly books again? Is it all going to be subconscious?"

"All the new interesting writing is," said Nicholas.

"Well, then—I'll ask you another. Don't you think there's too much about sex? I don't spend all my time wanting to fool about with women. Nor do most men. Now if some man would write a novel about wood-carving—*that* would be interesting."

"Yes, of course. But writing is an *art.*"

"Well," Charles said, "it's all too damned serious for me. Now *Jorrocks* is a good book—I've read it dozens of times."

They sat silent a little. Then Nicholas leaned forward and, smiling with the utmost good nature, said:

"You're a fine fellow, Charles. Don't you worry about the young generation. There's always got to be one, you know. Now look here, old man. I want to talk about things."

"Yes?" Charles said. He was thinking about his mother and the light that came into her eyes when he greeted her, and about Fanny and the light that came into *her* eyes when . . . Now both those lights were out. So he clung the more to Nicholas who, although a very clever man, found Charles worth while.

"I want to talk about the future. Soon I shall have been with you for a whole year. You've all been awfully good to me—well, all except Fanny. And that's part of what I want to talk about."

Charles's eyes darkened.

"Look here, old chap, don't you worry about Fanny. She isn't quite herself just now. Some damned silly thing has happened to upset her. I was the guilty party—I admit it—but she's making such a song and dance about it."

"What have you been doing, old boy?" asked Nicholas.

"Oh, nothing that matters to anyone but Fanny and myself."

"I see. If you told me I think I could help."

Charles hesitated.

"Oh, it's only—well, I wrote some letters to a woman. I wasn't really in love with her. It was a silly little affair while Fanny was away on a cruise. I've never done such a thing before. I certainly never shall again. Anyhow Fanny found one of the letters. It was among some of her papers in her room. . . ."

"Good heavens!" said Nicholas. "However did it get there?"

"I can't imagine. It was the worst luck in the world. Of course Fanny was upset. It was quite right she should be. I said how damned sorry I was. I tried to show her that it was nothing at all. But you know what women are."

"Yes, I know what women are," said Nicholas.

"I only told you this, Nick, old man, to show you that you mustn't pay any attention to Fanny just now. She's upset and not herself. In fact she's changed in the most extraordinary way lately. She was always so sweet and good-natured. But now she snaps up at everything. But women *are* queer. Let them get an idea into their heads——"

"I'm glad you've told me," said Nicholas frankly. "Because of course it hasn't been very comfortable for me. You see, Charles, I've come to a moment when I have to make up my mind. Whether I go or stay——"

"Oh, you're not going? You mustn't think of going."

"That's just it. I don't *want* to go, of course. Lizzie and I have been happier here than we've ever been anywhere." He stopped a moment and looked at Charles. What a *silly* old ass Charles was, and yet quite lovable. If he fell in with Nicholas's plans, Nicholas felt that he might love him very much. "You see, Charles, what I have in mind is that Lizzie and I should make our permanent home here. The children like me, you like me. Lizzie's devoted to Edward, and I feel that the time has come for her to settle down. She'll be growing up soon, and England's really her proper home. You know, Charles, I'm a worthless, wandering sort of vagabond, but Lizzie's everything to me. I'd do anything for her——"

He stopped, surprised at his own sincerity. For what he said was true. Lizzie *was* his passion.

"I know," said Charles. "I've seen how much you are to one another."

"My idea," said Nicholas, "is that I should pay for my share in the house just as Matthew and Grace do. I think I shall be in funds very soon. I've made a rather important acquaintance. A woman—a Mrs. Agar. She's in with everybody, behind the scenes in everything. She has already put me onto a thing or two, and I've done her a few small services. I think she might be useful to you, Charles, as well."

"What does she do?" asked Charles.

"You know what women are these days. They are as good financiers as men—better very often. She's as sharp as a needle. There are other things as well. I haven't been as idle all these months as some of you have thought."

"I've never thought you idle," said Charles.

"No, but you must have thought pretty badly of me, borrowing all that money——"

"That's all right, old chap," said Charles hurriedly.

"Well, you'll soon see that it *is*. You'll get your money back *and* with profit. I don't *want* to leave London, as things are, and I *do* want to stay here. If only Fanny——"

Charles felt indignant about Fanny. Was she master of this house or was he? Were they all to be upset simply because she was? And now that his mother was gone there was all the more room for Nicholas, who had livened the house up, was good for the children—yes, and good for himself, too.

"As far as I'm concerned, Nick," he said, "you're welcome to stay. I think it's a jolly good idea. Good for us and good for you. You must be sick of wandering all over the globe with no place to go to."

"Well, frankly I am. I'm a home-loving bird really. There's no place like old England when all's said and done." He added, looking affectionately at Charles: "You *are* a good chap, Charles."

"I'm glad there's someone thinks so," said Charles.

"Oh, don't you worry about Fanny," said Nicholas.

"No, I won't," said Charles.

2

First the snow, then the tempest, then the flood. England was cursed. As the sky hung, a thick blanket of malevolence, over the flooded fields, as the snow mounted hedge-high across the roads of the North, as the cold pierced to the very heart, the consciousness of doom crept through doorways, slimed the windowpanes, darkened lights at evening. There was no melodrama. That the world was about to end with a whimper rather than with a bang, that was only just, for man had lost his grandeur. He was so stupid that nothing was left for him but to rail against himself. He did not even rail with magnificence but, putting his head in a gas oven, made a quiet unspectacular exit.

Matthew, stung with the soft mischievousness of hesitating snow, walked the streets. The snow had a salt flavour about it and, touching the pavement, melted, for, like weak men of good will, it had no purpose. A thin mist veiled the houses. The traffic screamed, but men made no sound, as though shame were voiceless. Across the spaces of Hyde Park Corner the cars streamed between the statues, and Jagger's gun was the only reality.

Matthew had been on his way to a meeting with his friends but, halfway there, he had stopped his taxi, got out, dismissed it. He could not go to the meeting because God was no longer real to him. Nicholas had destroyed Him.

"He can never have been real if so slight a thing as vexation with my brother can blot Him out. I have been cheating myself with a sham, and that has been easy, because I have removed myself from life, sitting inside my cozy room with everything comfortable about me. And now at the first challenge I fail—I can do nothing. I am sterile. Nobody listens to me. In myself I have no courage. My brother mocks me.

"But even if I had courage it would be no better. For courageous, strong men do not believe in God any more. Only the old women and the hysterical and the superstitious. I thought that God was a cloud of fire and a pillar of smoke and a beautiful companion. Rather He is a fragment of wood that men once made into a cross, a sponge lifted on a spear, a star that has set. I believed in Him because I wanted Him. He can do nothing for me because He does not exist. And because men know this they too have become nothing. They have desperate courage because life now is a joke and death is nothingness. They laugh at one another because life without meaning is a silly stupid-faced thing. For centuries they cheated themselves with a faked nobility. They entered their Gothic cathedral and their hearts were enraptured—enraptured with a cheat. For the first time in the world's history they know that they are fooled, and so with the brave despair of the doomed they make a machine and, riding it, fling themselves into nothingness. . . ."

Nicholas had shown him this, not because he was clever, but because he had proved Matthew helpless: Matthew, a silly old man, a stuffed doll.

His agony was very terrible and, for any spectator, very ludicrous. He was a stout little man, decently dressed, walking past the railings of the Green Park. He carried a folded umbrella. He did not know where he was going. He had no destination. The snow fell more thickly, and there was a faint green growth, like a fungus, blanketing the sky.

Then, in his weariness, depression, futility, he had a vision. He was weary, he had eaten no luncheon, he had not slept properly for many a night. He suffered, as he always did under certain cold winds, from neuritis in his right leg. So he stopped and leaned against the railings and looked into the Park. The Park was covered with white birds. When he first looked they spread over the ground like a sheet of dazzling silver. But, even as he watched, they rose in a wind of splendour. Thousands upon thousands, they beat the air with their strong wings. Their whiteness was incredible, so pure and dazzling that it hurt the eye, and, through their whiteness, the light shone.

They were compact like a cloud. Then they broke and, in spirals of silver, rose higher and yet higher. They were strong as eagles, for they had no fear, no hesitancy, but, knowing what they had to do, marshalled in perfect discipline, flooded the grey air, charging it into broken foam as the sea is whipped with wind. Higher and higher they rose, and there stayed, far above the bare trees but still visible, now thinning into lines so that they threaded the sky with streams of light. Then they were gone and the snow was falling in a sudden blizzard of storm. All the sky was blotted out, and the snow lay now, hard and shiny, on the pavement. Soon the whole city would be canopied.

"It was only the snow," he thought. "The birds were only the snow. . . ."

He walked on.

"But how strong! How glorious! With what wings they beat the air! How magnificent their direction!"

He put up his umbrella. Soon it was clotted with the snow.

3

Edward on his side loved the snow. It was what, in London, he was always wanting and so seldom got—snow that would lie, that would glitter on wall and pavement and encrusted chimney with a thousand, thousand crystals. It was bad luck, of course, that it came after he had returned to school; there was one most glorious evening when the sun, just before it set, glittered across the roofs, the snow was a dazzling glory, and within the Westminster precincts there was a perfect hush, broken only by bells and the twittering of sparrows.

At the school gate he found, as he had hoped that he would, Lizzie and the dog. This was perfection, for he cared now for Lizzie and the dog beyond anyone else in the world except his mother.

That he should care for the dog was natural. Ever since he could remember he had longed to possess a dog, and now it irritated him to consider that he might have owned a dog years ago had he only been bold enough. The opposition had been nothing.

His father had said, "Wherever are you going to keep it?" Romney had said, "What do you want a dog for?" and his mother (who seemed to take less interest in her son that she had done: he was deeply hurt by this, but of course no one knew it) said nothing.

There might have been more trouble had the dog not been so perfect, had Mrs. Baldwin not at once taken a liking to him. This last fact had its danger, because dogs degenerate at once if the cook indiscriminately feeds them. But this dog *knew* that he belonged to Edward. He had, it appeared, no longing for his other home; when Edward went to fetch him he gave him one glance out of his deep brown eyes and then followed him home. At first he slept on a chair in the kitchen, but, after a night or two, quietly walked upstairs and settled himself in a chair in Edward's room. He was elegantly house-trained and apparently his only aberration (and possibly it was *not* an aberration) was that there was a rat somewhere in the pantry. For this, his body crouched, his nose twitching, he would patiently wait by the hour.

They say that dogs frequently resemble their masters and mistresses. This dog certainly resembled Edward. He was plain and self-contained. He did not believe in showing his emotions. He was a quiet dog but, like his master, always knew what he was about. He was also courageous like his master—yes, with one notable exception. For he was terrified, from the beginning, of the cat, Becky Sharp.

This was the more strange in that the cat paid him no attention at all. The cat walked past him as though he did not exist.

During the day, while Edward was at school, other members of the family would take the dog for a walk. He behaved excellently in the streets, being town-trained, and gave no trouble, but it was only to Edward that he belonged; he would leave anything or anyone for Edward. He was a one-man dog.

When Edward came out of the school gate he jumped about, ran around, sniffing for smells, barking a little, prancing on the snow like a thoroughbred charger. Then he walked close to his master's heels, thoroughly satisfied with the world as Edward (he was convinced) had so cleverly made it.

Edward, today, knew at once that Lizzie had something on her mind. With all his quiet plainness he was remarkably perceptive for a boy of his age. One of the reasons for the close friendship of the two children was that they both perceived more than they ever said and when they spoke spoke with honesty.

"Look here," Edward said, "we can go to the Park and see how frozen the water is and get home by five. Mother will be in today, so I mustn't be late. I say—who was Casanova?"

Lizzie told him.

"It's only Humphries says he has a book about him and he was the wickedest man in history. His father would be wild, Humphries says, if he knew he had the book. Have you read it?"

Yes, Lizzie had read it and didn't think much of it. When they had crossed the street in safety and saw the snowy ground sparkle, under the last long yellow ray of the sun, in front of them, Lizzie unburdened her mind.

What she had to say was sufficiently startling.

She was going away—not with her father, not with anybody, by herself—and for ever.

"Gosh!" said Edward.

He looked at her and knew that he cared for her more, yes, far, far more, than he had ever cared for anyone in his life except his mother. (And his mother lately had been different.) It was amazing to him that he could care for a girl so much. But Lizzie was like no other girl that he had ever seen.

He saw her now, standing there on the snowy ground, looking gravely at two solemn birds, crimson-winged, grey-necked, that walked delicately, like Agag, picking up first one twiggy leg, then another. The scarlet wings flamed against the white. Her small pale face, sharp nose, little restrained independent body—how well he knew these things!

"Going away!" he gasped.

"I think I shall go to Paris," Lizzie said.

"And not come back?"

"No. I have some money. There's a lady I know in Paris."

The dog, as though he knew that something serious was toward, came and sat on his haunches beside them.

"You're not to tell anyone, Edward," she said quickly. "Not my father."

"No. Of course. But you can't leave Uncle Nicholas, can you?"

She nodded her head.

"I must."

"Why? Doesn't he want you?"

"Yes, he wants me—when he thinks about it." She drew a deep quick breath. "Edward, have you seen a man in our house sometimes, a little man with a yellow face?"

Yes, Edward had—once.

"I hate him. I've always hated him. He's followed us for years and years, wherever we've been. When I was small it didn't matter, but now it does. He speaks to me in the street, in the house, and I've told Father, but he does nothing. He's called Abel," she ended.

"What does he speak to you about?" Edward asked.

Lizzie became impressive. She caught Edward's arm and stood close beside him, a thing that she never did, for she hated contact with anybody.

"He's bad," she said. She raised her head and looked out far across the snow. "They always say I'm old for my age. Going about with Father makes me old. Other children always seemed so stupid. But in your house things have been quite different. Your mother is good, and you are, too, Edward, although you are very silly sometimes. You none of you know *at all* what the world is like. At first I thought how silly that was, but now I don't think it so silly."

"But you love your father, don't you?" asked Edward.

"I don't know. . . ." She turned away. "Often I hate him—and he shouldn't let Abel come so close, because I'm growing older. I won't be touched by anyone. *You* can, Edward, because you don't know what grown-up people do."

"Oh, yes, I do," said Edward.

"No, you don't. Not what they really do. People are horrid except in your house. And if Father won't see that they don't touch me, then I must see myself."

"What will you do in Paris?" asked Edward, his eyes very wide open.

"This lady always said if I was unhappy I could come to her. I'll learn to be a secretary or a nurse or drive a car. I shall soon be fourteen, and fourteen is grown-up in France if you're not French."

"Won't you tell *anybody* that you're going?" Edward asked.

"No. I shall just go to Victoria Station."

"Oh, gosh!" Edward said. "I'd like to go, too—just for a day or two. It wouldn't matter. . . . Mother wouldn't mind."

"Of course your mother would mind," Lizzie said indignantly.

They turned homewards.

Edward frowned. "I don't know. Everything's different at home now. Romney won't do a thing, and Father's always grousing and Mother loses her temper. If I went off for three days they'd open their eyes a bit."

Lizzie said: "And what about the school?"

"Oh, there are lots of schools," Edward said airily. "And chaps leave ever so early now. Burton Minor went last term, and it was partly because he ragged old Pons and put those eggs in his desk, but he said he didn't care and he was going to be an airman as soon as he could. I wouldn't go more than a day or two, but I'd see France and there are lots of things I could be. I know a chap was a cabin boy, and what's the use anyway of all the rot they teach you at school?"

Lizzie shook her head.

"You love your mother, don't you?" she asked.

"Of course I love my mother," he answered indignantly.

"Then you mustn't leave her even for a day."

"But you love your father, don't you?"

"Yes. But no one shall touch me. He always thinks for himself. Now I shall think for myself."

"When do you think you'll go?" said Edward.

"I don't know. You swear you won't tell anyone?"

"I swear."

"Then when I live in Paris, later on you can come."

"Perhaps I'll fly over," said Edward excitedly.

When he came into his room again he felt quite swollen with his secret. Everything was changed since Lizzie had come. He was no longer only a boy. He was something else as well, and there was a world beyond the school, a world that he was now, like a grown-up man, beginning to enter.

Yes, a world crystallized with snow—but they couldn't tell, although they might guess, that with a breath the glitter would be gone and, instead, a cold, bitter tempest, a torrent of rain, fields flooded and the kitchen swimming in water, the London trees beaten with rain—nor could they tell that, after this, there must follow the loveliest spring, the most sumptuous summer that England had ever, in living memory, known, *such* spring evenings and then so rich a sun that the ground is fiery with harvest and the long nights stained with moonlight. . . .

But this is only background. First the Spring Evening must be fought for. It does not come only with longing. Moments of crisis are heralded by the step of Hercules. As with Pholus:

Here Pholus lived:
One dove-breast noon,
Cloudless blue as that of fircomb-smoke,
Hanging so still above the Centaur hearth,
His house of wood gleaming in its new-sawn grain,
With resin in the knots of it;
There came a step,
A heavy footfall down among the pines,
Heavy as a bear. Nearer, nearer came,
With snapping of branches, of pine-needles trodden,
Coming up the wood to him, till Pholus stood
At his high doorway (for a man on horseback),
In the winter stillness. It came up from the world,

As from deep of ocean, to the cell of Pholus,
A man with measured step, a giant in the pine-wood;
He showed, he came forth, he was Hercules.

On an afternoon of pouring rain all the family were engaged, and all, for a brief moment, through traffic and the clang of the street drill and the voices of women shopping and the four unemployed young men singing Welsh songs in Piccadilly, were aware of the approaching measured step.

Lottie said to Nell, who had appeared "for only five minutes": "Hector's in the other room changing. He thinks on a beastly wet afternoon like this you *have* to change. What do you think, darling?"

Nell, looking at Lottie, knew that she had arrived at some decision. What was she going to do? She was no longer friendly, although more demonstrative than ever. Nell was terrified—she was also relieved. It was then that she heard the step, as though beyond the windows a whole army were marching. It was doubtless the rain.

"I'm going to leave you two," Lottie said. "I've got a date with a gentleman. You're such good friends I know you won't be bored."

At the door she added:

"I saw your Uncle Nicholas last night."

"Oh, did you?" said Nell. "Where?"

"Oh, at a party. He was most amusing—and he gave me some good advice."

When Hector came in Nell said: "It's come, Hector."

"What's come?"

"Lottie's decided on something."

"How do you know?"

"Oh, by what she said, the way she looked."

Hector caught his breath.

"I believe you're right. She's been everywhere lately with Ellstein, the film man. It's paradise itself to her to be able to go to films all day and every day for nothing. I think she may leave me!"

"Oh!" Nell drew a deep breath.

"Yes—but she'll do something devilish first."

They sat on the sofa close together. They looked extremely young but not helpless.

Hector said: "What would you mind her doing most?"

"Telling Mother," Nell said. "But perhaps not. It's time we had everything out at home. You can't think what it is at home now, Hector. We've all lost touch with one another, and it can't go on. There's going to be an unholy row any minute."

"I'm frightened about *you,*" Hector said. "I haven't a job. There isn't one in sight. Nearly everyone I know is out of a job. What's going to become of us all? I'm young, fairly intelligent, ready to do anything, and no one will give me even two pounds a week. Nine out of ten of us are superfluous and will be for evermore. Frightening? I tell you it turns your bones to water."

She put her arms round him, holding him very close.

"Once we've had our row at home," she said, "and got rid of Lottie, we'll go on all right. I've got heaps of ideas. There's your poem, there's the theatre. I've got a notion of a new sort of shop——" She listened. "Isn't it funny? The rain's like an army marching. I've a kind of feeling, Hector, that tonight's the night."

He kissed her. "What sort of night?"

"I don't know. But a scrap, a climax. Since Granny died it's been piling up. When I see you tomorrow I shall have something to tell you, I'm sure."

"Will you telephone if you want me? I'll come straight along and face the whole family."

She laughed.

"I expect I can manage. It's really only Mother. She's always been so gentle, lived only for us, been always so sure that everything would go right so long as we all loved one another. Old-fashioned, and I suppose *I'm* old-fashioned caring so much about the family. But *we're* going to have a family, aren't we?"

"Of course," said Hector.

"Then I shall care in my own way just as much as Mother does. I can't see that anything changes—except that my generation says 'bloody' sometimes and wears no clothes if possible and is open-minded about sex. The feelings underneath are the same. When I have a child by you I shall love it just as much as Mother loves me and Romney and Edward. I'll want it to be good and happy and have enough to eat. And when it goes off and leaves me I shall find it just as hard as Mother is finding it now. Don't you think so?"

"I hope so," said Hector. "The only difference will be —how are we going to feed our children? We oughtn't to have any if we can't feed them."

"Yes," Nell said, meditatively. "They won't be able to be lazy, that's certain. And they won't have to mind what they do. But we'll make them ready for anything and teach them not to grumble. It's my idea that *their* generation will be the bravest there's ever been *and* the most adaptable *and* the most hygienic."

"You're a bit of an optimist, darling," Hector said.

"Yes, I am. Because I love you and because I think people don't see far enough."

"I read a book last week," Hector said, "about people on the dole. They are *ready* to be brave and work hard and all the rest of it, but there's simply no place for them, no place at all."

"By the time *our* children come along," Nell said, "there *will* be a place for them. We're all too impatient perhaps. Thirty years from now all this confusion will have arranged itself in some new order. It's our job to see that it does. Even now there are more happy people in the world than there were a hundred years ago or even fifty. People *care* now about housing and employment and disease far more than they did before the war. We *want* to make things different. Father's mother when she was a girl didn't give a damn."

An hour later, before she went home, she took Hector's face between her hands and, looking into his eyes, said:

"Every hour I love you more. Every day I know better that this is for ever."

Then she came suddenly to a decision.

"I'm going straight back to tell Mother."

Hector looked frightened.

"Wait," he said. "Think what——"

"No. I've thought long enough. Do you know one thing—very curious? The longer we go on like this, the more I'm under Uncle Nicholas's influence. Perhaps it's because *he* knows and the rest of the family doesn't. Again and again, I find myself saying something to Mother as though *he* wanted me to. I've come to the conclusion he hates her."

"Why, I thought they adored one another," Hector said.

"He doesn't adore *her*. He's always forcing one to take sides. He seems to have some sort of power over me because he knows about us. So Mother must be told."

She went with Hector's blessing.

Meanwhile Nicholas had tea with his lady of Fortnum & Mason's. He went because you never know when a friend in need may be useful. He stayed very much longer than he had intended because everyone found him so charming. His hostess, her husband, her brother, a lady calling, an old aunt, he captured them all. It was easy work for him, like cutting butter with a knife. He found that they were rich, generous and, by his intellectual standards, extremely stupid.

"You *must* come and stay with us in the country," said his hostess.

"Indeed I will," Nicholas said.

"And bring your little girl."

"I never go anywhere without her."

Was this a waste of time? he asked himself, as he hailed a taxi in the rain.

It was, of course, if he had made his permanent home in Westminster. As indeed he had. He thought of them all, sitting comfortably back in his taxi, as a trainer thinks of his lions and his tigers: Fanny, Charles, Grace, Matthew, Romney, Nell. . . . Yes, he had settled down at last.

He paid a visit to Abel, who now had two scrubby little rooms in a street off Portland Place. Abel liked to be scrubby. He made a jungle of civilization. Anywhere that he lived acquired very quickly a musky fœtid air, something indescribable, something like an animal shop where the birds' droppings, the scent of stale water, the closeness of the cage, defy light and air and the changing of the hours. On the table were the remains of a meal, clothes were thrown onto chairs, the windows were close shut.

And now their relations were changed, although Nicholas did not notice it because he himself was changed.

"I suppose," Nicholas said, "the only way I shall ever get rid of you now, Abel, is to murder you."

(He might do it one day if there was an easy, safe

method. It would be no crime. He looked at him, speculating about methods.)

Abel grinned.

"Why? I'm your best friend."

"If you speak to Lizzie again I *shall* murder you. That's what I've come to talk about. We're going to stay in London now, to stay for evermore. I suppose you're a permanency. All right. But on condition that you never speak to my daughter. You've been bothering her, she tells me."

"Ah, she's a nice girl," Abel said. "She's growing up. Why shouldn't I speak to her sometimes? I've known her since she was a baby."

"It's just because she's growing up that I won't have you near her. You're a nuisance to her. She hates the sight of you."

Abel sat forward in his chair, his body gathered taut, as though he were about to spring.

"Captain—listen. What I do, what I don't do—what can *you* do about it? I think things are different now. You are settled here in London. I too am settled. I make some money independent of you. I have a nice girl—perhaps two nice girls. I care for you, Captain, very much. How should I not when I know you so very well? You say you murder me one day? But you cannot. You murder yourself. I am a part of you now. I am Abel, but I am also Captain Nicholas Coventry. We have become so close that we are now one man. And, as the time passes, I will be more and more of you. I am inside your body."

And, in this room, it seemed almost to be so. Some of the West Indian heat was here. Without his clothes Nicholas moved, under the checkered sunlight, through the scrub while the palms, the banana trees closed above his head and, in a sudden clearing, he saw the surf break, far below, on the border of that wine-dark sea. Abel was close to him. His knees projected forwards, and on them his brown hands clenched the bones.

"God, it's close in here!" Nicholas said. "Why do you never open a window?"

"I like it warm. And so do you, Captain. I know you. You have that good, quiet English family in your hand, but that is not real except that it is convenient to have them there because of what you get from them. I am your real life, Captain. We have grown closer and closer. I am very happy about it."

He got up, knelt on the floor at Nicholas's feet, put his brown hands on Nicholas's chest, touched, for an instant, with the light flicker of a bird's wing, Nicholas's cheek. Then he got up.

"Have a drink, Captain?"

Nicholas said: "I don't mind, and for God's sake open a window, you dirty little swine."

And Romney? Romney's afternoon was not so good. First he was at the Galleries, then he went to the Book Club and had a word or two with his Mary Benson, then in the street outside the Book Club he had some bad news, then he went home and saw his mother. But before he saw his mother *she* saw someone else. All these things were of importance.

Even time (although it does not exist) was on this eventful day important. As thus:

Lottie said good-bye to Hector and Nell at five minutes to four. Nicholas drove to Abel's at five minutes to five, Fanny received her visitor at ten minutes past five, Romney had his piece of bad news at a quarter to five.

During this same period of time from 4 to 6 P. M., there was a riot in Rio de Janeiro (thirty people killed), shops looted in Havana (Machado not at all popular), five peasants murdered in the Ukraine, and a frontier battle in China. Other pleasanter things happened, too, like Edward getting ninety out of a hundred for his essay on the Panama Canal.

Meanwhile everything continued to go wrong with Romney. At the Galleries he was greatly irritated by the visit of two novelists. They did not come together, but met by accident. One was thin, one was fat. As it should be, the thin one was cynical, the fat one exuberant. They pretended to be delighted at the meeting and pressed visits the one on the other. Nevertheless they succeeded in a very short time in planting daggers. Romney, overhearing, disliked the exuberant one the more. He was kind, charitable, and modest. He was having luck that he did not deserve in these bad times. His forthcoming work had subscribed at the booksellers' quite amazingly. No, he did not deserve it. After all he had been writing for thirty years and it was sheer luck for him that people still read him. To which the cynical one: He *was* glad that *someone* at least was selling and especially his dear fat friend who so thoroughly deserved it. He never could understand *why* the more modern critics were so spiteful to his fat friend—jealousy in all probability—but it must be *maddening* to be so malignantly treated. To which the fat one: Ah, well, he was a philosopher by now. And he did not know that he *was* so badly treated. The quite *new* generation was rallying to his side. Had the cynical one seen a review of his work by young Tom Noddy? Fresh from Oxford and most appreciative. To which the cynical one: No. He hadn't seen it. He was delighted. Young Noddy would get on. He knew on which side his bread must be buttered.

And so on. They did not look at the pictures.

Romney was revolted, and in his five minutes with

Mary (for she was busy today and could give no more) poured out his bitterness.

"Writers are *disgusting* with their bitterness and meanness and jealousy. They are worse than painters or musicians."

Mary did not think so today. *All* artists are sensitive, egoists, fighting for their lives. They create and, living with their creations as they do, think them important. They are children, building castles on the sand. And now Romney must go. She smiled at him as though she loved him—which, secretly, she was beginning to do.

Then, in the street outside, he met Westermarck, an old friend of his and Harry's. On seeing him his heart leapt. He had heard nothing of Harry for so long. Now there would be news. There was. Harry had died, three days before, of pneumonia.

Romney walked on, not knowing his destination. The rain poured down upon him, spat upon him from the pavement, umbrellas brushed his hair, cars hooted at him. He did not perceive. Harry was dead.

His love for Harry swept over him like a fire. For it had been a real love, going deep beyond flesh and blood, into the only true world. The foundation of that love had been Harry's strength. Harry might be, intellectually, a fool, having no imagination, no taste, no true sympathy, but he had been strong, his feet set full-square, his courage almost divine, his simplicity superhuman. Whatever went, however beastly this rotting world might be, Harry remained, for he had cared for the real things. He had known what the real things were. Now, with a breath, with a puff of wind, Harry was gone. Westermarck, who had been a friend, spoke of him casually. These hurrying multitudes faltered no whit because Harry was dead. His leather armchairs, his pipes, his golf, his laughter were already forgotten. He would never now marry the charming girl, take his young son to Rugby matches, be proud of his beautiful daughters.

Romney had loved him. He would never love anyone again like that. All the world was shadow, and life—oh, life was cursed and rotten and false! This was the end.

So when, wanting only to be alone, he went to his room and found his mother counting his shirts and collars, he saw her as nothing but an intolerable disturbance.

He saw her kindness and mildness and gentleness and awkwardness as insults to his own state. Her tall figure in its dark grey dress with the black cuffs, a wisp of her hair straying into one eye, her face flushed—all these things were his past life, belonging to a dead and gone world; he loved her of course, but as one loves part of oneself that is now more recollection than conscious present. So he saw her as, carrying Harry with him, he came into his room to be alone.

He could not know that at this very moment the crisis of her whole life was upon her because of the visitor who had left her. He also could not know that never after today would he think his mother old-fashioned again. She herself, looking up, scarcely saw him, so deeply preoccupied was she with her own problem.

She said: "Oh, Romney!" Then, her mind altogether away from this, she went on: "I *think* the shirts are all right. There's a black-and-white one——"

"Something awful's happened," he began.

"Oh, what is it?" she cried, and had he not been so intent on his own circumstance he would have known that she was alive, just then, to danger—danger from any corner. . . .

"Oh, nothing—I can't tell you, I can't tell anyone——"

She said then a strange thing, straightening her body, putting her hands to her hair.

"You, too. No one here tells one anything. It comes from outside."

But he was not listening. He went up to her.

"Look here, Mother. I've got to go away."

"Go away? Have you done something, too?"

"I? No, nothing. Of course not. But I must get out of England. I must find a job somewhere abroad——"

"Why!" She put her hands on her breasts. "What *have* you been doing?"

"I tell you I've not been doing anything. But I hate England. I hate this house. I'm not interested in my job any more. I'm no good at it . . . I——"

"What has Nicholas been saying to you?" she interrupted him fiercely.

"Uncle Nicholas? What has he got to do with it?"

"Everything." Then she went on: "Perhaps you *had* better go. Perhaps we'd all better go! Sell the house. Separate. We are no use to one another any more."

He thought she was going to cry. She stood there, her eyes shining, her head up, "almost like a crazy woman," he thought afterwards when he looked back on it. For now he *did* perceive that something was wrong with her and that his was not the only trouble in the world. And behind his own distress there stirred the eternal truth that he loved her, that life without her would be impossible. And it might be that during these last months he had been forgetting her and . . .

But she gave him no time for repentance. She took two of the shirts that she was holding and threw them on the bed.

"Look after your own clothes, Romney," she said and left him extremely astonished.

Fanny had in truth very good reason to be upset, for but now she had had (and from her own daughter) terrible news.

She had been sitting in the drawing room waiting for tea. She would be, she expected, alone unless Grace was in. She would be glad to be alone, for she was nearly at the end of her endurance.

Then Nell came in.

"Hallo!" she said. "Anyone for tea?"

"No one but ourselves," said Fanny.

"That's good." (She went straight for it because she was frightened.) "Mother, I've come straight back to tell you something. I've been struggling to for months. I've simply been too cowardly."

("More trouble," thought Fanny.)

They sat down together on the sofa, hand in hand.

"It's just this," said Nell. "For six months now I've been living with a married man."

"Oh, dear!" Fanny cried, and then from the very bottom of her heart: "Oh, you shouldn't!"

Her brain turned. The room turned over, and in this whirligig she saw pictures: Nell playing as a little girl with a dog on the lawn, Nell—aged fourteen or so—asking her certain questions, Nell kissing her good-night. Then with these some slim gentleman, dressed in a frock coat, saying to her: "You've got to be modern now . . ."; a sentence from some book: "Science and hygiene have altered all this."

Then sheer alarm and panic. Nell was going to have a baby. Nell would be in a divorce case. Nell would run away to China or Africa; and then morality—Nell was wicked, Nell had broken the Law, Nell was wicked; and then all these lost in the one thought that Nell must be protected, be cared for, be defended against the world.

At last, when the room had settled down and her heart was beating less violently, she said:

"Oh, Nell—you! I never would have dreamt it!"

Nell then, very white in the face, told her about it. She told her about Hector, she told her about Lottie.

"She doesn't care for him, not a little bit. She's going off with another man. Hector and I love one another quite terribly, Mother."

"Why did you tell me now," Fanny asked, "when for so long you haven't done?"

(Afterwards, thinking about it, she was shocked to remember that it was not Nell's sin but Nell's silence that hurt her most.)

"I was afraid to," Nell said. "Girls of my generation aren't supposed to be afraid of a little thing like this, are they? But I was. I didn't think the thing itself wrong. After all, I wasn't cutting anyone out. Hector was miserable with Lottie. But the deceit has been hateful."

"It needn't have been," Fanny said.

"I *couldn't* tell you. Only Uncle Nicholas knew."

Fanny said: "Nicholas."

"Yes. He knew Lottie. He gave Hector and me lunch and found out all about it. And the more he knew and you didn't, the more——"

She got up and said in a shrill, small voice, the defiant voice that she had as a child when she had done wrong:

"Well, I've told you."

"Nicholas knew—and you were lying to us all the time."

"Not lying."

"Yes—on those week-ends you said you were going to friends."

"Hector *was* a friend."

The look of misery on Fanny's face beat Nell down.

She was on her knees holding her mother, looking up into her face.

"It's all right—Hector and I will marry soon. Oh, Mother! *don't* look like that!"

But Fanny said: "What use am I to any of you? You all deceive me—and for *you* to do this, Nell—so secret, so false . . . What has happened to everybody?"

She got up. She put her hand to her forehead.

"I'm bewildered. I don't know *what* I shall do——"

She went to Romney's room and began mechanically to tidy his clothes. Thus Romney found her. . . .

Then, half an hour later, after throwing Romney's shirts onto the bed, Fanny went back to the drawing room. It was as silent as the South Pole. There are crises in the lives of all of us when everything rushes to a single point of action. It is only a moment of time that we are given, but our fate is now to be decided. We are fortunate if, at this crisis, the alternatives are clearly presented to us. Often they are confused. But at this, the most important hour of Fanny's life, the issues were perfectly clear.

During this time no other person entered the room. It remained bare for her to make her decision. Some small things acted with her—the Japanese screen and two figures in it, a man raising a sword, a woman standing beside a tree in blossom. Also a small painting hanging on the left of the fireplace that presented a bonfire burning in a clearing of a wood. And the rings on her fingers.

At first she could think of nothing but Nell. Nell, whom she had believed pure and perfect, had for months past been a married man's mistress. Then the other figures crowded about her: Charles who had been unfaithful to her, Romney who wanted to leave her, Edward who had some secret from her.

They had all betrayed her. That was the first thing that she saw.

Her emotions then were wildly revengeful. She had always been considered a mild, sweet, loving woman. She was not mild nor sweet nor loving. At that first moment, moving as it seemed into the very heart of the screen so that she stood beside the man with the sword, she hated them all! They had betrayed her. What could she do to punish them? Old, forgotten, submerged rages rose in her. She was one with herself as a small child who had bitten her governess's finger through to the bone. She was again stamping on the floor of her bedroom, throwing the china to the ground until it lay in fragments about her. Once again she hit Grace on the mouth and made her lip bleed. Once again she cried, as she had done once on a Sunday: "I hate God! I hate God! He's a beast!"

She was sitting forward on the sofa, her body very still, her hands clenched, but she took the sword from the warrior's hand and, raising it, waited for the enemy. But no enemy came. Only the clock ticked. The coals stirred in the fire.

An immense desolation seized her. All sentimental people who are sensitive to the opinions of others are frequently desolate. Fanny had often been so. But this was something other. This was the solitariness of the woman under the blossoming tree, whom beauty and life surrounded, and she herself was isolated!

And *what* isolation! Only Janet in the whole world still needed her. At the thought of Janet she rose from the sofa and began to pace the room, her eyes staring at the wall paper, the pictures, the furniture, seeing none of them and yet photographing them so intensely on her mind that she would never see them again without thinking of this hour.

She would run away to Janet! She would leave the whole lot of them and Nicholas could do what he liked. Charles? . . . Edward? . . . Leave Charles, leave Edward? Why, yes, if they cared for her so little!

And once she was gone she would never come back! She would make her own life and they could make theirs.

"My own life! My own life!" she cried aloud to the listening chairs, the watching mirror, the picture of the bonfire in the wood.

Wasn't that what every woman of middle age demanded and never got? There she had been for years and years sacrificing herself, enduring the pains of childbirth, submitting herself unselfishly to her stupid, greedy husband's desires (for Charles *was* stupid—yes, and greedy, too), serving his children, slaving for him—and what did they do? How did they repay her? How had Charles repaid her?

Well, she had had enough of sweetness and goodness and submission. She would go to Janet; but did Janet care for her any more than did the others? Had not Janet left her at a moment's provocation? Ah, but then, Nicholas . . . Janet had hated Nicholas from the first, Janet had foreseen . . .

At the thought, at the name—Nicholas—Fanny stopped her walking. She stood staring into the Japanese screen.

It was Nicholas who had done all this.

Her desire for vengeance, her sense of desolation, fell from her. She stepped one further pace, out of her own heart, away from her egotism, into a truer reality. Yes, Nicholas had done this, but *could* he have done it were she the woman she thought herself? *What* did she think that she was? She said often about herself that she was untidy, poorly educated, forgetful, enthusiastic at the wrong time, too talkative, often foolish in company. She admitted these things because people forced her to admit them. But in her heart she made allowances for all of them. And besides the allowances, she had, as so many of us have, the secret belief that if only everyone knew the whole truth the world would be amazed at our integrity, our inner wisdom, our courage under superhuman difficulties. Her religion even was in part built of this. Even in a quite trivial moment when Mrs. Frobisher would say, "But, Fanny! Esthonia's nowhere *near* China!" she could think: "God sees me. He knows what a fine nature I have, and it's only He who has seen my triumph over temptation, the way that I have made ends meet, my patience with Charles."

She did not say to herself consciously, as she undressed at night: "Yes, I'm a *good* woman—fine, if only one knew the truth." She was not at all a vain woman, but she must defend herself, as we all must, and the battlements of her castle she had built with her own hands.

Now—and this was the real crisis for her of this whole sequence of events—at the thought of Nicholas and what he had done she beheld herself as she was.

"If I had been a different woman—stronger, wiser, less selfish, more far-seeing—could he have had this power?"

No. He could not. The power that anyone has over oneself is a criticism of one's own lack of power.

It had been easy enough when all had gone well to think herself sweet, charming, unselfish, a perfect wife and mother. They had, all of them, encouraged her in that belief.

When, nearly a year ago, she had told that little woman in the shop that all was beautifully well at home she had, unconsciously, reflected on her own virtues. And with that public statement had come the challenge.

It was as though God had been listening to her and had said: "You think you're fine, do you, and have done everything well? Now we'll see."

She had spent the last six months in accusing the family. She had been aghast at the things they had done. But would any of this have happened had she been a finer woman? And if they *had* happened would not a finer, stronger woman have bravely dealt with them?

Would Nicholas have had the power had she herself been more powerful? She looked at the screen, at the picture, and they had a deep significance for her. She had not wielded the sword, she had not known the patience of the woman by the tree, she had neither the beauty nor the strength of the fire in the wood.

She sat down on the sofa again. Quieter now, moving in a wider, freer, less selfish world, she gathered her strength. It was not too late, although not a moment was to be lost. It was her strength against her brother's. She must challenge him at once. Either she would go or he would.

In connection with Nicholas two things had happened yesterday. Charles, in that shy, defensive manner that he adopted now to her, had mentioned that Nicholas would probably remain in the house indefinitely.

"It seems he likes being here," Charles said. "He'll pay his share of the housekeeping."

And the other was that, walking home, she had passed a curiosity shop, and there, in the window, very chastely displayed, was her own gold snuffbox! She had stared and stared. She could not believe her eyes. Then she had entered the shop and made enquiries. . . . Nicholas himself had sold the snuffbox. She did not enquire the price he had received.

There must then be no delay. Either she went or Nicholas went. She would make the challenge at once: no time better than this evening, after dinner. They would be all at home tonight.

Having come so far, her heart began to beat wildly with sheer panic. Like Charles she detested scenes. Anything like public melodrama appalled her and seemed to her in the very worst taste.

But this . . . what was it but melodrama?

"Well, all of you. Here we are. Now you can choose. Either Nicholas or I leave the house tomorrow——"

What a thing for a sister to say about her brother—in public—in front of her own family! And suppose then that they said: "All right, dear. You go. You needn't stay away for long. You've been very queer lately and certainly need a holiday." They would not take her seriously. Of course not. They never had. After that she must go. She would go to Janet. And then suppose that after all they did not want her to return?

Odder things than that had happened. Nell was in love and would be married. (Somewhere, deep within herself, she was appalled that she was not more truly shocked at Nell's conduct.) Romney had told her that he wanted to go abroad. And Charles? Could it be that after all these years of married happiness they would separate? It could. Had not, only last year, the Daniel Caines separated after twenty years of happy marriage? Incompatibility. Charles was tired of her. Had he not been unfaithful to her within the last year?

She would go. She might return. And to what? To find Nicholas now completely established and all of them contemptuous of her for her melodrama and weakness.

But what was the alternative? To say nothing. To submit. To be sweet and domestic and careless and indulgent once more. To behave to Charles and Romney and Nell as though nothing had occurred. And Nicholas established here for ever. . . .

She could tell them about the snuffbox. That might shock them a little. But no. She would use no extra weapon. As her thoughts marched the issue became ever clearer. She was fighting for her family against Nicholas. If her family did not truly love her, above all, if Charles did not love her, then she might as well go. Nicholas should remain.

And she knew that a challenge would tell her everything. She would make them perceive that this was *real* and that all the events of the past year had led to this. Nicholas, too, would perceive it. He was much too clever not to.

At the thought of his cleverness, her blood, to quote the good words of innocent narrators, "ran cold." She began to shiver. She was seized there, on the sofa, with violent trembling. From the very beginning she had been afraid of Nicholas. During his ten years' absence she had forgotten and at the first sight of him she had rejoiced, but he had not been in the house a day before she began to remember.

Now the thought of facing him in the open horrified her. He would have some plan. He would influence the others to mock. He would defeat her scornfully.

She looked at the screen, at the man with the sword.

If she were defeated it would not be because Nicholas had defeated her. It would be because, with all these years, she had not lived so that her husband and children loved her She had not been fine enough to make them do so.

If she were defeated it would be because of herself.

She nodded her head at the screen. In this room, after dinner tonight, the man with the sword should see which way it went.

Then of course the door opened and it was Nicholas who looked in.

"Hullo, old dear. Sitting all by yourself?"

She went towards him, smiling.

"Yes. I've been dozing, I think."

He put a hand on her arm and lightly kissed her cheek.

"You'll be in to dinner, won't you?" she asked.

"Yes. I'm getting ever so domestic."

"We'll all be in. How nice! It's quite a long time since we have been."

They went out of the room together.

4

Dinner that evening was very gay. They had not been all of them together for that meal since the Old Lady died. Nicholas was most amusing and told one story after another, most of them merry, but one, over the dessert, very sinister about a house in Jamaica once lived in by a slave owner, and still a thin negro, with head on one side, his legs bound in rags, cries from an upper room pitifully as his back is lashed, and dogs howl, but there are no dogs, no negro, only the sea beating almost to the broken doors of the deserted house.

When they went up to the drawing room he said that they must play *vingt-et-un*. He took charge of them all, arranging the table, telling them where they were to sit, pouring the counters onto the cloth, saying that he would be Bank.

He made Grace sit by him, and she, smiling, for she dearly loved any game of chance, but terrified of Nicholas, submitted as though she were hypnotized by him.

Fanny was at the opposite end of the table from

Charles. He looked at her once, his eyes staring at her out of his round ruddy face. She knew what he was saying to her.

"How long is this silly farce to continue?" She knew that he was beginning to be angry as a boy is who is lost in a maze. "Why don't you do something about it?" he asked her. "Forgive me or scold me. I'm losing my patience."

And she looked at Nell who was laughing and joking as though she had no conscience at all. She was on Nicholas's other side, and he made little jokes to her in her ear.

Once or twice he told Fanny what to do, as though he possessed her, too. She had the Bank and he wanted to buy it from her. She refused to sell.

"Oh, come on, Fanny. You don't want it. You'll be much safer without it."

Then suddenly she let him have it, and she could see that he was thinking: "You poor silly creature! I can do what I like with you."

As his spirits rose and his consciousness of commanding them all grew, he developed in his mind the amusing fancy that they were in fact all his puppets. He had seen once, at a music hall, a mesmerizer who put his subjects through absurd antics, making one crawl upon the floor, another drink from an empty glass, tilting it until he had swallowed the last drop, another dance as though to a hornpipe. How amusing if he could do this with them now, making Grace crawl on her knees, and Charles strip himself to his shirt, and Fanny—what would he make that big, flushed, silly, amiable sister of his do?

"What about another, Charles?"

"Pass," said Charles.

"Come on, Grace. One more."

"Oh, I don't think I ought to. . . . I don't think . . . Oh, well, I'll risk it. There! I knew I shouldn't!"

Only with Matthew he could do nothing. That thickset little brother of his spoke very seldom, seemed not to take much interest in the game.

"By Jove, how he hates me!" Nicholas thought. "I'll have him out of the house before much longer. His monkey religion can go elsewhere."

"Come on, Matthew, be a sport. Have another."

"No, thank you, Nicholas."

He looked at his own cards.

"Pay twenty," he said.

It was not, of course, long before he had accumulated in front of him a great pile of counters. In games of chance he had always an uncanny luck. Anything that did not matter. But, even in a small, unimportant thing like this, it was pleasant to win, and there was great comfort in the thought, present with him tonight more than ever before, that here at last he was settled down. Here was a safe refuge for himself and Lizzie. It would not be long before he could persuade old Charles (of whom he was really very fond) into a number of most profitable schemes. He would turn Matthew out and take his room for a private sitting room. Nell would marry, Romney marry or go abroad—and then with Fanny and Charles and Grace slipping into an obedient, submissive old age, the house would be his. It would suit him very well.

"Come on. Pay up, all of you," he said, laying his cards on the table. "I doubled you, remember."

The clock struck half-past ten. Fanny got up.

"That's half-past ten," she said. "That's enough for tonight."

They were all very startled. She stood, her hands pressing the table, looking at them. There were loud protests.

"My dear Fanny!" Nicholas said. "We were only just beginning."

"I say, Mother!" cried Romney.

"No," she said. "Settle up. It's time we stopped."

Her voice was changed. They all noticed it—and not only her voice, but the way she stood, something tense in her carriage. Charles said:

"All right, Fanny. If you think so."

They settled up, paid their debts. The cards were slipped into the drawer of the table.

"Well, good-night, all," said Romney. "I'm for bed."

"No—wait a minute," Fanny said. "I want you all to stop a minute. There's something we've all got to discuss."

She, above the terror in her heart (for now she was committed to the event, whether she would or no), saw them all transfixed in their different movements. Grace was still in her chair by the table, Matthew had gone quietly to the armchair near the fire, Charles, his legs apart, stood, his hands in his pockets, staring at her, Nell was on the sofa and Romney beside her. Nicholas stood by the fireplace, lighting a cigarette.

She herself sat down in the chair nearest to her, for her limbs were trembling. It was placed in front of the Japanese screen, which she could not therefore see.

"Here, Fanny—what's all this about?" Charles asked.

It was he at whom she looked when she went on:

"I won't keep you very long. But this is the first night we've all been together for weeks. There's something I want to say."

She paused. Nicholas, looking at her with an amused friendly smile, thought: "Whatever has the old girl got in her head now?"

Then she made her plunge.

"It's this. Nicholas," (she looked directly at him) "isn't it true that you mean to settle down with us now, to live with us altogether? *You* haven't told me, although I think you might have done. Charles——"

Charles came forward. "Look here, Fan, what the devil's the matter with you? This isn't something for all of us. It's got nothing to do——"

"I think it has," she said quickly. "With all of us. I think we all ought to hear what Nicholas is going to do."

Nicholas jingled his coins in his pocket.

"My dear Fanny, I think Charles is right. I don't see what my staying here has to do with the family. I don't imagine they'll any of them object if I *do* stay."

"No," said Fanny. "But I want you to tell us all—just what you mean to do."

He gave her a sharp look. She remembered how, in the long-ago past, he had shot those glances at someone who might, he fancied, be in his way.

"If that's all," he went on, "it's soon said. I'm sorry I didn't mention it to you, Fan. I thought it mainly Charles's business." He looked round upon them all with exceeding friendliness. "The fact simply is—although it embarrasses me a bit to make a public declaration of it—that Lizzie and I have been so happy here, you've all made us both so comfortable, that the other day I suggested to Charles that the arrangement should be permanent. I've got a bit of a job now in London, and it suits me to stay here. I'd rather be in this house than anywhere else. Of course I'll pay my shot in the upkeep and all of that. I hope you none of you mind——"

"Mind!" Romney broke in. "Why, I should think not, Uncle Nick! It's a grand idea."

And Charles said: "And that's that. I don't know what Fanny's notion was in making this into a kind of public meeting. But as we *are* all here I may as well say that Nicholas and Lizzie have been grand additions to the family. And now that the poor Old Lady has gone there's lots of room. Stay as long as ever you like, Nick, old boy, and welcome. And now—what about a drink?"

He moved towards the tray where were the whisky, the siphons, Grace's milk, and the jug of barley water.

"And now," said Fanny, "I'll tell you why I wanted you all to be here."

Charles stopped, turned, and looked at her.

"It's more important than you imagine—at least for myself. It's something you all must decide. It's just this: if Nicholas stays, I go."

The first remark was a horrified "My God!" from Charles.

Then Nicholas did his turn.

"If Fanny feels like that," he said, "the matter's settled." He moved towards the door. Charles caught his arm.

"By heaven, you don't!" he cried. "Fanny, are you mad? What craziness——" He stopped, collecting his words. "Do you know what you've done, insulting a guest in our house, your own brother, too? You're ill. You've been upset for months." He put his hand on Nicholas's shoulder. "I apologize, Nick—and so shall Fanny when she comes to her senses. Meanwhile the sooner we all clear out——"

But Fanny went on:

"I know that it seems very rude. But I can't stop to think whether I'm rude or not. Besides, we're only the family, aren't we? There are no outsiders here. It's no use blustering, Charles. I don't see why anyone should get excited. It's simply as I said. If Nicholas stays, I go—and I want you all to decide which it shall be."

Nicholas came over to her.

"Now, Fanny," he said, "I'm sure you're right. I'm not angry, and nobody else is. Only it's pretty serious for me—that you should feel so badly about me, I mean. What have I done? I think it's fair we should all know."

He was thinking: "This is the greatest surprise of my whole life. I never dreamt she had it in her." And quietly, realizing at once that their whole past life together was involved in this, he settled down to fight her.

She looked up at him.

"There's no need to make this personal. Much better for all of us that we shouldn't. When you first came here a year ago I was delighted to see you. I didn't know, of course, that you were going to stay so long, and I had forgotten, in the ten years, how much we'd always disliked one another——"

"My dear Fanny——"

"Oh, yes. You know it as well as I. But this isn't to be personal. I don't want to discuss or account for anything. Since you have been here I have been increasingly miserable, and now it has reached a point when we can't be in the same house together any longer. So long as I thought that you were only on a visit I could wait, but when I knew that you meant to stay altogether, I thought what it would be best to do. I could have gone away without saying anything, but that would have been cowardly. I could have discussed it with Charles. He would have thought me simply ill or mad or something because I couldn't have given him my real reasons. I could have asked you to go. Well, I did ask you. You laughed at me.

"But there are other reasons for making it a family

discussion. During your year here you have, as I think, influenced all of us and all of us badly. Matthew and Grace and I know you better than the others do. It's a matter for all of us, not only for Charles and yourself, as to whether you are going to live here or not."

Romney interrupted: "All right, Mother, if this *is* to be a family discussion, then we'll say what we think. And what *I* think, Uncle Nicholas, is that this house has been a different place since you came—twice as jolly, twice as lively——"

"I must say," Nell said, "*you* haven't been very lively lately, Romney."

"All right. Leave me out of it. I've had my own troubles that have nothing to do with Uncle Nicholas. I say that he's shaken us all up and a damn good thing, too. We needed it."

Then Grace surprised everyone by speaking. She looked up, gave a frightened glance at Nicholas, then said:

"But of course, Fanny, you're not going—not even on a visit. We missed you terribly when you went on that cruise. I know Charles did—and all of us."

That made Charles burst out:

"Good Lord, this is all absurd! Of *course* Fanny isn't going, nor Nicholas either. And it's damned bad taste to discuss it, all of us like this. It makes me as shy as anything. What *you* want, Fan, is a good night's rest. Come on. Let's have a drink and stop this nonsense."

Fanny spoke, and somehow, whether by the quiet determination of her position, sitting back in her chair, not moving, or by some inflection in her voice, it came to them all that this was serious, that it *really was* about something, and that they had never in all their lives seen Fanny like this before.

"I'm sure," she said, "it's very rude to discuss Nicholas

in front of himself; I'm equally sure that he likes it very much. Do you remember, Nicholas, how once at a children's party at the Dermotts' they were talking about two little girls, how pretty they were and so on?—you broke in with 'And what about me?' But we're *not* discussing you, Nicholas. This ill-mannered business needn't go on another five minutes. I simply want everyone to say whether they'd rather have me or you in the house. Because we *can't* stay in it together. No. Not another twenty-four hours."

Nicholas now showed his extraordinary charm. It was as though he wanted them all to understand that, beneath his badinage and gaiety, he was a very genuine person, a rather wistful and lonely person if all the truth were known.

"Look here, all of you. Never mind about my being embarrassed. I'm used to it. Only—I must confess—this has been a tremendous surprise to me, simply taken my breath away. If Fanny feels like this, Lizzie and I have to go—that's all there is to it——"

"By God, you don't!" Charles broke in.

"Oh, yes, Charles. Of course we have. We're quite used to moving on. I don't think that Fanny is quite fair to me in one thing, though. When Lizzie and I came here first we didn't *mean* to stay—really we didn't. We weren't sure even that you'd want us at all after I'd behaved so badly in being silent so long. But you were all so good to us, so awfully kind to us, that we stayed on and on. And then I found some work to do. And then Charles seemed to like the idea of our staying—so there you are! Honestly I hadn't any notion that Fanny felt like this. And that's why"—he turned directly to Fanny—"I think you owe it to me to give some reasons for feeling as you do."

She knew that if, at that moment, she had turned to

Charles and said: "Which is it to be?" he would have roared at her: "You can damned well go on a visit somewhere! I'll never forgive you for this scene, this bad taste, this abominable rudeness to a guest of mine." She could see quite clearly that that was what he was feeling. Nevertheless she had now a new kind of strength; she was afraid of no one, not even of Nicholas.

"It's like this," she said, leaning forward a little. "In the first place, Nicholas, it isn't true that you meant to stay only for a day or two. You meant to stay as long as you could. It isn't true that you didn't know what you were doing. You've always known exactly what you were doing. We've talked about this before, so that you can't pretend that you don't know what I think. I want you to go simply because I want us all to stay together. When you came we were very happy, we believed in one another, we trusted one another. Now we don't any more. I myself have been more unhappy in the last six months than in all the rest of my life. That is partly my own fault. But not entirely. We are all unhappy here even though we mayn't like to admit it. And that's because you've done your best, Nicholas, to take away everything that made us happy. You think that family life and old-fashioned ideas like fidelity and religion are absurd now. The world has grown out of them. You've laughed at us for still believing in them. That's why I want you to go—or, if you don't go, why I must."

Nicholas laughed, gently and with great kindliness.

"You make me out a perfect villain, Fan. This is like a Salvation Army meeting. I *don't* laugh at your ideas. I think they're fine. I can't tell you what it's been to me, after wandering about the world as I've done, to settle down with people who believe in the things you do. It's made a new man of me."

And that was his first mistake. Romney, Nell, and even Charles had heard him express such very different sentiments! He *didn't* admire fidelity and old-fashioned beliefs. Hadn't he told Romney that he was a rascal and gloried in it? Hadn't he advised Charles to wake up and see the world as it now was? Hadn't he chaffed Charles about this very old-fashionedness of Fanny's?

His second mistake was that he said to Charles:

"Come on, Charles. Stand up for me a bit. *You* know that I'm not as bad as Fanny paints me."

They all knew that in fact it was between Charles and Fanny and Nicholas. The others didn't count in the real issue, which was also something deeper and more general than even Nicholas and Fanny.

Charles himself was in a fine confusion. The public drama of the thing disgusted him. He was *really* ashamed of Fanny. Before Nicholas spoke he had been ready, as she knew, to cry out: "All right, Fanny—go if you want to! Stay with your old Janet for a week or two and see how you like it!" For, of course, she wouldn't go for long. A week would be all *she* could stand, and it might do her all the good in the world. She would begin to realize then how much they all meant to her, that she couldn't play tricks with them as she had been doing lately, order people out of the house as though she were mistress of it.

But, looking at her out of the corner of his eye, he seemed to see a new Fanny. Absurd and unreal though this scene was, it *meant* something. It *was* true that they had none of them been happy. It *was* true that Nicholas had some damned odd ideas. And then when Nicholas spoke, appealing to him, he remembered a number of things—the money that he had borrowed (if he was in a job now why hadn't he attempted to repay any of it?), some of the things that he had said and the stories that he had told.

So that when Fanny made, at last, her real challenge —the challenge, if he had known it, all their lives depended on—he was altogether of two minds. On the one hand to teach Fanny a lesson for forcing this scene on him, for behaving so badly to him during these last weeks, for, in general, being so unlike the Fanny whom he loved; and, on the other hand, to show Nicholas that *he* wasn't master here either (and maybe, after all, it wouldn't be altogether a good thing if Nicholas lived here for always).

Fanny got up from her chair.

"We aren't going to discuss it any more," she said. "I'm going tomorrow morning. It's time I led my own life for a bit. I know what you've been thinking of me for years back. Dear old Fanny who doesn't know Epstein from Einstein, who loses her temper at cards, who may make us ashamed at any moment by the silly things she says—and the rest of it. Why should a woman expect, when she's middle-aged, to hold her family any more? She's done her job. There's no reason for them to care for her any longer if they *don't* care for her. The only way I could hold you is because you love me. Why should you love me if I'm not the sort of person you *can* love? I'm sure it's very embarrassing for you all to talk in this way, but once in forty years it's not a bad thing for us to say what we think. Just about this time last year I told a woman in a shop that we were the most united family in existence. I see how silly I was. Nicholas is right, I expect, when he says that we spend all our time shamming. We're not shamming tonight." She went on, standing in the middle of them: "You know, I owe something to myself, too. I've tried to be a fine mother and a good wife—just as though I were one of those plain, good family women in one of the American films. I give it up. Nicholas says no one needs fine mothers and good wives any more. I expect he's right. I'm going to be something on my own now—study myself a bit. You can all pay me visits sometimes and see how I'm getting on."

She walked to the door. Everything depended on Charles. Even as her hand was on the door knob he was still of two minds. Let her go! She'd come back running! What right had she to order Nicholas out of the house just because she didn't like him? But would she come back? What would he do without her? What would this house . . . ?

His whole life long with Fanny drove him forward. He put his hand on her arm as, only twenty minutes before, he had done to Nicholas.

"Don't be an ass, Fan. Of course you can't go. We wouldn't know what to do without you. . . ." He held her with his hand. They all waited in extreme embarrassment. Romney lit a cigarette.

Then Charles said: "I'm awfully sorry, Nicholas, old man, but if Fanny feels like this . . . perhaps it would be better. . . . And now have a drink, everybody. What's yours, Matthew? Have a drink, Nick. . . ."

"Thanks, old man," said Nicholas, coming forward. "Fanny, don't go. There's something *I* want to say now. Yes, Charles. Thanks. Soda right up."

Fanny turned back. Nicholas nodded at her.

"All right, old girl. You've won."

All she knew was that she was dreadfully tired—and, after that, that she never wanted to see any of them again.

She wanted just then to leave them, whether Nicholas went or didn't go. She sat down just where she happened to be. It was the sofa, and she was surprised to find that Nell had taken her hand.

But she *did* murmur: "I'm sure we're all so very tired. Hasn't this gone on long enough?"

"Only five minutes more, my dear," said Nicholas, holding his glass of whisky up against the light and looking at it. "I want to tell you all something before I go. Tomorrow morning I depart and, after what I'm going to say, you won't want, any of you, to say good-bye to me."

Charles, very uncomfortable, broke in:

"I say, old chap, don't think because of what I said—what I mean is that after a bit you'll come and stay again. Fanny didn't mean——"

"Oh, yes, she did," said Nicholas. "She meant every word of it. She's wanted to see the last of me for months. So have Grace and Matthew. Only I didn't think they'd have the pluck to say so. I banked on that. I never was more surprised in my life than I was at Fanny's outburst. Only an hour ago I thought I was nicely settled here. Of course I knew what my own family thought of me, but I argued that they'd do anything for a quiet life. I really didn't know you had it in you, Fanny, my dear."

She looked at him and realized how greatly he was enjoying this. It had always been the same. If he couldn't have one thing he'd have another. If he couldn't be the centre of the stage, whether seen or unseen, one way, then he'd be it another. Vanity and selfishness, she thought, and (to give him his due) a sense of humour.

"Now listen, all of you," he said. "This is my last will and testament. Once more I make my bow, only this time, as it's all among the family, I can speak the truth.

"I must thank you for a very pleasant year here. Often you've bored me—oftener you've amused me. I stayed—

and I wanted to go on staying—for two reasons. One because I thought this a nice place to settle into, and the other, quite altruistic, because I felt that I was good for all of you."

Matthew murmured something.

"Yes, even for you, Matthew. You don't know it, but you are, all of you, as remote from real life as the Hebridean cuckoo. I don't mean that insultingly. I'm not being vindictive because you're turning me out. I've no malice in my nature, although I would like to do *you* a bad turn before I go, Matthew, if I could."

Charles, who saw Nicholas growing into a different man before his eyes said:

"I say, Nicholas, hold on."

"No," said Nicholas. "I don't mean to hold on or hold off. If Fanny hadn't arranged this little dramatic scene you wouldn't have found me so honest, but as it is—as I'm going anyway—I may as well let you have the truth.

"I came here on a visit—a sort of rest house until times were easier. And then I found you very amusing. I found you loaded up with a lot of old-fashioned ideas dating from the Ark: Matthew's religion, Fanny's domesticity, Grace's—shall I tell them what *your* amusement was, Grace dear?"

Grace burst out:

"I don't care what you tell them. I'll tell them myself. I'm not ashamed——"

"All right, I won't tell them. Let me explain. I loved getting you all to do as I wished. It was the greatest fun. And then I was spoiling the Egyptians—a thing I've always loved doing. What do I owe you, Charles? Never mind, you'll never see any of it——"

"If you think——" said Charles indignantly.

"Oh, no, I don't. You're a generous fellow—as weak

as butter. You're all weak, and you're a lot of lambs complacently living in a world of lions and tigers. When I've finished you'll think me a very wicked man, I don't doubt. But I'm not—no wickeder than the next man—only more honest. I hate humbugs, and you're all the nicest people in the world, but damnable humbugs."

"What's the use of all this?" said Charles. "You aren't making things any better, Nicholas, you know."

"Oh, yes, I am," said Nicholas, "much better. And I'm enjoying myself. You can't be so unfair as to deny me these last words, positively the very last you'll ever hear from me. What was I saying? Oh, yes, the world has changed, but you none of you know it. God is as dead as Queen Anne for one thing—morality is a matter only of social convenience for another. But I'm not going to preach. I soon found that you were all up to your own little games like every other family I've ever seen. So I used you, loving you all very much, of course. For instance, I took one or two things that were just as much mine as yours really. A picture or two, and the gold snuffbox. Do you know what I sold it for?"

"You sold it?" Romney cried.

"Indeed I did. And for two hundred pounds."

"Two hundred pounds!" Grace gasped.

"Yes. You didn't think it was worth so much, did you? Well, nor did I. But it was. And you'll never see either the money or the snuffbox again."

"As a matter of fact," said Fanny, "I knew you'd sold it. I saw it in a shop window two days ago and went in and enquired about it."

"Well, did you really?" said Nicholas. "And didn't say anything about it just now. Upon my word, I admire you for that, Fanny." He looked as though he were going to pat her on the shoulder, but he went on. "And that letter, Charles——"

Charles started, turning to Fanny.

"Oh, it's all right. I'm not going to tell anyone about it. But it was I who put it in Fanny's room. I found it in an old dressing gown."

"You blackguard!" Charles cried. "If I'd known it was you——"

"Yes, but you didn't. You never dreamt of it. Now you'll never forgive me, but it doesn't matter because you'll never see me any more, dear Charles. I did it because I thought it time you and Fanny were up against something that really mattered. After years of marriage things get sleepy, don't they? And then it amused me, of course, to see what you would do. And then I was irritated with Fanny—I wanted to teach her a lesson. I've taught you all a lesson if it comes to that. Life's real, you know, full of rogues and sudden death and cancer and murder. Not at all the pretty sentimental thing you fancy it is. And as to your God, Matthew, He's been a pretty good failure in this case, hasn't He?"

"It isn't God that's failed but myself," said Matthew indignantly. "I got to hate you so these last months that He was removed from me." He went on: "I'd only say this, Nicholas. By your own account, from what you've told us now, you're a pretty good scoundrel. But don't think that God doesn't exist. Your being a scoundrel isn't important nor my weakness. It goes much deeper than what *we* are."

"Well, have it as you like," said Nicholas impatiently. "I've finished. Only remember I've done you a good turn. You'll all of you go about the world now with your eyes a bit more open."

He smiled on them all, finished his whisky, went to the door.

"Good-bye. Good-bye. Lizzie and I will go to a hotel in the morning, and we don't want to be seen off."

5

He went to his room, greatly pleased with himself, very conscious of the way in which he had held them all spellbound. But *in* his room, the door closed behind him, the atmosphere changed. He looked about him at the familiar things.

After all, what a bore! Such a little time ago to dinner when he had seemed so securely settled, so happily placed! But he was well accustomed to these changes. He rememberd at Rome, in the Aldebrondi villa, how, after dinner, there had been a scene very like this—only of course more temperamental, and Laura had thrown the candlesticks at him. . . .

He must tell Lizzie. He went up into her room and woke her up. She roused herself from her deep sleep as quietly as though, through the evening, she had been expecting him.

He sat on the bed, put his arm around her, drew her towards him. The only creature in the world whom he loved!

"Lizzie darling—I'm sorry to have woken you. But I had to tell you. We're leaving tomorrow morning."

"Leaving here?"

"Yes, dear—there's been a row."

"Oh, dear—another?"

"What do you mean—another?" he said crossly. Then he kissed her, held her close to him, stroking her dark hair.

"Your Aunt Fanny doesn't like us. She says we've got to go."

He was aware that her body trembled.

"Where do we go this time?" she asked.

"Oh, to a hotel for a day or two. Then there's a nice place in the country—some new friends I've made."

As she said nothing (she had always before played up to his plans whatever they might be): "You'll like it awfully there, dear. They're very nice people. It will be *much* better than here. After all, it *was* beginning to be boring here. Wasn't it?"

She didn't respond to him at all.

"I don't know. I have been happy here."

"Oh, darling, you couldn't be. Although they are my relations they *are* so stupid!"

"What did Aunt Fanny say? Did she say that she hated us?"

"Oh, not that of course. English people aren't like that. They may hate you ever so much, but they don't say so."

"Did she say that she wanted me to go?"

"No, she never mentioned you. But of course if I go you do."

He thought that she was going to cry. He had never in his life known her do so. She did not now. She gave a deep sigh. Then she said:

"Can I say good-bye to Edward in the morning?"

"Of course, dear, if you catch him before he goes to school."

Very quietly she drew away and lay down. She turned on her side. He waited. No word came from her.

A fear, as acute as any he had ever known, attacked him.

"Darling—you aren't angry with me? It wasn't my fault. Kiss me."

She turned her head and allowed him to kiss her. Then she turned away again.

He waited. There was no sound. He went back into his room. Had they after all won the only victory over him that really mattered? With their damned hypocrisy and soft ways had they taken Lizzie away from him?

He hesitated. Should he go back to her and *make* her show her love for him?

He had never felt quite so lonely before.

In their room, Charles, half undressed, burst out to Fanny:

"But I can't understand! I *never* was so taken in by anyone in my life! And he seemed to glory in it! Putting that letter——"

She came to him, kissed him, sat beside him on the bed, her arm about him.

"Charles, darling, let's go to sleep. I don't think I've ever been so tired in my life."

"The damned scoundrel——" Charles went on.

She clung to him like a child, holding his hand as though she were terrified that it would disappear.

"It doesn't matter. Nicholas isn't our sort anyway. It will always be a battle between our sort and his—but it *doesn't* matter. Love me. Charles, love me as though you had met me for the first time yesterday."

Later, in his arms, she murmured, just before she went to sleep:

"I'm sure it will be fine tomorrow."

And one more.

Matthew Coventry stood, his head bent, in his room and, in a silence more profound, it seemed to him, than any that he had ever known, heard the tap of the hesitating branches against the window pane.

He had not turned on the electric light but lit two candles on his table, and in their light that wavered with the breeze from the just-open window, the "Virgin of the Rocks" came to life, moving like green water against the shore. He raised his head and looked at it. He looked, as he so often did, to the left-hand corner of the picture where a world of beautiful dream began in a faint blue light—a world that had no limit, no sound, nothing but peace.

He was bitterly humiliated. Fanny, whom he dearly loved but had never thought greatly courageous, had done what he should have done. It was he who should have liberated the family. Had he not, in his heart, always prided himself that he was nearer to God than they? Had not this fight with Nicholas been exactly *his* fight, for it had been about the existence of God although they themselves might not know it? But *he* knew it. God knew it. At last, after years of preparation, God had tested him and he had altogether failed. He had failed because he had hated. His hatred of Nicholas had paralyzed him, as hate always paralyzes right action.

He undressed. He came back from his bedroom and stood in the little breeze, under the picture by the fluttering candles, a white-skinned, flabby, bare, forked little creature who was worth without God no more than the ashes that he would soon become.

He sank on his knees and, naked as he was, prayed. He surrendered himself, as he had so often done before, to God. But this time more truly. For he began now from the bottom. All the climb had to be made again.

On his knees he remembered the words of Epictetus: "But the tyrant will bind thee. What will he bind?—the leg. He will rob thee of what?—the head. What though can he neither bind nor take away? The will. Thyself.

That is why the ancients said—know thyself." Know thyself. Surrender thyself. Love thy fellow men. On these words the new world was to be built.

He rose, put on his pyjamas, brushed his teeth, went to the window and thought of the Tree.

"I begin again and, all the world over, men are beginning again.

"The door is open and God speaks. Depart. But whither? To nothing terrible but rather to the place where you belong—to everything that is friendly and akin——"

Submission to God's will to act as He orders. Love of men. Companionship with all the world of nature. . . .

He would start again from the beginning. . . .

6

Nicholas came down to breakfast. Only Nell was present. He was not at all embarrassed but helped himself generously to kidneys and bacon. Nell gave him his coffee.

"I may as well have a good meal, as it's my last in this house," he said. "Nell, dear, you look blooming. Hector will be delighted at your loveliness."

Nell, leaning on her elbows, looked at him across the breakfast table. He was extremely spruce and had a flower in his buttonhole, a flower that he had undoubtedly taken from the bowl in the drawing room.

"Uncle Nicholas, tell me," she said, "why did you burst out with all that last night? Did you *like* us knowing how bad you'd been?"

"I did it, my dear," said Nicholas, "because it amused me."

"Do you do everything because it amuses you?"

"Pretty well everything."

Then she said: "We're probably not such fools as you think."

"And I'm probably not so wicked as you think."

"I'm sorry," Nell said, "Lizzie's going. She's a darling."

But he didn't answer that. That was serious.

He kissed her good-bye. She was the only member of the family whom he saw.

Oh, yes, he saw Romney.

Romney ran down the stairs, shook him by the hand and said: "Uncle Nicholas, you haven't taken the negress, have you?"

"No. But I wanted to," said Nicholas.

"Sometime," said Romney, "when you're in town again, let me know. We'll have lunch. There's a girl I'd like you to meet."

"All right, I will," said Uncle Nicholas, grinning. Romney looked happy again, he noticed a little wistfully.

For the rest there was only Becky Sharp. She was on the steps to see them go.

She watched them with intensity. When the cab was out of sight she started, with that absorption that gives the solemnity of a religious rite to a cat's ablutions, to wash her whiskers.

7

A week later on a lovely spring morning, somewhere in Herefordshire, the lady who had shopped at Fortnum's was arranging the flowers.

The maid, Isabel, came and said: "Someone on the telephone, madam."

At the telephone the lady said (her daughter was teasing the Pekinese close beside her), "A call from London? . . . Yes . . . Yes? . . . Who is that speaking? . . . What? I can't quite hear. . . . Oh! Captain Coventry? Why, how delightful! I hoped that . . . Yes—I can hear perfectly. Why, how are you? . . . I'm splendid, thank you—yes, splendid . . . What? A visit? Why, of *course*. How perfectly splendid! . . . Oh, definitely! Quite delightful! . . . Oh, yes, and bring your little girl! . . . No, there's no one here except the family. For as long as you like. Of course we shall be enchanted! As *long* as you like! . . . This afternoon? Why, certainly. There's a very good train—three-thirteen from Paddington. We shall be *delighted*. The car shall meet you. That's perfectly splendid."

Radiant, she turned to her little girl.

"What do you think? It's that charming Captain Coventry. He's coming this evening. And he's bringing his little girl, so you'll have a companion. . . . I *am* glad! I do hope he stays quite a while. . . ."

8

The lovely spring sunshine flooded the street. Within the station there was a warm radiance. Nicholas and Lizzie were in plenty of time.

"I've taken first-class tickets, darling. So like me when I haven't a bean. Still, we won't be poor for long. Have you got the papers you want?"

"Yes, thank you," said Lizzie.

She was staring down the platform. She had written to Edward giving him this new address, telling him the train by which they were going. Of course he could not be here. It would be a half-holiday, but they would make him play one of those silly games. Nevertheless she stared down the platform.

"That right, porter?" said Nicholas. "Have we got everything?"

"I think so, sir," said the porter.

Nicholas considered him.

"You look very tired. Been up all night?"

"Well, sir—my wife's bad. 'Ad an operation last week —all her inside taken out."

"I say, that's bad," said Nicholas. He took out his pocketbook. Smiling, as one friend to another, he gave the man ten shillings.

9

Just as the train was beginning to move, a small, thick-set man with a brown face, clothed in a black suit, came running down the platform.

He jumped into a third-class carriage.

THE END